A RADICAL SHIFT of GRAVITY

created by

NICK TAPALANSKY & KATE GLASHEEN

A RADICAL SHIFT OF GRAVITY
© 2020 Nick Tapalansky and Kate Glasheen.

ISBN: 978-1-60309-458-0   23 22 21 20   1 2 3 4

Published by Top Shelf Productions, PO Box 1282, Marietta,
GA 30061-1282, USA. Top Shelf Productions is an imprint
of IDW Publishing, a division of Idea and Design Works,
LLC. Offices: 2765 Truxtun Road, San Diego, CA 92106.
Top Shelf Productions®, the Top Shelf logo, Idea and Design
Works®, and the IDW logo are registered trademarks of
Idea and Design Works, LLC. All Rights Reserved. With
the exception of small excerpts of artwork used for review
purposes, none of the contents of this publication may be
reprinted without the permission of IDW Publishing. IDW
Publishing does not read or accept unsolicited submissions
of ideas, stories, or artwork.

Editor-in-Chief: Chris Staros.
Designed by Gilberto Lazcano.

Visit our online catalog at
www.topshelfcomix.com.

Printed in Korea.

A RADICAL SHIFT of GRAVITY

created by

NICK TAPALANSKY & KATE GLASHEEN

Top Shelf PRODUCTIONS

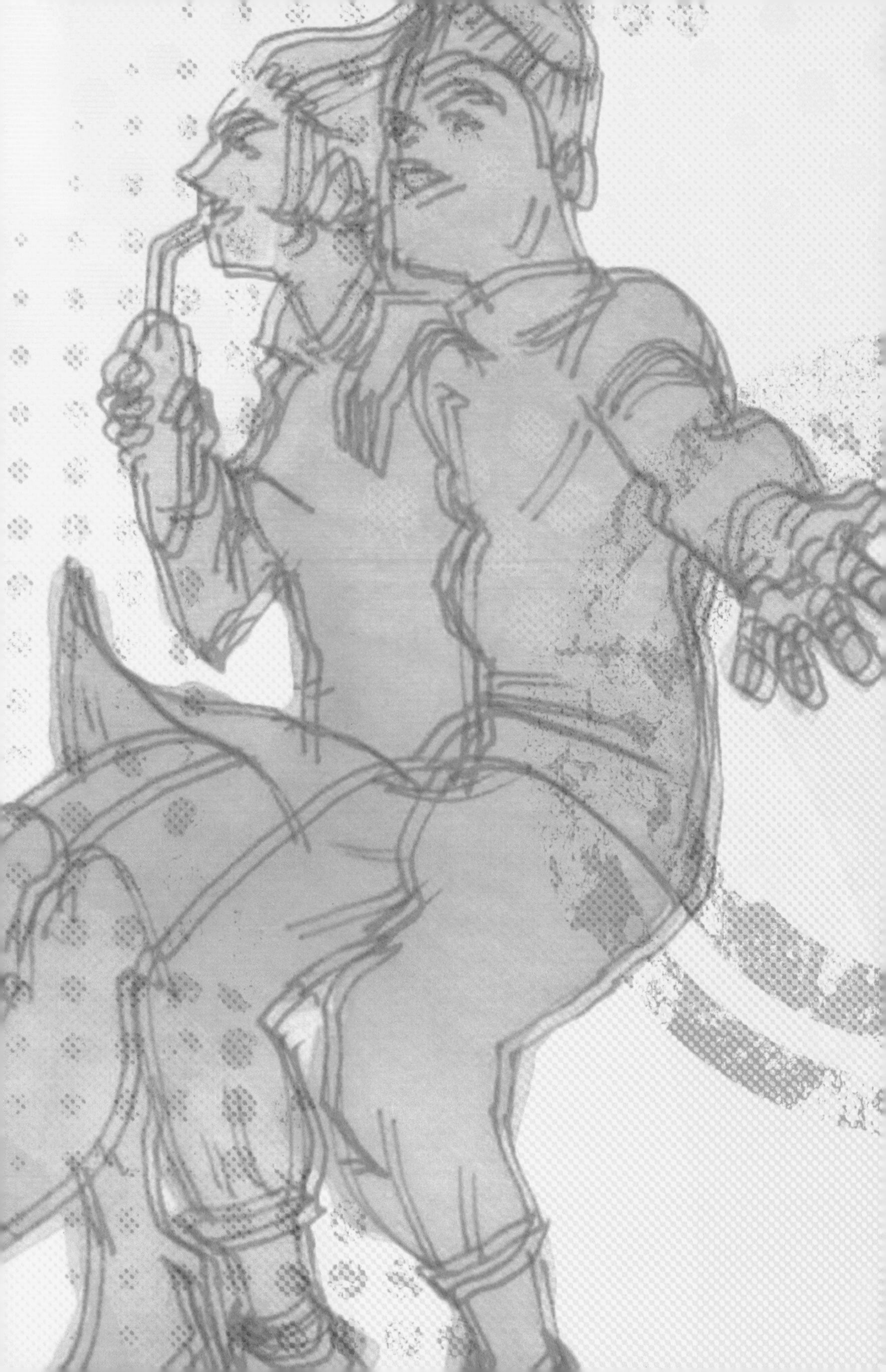

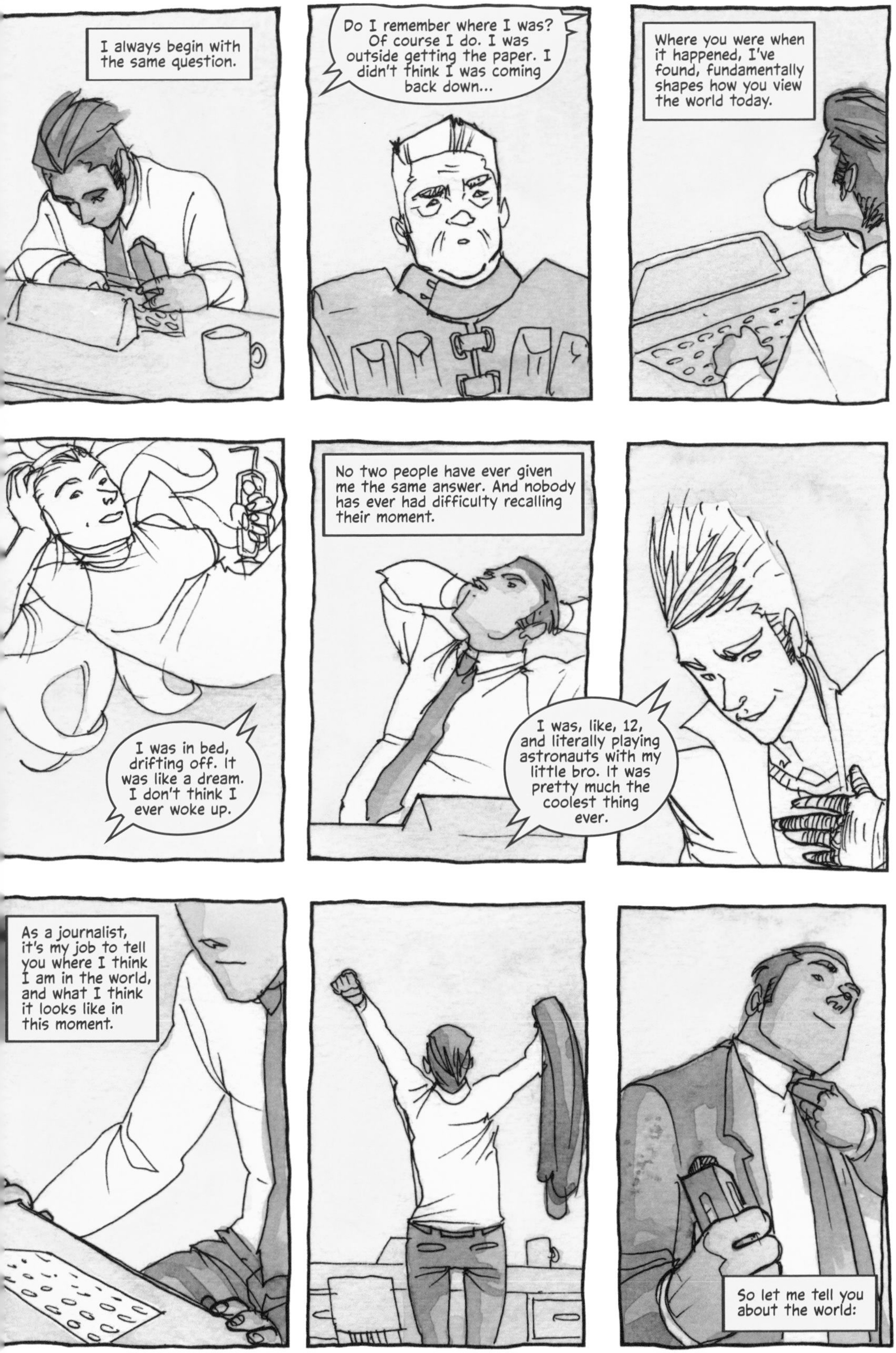
I always begin with the same question.
Do I remember where I was? Of course I do. I was outside getting the paper. I didn't think I was coming back down...
Where you were when it happened, I've found, fundamentally shapes how you view the world today.
I was in bed, drifting off. It was like a dream. I don't think I ever woke up.
No two people have ever given me the same answer. And nobody has ever had difficulty recalling their moment.
I was, like, 12, and literally playing astronauts with my little bro. It was pretty much the coolest thing ever.
As a journalist, it's my job to tell you where I think I am in the world, and what I think it looks like in this moment.
So let me tell you about the world:

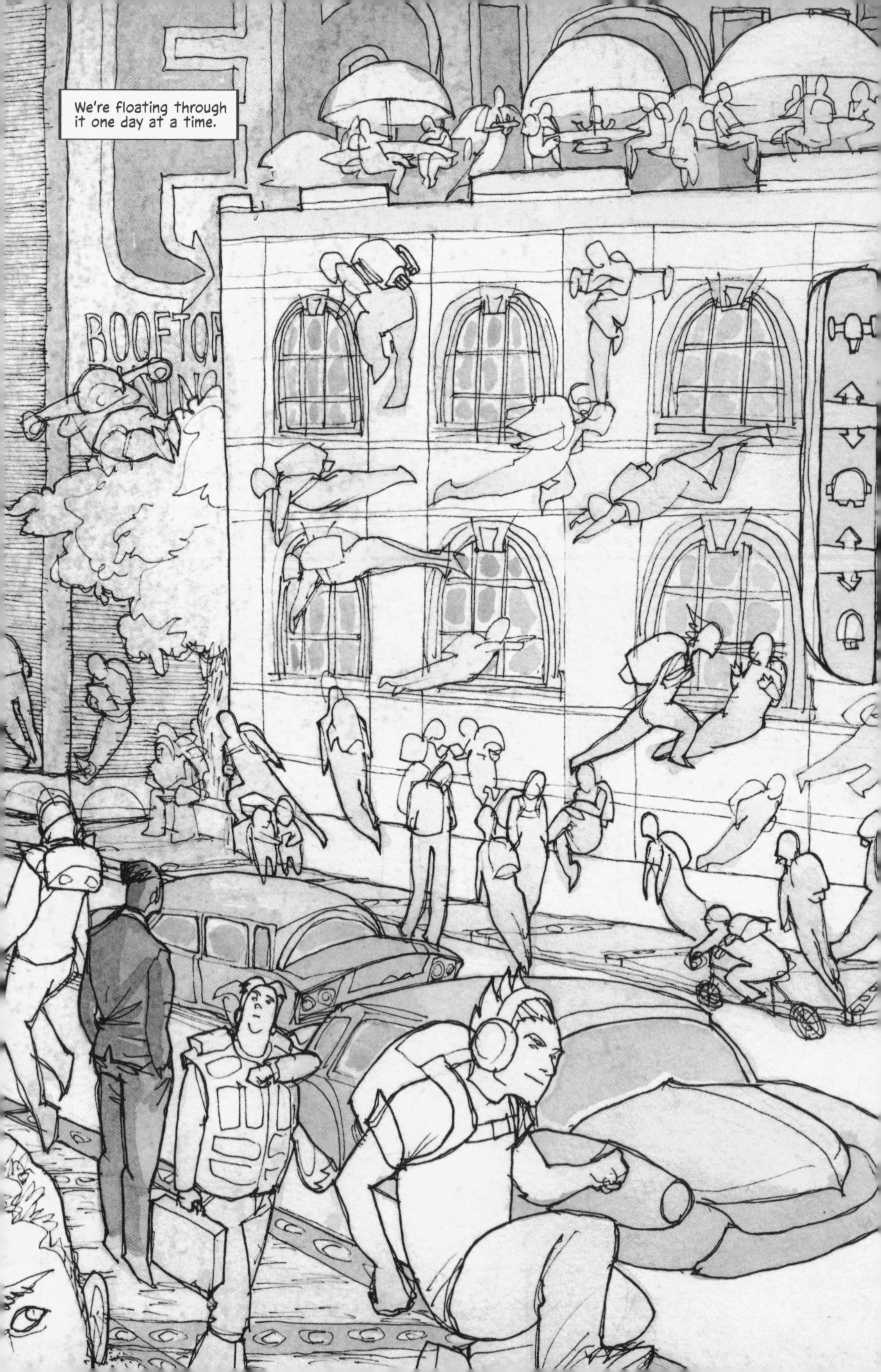
We're floating through it one day at a time.

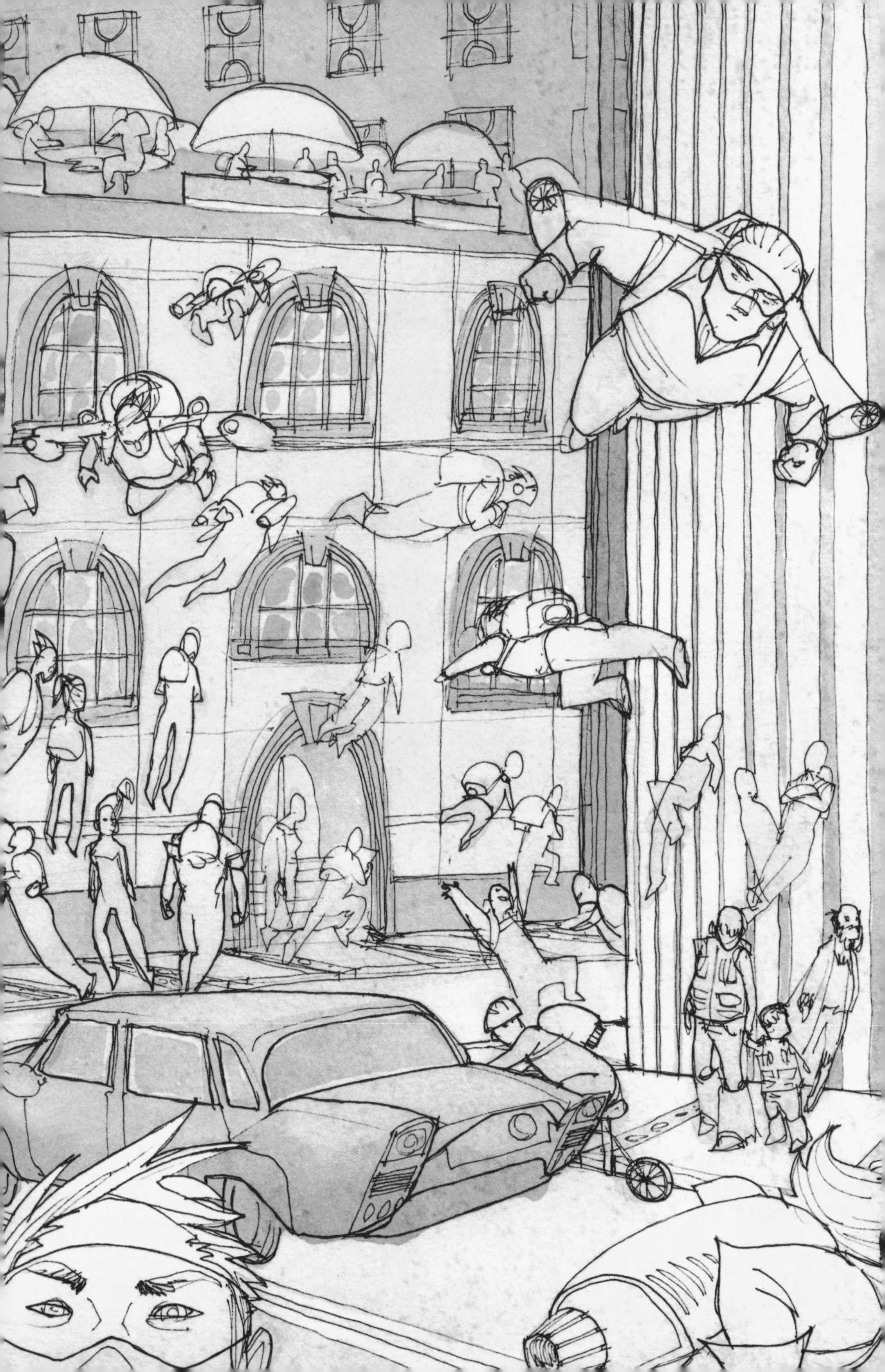

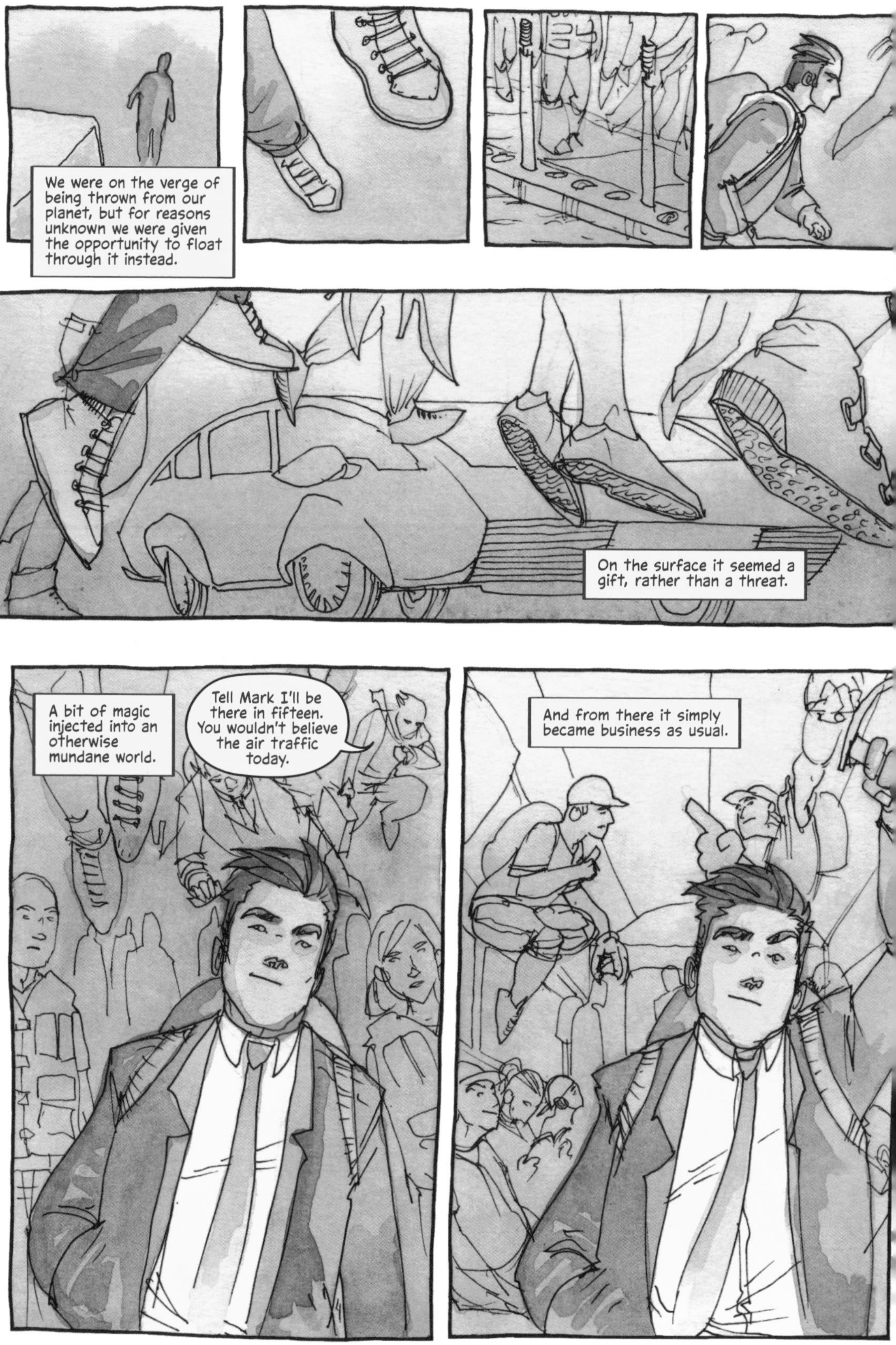
We were on the verge of being thrown from our planet, but for reasons unknown we were given the opportunity to float through it instead.
On the surface it seemed a gift, rather than a threat.
A bit of magic injected into an otherwise mundane world.
Tell Mark I'll be there in fifteen. You wouldn't believe the air traffic today.
And from there it simply became business as usual.

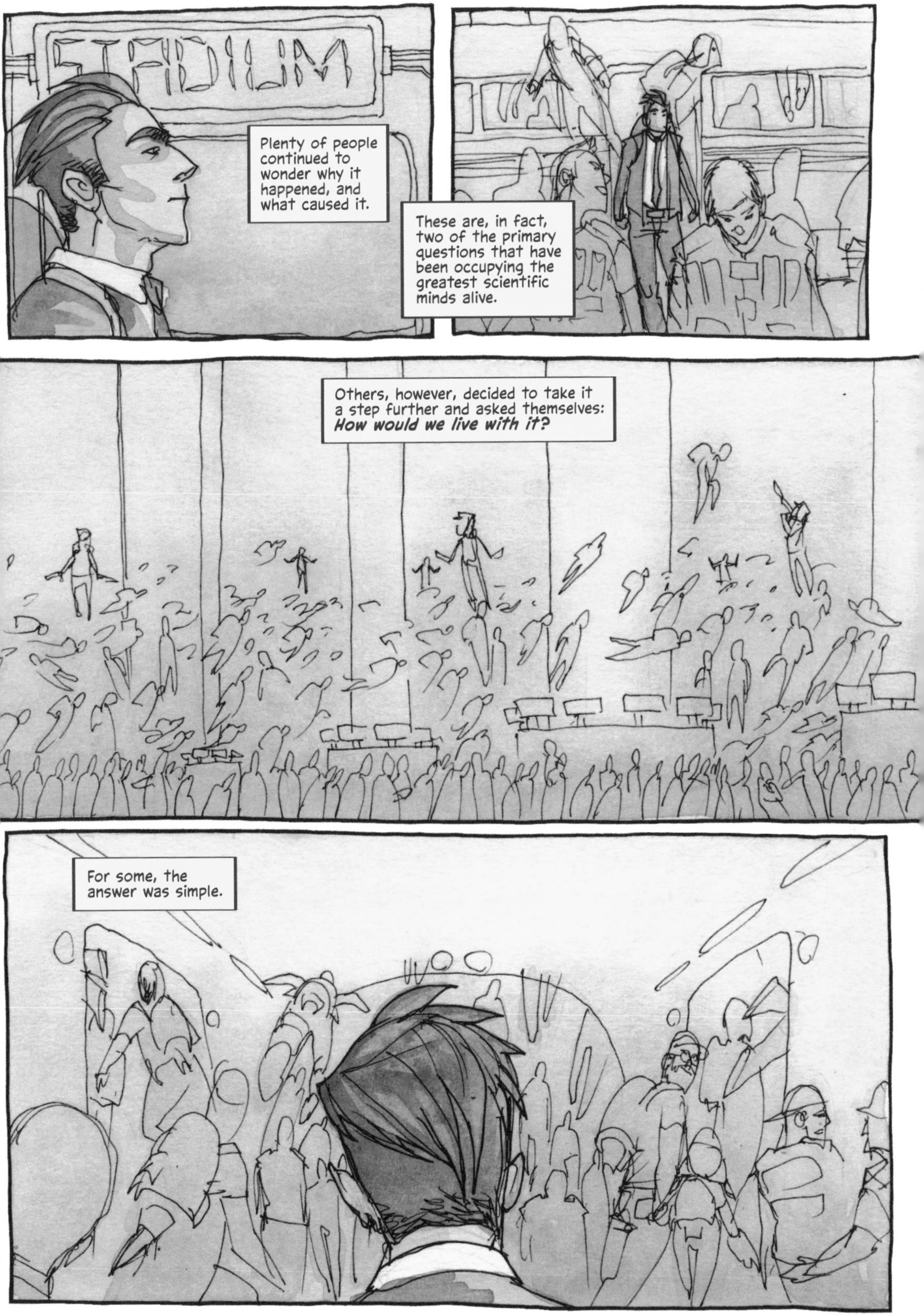
STADIUM
Plenty of people continued to wonder why it happened, and what caused it.
These are, in fact, two of the primary questions that have been occupying the greatest scientific minds alive.
Others, however, decided to take it a step further and asked themselves: *How would we live with it?*
For some, the answer was simple.

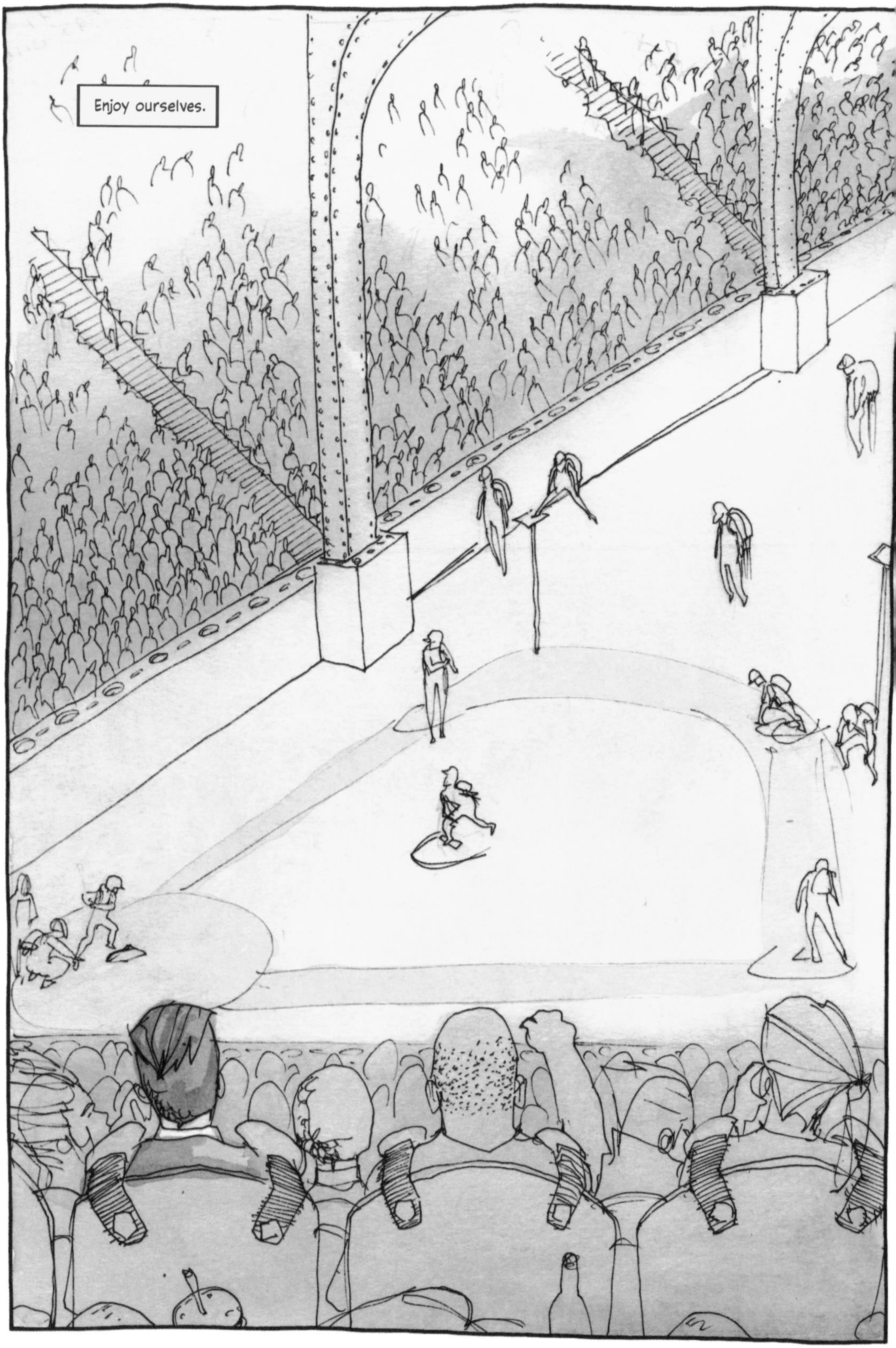
Enjoy ourselves.

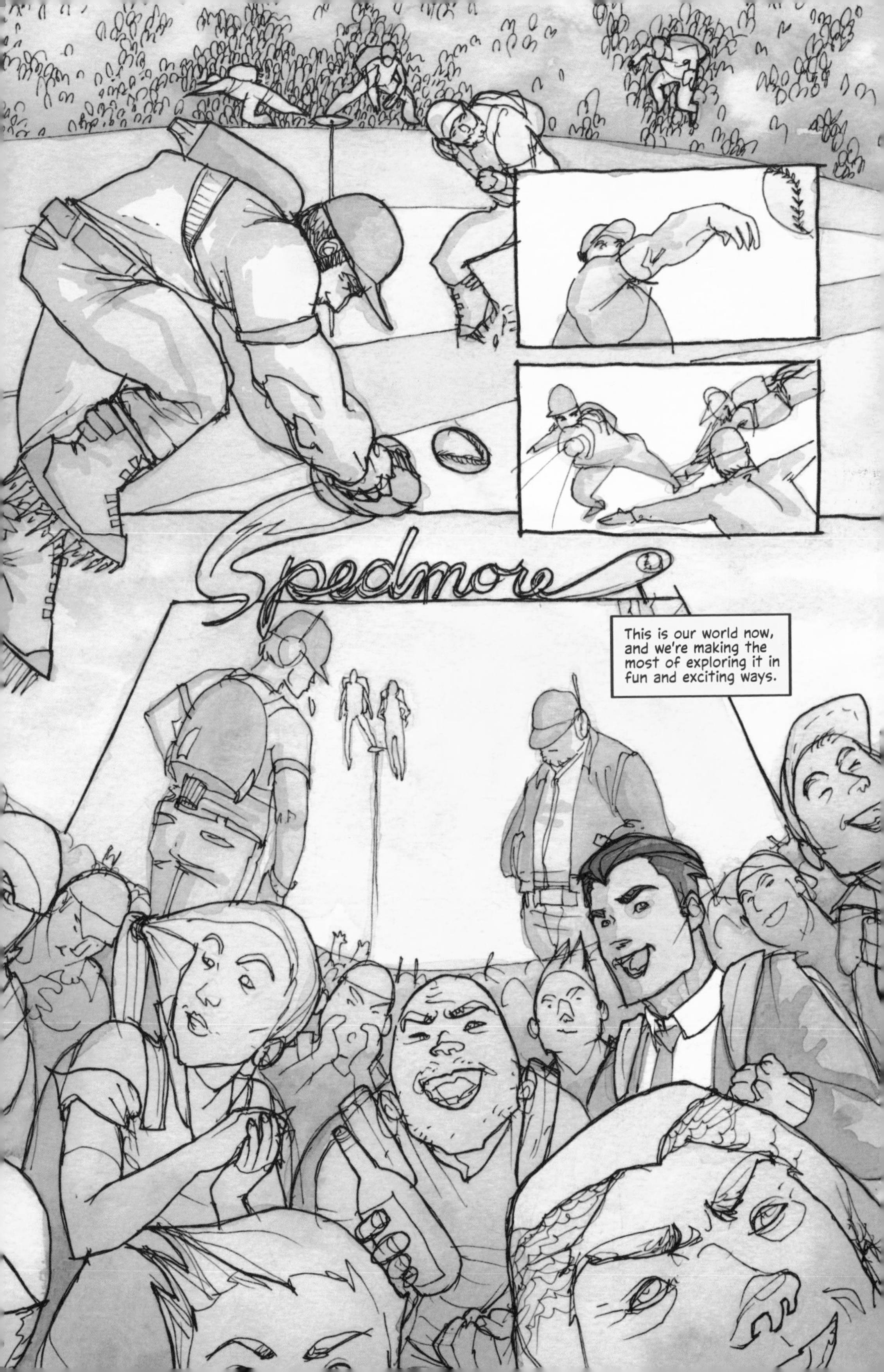
Spedmore
This is our world now, and we're making the most of exploring it in fun and exciting ways.

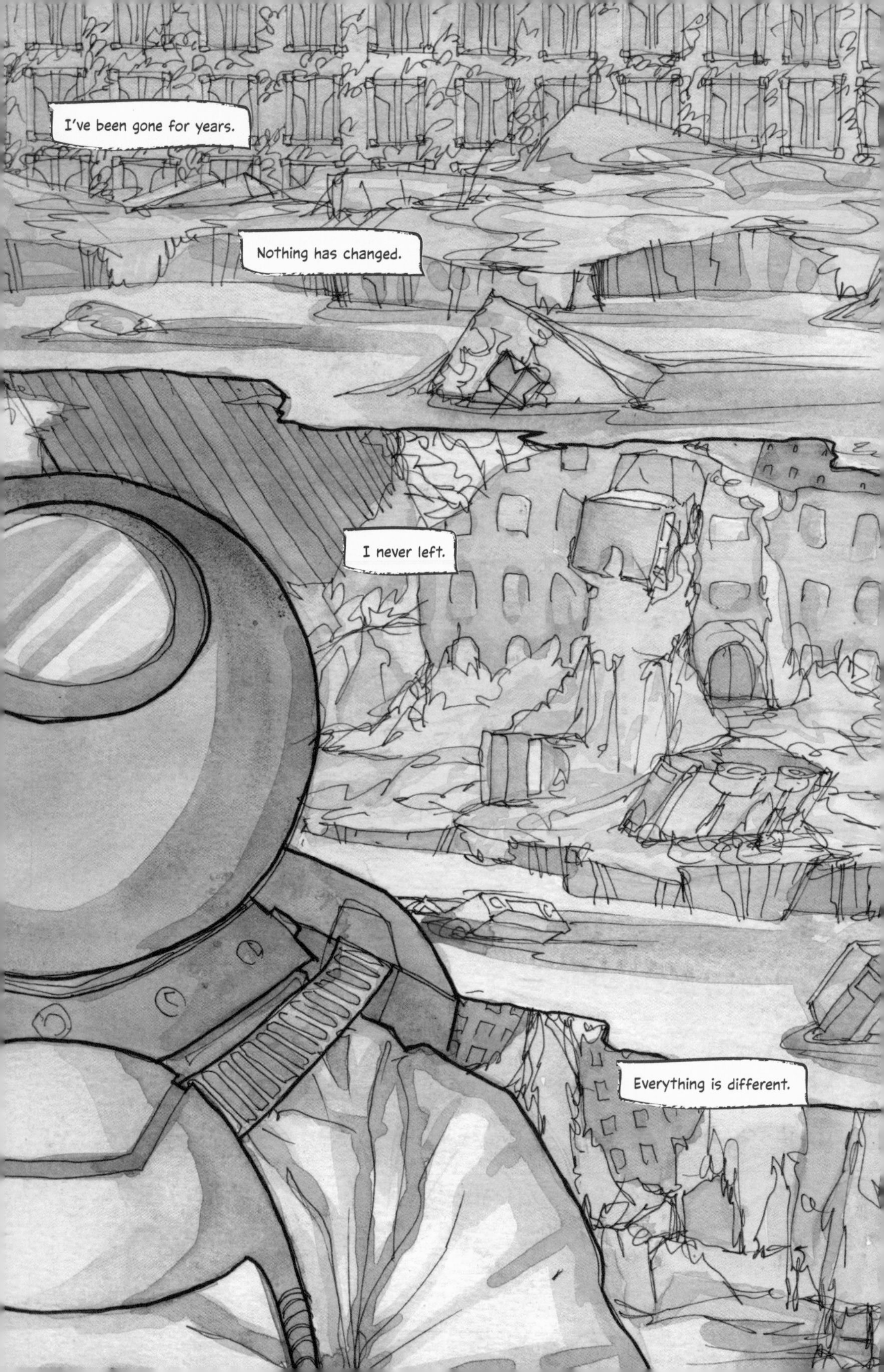
I've been gone for years.
Nothing has changed.
I never left.
Everything is different.

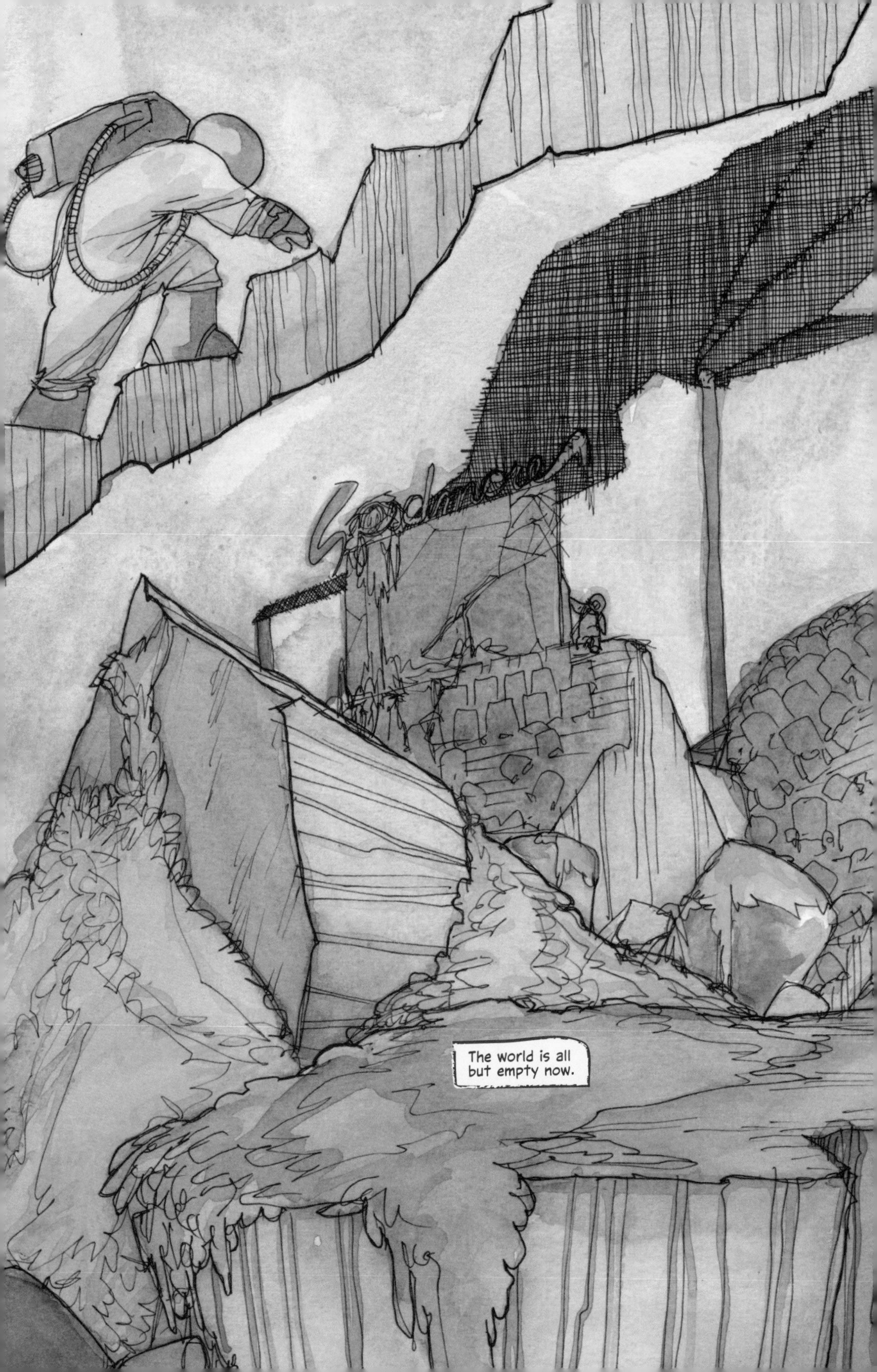
The world is all but empty now.

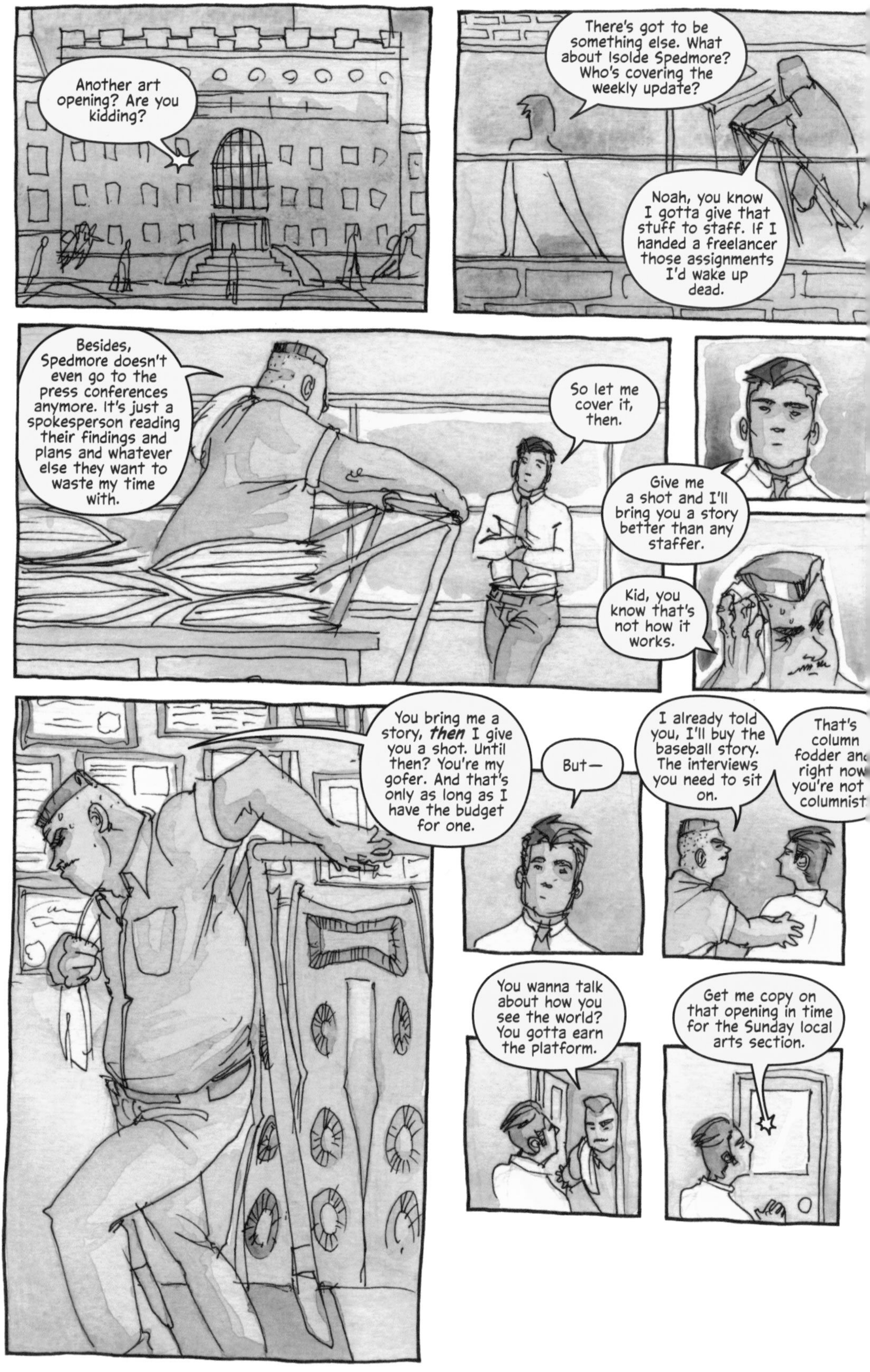
Another art opening? Are you kidding?
There's got to be something else. What about Isolde Spedmore? Who's covering the weekly update?
Noah, you know I gotta give that stuff to staff. If I handed a freelancer those assignments I'd wake up dead.
Besides, Spedmore doesn't even go to the press conferences anymore. It's just a spokesperson reading their findings and plans and whatever else they want to waste my time with.
So let me cover it, then.
Give me a shot and I'll bring you a story better than any staffer.
Kid, you know that's not how it works.
You bring me a story, *then* I give you a shot. Until then? You're my gofer. And that's only as long as I have the budget for one.
But—
I already told you, I'll buy the baseball story. The interviews you need to sit on.
You wanna talk about how you see the world? You gotta earn the platform.
Get me copy on that opening in time for the Sunday local arts section.

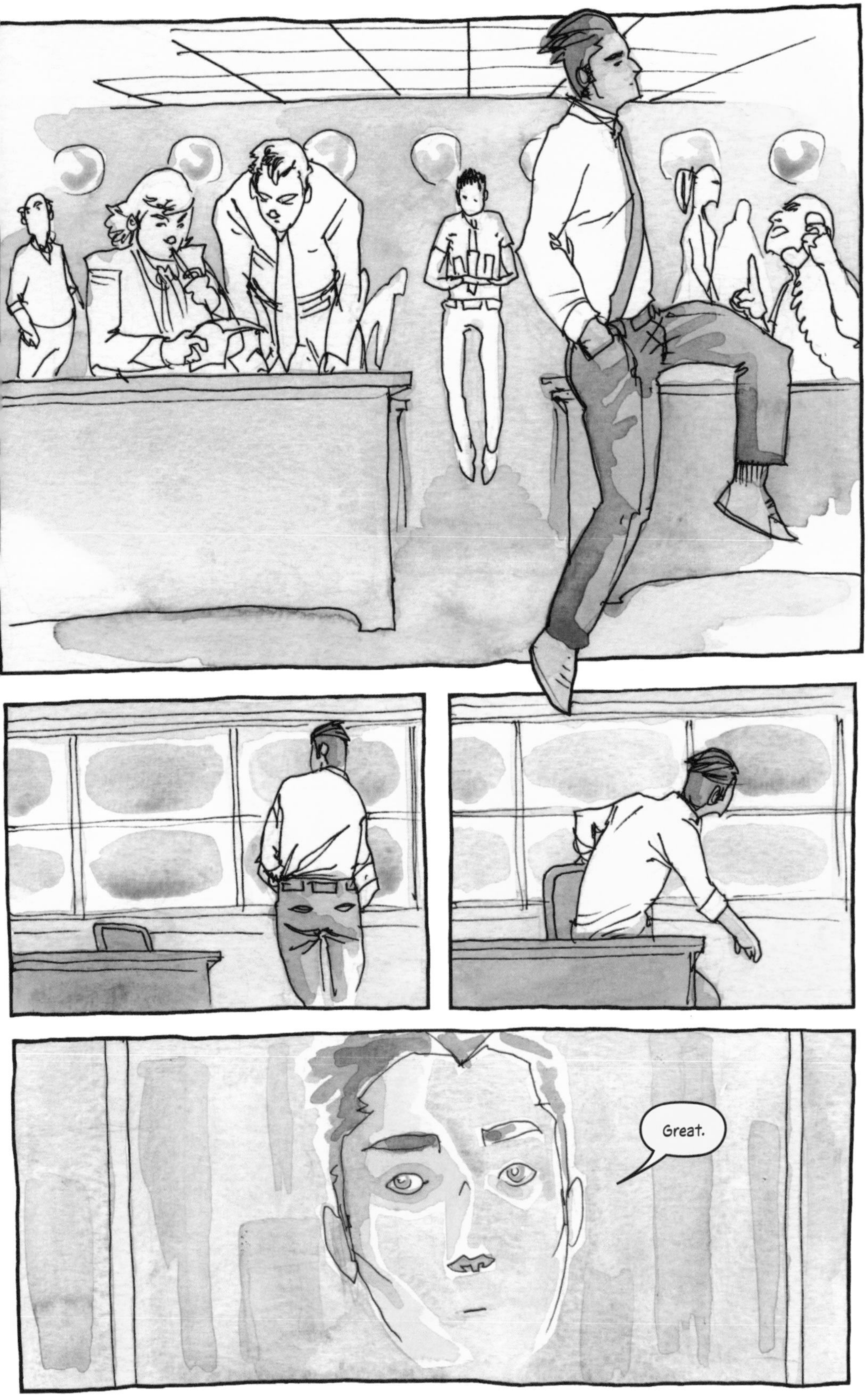
Great.

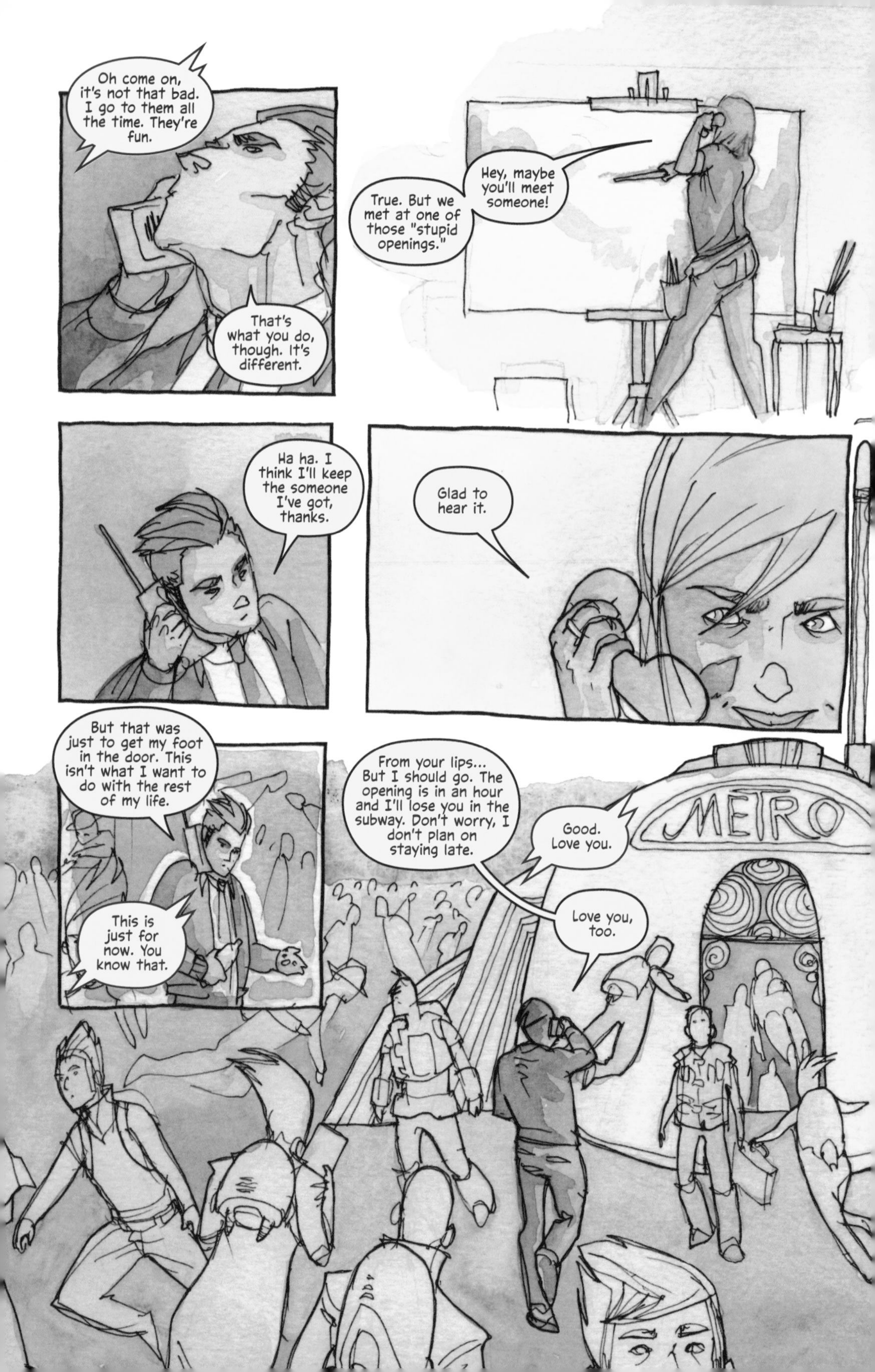
Oh come on, it's not that bad. I go to them all the time. They're fun.
That's what you do, though. It's different.
Hey, maybe you'll meet someone!
True. But we met at one of those "stupid openings."
Ha ha. I think I'll keep the someone I've got, thanks.
Glad to hear it.
But that was just to get my foot in the door. This isn't what I want to do with the rest of my life.
This is just for now. You know that.
From your lips... But I should go. The opening is in an hour and I'll lose you in the subway. Don't worry, I don't plan on staying late.
Good. Love you.
Love you, too.
METRO

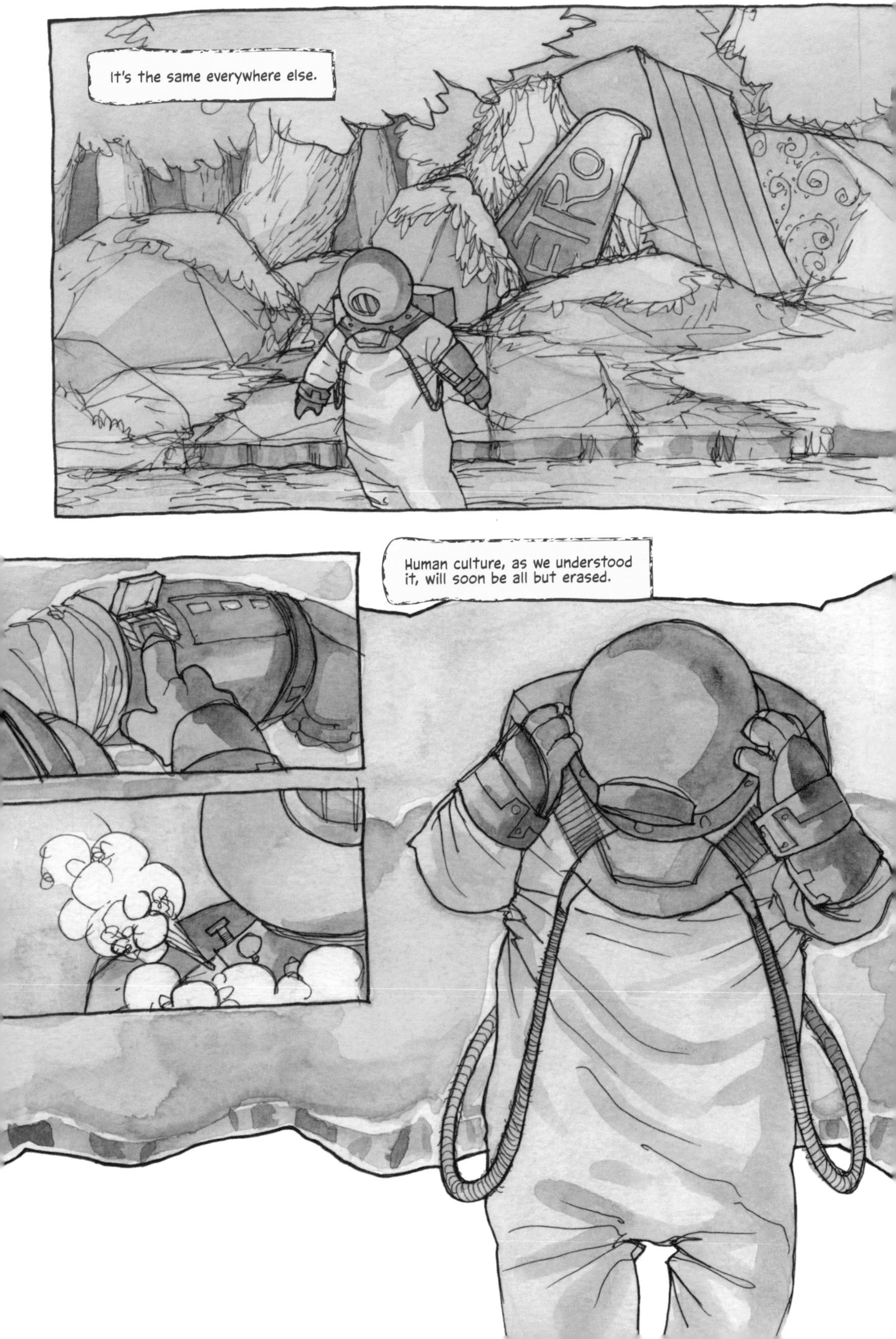
It's the same everywhere else.
Human culture, as we understood it, will soon be all but erased.

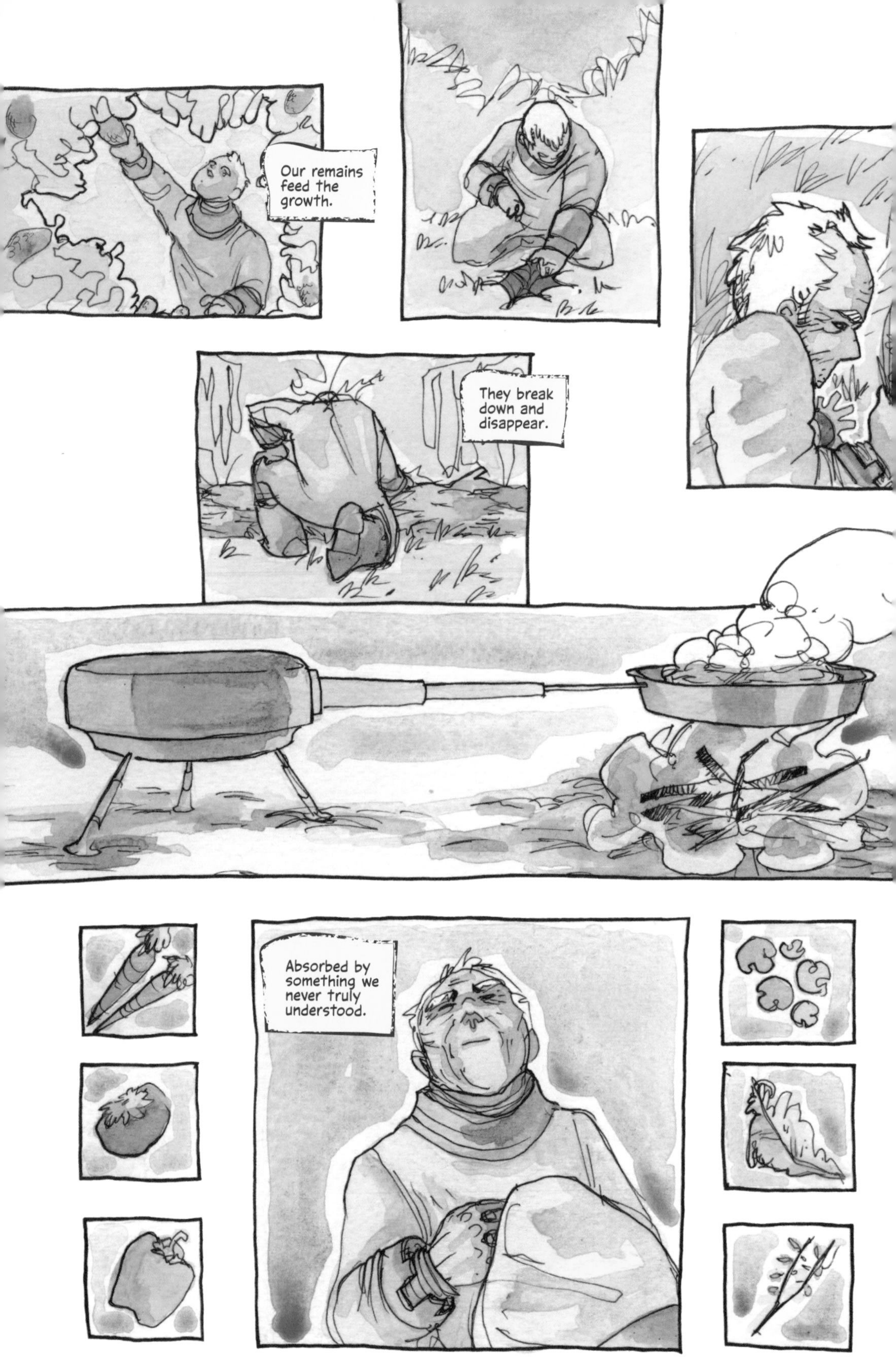
Our remains feed the growth.
They break down and disappear.
Absorbed by something we never truly understood.

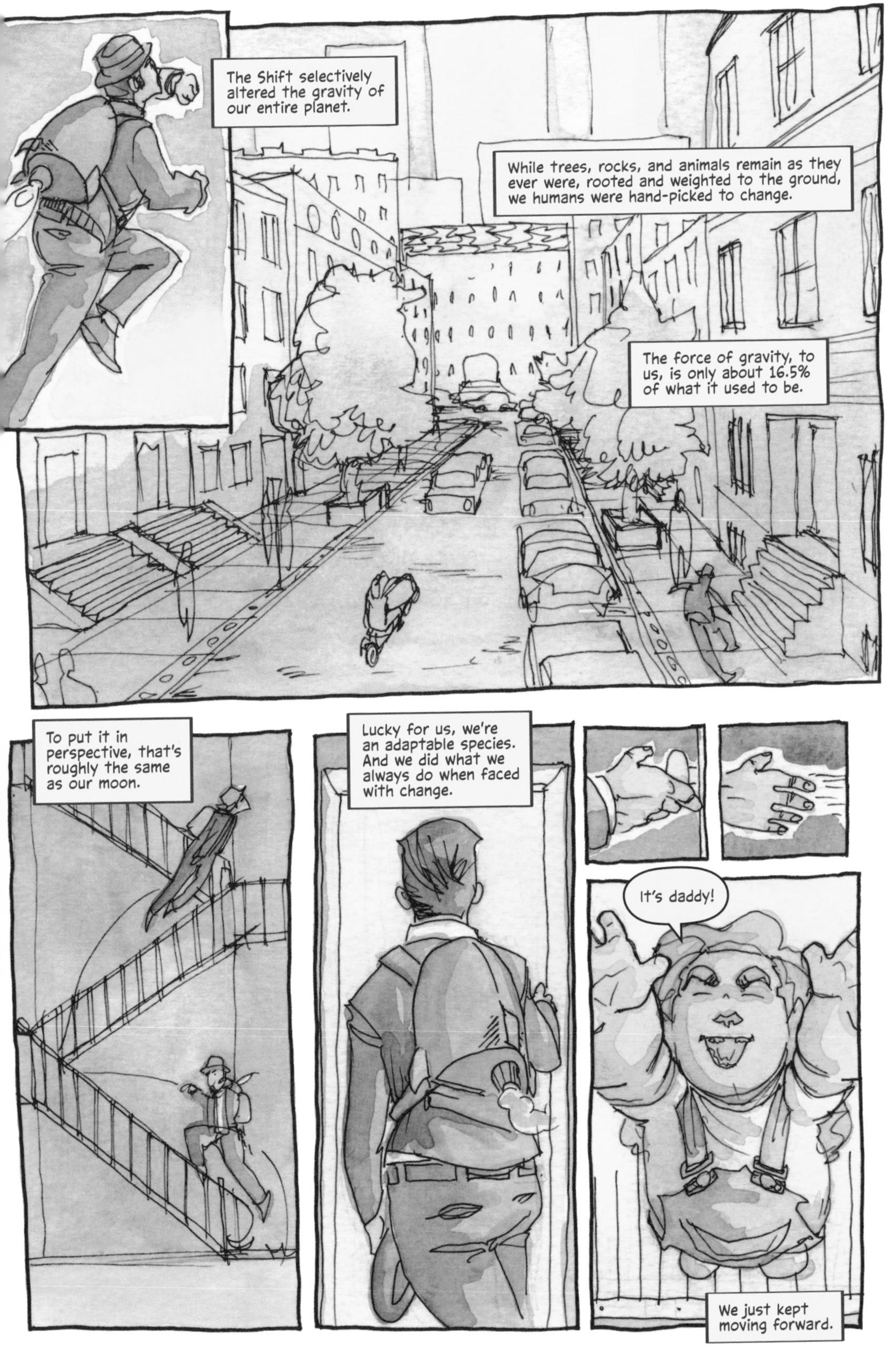

The Shift selectively altered the gravity of our entire planet.
While trees, rocks, and animals remain as they ever were, rooted and weighted to the ground, we humans were hand-picked to change.
The force of gravity, to us, is only about 16.5% of what it used to be.
To put it in perspective, that's roughly the same as our moon.
Lucky for us, we're an adaptable species. And we did what we always do when faced with change.
It's daddy!
We just kept moving forward.

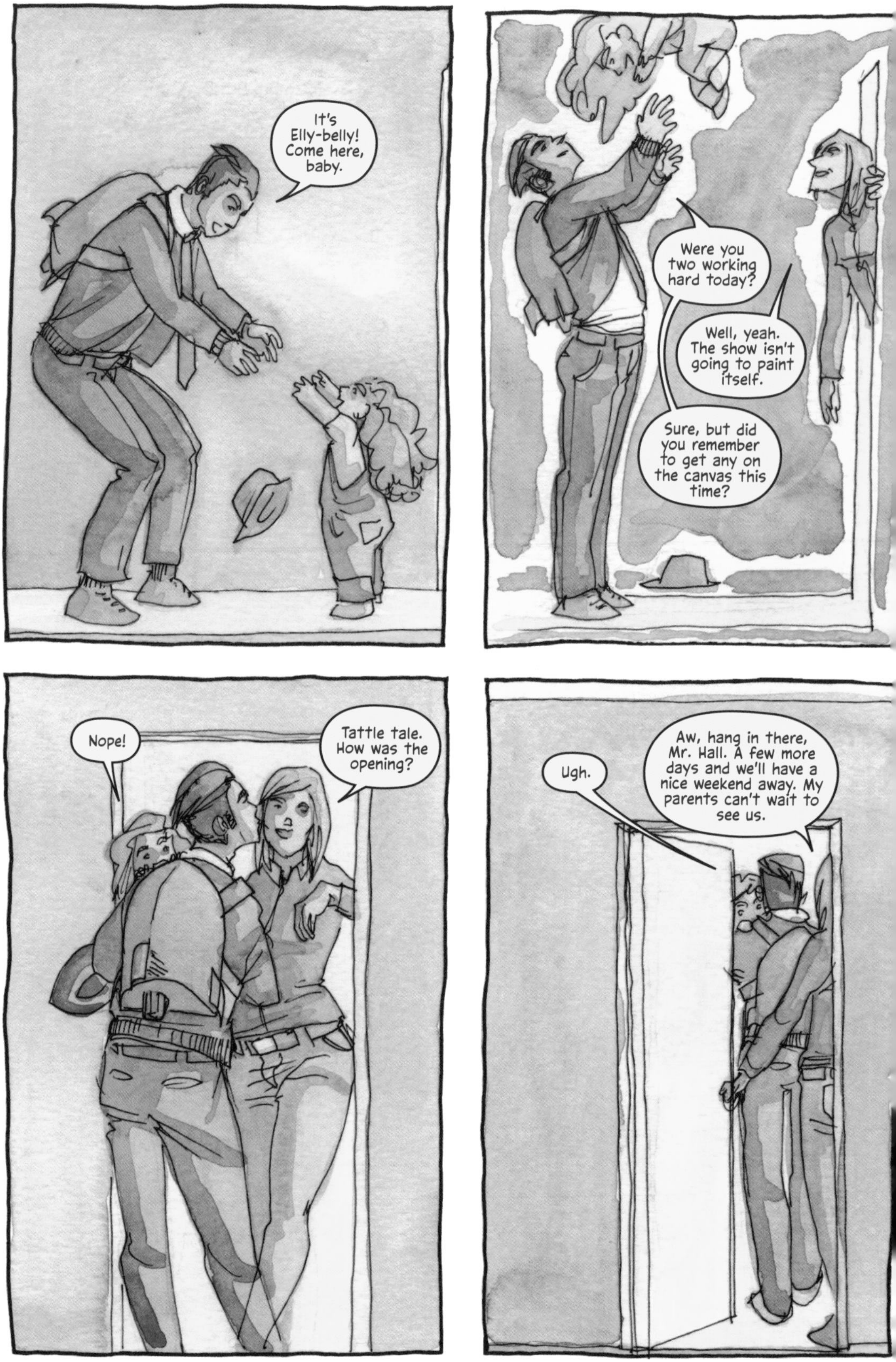
It's Elly-belly! Come here, baby.
Were you two working hard today?
Well, yeah. The show isn't going to paint itself.
Sure, but did you remember to get any on the canvas this time?
Nope!
Tattle tale. How was the opening?
Ugh.
Aw, hang in there, Mr. Hall. A few more days and we'll have a nice weekend away. My parents can't wait to see us.

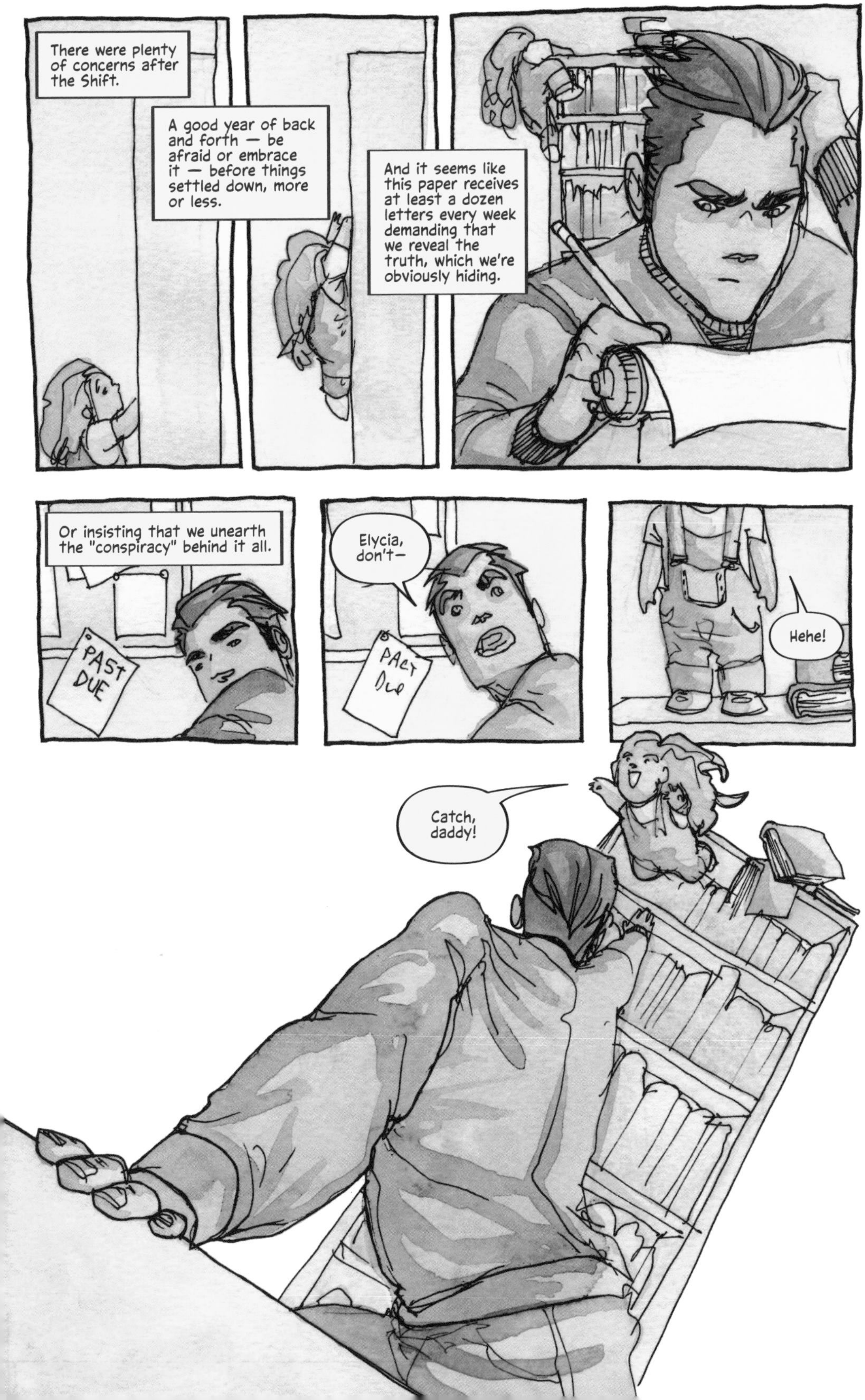
There were plenty of concerns after the Shift.
A good year of back and forth — be afraid or embrace it — before things settled down, more or less.
And it seems like this paper receives at least a dozen letters every week demanding that we reveal the truth, which we're obviously hiding.
Or insisting that we unearth the "conspiracy" behind it all.
PAST DUE
Elycia, don't—
PAST DUE
Hehe!
Catch, daddy!

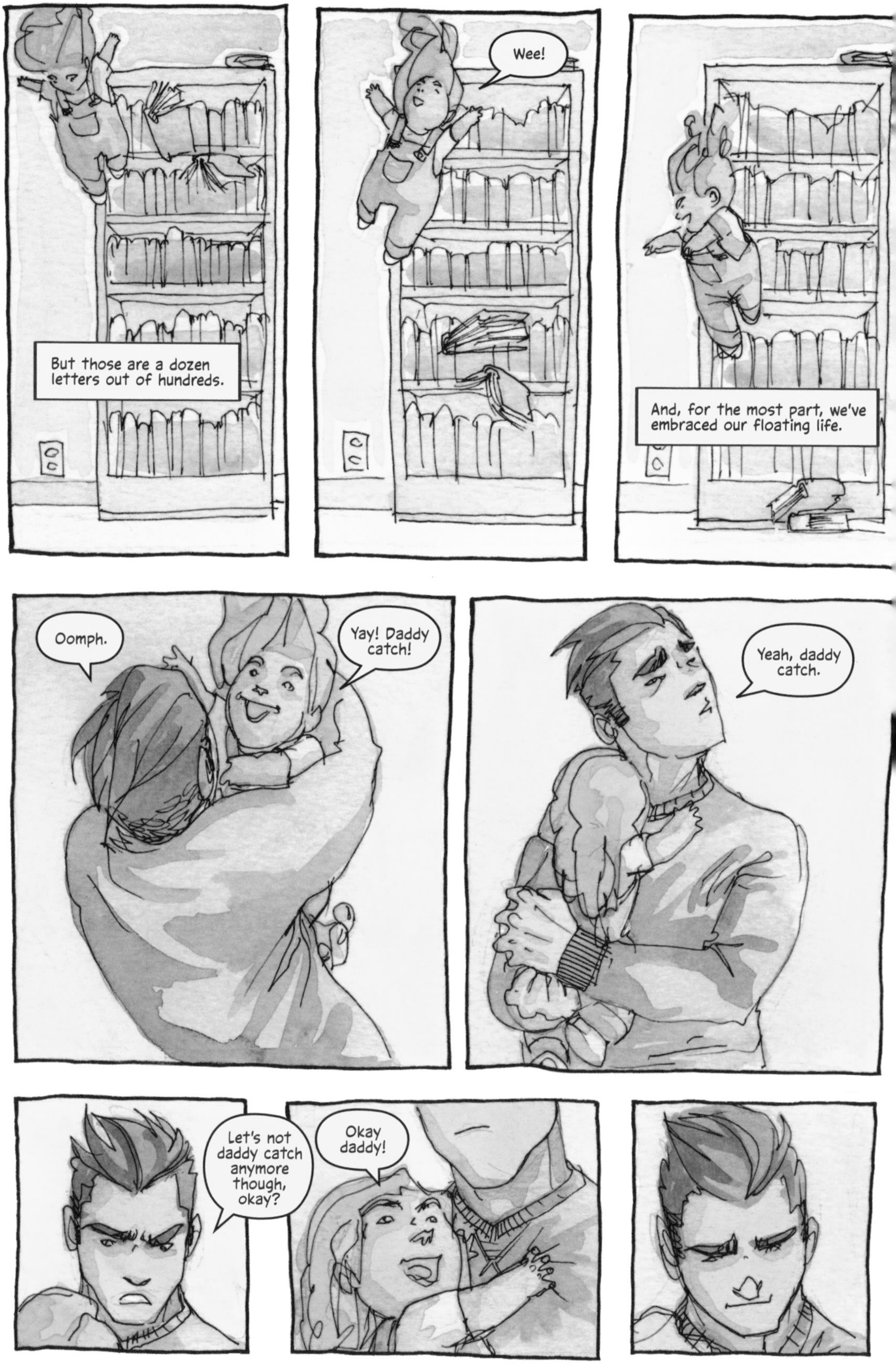
But those are a dozen letters out of hundreds.
Wee!
And, for the most part, we've embraced our floating life.
Oomph.
Yay! Daddy catch!
Yeah, daddy catch.
Let's not daddy catch anymore though, okay?
Okay daddy!

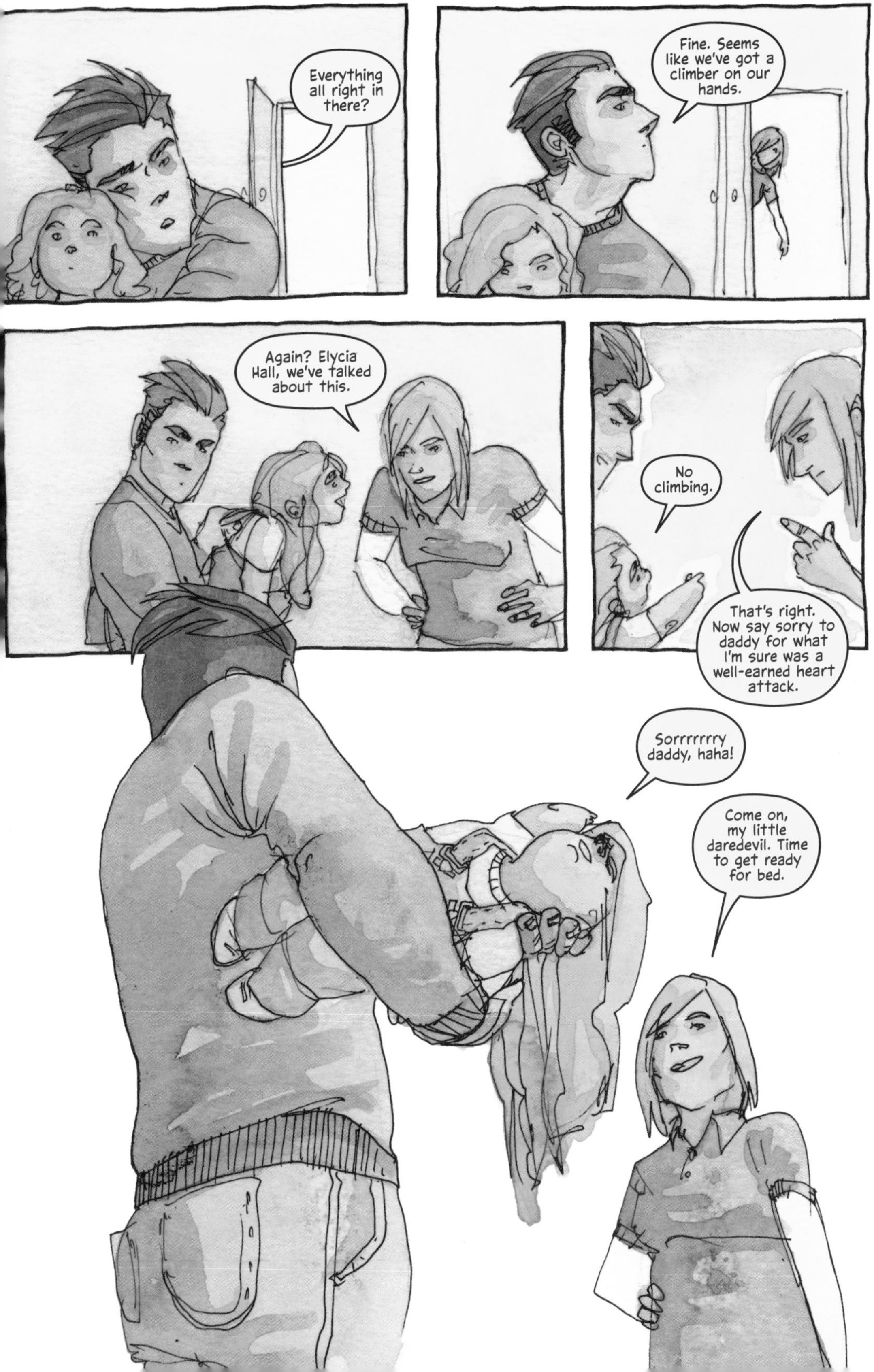
Everything all right in there?
Fine. Seems like we've got a climber on our hands.
Again? Elycia Hall, we've talked about this.
No climbing.
That's right. Now say sorry to daddy for what I'm sure was a well-earned heart attack.
Sorrrrrrry daddy, haha!
Come on, my little daredevil. Time to get ready for bed.

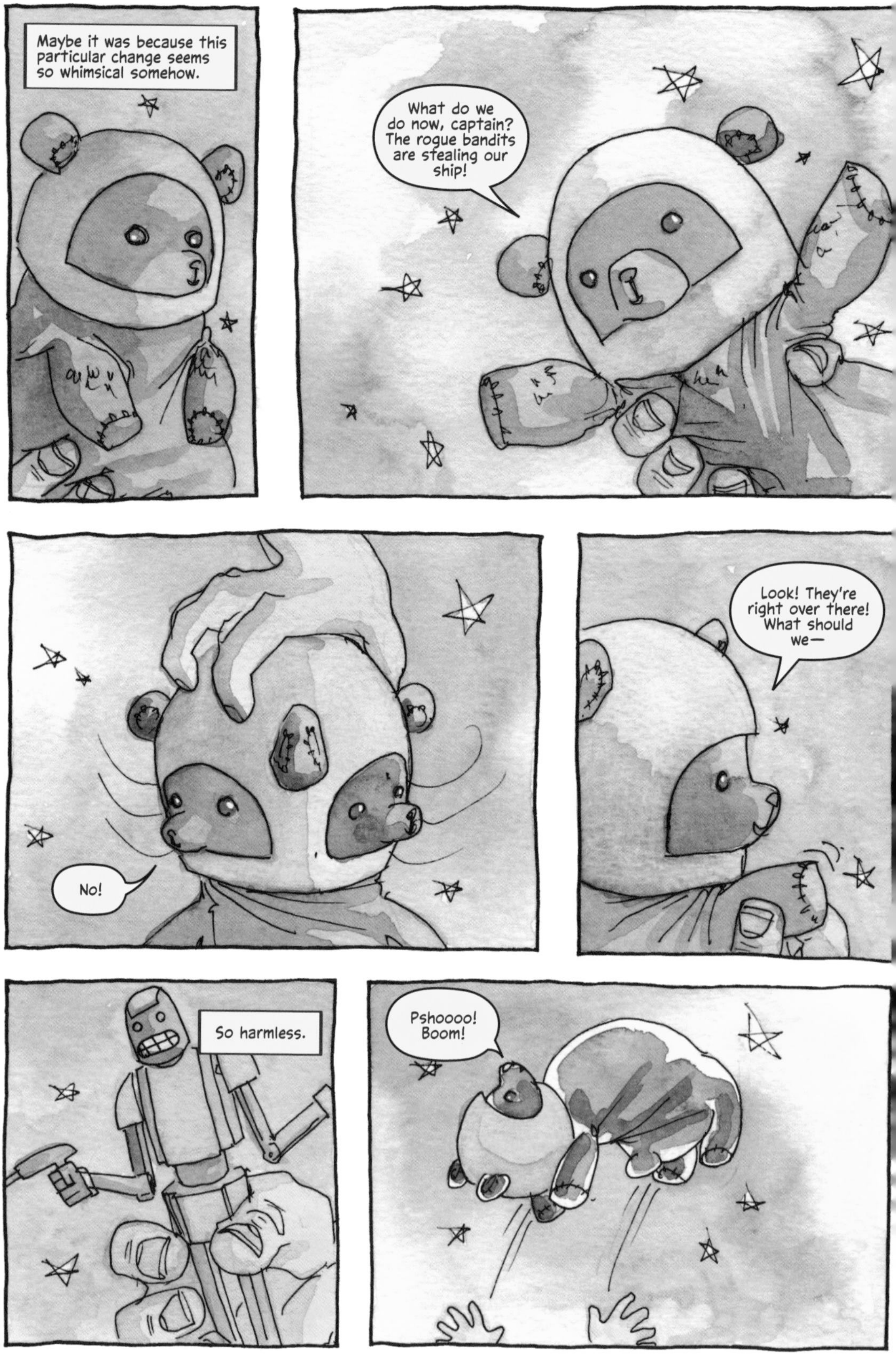
Maybe it was because this particular change seems so whimsical somehow.
What do we do now, captain? The rogue bandits are stealing our ship!
No!
Look! They're right over there! What should we—
So harmless.
Pshoooo! Boom!

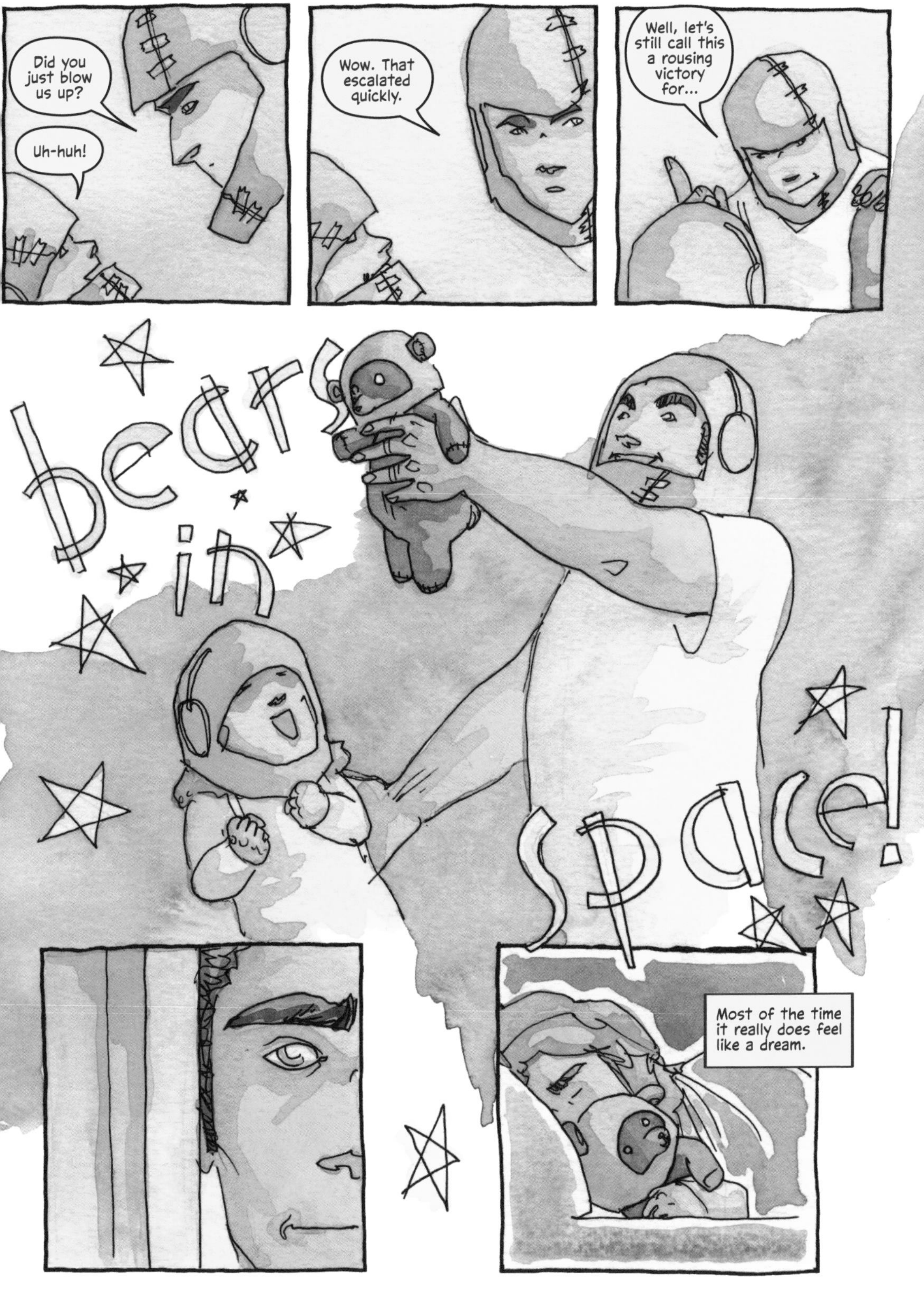
Did you just blow us up?
Uh-huh!
Wow. That escalated quickly.
Well, let's still call this a rousing victory for...
bears in space!
Most of the time it really does feel like a dream.

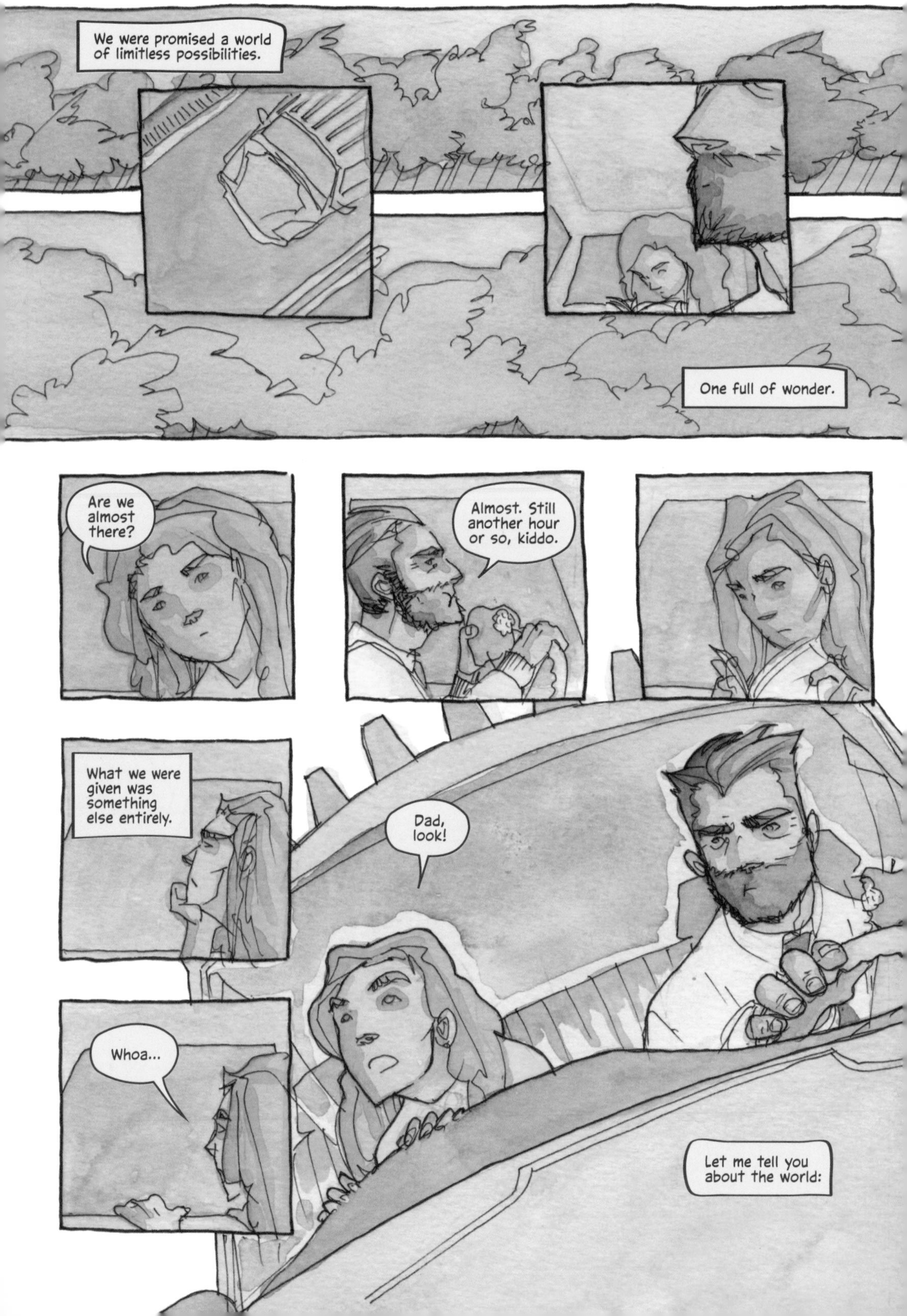
We were promised a world of limitless possibilities.
One full of wonder.
Are we almost there?
Almost. Still another hour or so, kiddo.
What we were given was something else entirely.
Dad, look!
Whoa...
Let me tell you about the world:

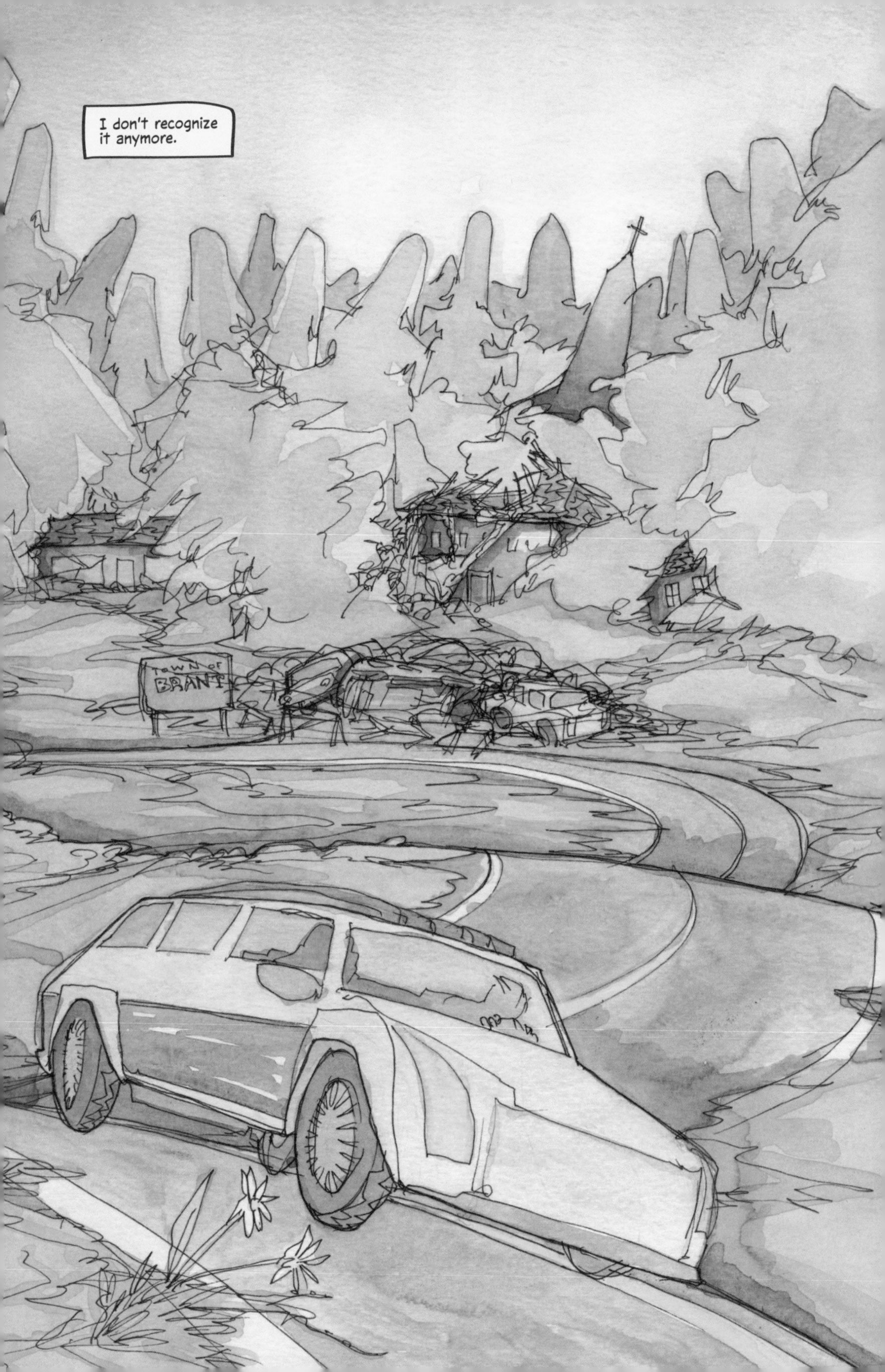
I don't recognize it anymore.
TOWN OF BRANT

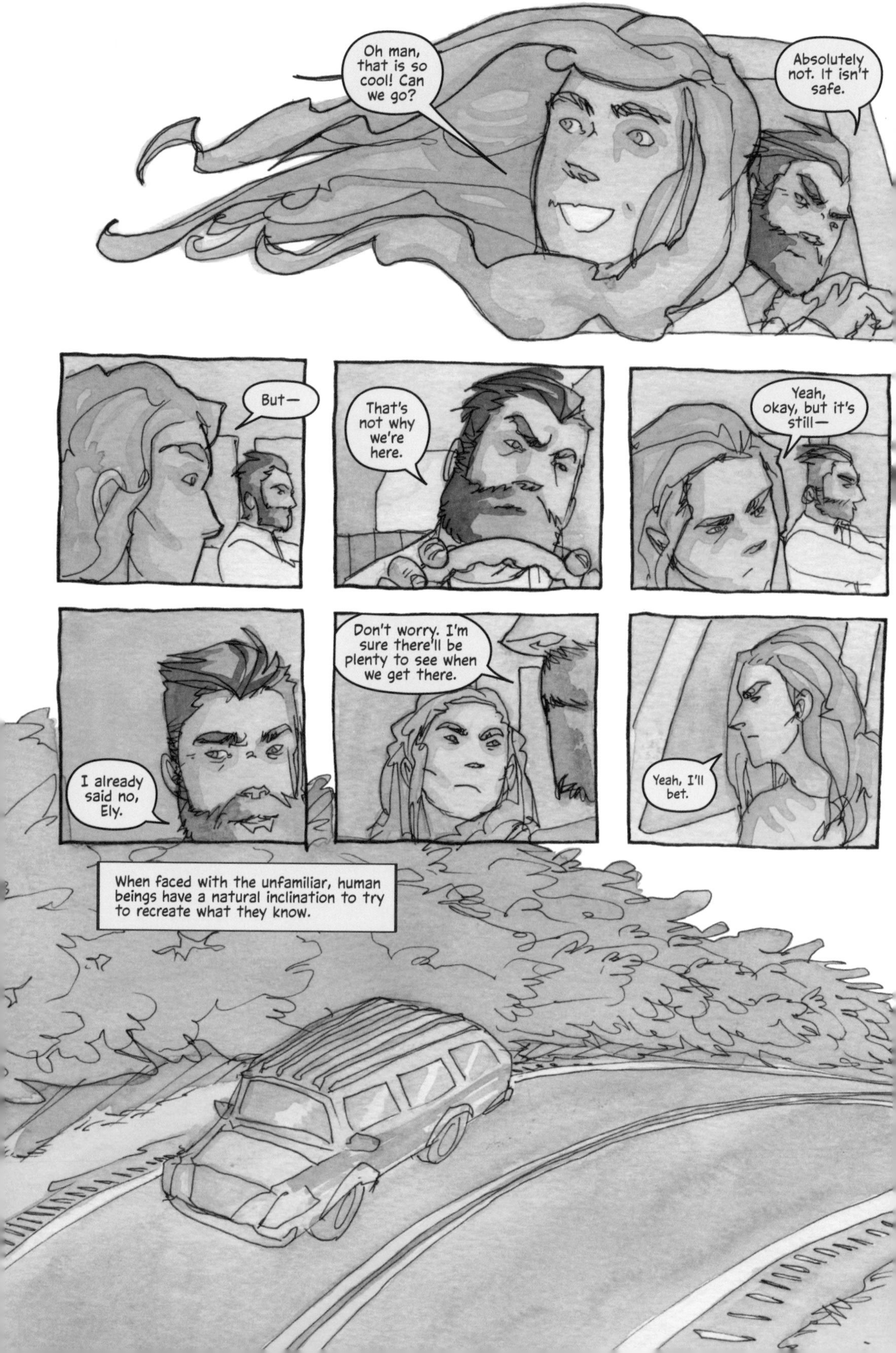
Oh man, that is so cool! Can we go?
Absolutely not. It isn't safe.
But—
That's not why we're here.
Yeah, okay, but it's still—
I already said no, Ely.
Don't worry. I'm sure there'll be plenty to see when we get there.
Yeah, I'll bet.
When faced with the unfamiliar, human beings have a natural inclination to try to recreate what they know.

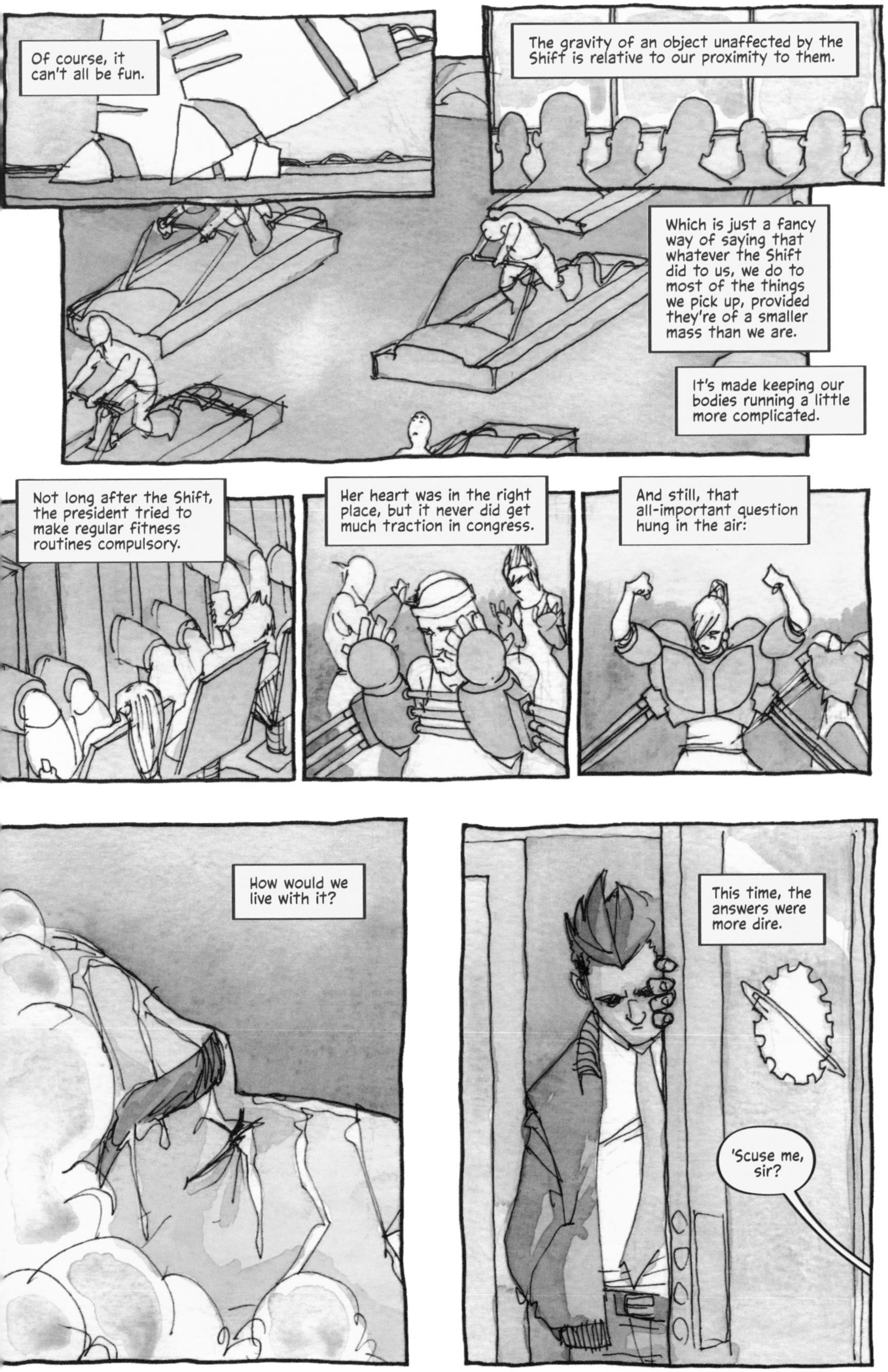
Of course, it can't all be fun.
The gravity of an object unaffected by the Shift is relative to our proximity to them.
Which is just a fancy way of saying that whatever the Shift did to us, we do to most of the things we pick up, provided they're of a smaller mass than we are.
It's made keeping our bodies running a little more complicated.
Not long after the Shift, the president tried to make regular fitness routines compulsory.
Her heart was in the right place, but it never did get much traction in congress.
And still, that all-important question hung in the air:
How would we live with it?
This time, the answers were more dire.
'Scuse me, sir?

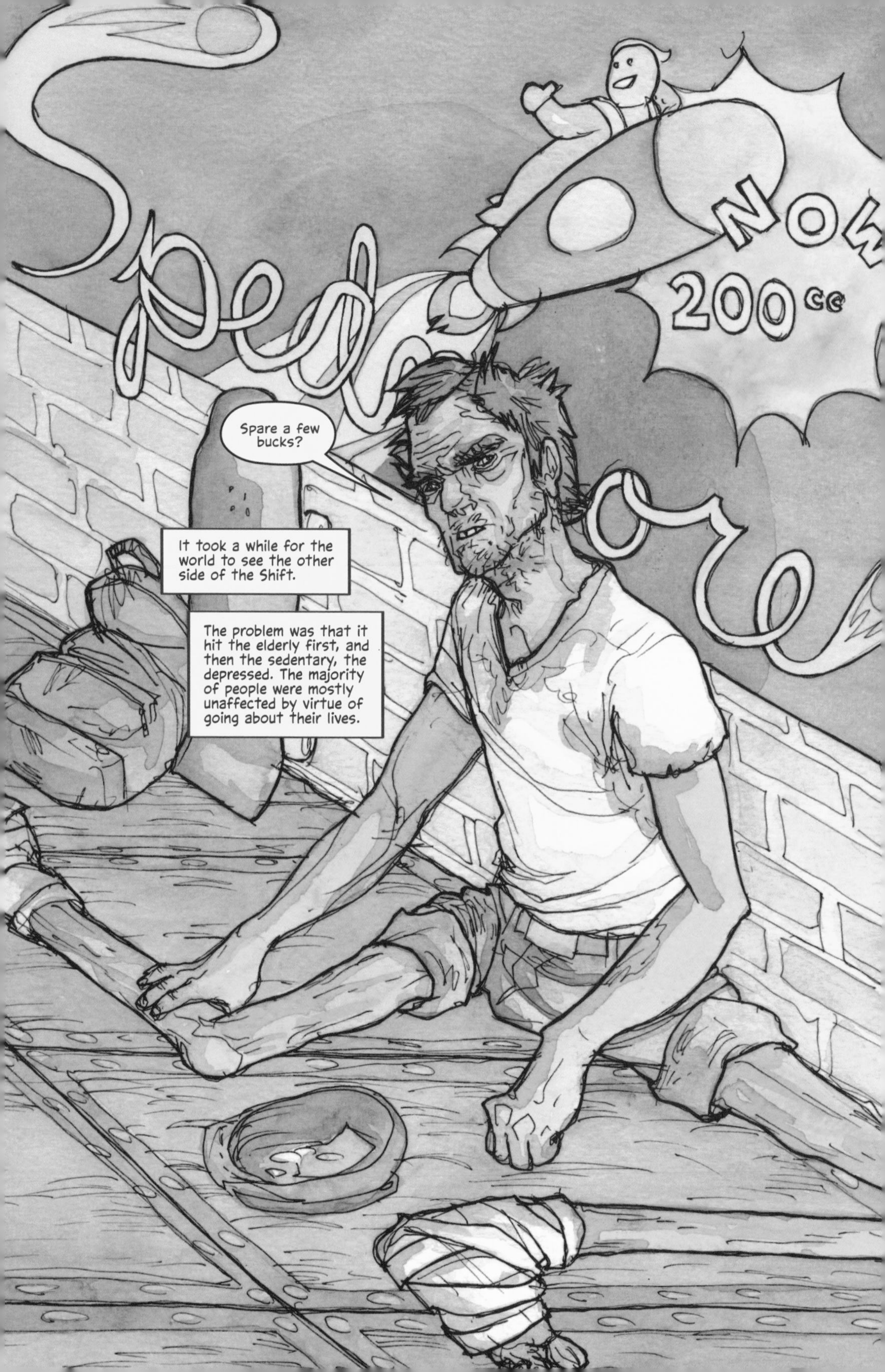
NOW
200cc
Spare a few bucks?
It took a while for the world to see the other side of the Shift.
The problem was that it hit the elderly first, and then the sedentary, the depressed. The majority of people were mostly unaffected by virtue of going about their lives.

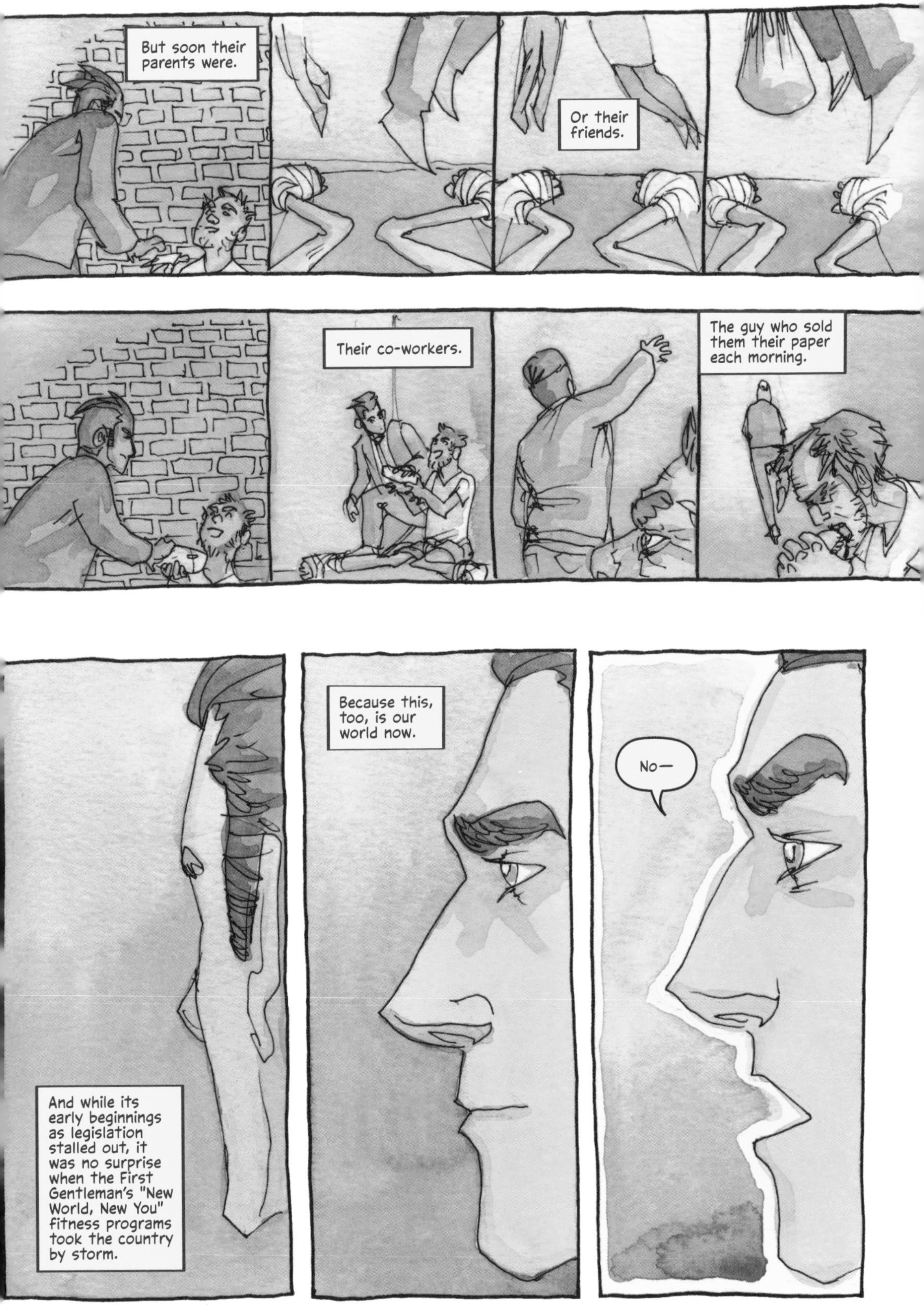

But soon their parents were.
Or their friends.
Their co-workers.
The guy who sold them their paper each morning.
And while its early beginnings as legislation stalled out, it was no surprise when the First Gentleman's "New World, New You" fitness programs took the country by storm.
Because this, too, is our world now.
No—

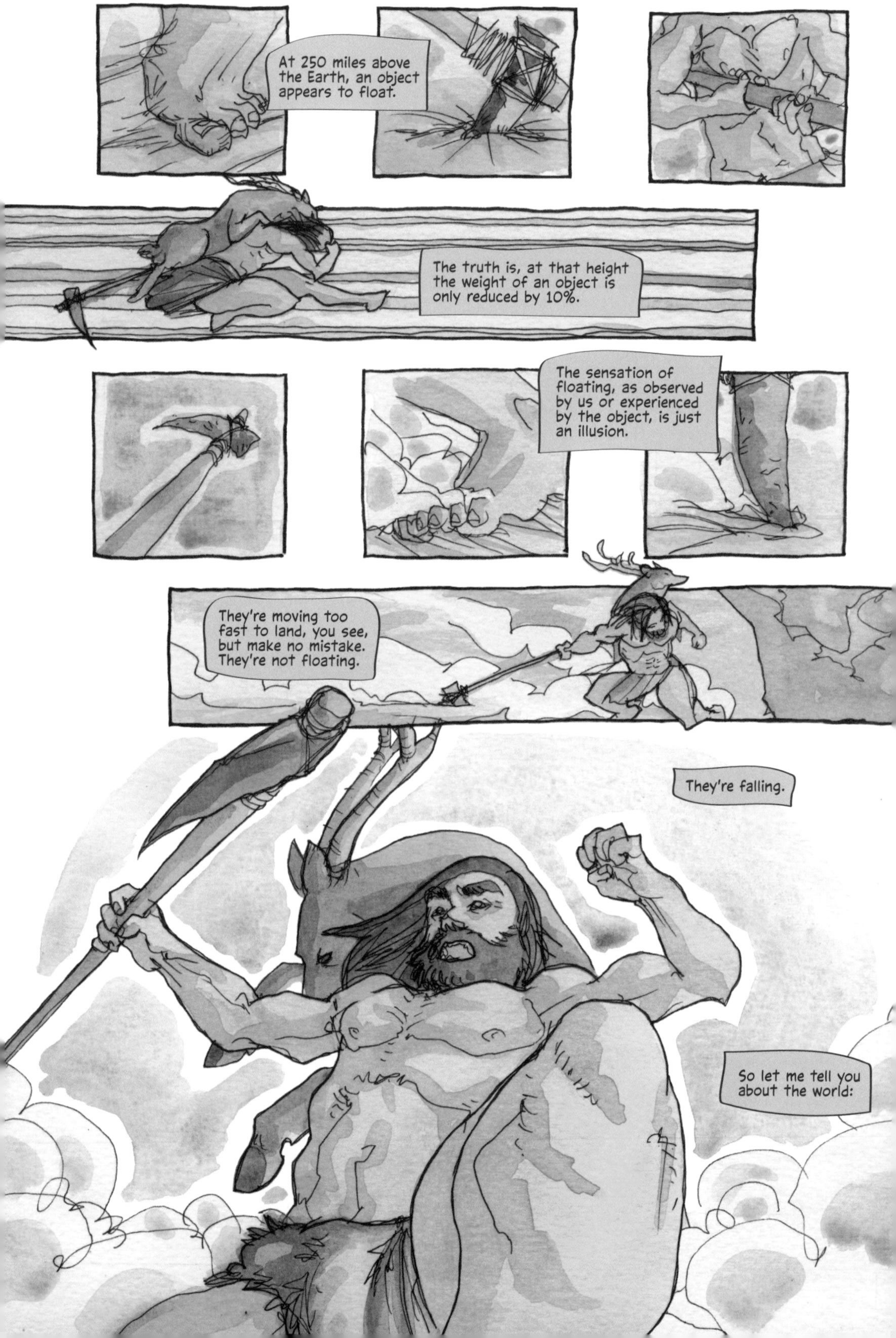
At 250 miles above the Earth, an object appears to float.
The truth is, at that height the weight of an object is only reduced by 10%.
The sensation of floating, as observed by us or experienced by the object, is just an illusion.
They're moving too fast to land, you see, but make no mistake. They're not floating.
They're falling.
So let me tell you about the world:

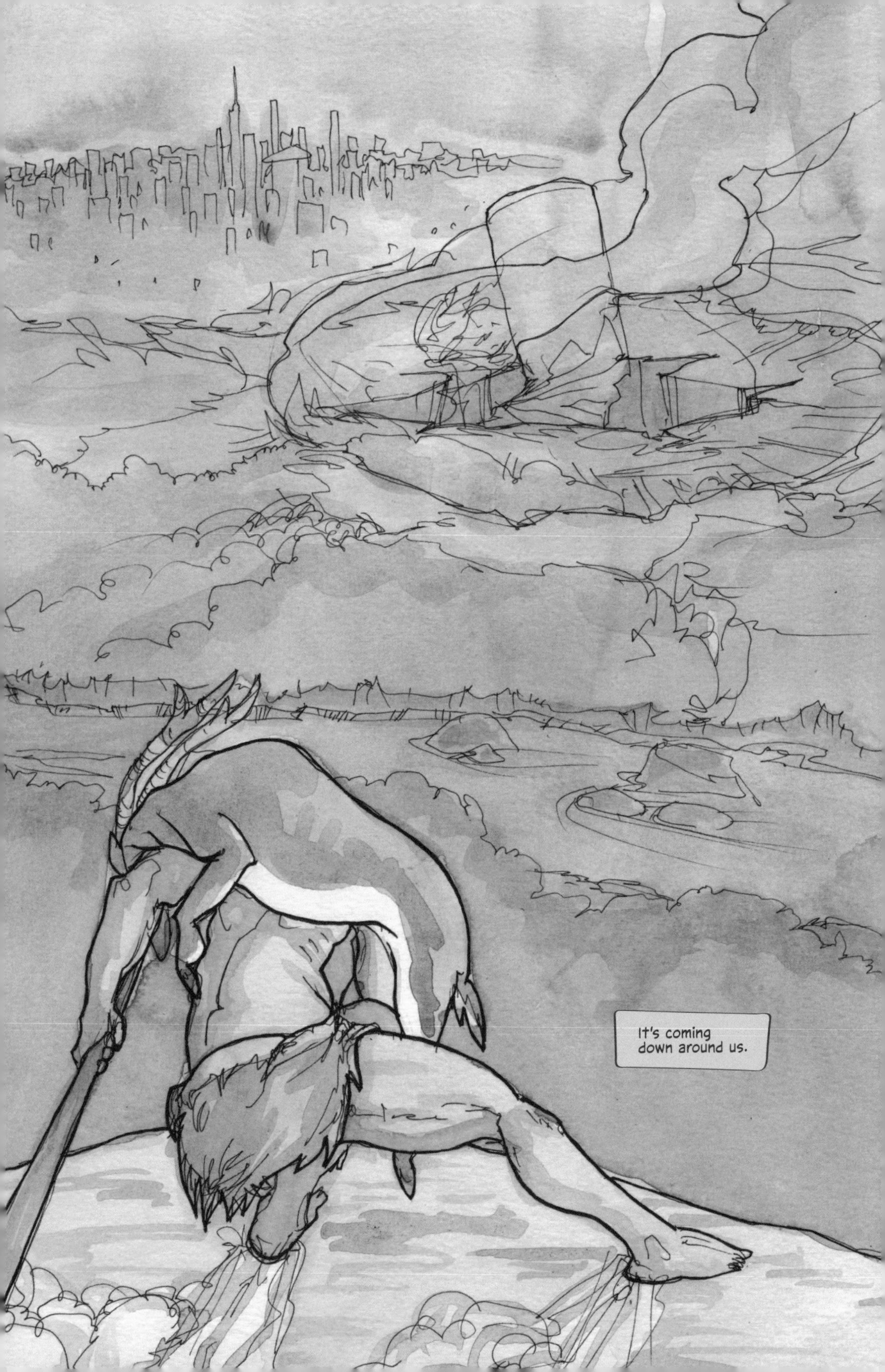
It's coming down around us.

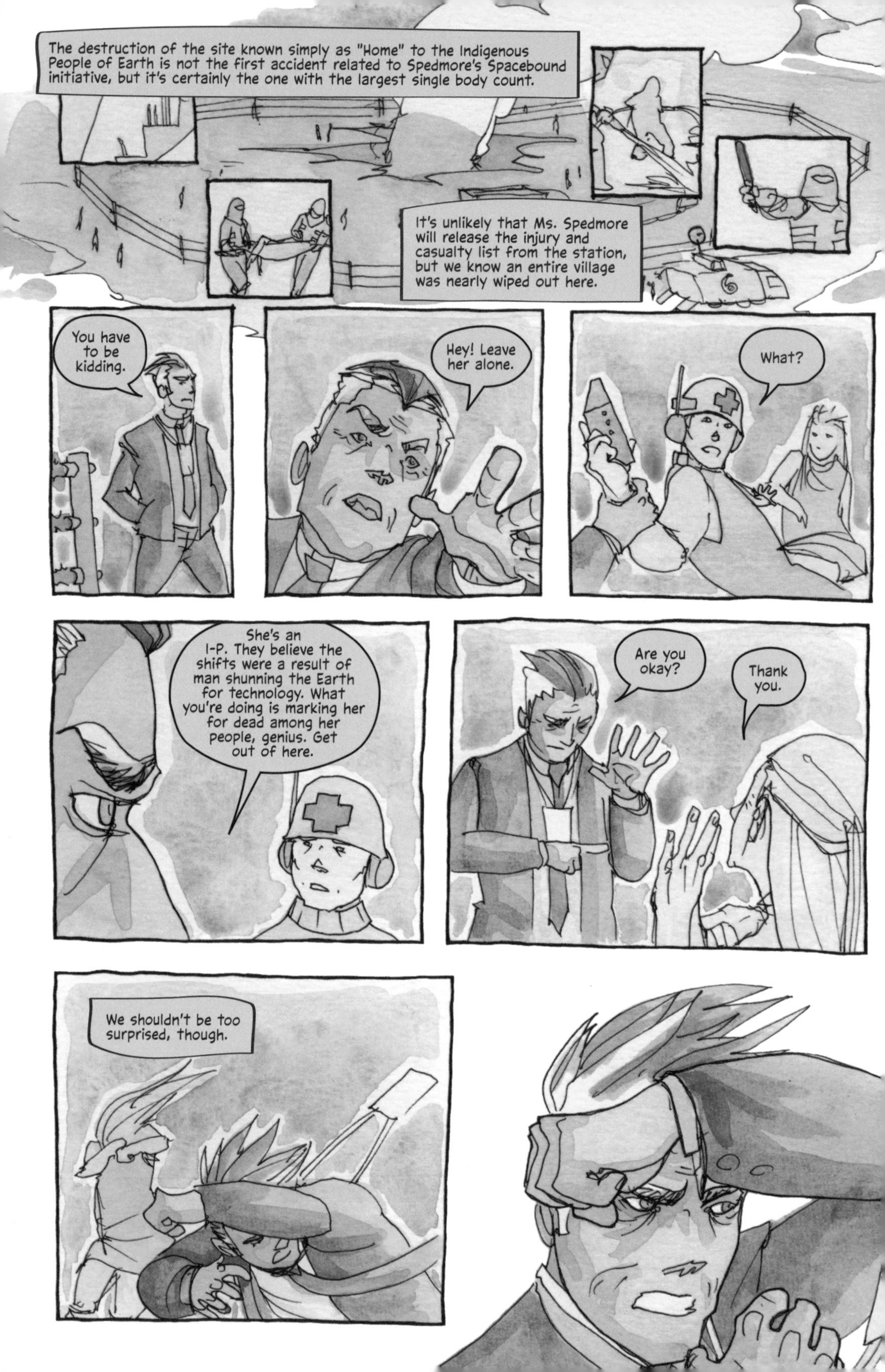
The destruction of the site known simply as "Home" to the Indigenous People of Earth is not the first accident related to Spedmore's Spacebound initiative, but it's certainly the one with the largest single body count.
It's unlikely that Ms. Spedmore will release the injury and casualty list from the station, but we know an entire village was nearly wiped out here.
You have to be kidding.
Hey! Leave her alone.
What?
She's an I-P. They believe the shifts were a result of man shunning the Earth for technology. What you're doing is marking her for dead among her people, genius. Get out of here.
Are you okay?
Thank you.
We shouldn't be too surprised, though.

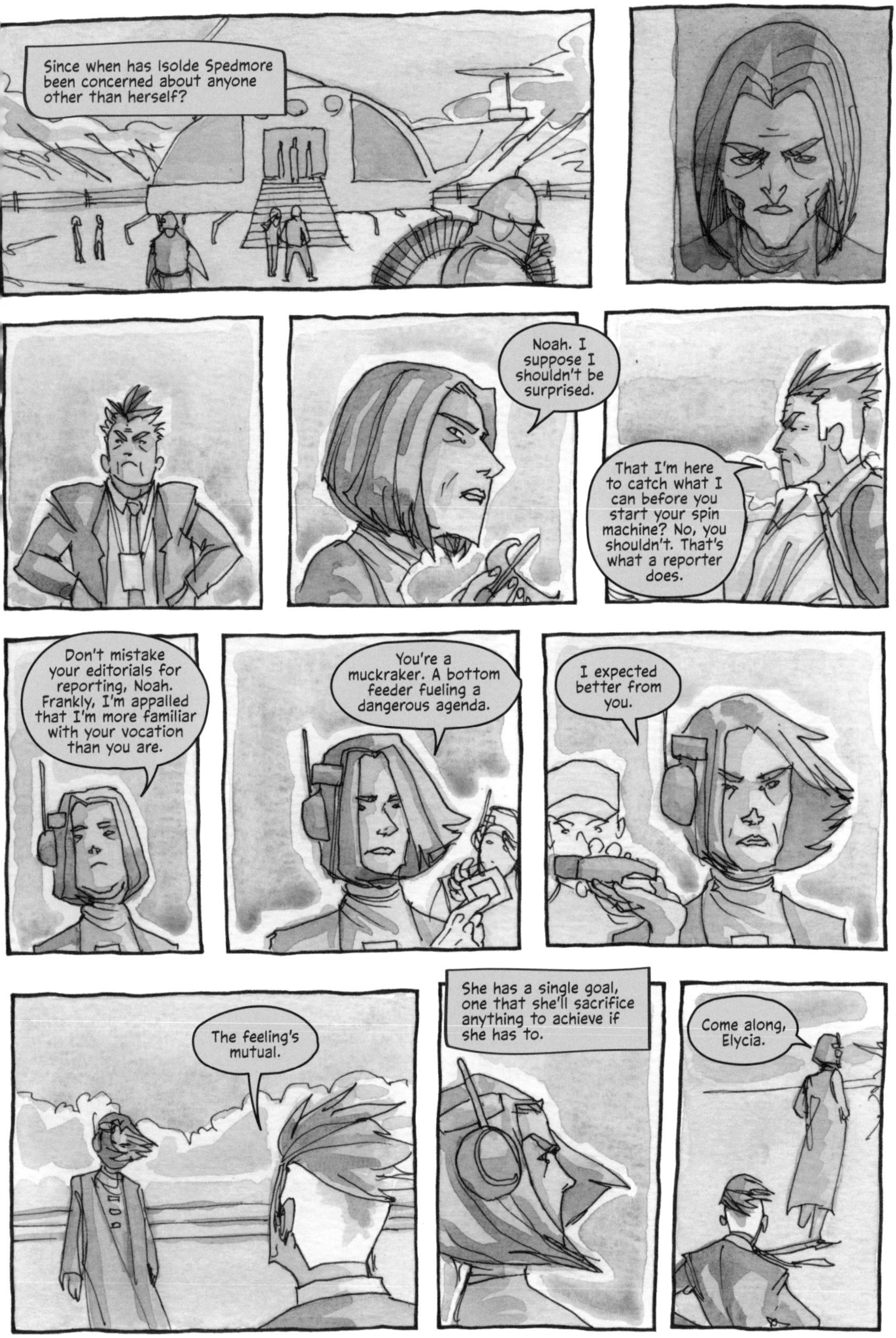
Since when has Isolde Spedmore been concerned about anyone other than herself?
Noah. I suppose I shouldn't be surprised.
That I'm here to catch what I can before you start your spin machine? No, you shouldn't. That's what a reporter does.
Don't mistake your editorials for reporting, Noah. Frankly, I'm appalled that I'm more familiar with your vocation than you are.
You're a muckraker. A bottom feeder fueling a dangerous agenda.
I expected better from you.
The feeling's mutual.
She has a single goal, one that she'll sacrifice anything to achieve if she has to.
Come along, Elycia.

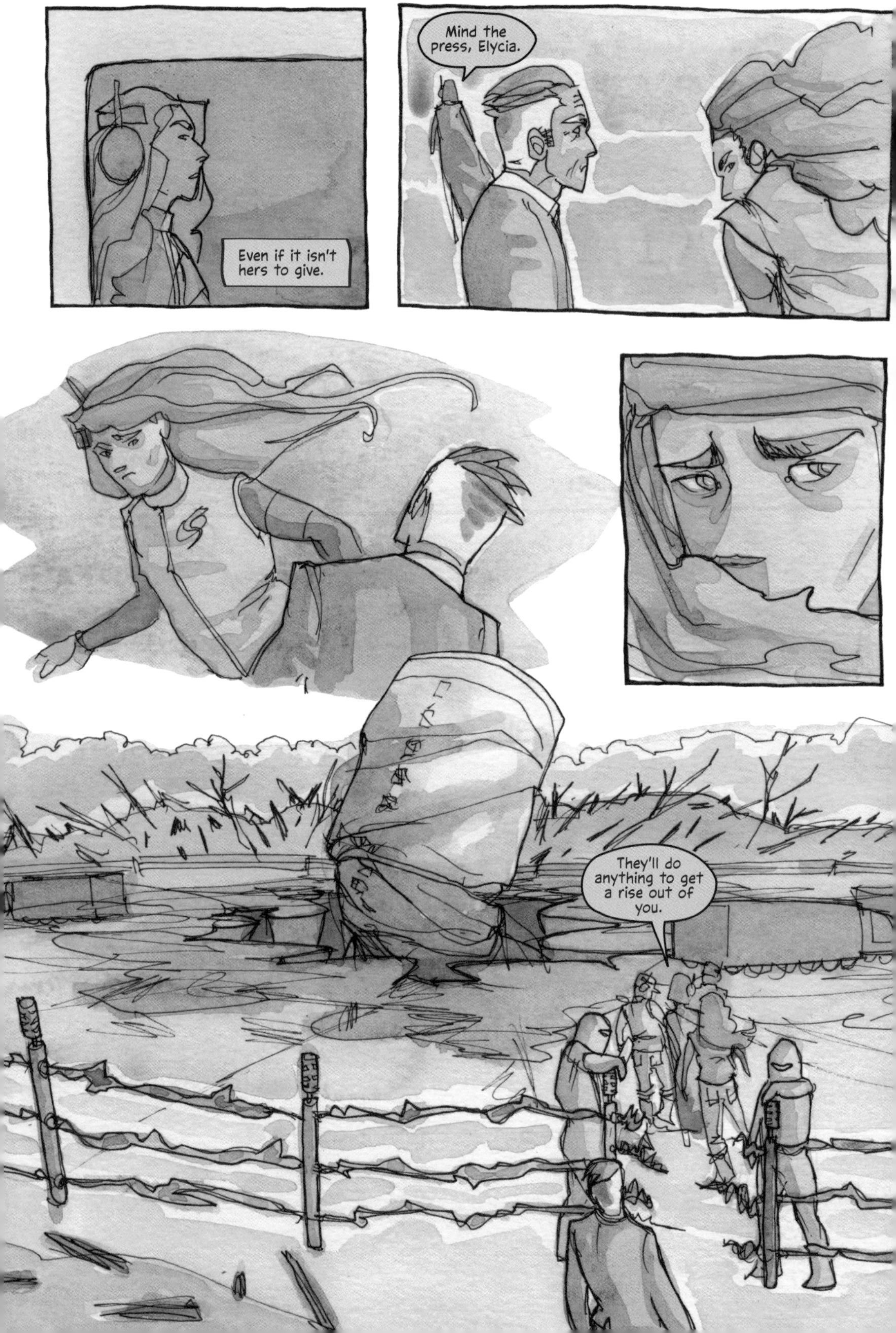
Even if it isn't hers to give.
Mind the press, Elycia.
They'll do anything to get a rise out of you.

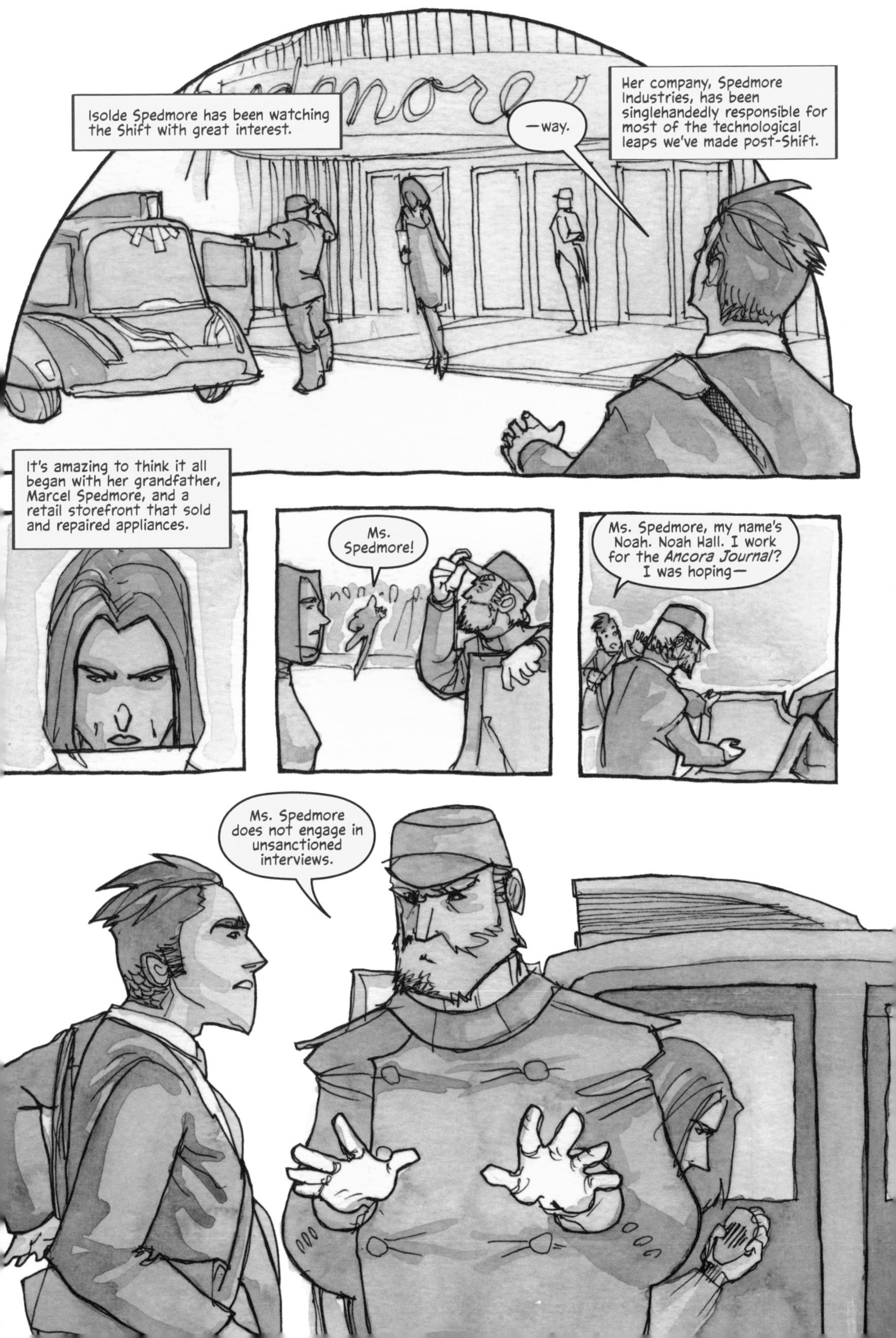
Isolde Spedmore has been watching the Shift with great interest.
—way.
Her company, Spedmore Industries, has been singlehandedly responsible for most of the technological leaps we've made post-Shift.
It's amazing to think it all began with her grandfather, Marcel Spedmore, and a retail storefront that sold and repaired appliances.
Ms. Spedmore!
Ms. Spedmore, my name's Noah. Noah Hall. I work for the *Ancora Journal*? I was hoping—
Ms. Spedmore does not engage in unsanctioned interviews.

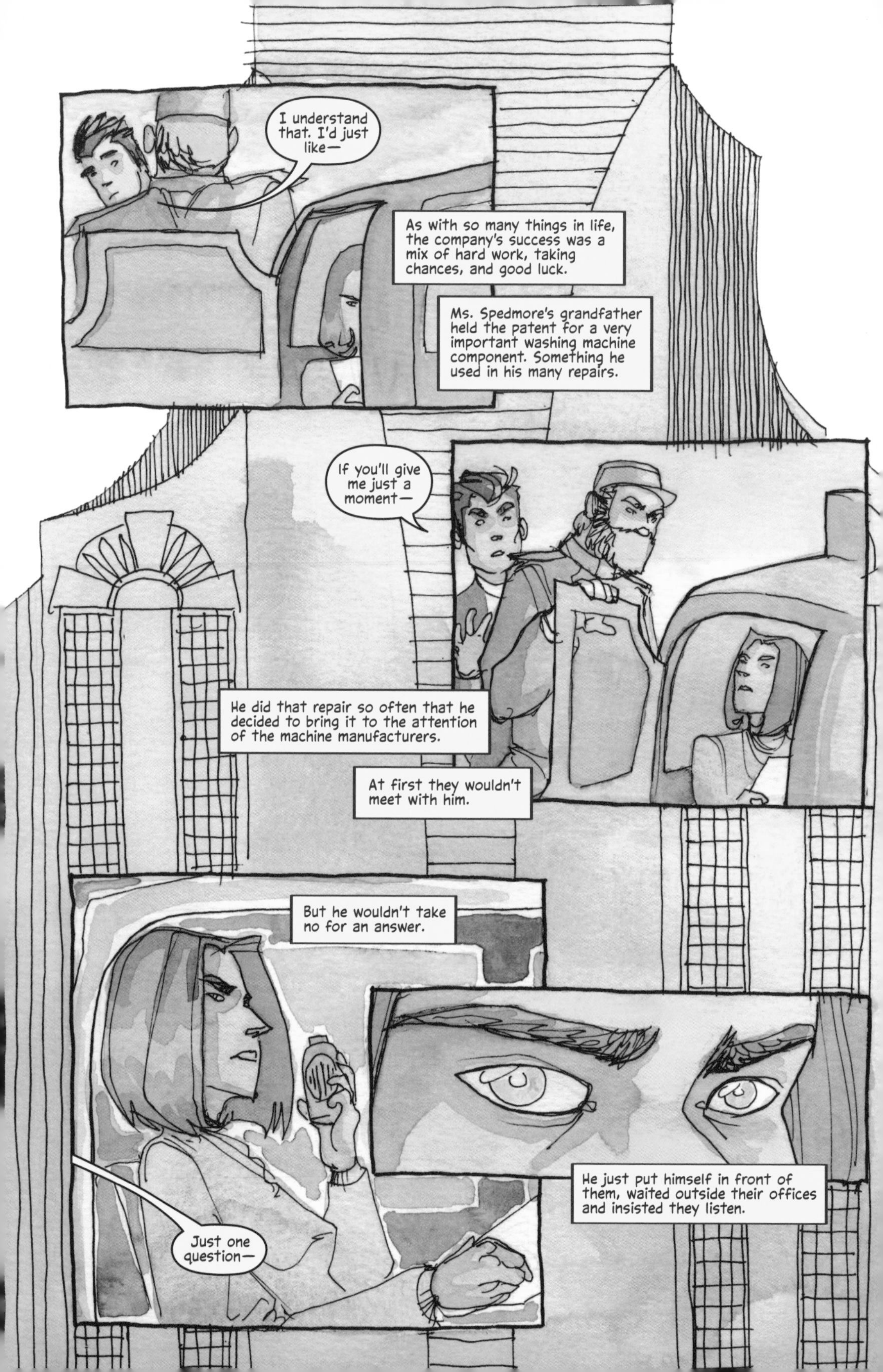
I understand that. I'd just like—
As with so many things in life, the company's success was a mix of hard work, taking chances, and good luck.
Ms. Spedmore's grandfather held the patent for a very important washing machine component. Something he used in his many repairs.
If you'll give me just a moment—
He did that repair so often that he decided to bring it to the attention of the machine manufacturers.
At first they wouldn't meet with him.
But he wouldn't take no for an answer.
Just one question—
He just put himself in front of them, waited outside their offices and insisted they listen.

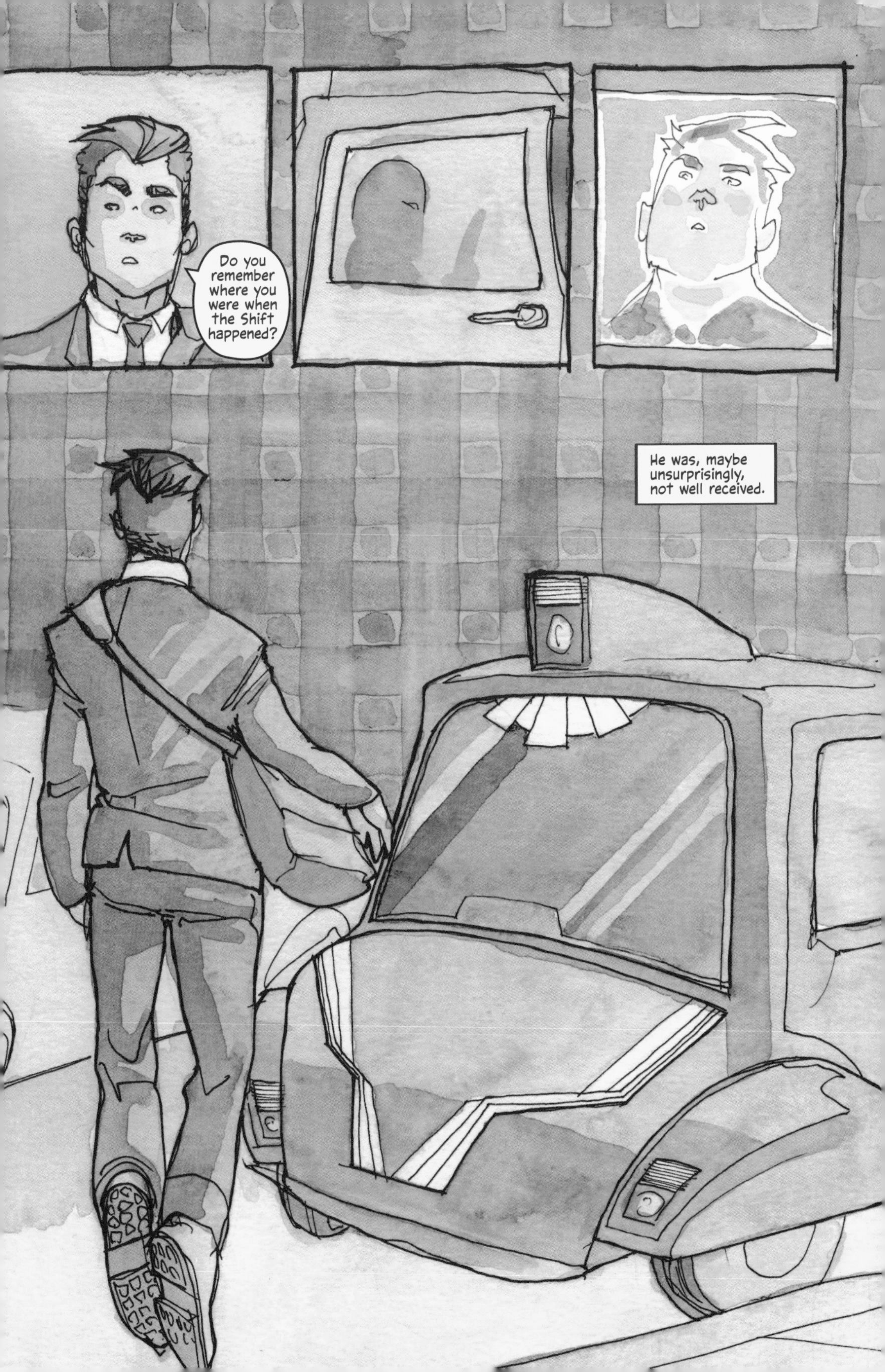
Do you remember where you were when the Shift happened?
He was, maybe unsurprisingly, not well received.

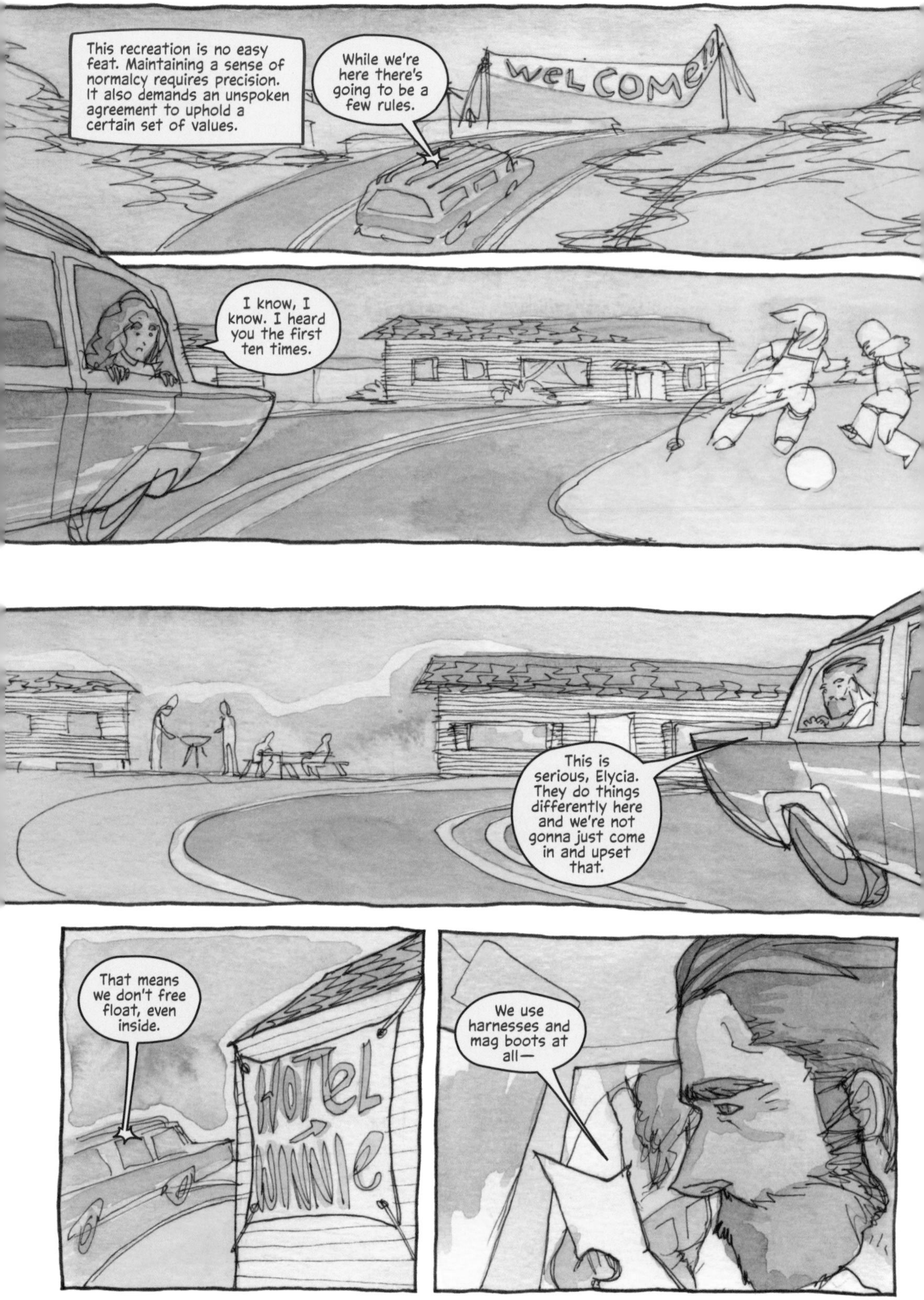

This recreation is no easy feat. Maintaining a sense of normalcy requires precision. It also demands an unspoken agreement to uphold a certain set of values.
While we're here there's going to be a few rules.
WELCOME!!
I know, I know. I heard you the first ten times.
This is serious, Elycia. They do things differently here and we're not gonna just come in and upset that.
That means we don't free float, even inside.
HOTEL WINNIE
We use harnesses and mag boots at all—

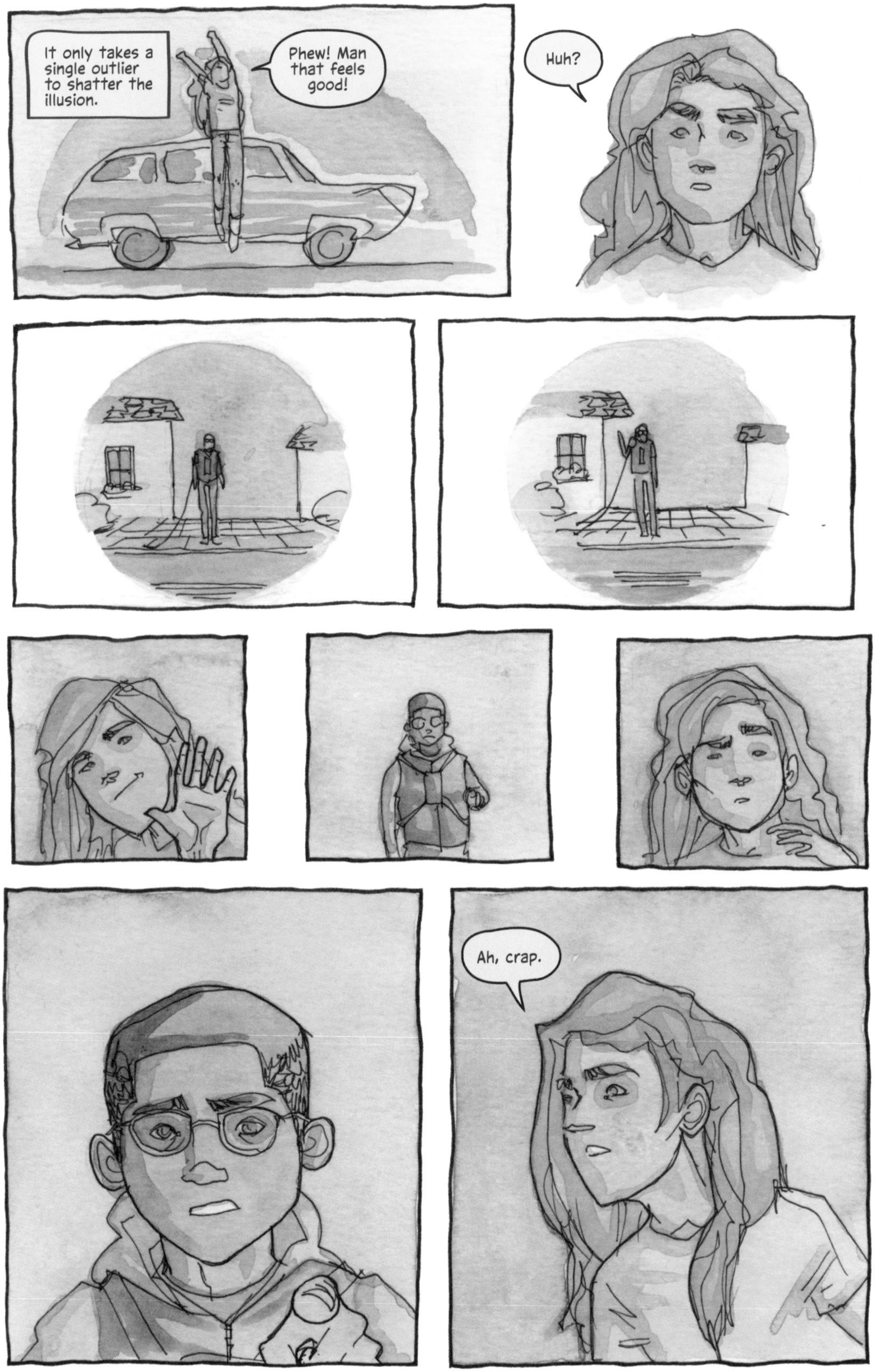
It only takes a single outlier to shatter the illusion.
Phew! Man that feels good!
Huh?
Ah, crap.

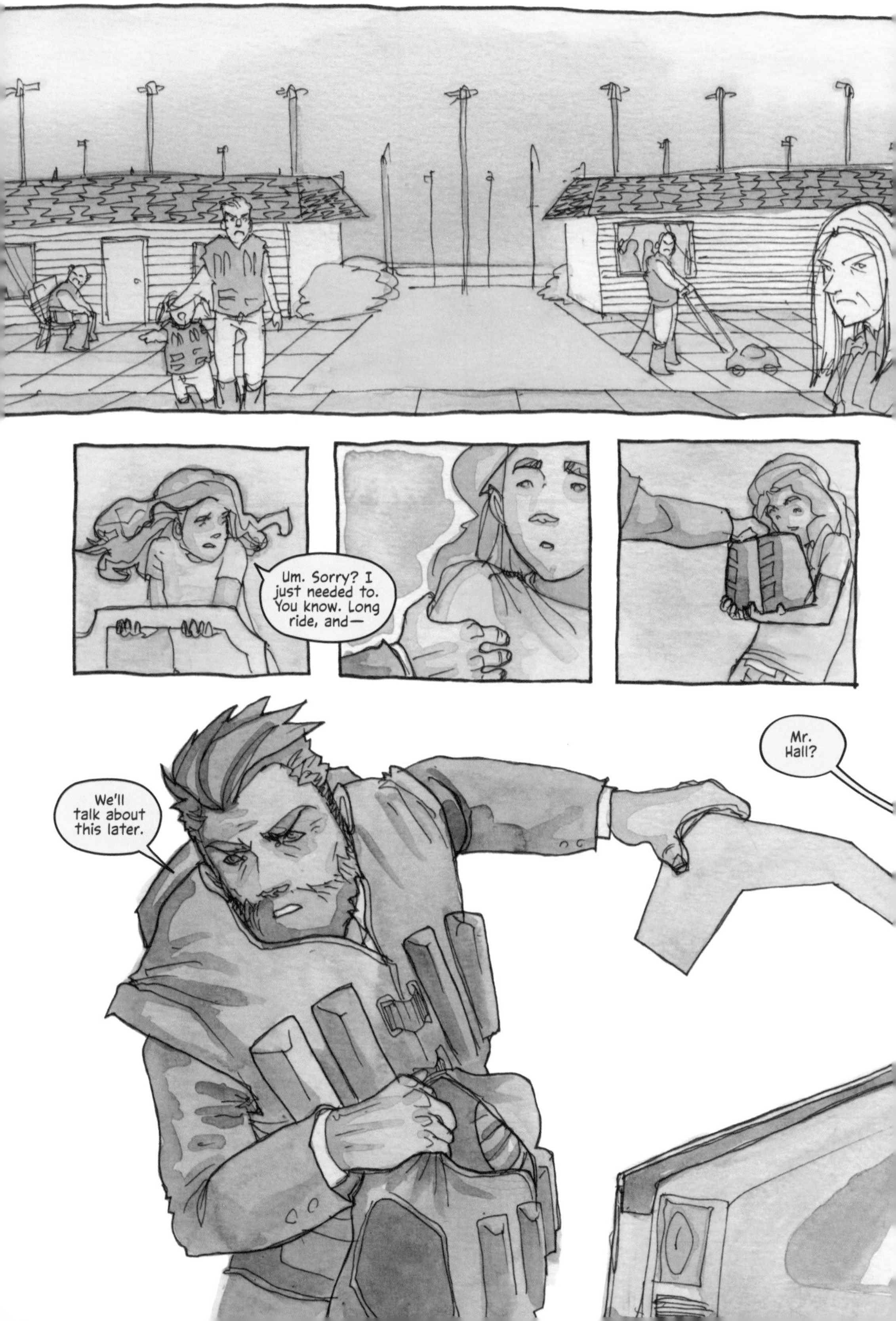
Um. Sorry? I just needed to. You know. Long ride, and—
Mr. Hall?
We'll talk about this later.

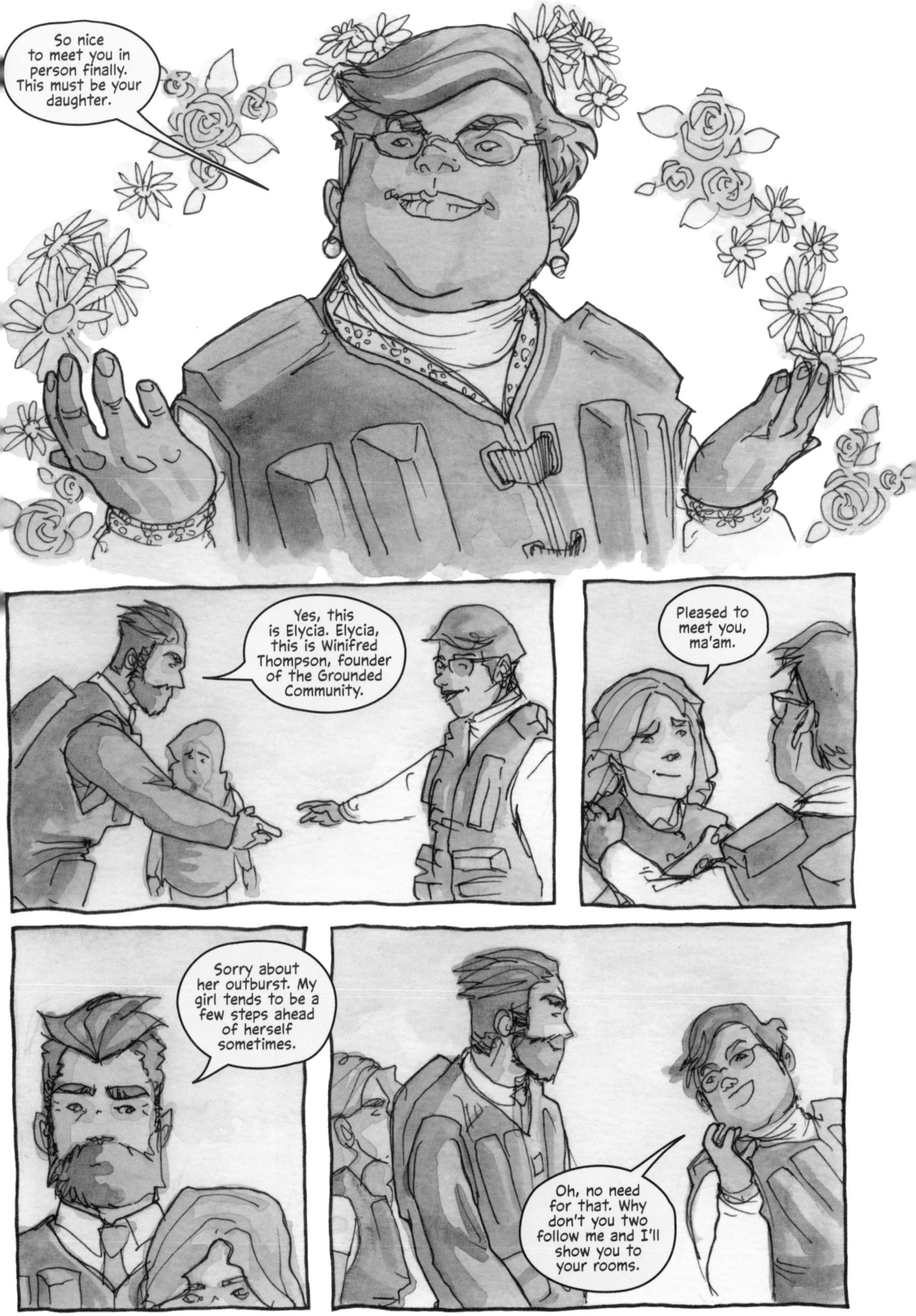
So nice to meet you in person finally. This must be your daughter.
Yes, this is Elycia. Elycia, this is Winifred Thompson, founder of the Grounded Community.
Pleased to meet you, ma'am.
Sorry about her outburst. My girl tends to be a few steps ahead of herself sometimes.
Oh, no need for that. Why don't you two follow me and I'll show you to your rooms.

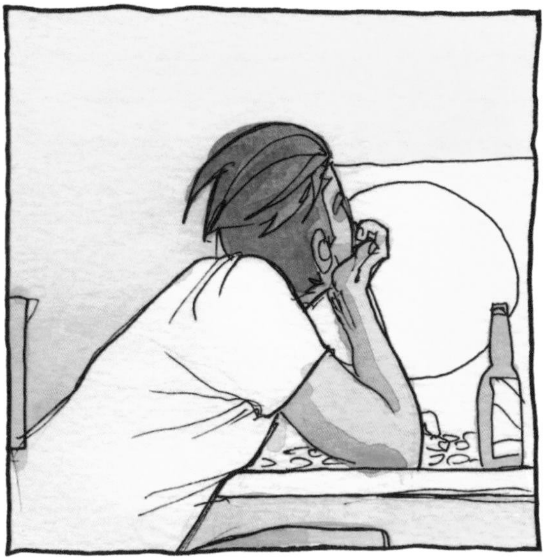

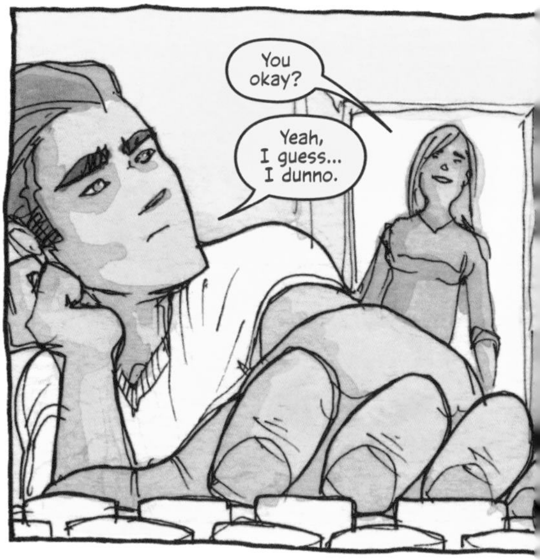
You okay?
Yeah, I guess... I dunno.

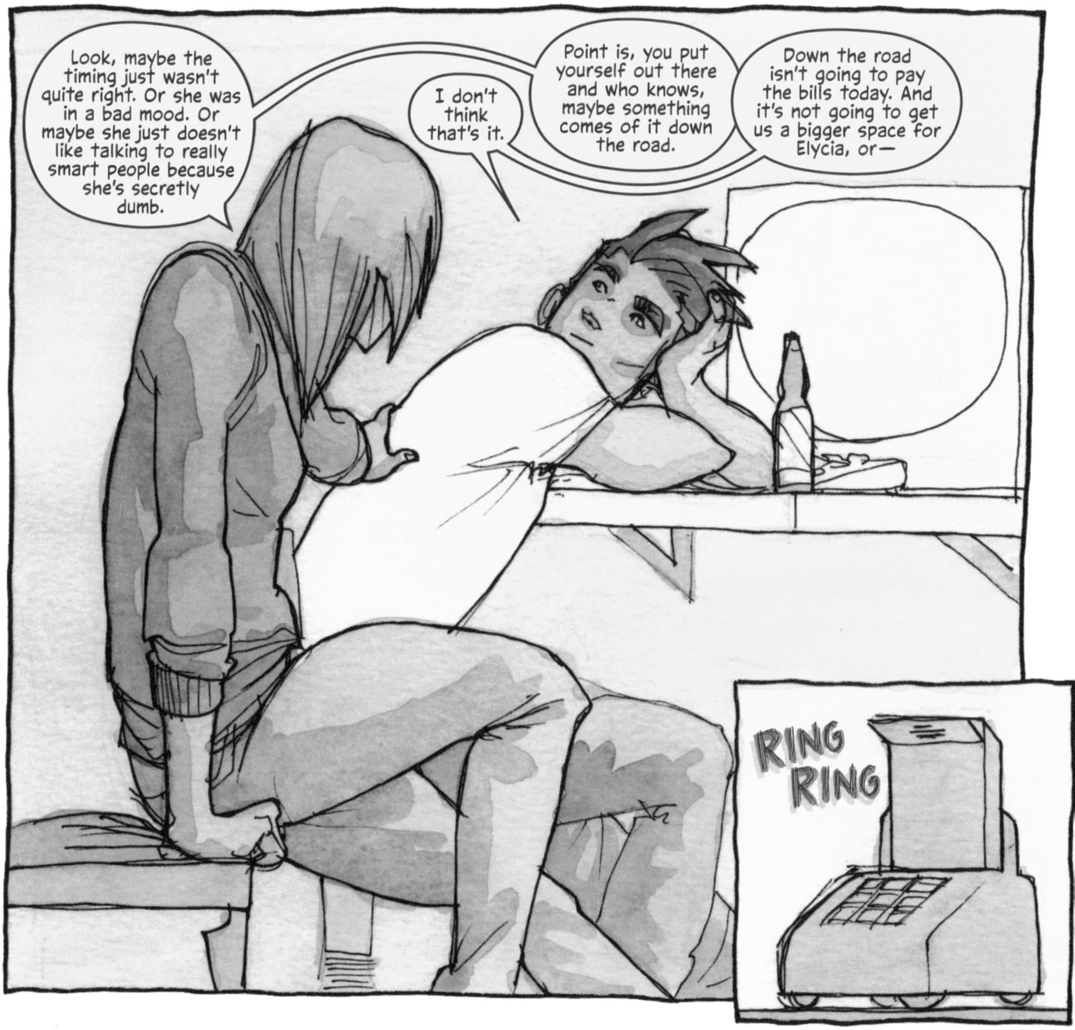
Look, maybe the timing just wasn't quite right. Or she was in a bad mood. Or maybe she just doesn't like talking to really smart people because she's secretly dumb.
I don't think that's it.
Point is, you put yourself out there and who knows, maybe something comes of it down the road.
Down the road isn't going to pay the bills today. And it's not going to get us a bigger space for Elycia, or—
RING RING

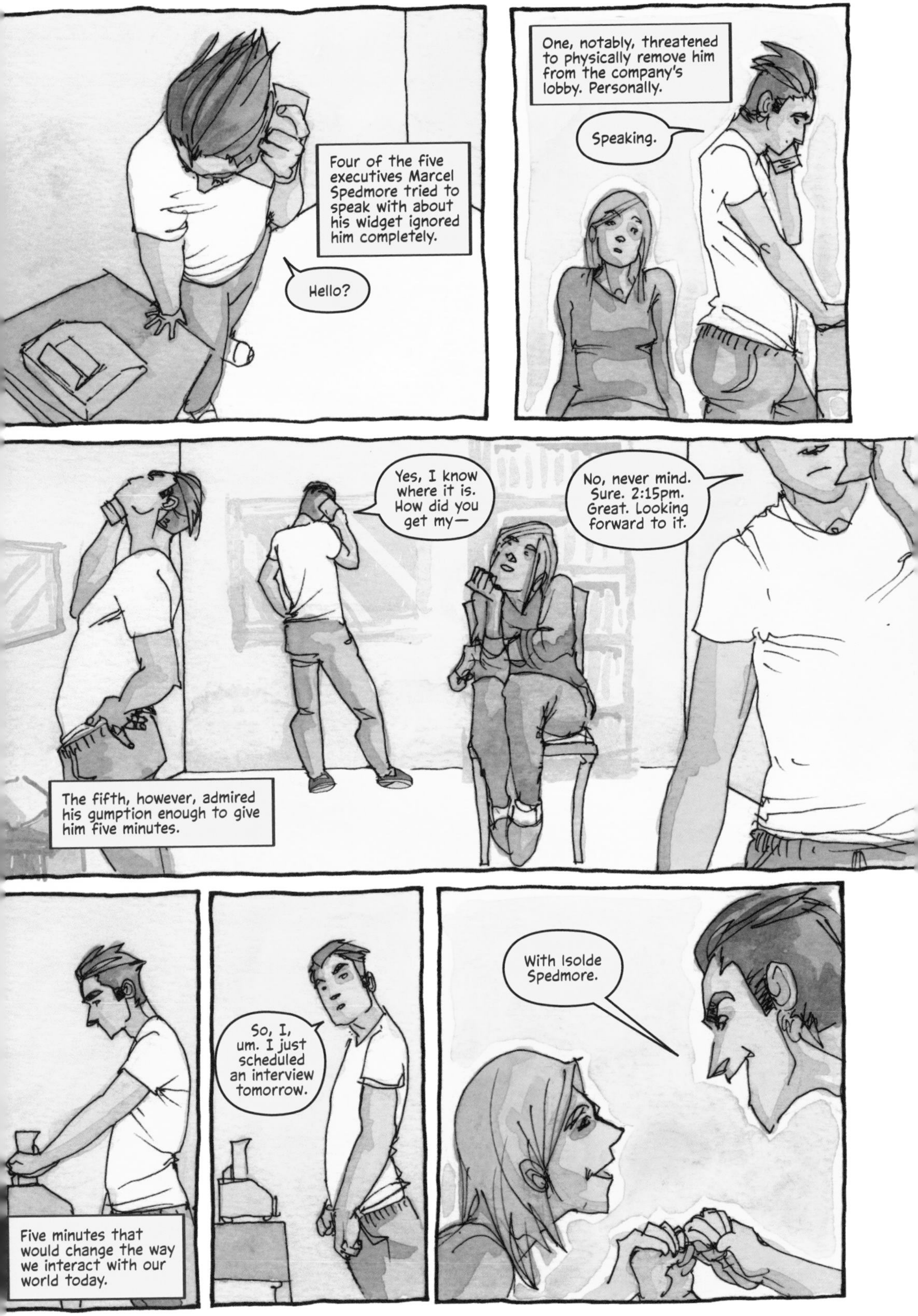
Four of the five executives Marcel Spedmore tried to speak with about his widget ignored him completely.
Hello?
One, notably, threatened to physically remove him from the company's lobby. Personally.
Speaking.
The fifth, however, admired his gumption enough to give him five minutes.
Yes, I know where it is. How did you get my—
No, never mind. Sure. 2:15pm. Great. Looking forward to it.
Five minutes that would change the way we interact with our world today.
So, I, um. I just scheduled an interview tomorrow.
With Isolde Spedmore.

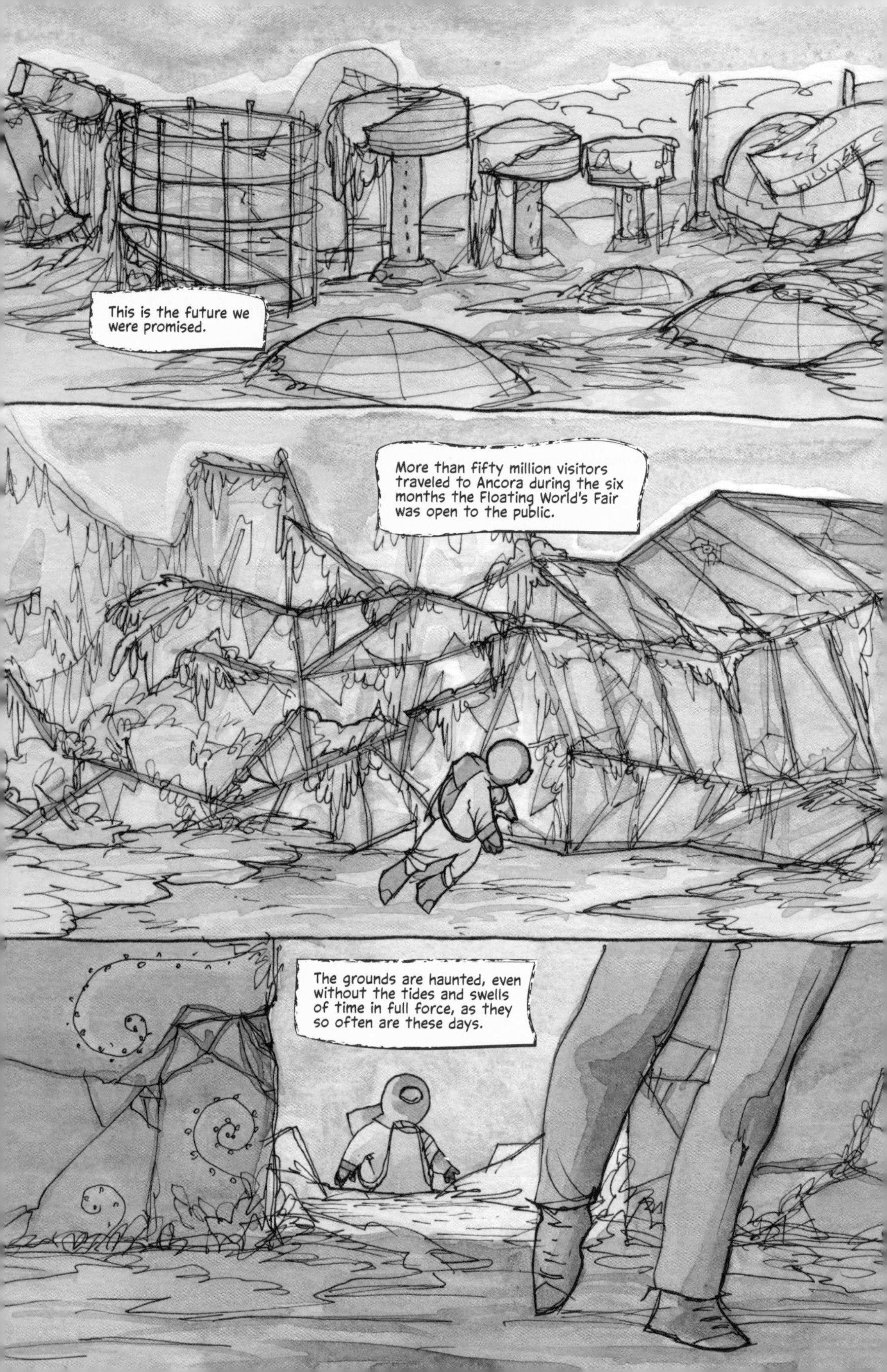
This is the future we were promised.
More than fifty million visitors traveled to Ancora during the six months the Floating World's Fair was open to the public.
The grounds are haunted, even without the tides and swells of time in full force, as they so often are these days.

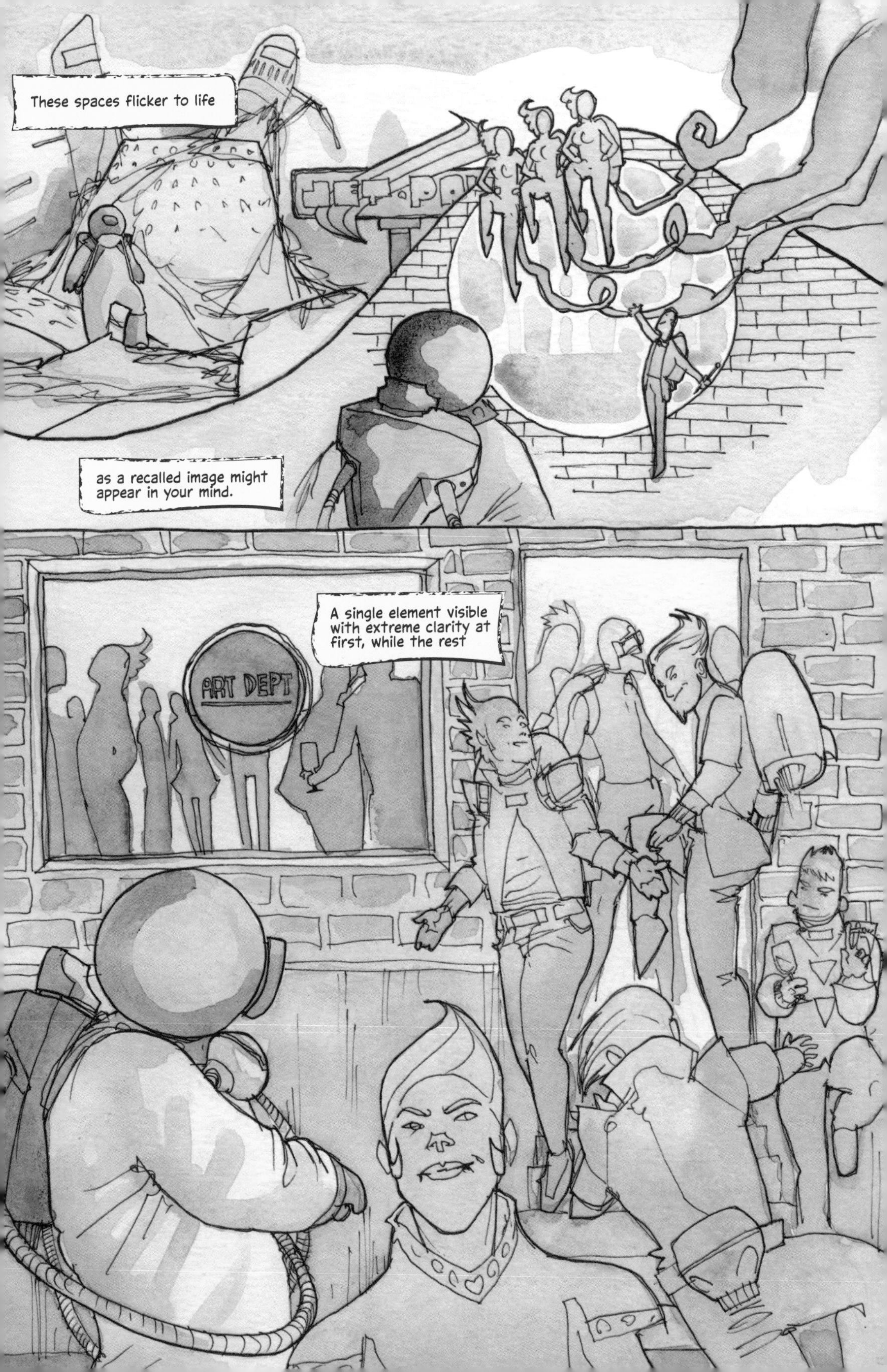
These spaces flicker to life
as a recalled image might appear in your mind.
A single element visible with extreme clarity at first, while the rest
ART DEPT

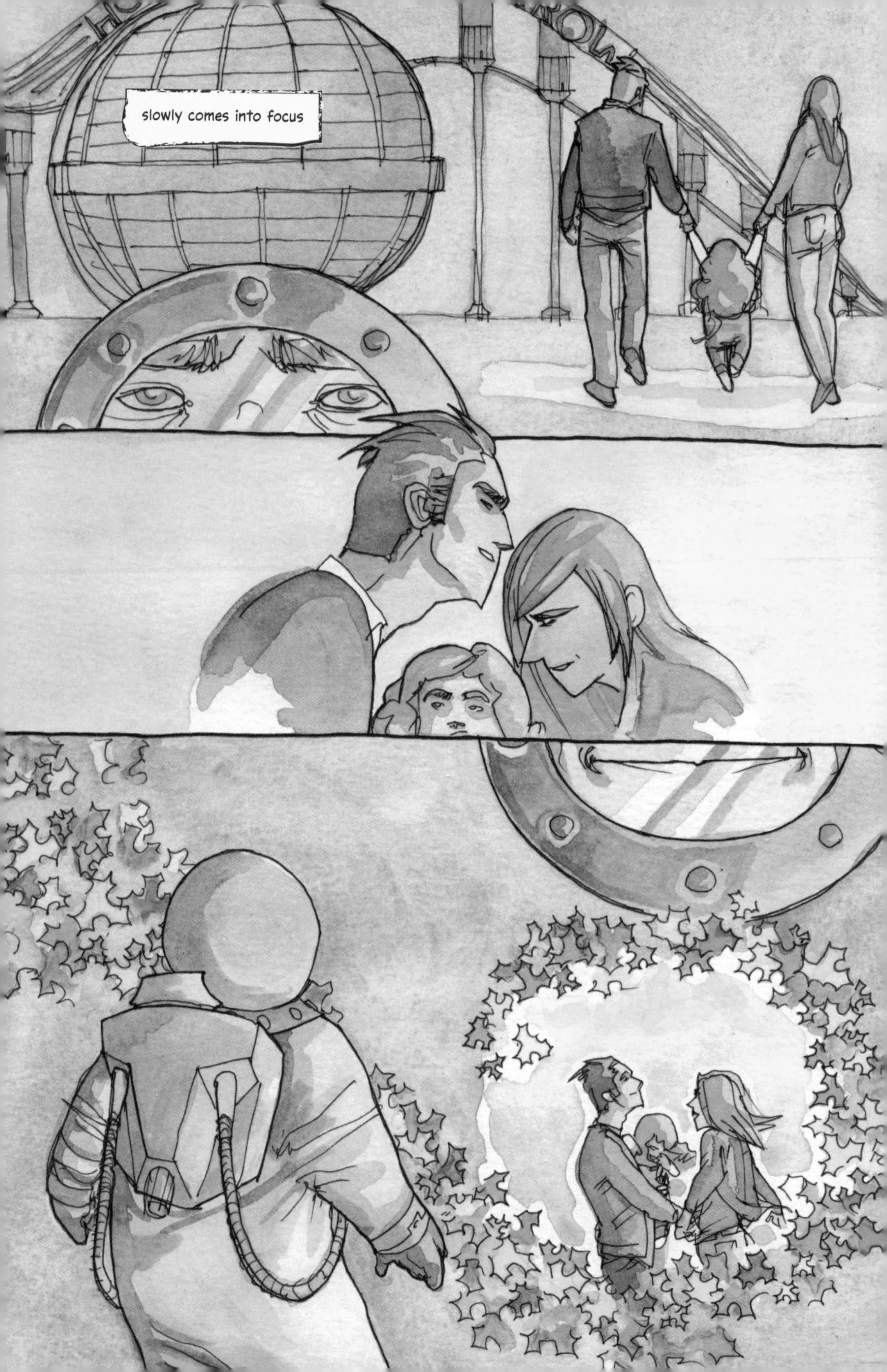
slowly comes into focus

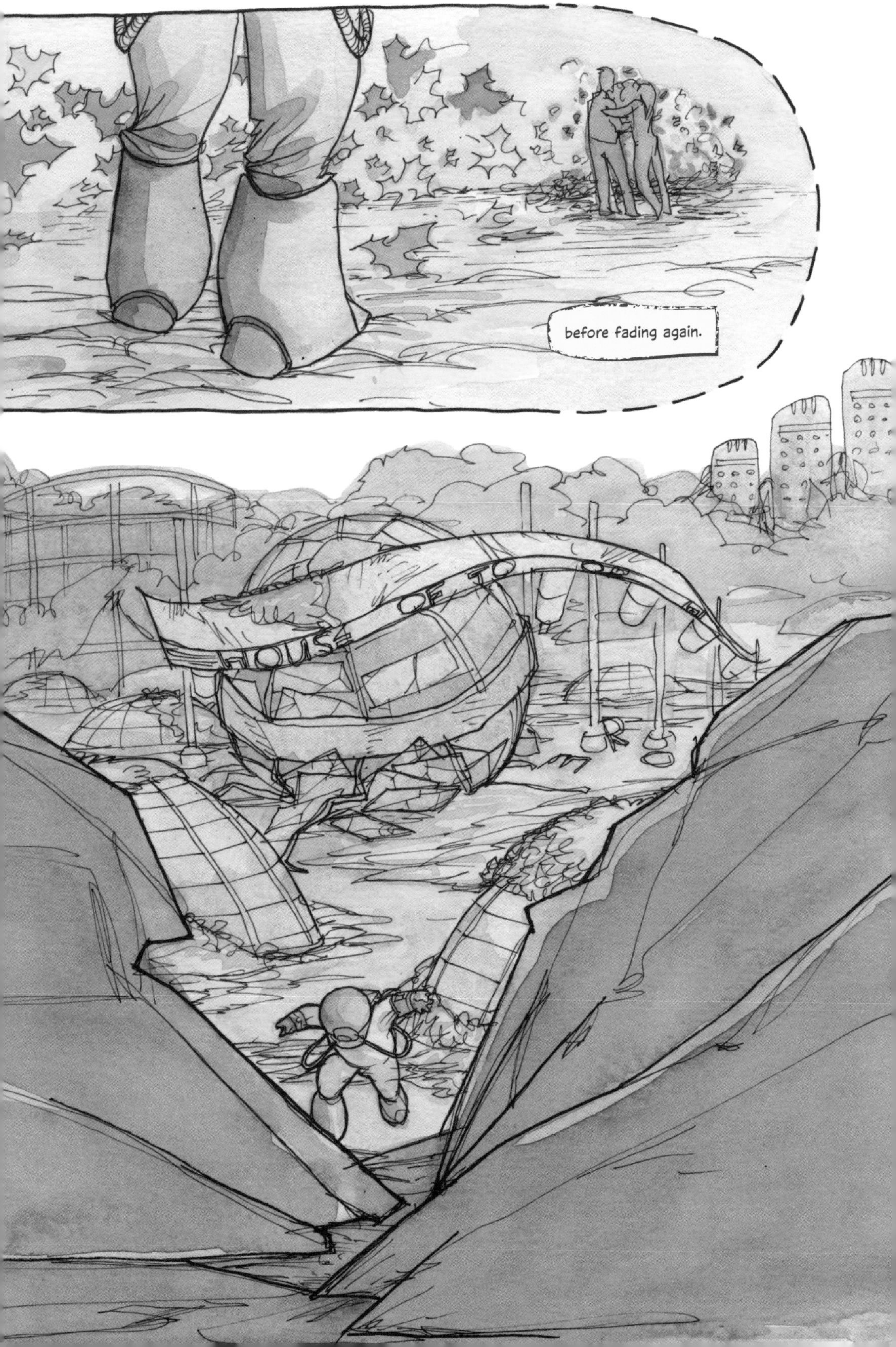
before fading again.
HOUSE OF TO

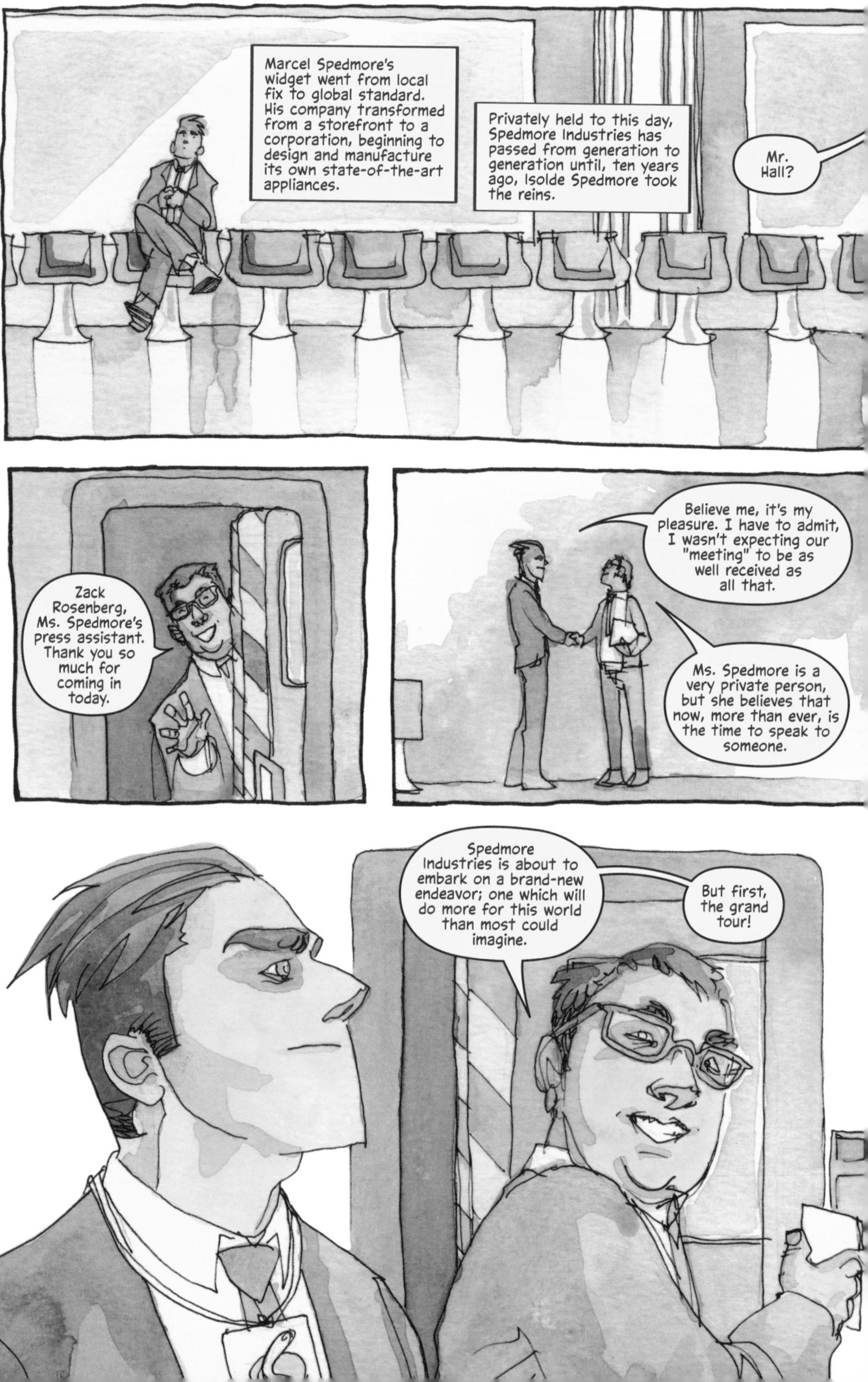

Marcel Spedmore's widget went from local fix to global standard. His company transformed from a storefront to a corporation, beginning to design and manufacture its own state-of-the-art appliances.
Privately held to this day, Spedmore Industries has passed from generation to generation until, ten years ago, Isolde Spedmore took the reins.
Mr. Hall?
Zack Rosenberg, Ms. Spedmore's press assistant. Thank you so much for coming in today.
Believe me, it's my pleasure. I have to admit, I wasn't expecting our "meeting" to be as well received as all that.
Ms. Spedmore is a very private person, but she believes that now, more than ever, is the time to speak to someone.
Spedmore Industries is about to embark on a brand-new endeavor; one which will do more for this world than most could imagine.
But first, the grand tour!

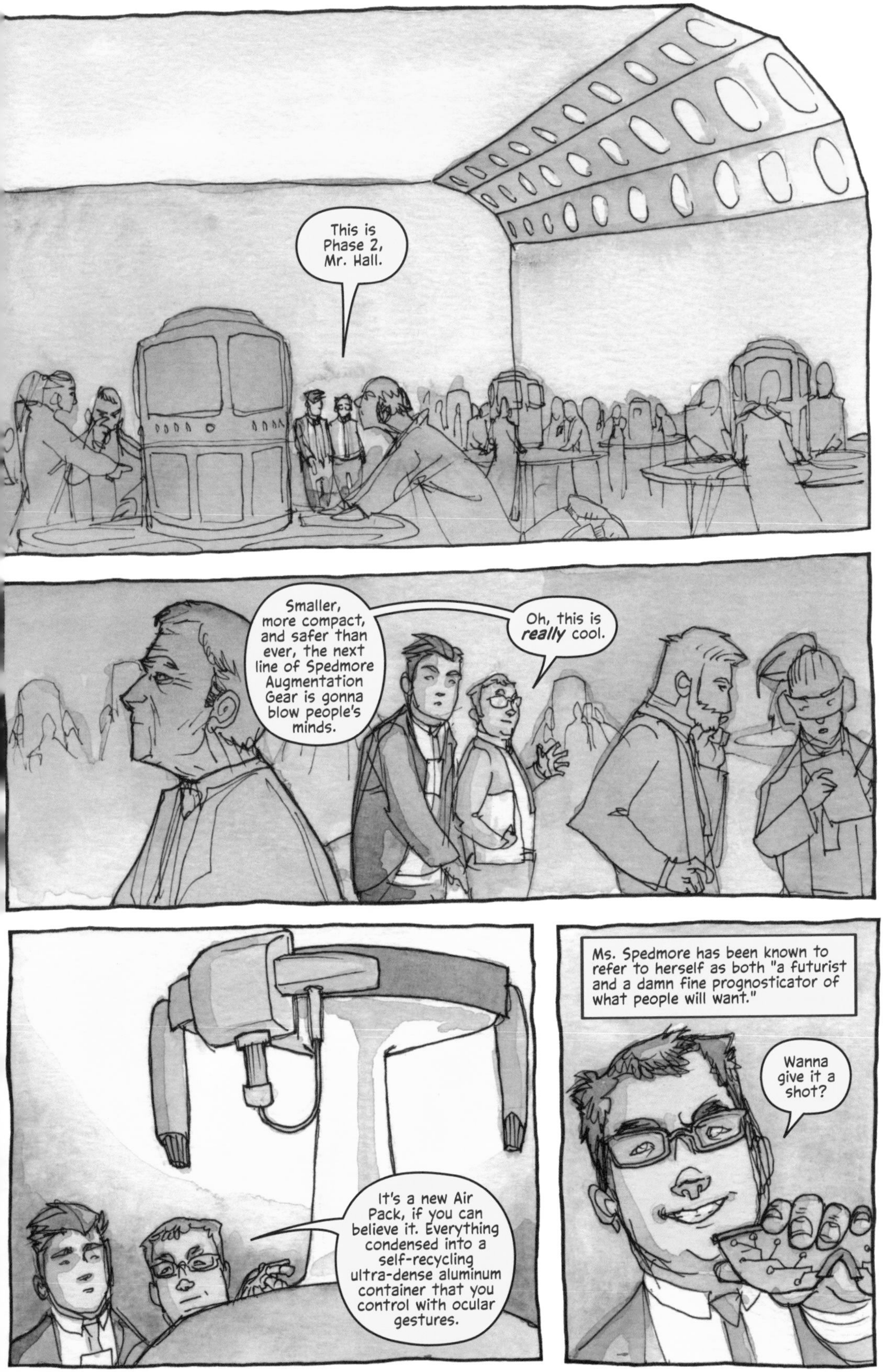
This is Phase 2, Mr. Hall.
Smaller, more compact, and safer than ever, the next line of Spedmore Augmentation Gear is gonna blow people's minds.
Oh, this is *really* cool.
It's a new Air Pack, if you can believe it. Everything condensed into a self-recycling ultra-dense aluminum container that you control with ocular gestures.
Ms. Spedmore has been known to refer to herself as both "a futurist and a damn fine prognosticator of what people will want."
Wanna give it a shot?

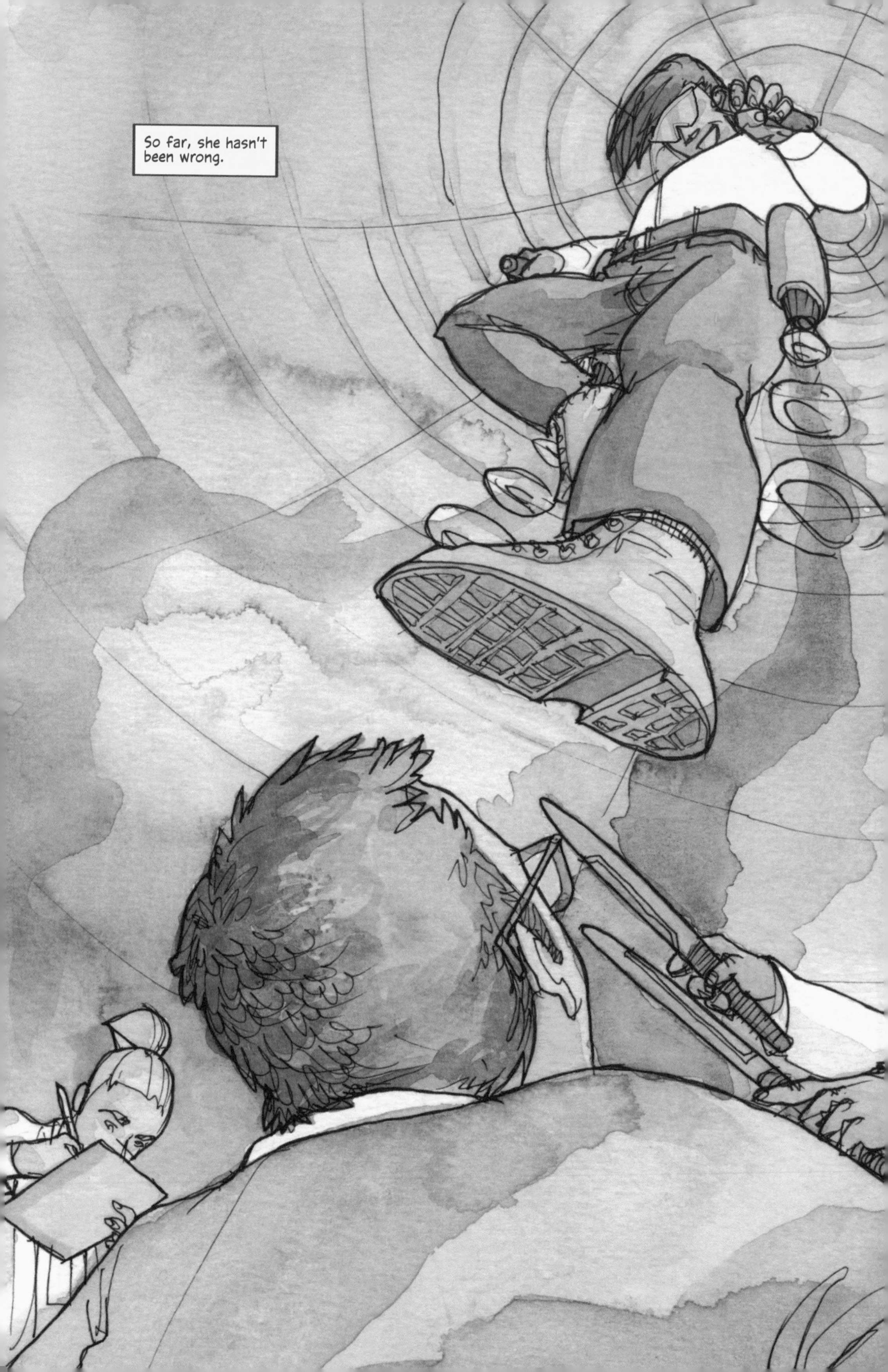
So far, she hasn't been wrong.

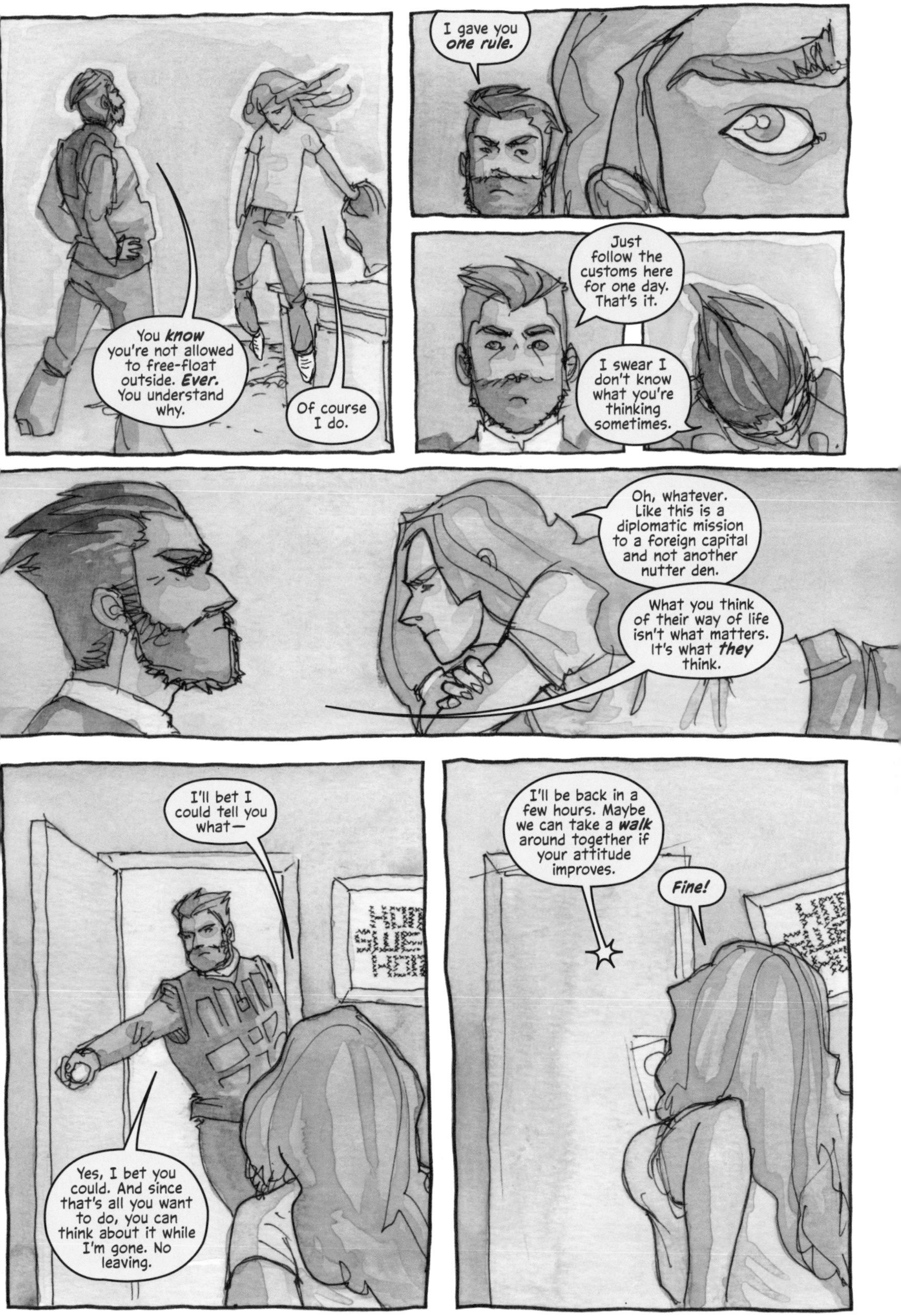
You **know** you're not allowed to free-float outside. **Ever.** You understand why.
Of course I do.
I gave you **one rule.**
Just follow the customs here for one day. That's it.
I swear I don't know what you're thinking sometimes.
Oh, whatever. Like this is a diplomatic mission to a foreign capital and not another nutter den.
What you think of their way of life isn't what matters. It's what **they** think.
I'll bet I could tell you what—
Yes, I bet you could. And since that's all you want to do, you can think about it while I'm gone. No leaving.
I'll be back in a few hours. Maybe we can take a **walk** around together if your attitude improves.
Fine!

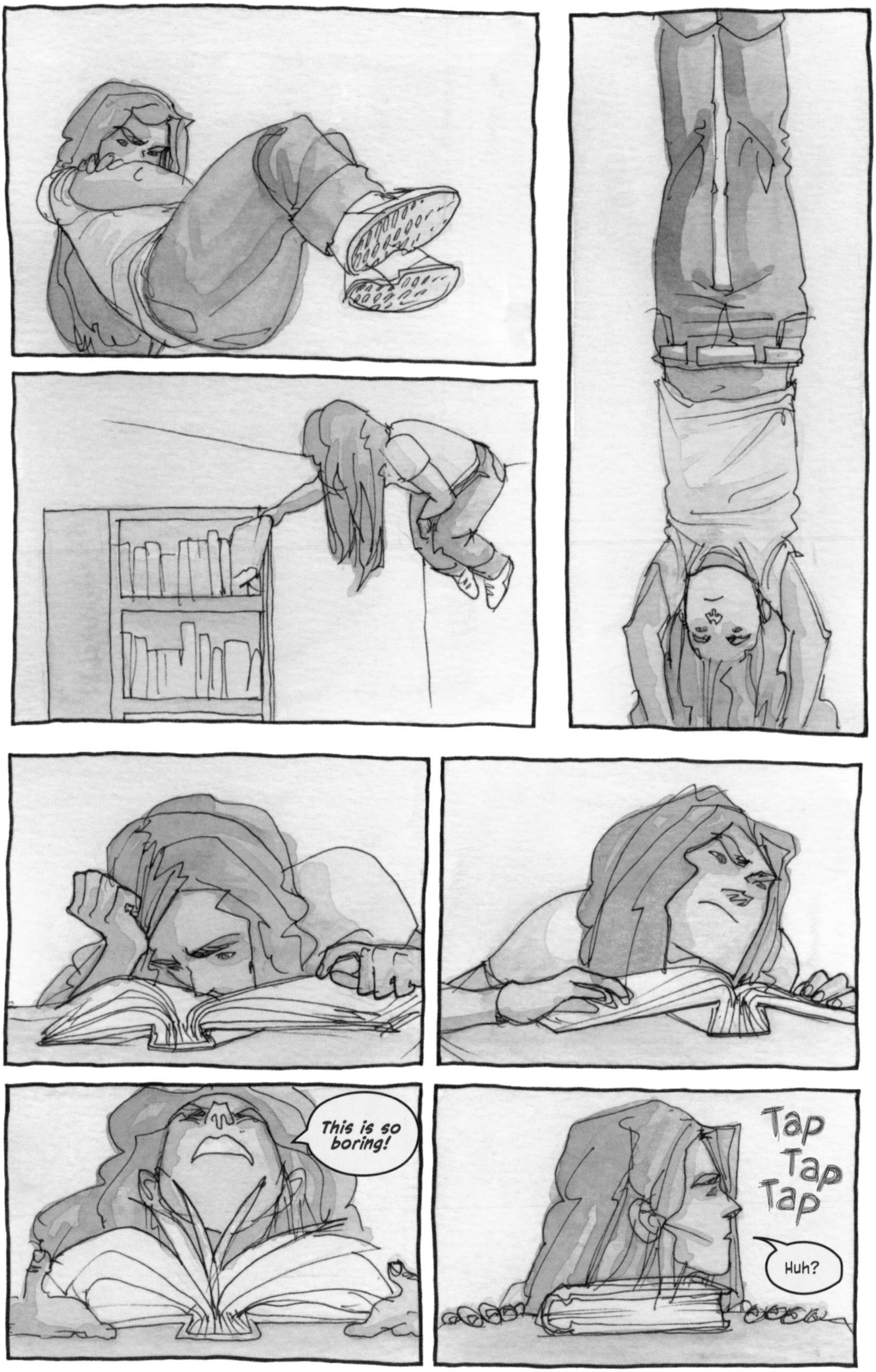
This is so boring!
Tap
Tap
Tap
Huh?

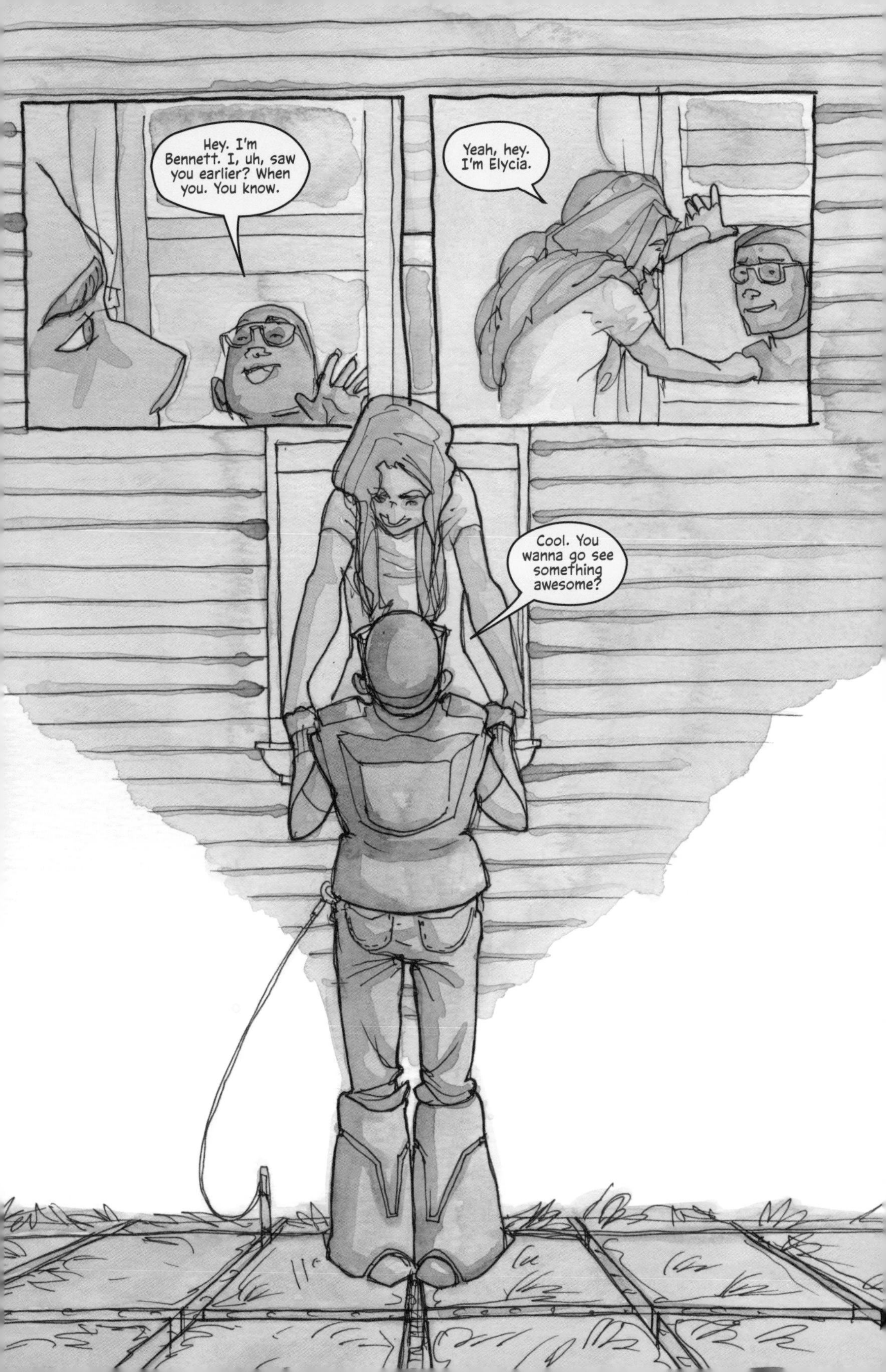
Hey. I'm Bennett. I, uh, saw you earlier? When you. You know.
Yeah, hey. I'm Elycia.
Cool. You wanna go see something awesome?

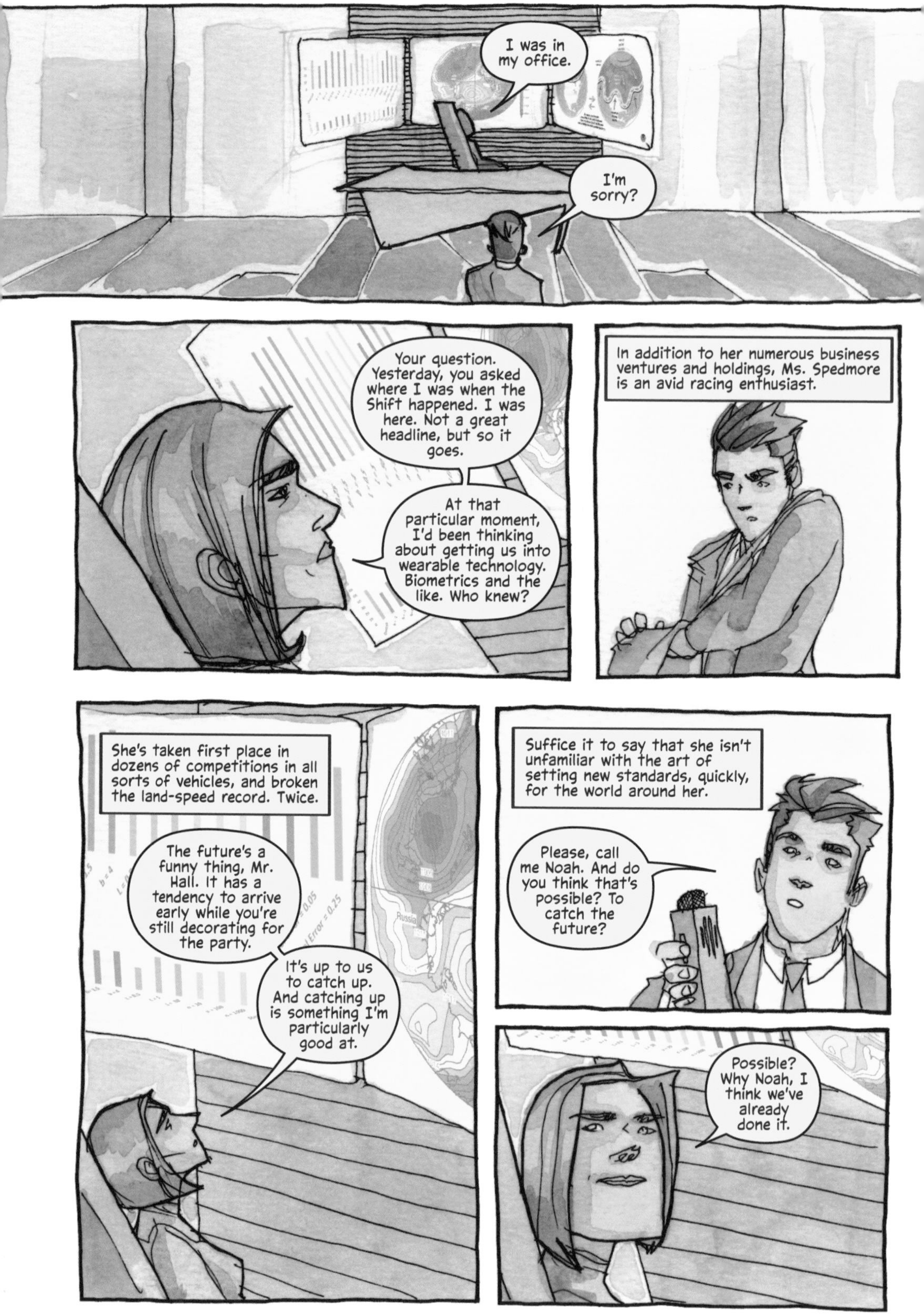
I was in my office.
I'm sorry?
Your question. Yesterday, you asked where I was when the Shift happened. I was here. Not a great headline, but so it goes.
At that particular moment, I'd been thinking about getting us into wearable technology. Biometrics and the like. Who knew?
In addition to her numerous business ventures and holdings, Ms. Spedmore is an avid racing enthusiast.
She's taken first place in dozens of competitions in all sorts of vehicles, and broken the land-speed record. Twice.
The future's a funny thing, Mr. Hall. It has a tendency to arrive early while you're still decorating for the party.
It's up to us to catch up. And catching up is something I'm particularly good at.
Suffice it to say that she isn't unfamiliar with the art of setting new standards, quickly, for the world around her.
Please, call me Noah. And do you think that's possible? To catch the future?
Possible? Why Noah, I think we've already done it.

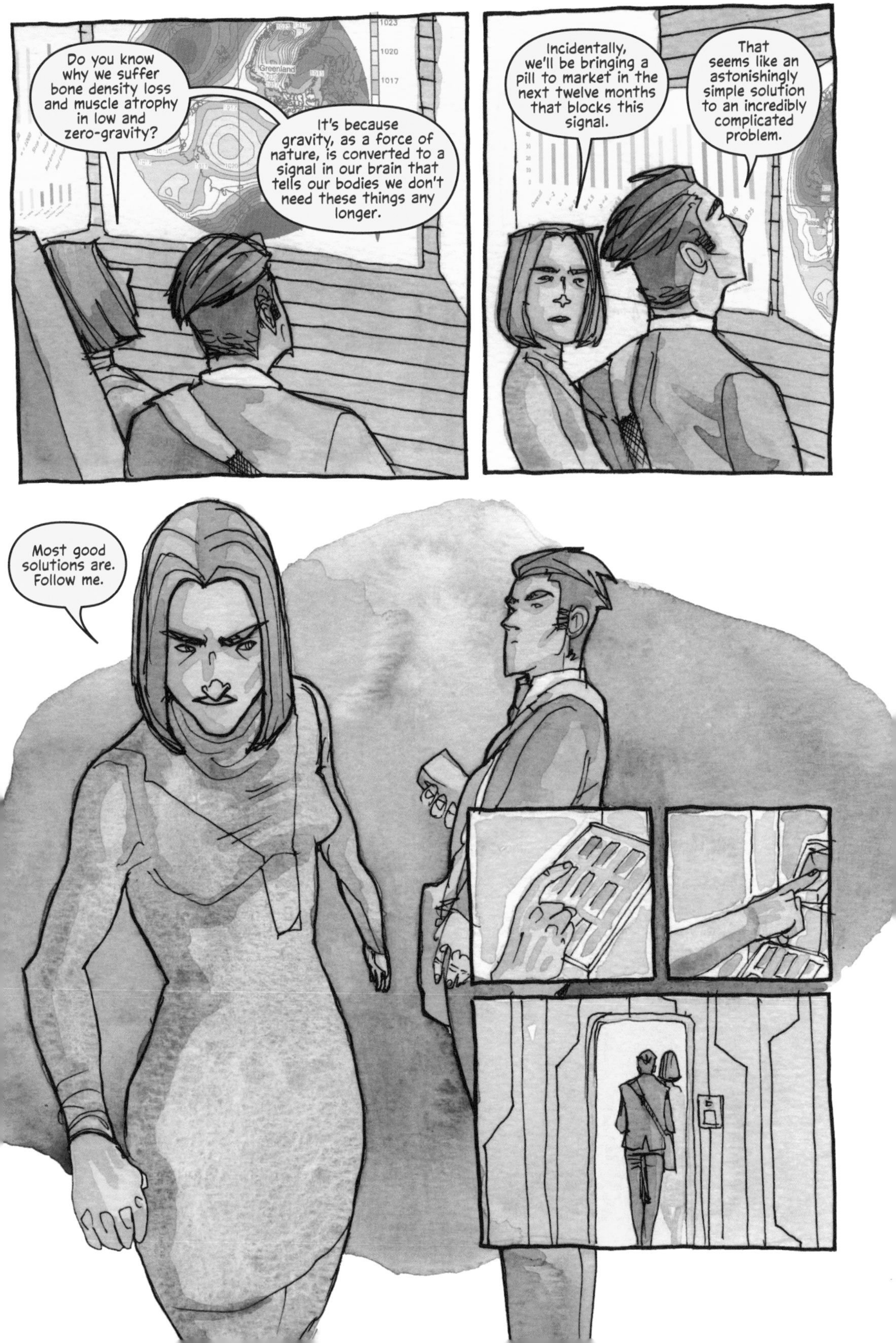
Do you know why we suffer bone density loss and muscle atrophy in low and zero-gravity?
It's because gravity, as a force of nature, is converted to a signal in our brain that tells our bodies we don't need these things any longer.
Incidentally, we'll be bringing a pill to market in the next twelve months that blocks this signal.
That seems like an astonishingly simple solution to an incredibly complicated problem.
Most good solutions are. Follow me.

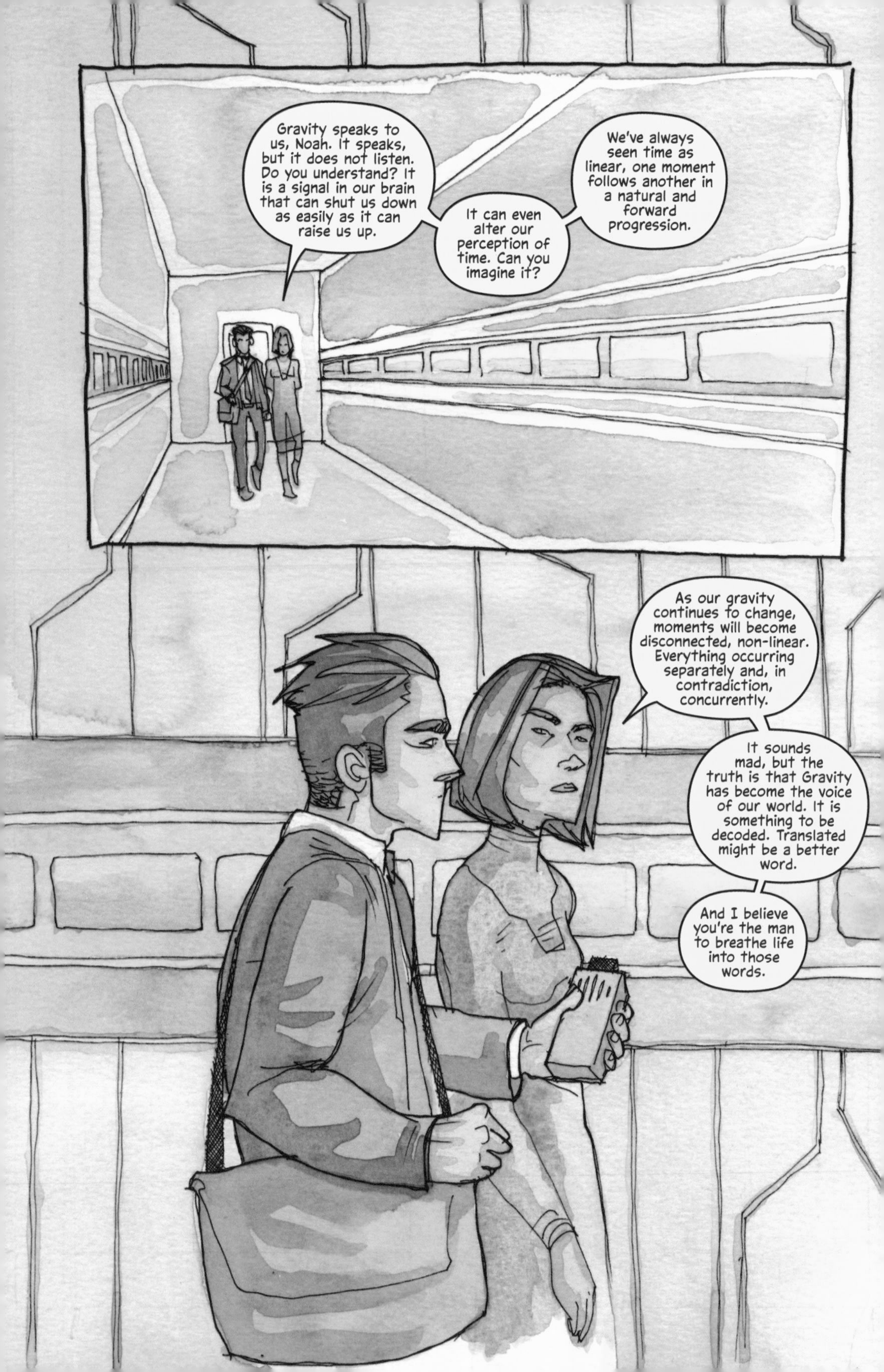
Gravity speaks to us, Noah. It speaks, but it does not listen. Do you understand? It is a signal in our brain that can shut us down as easily as it can raise us up.
It can even alter our perception of time. Can you imagine it?
We've always seen time as linear, one moment follows another in a natural and forward progression.
As our gravity continues to change, moments will become disconnected, non-linear. Everything occurring separately and, in contradiction, concurrently.
It sounds mad, but the truth is that Gravity has become the voice of our world. It is something to be decoded. Translated might be a better word.
And I believe you're the man to breathe life into those words.

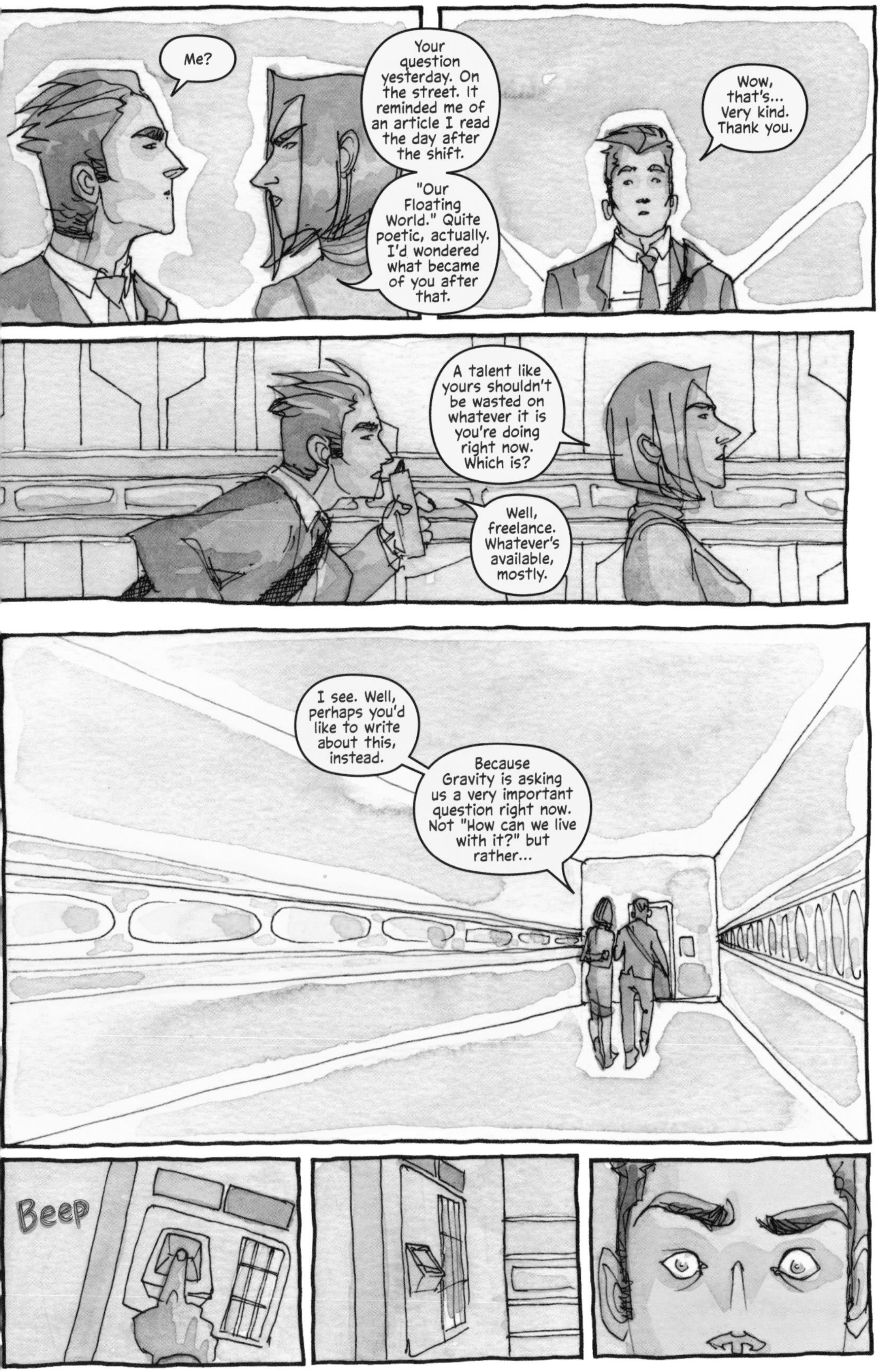
Me?
Your question yesterday. On the street. It reminded me of an article I read the day after the shift.
"Our Floating World." Quite poetic, actually. I'd wondered what became of you after that.
Wow, that's... Very kind. Thank you.
A talent like yours shouldn't be wasted on whatever it is you're doing right now. Which is?
Well, freelance. Whatever's available, mostly.
I see. Well, perhaps you'd like to write about this, instead.
Because Gravity is asking us a very important question right now. Not "How can we live with it?" but rather...
Beep

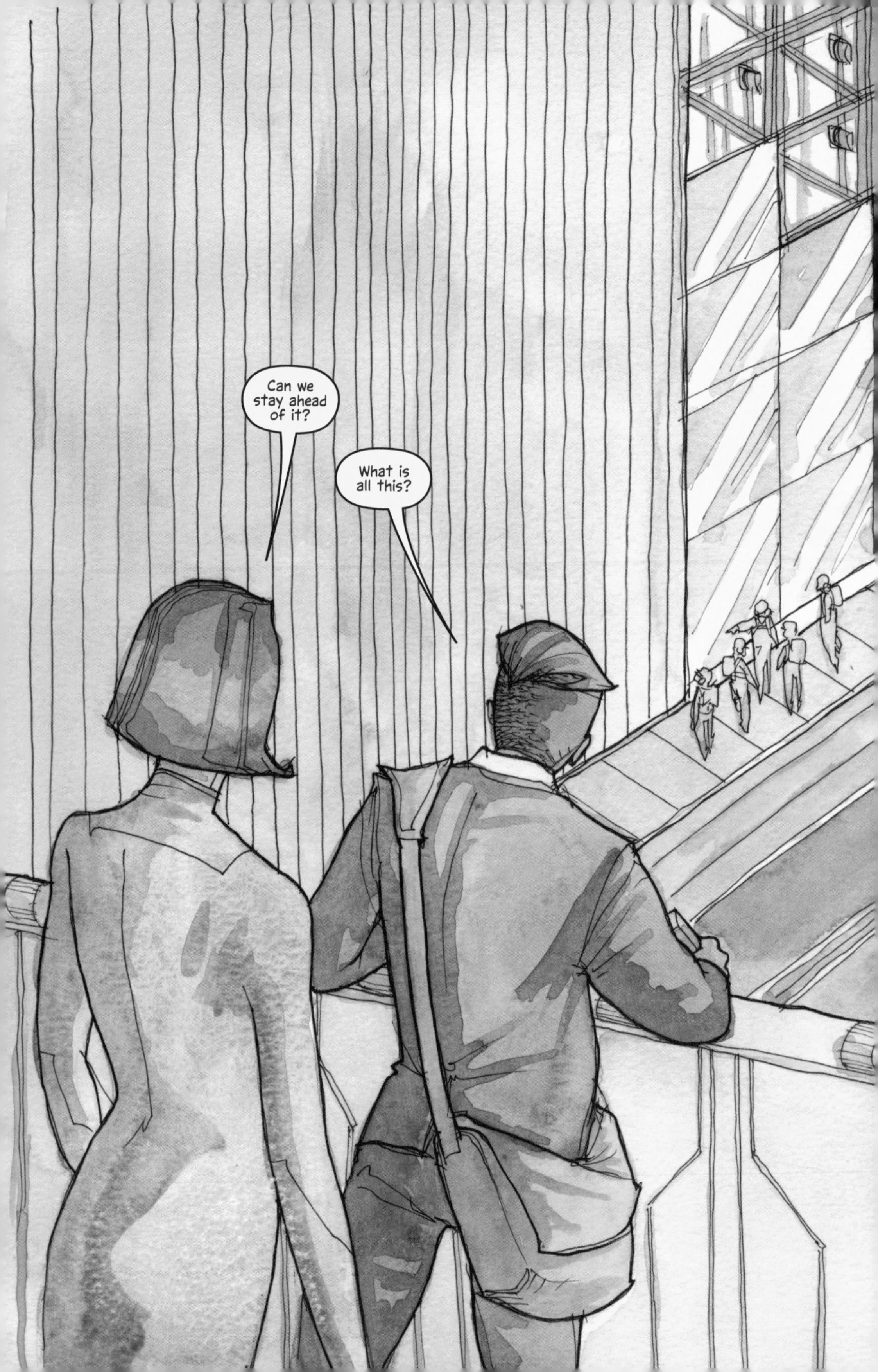
Can we stay ahead of it?
What is all this?

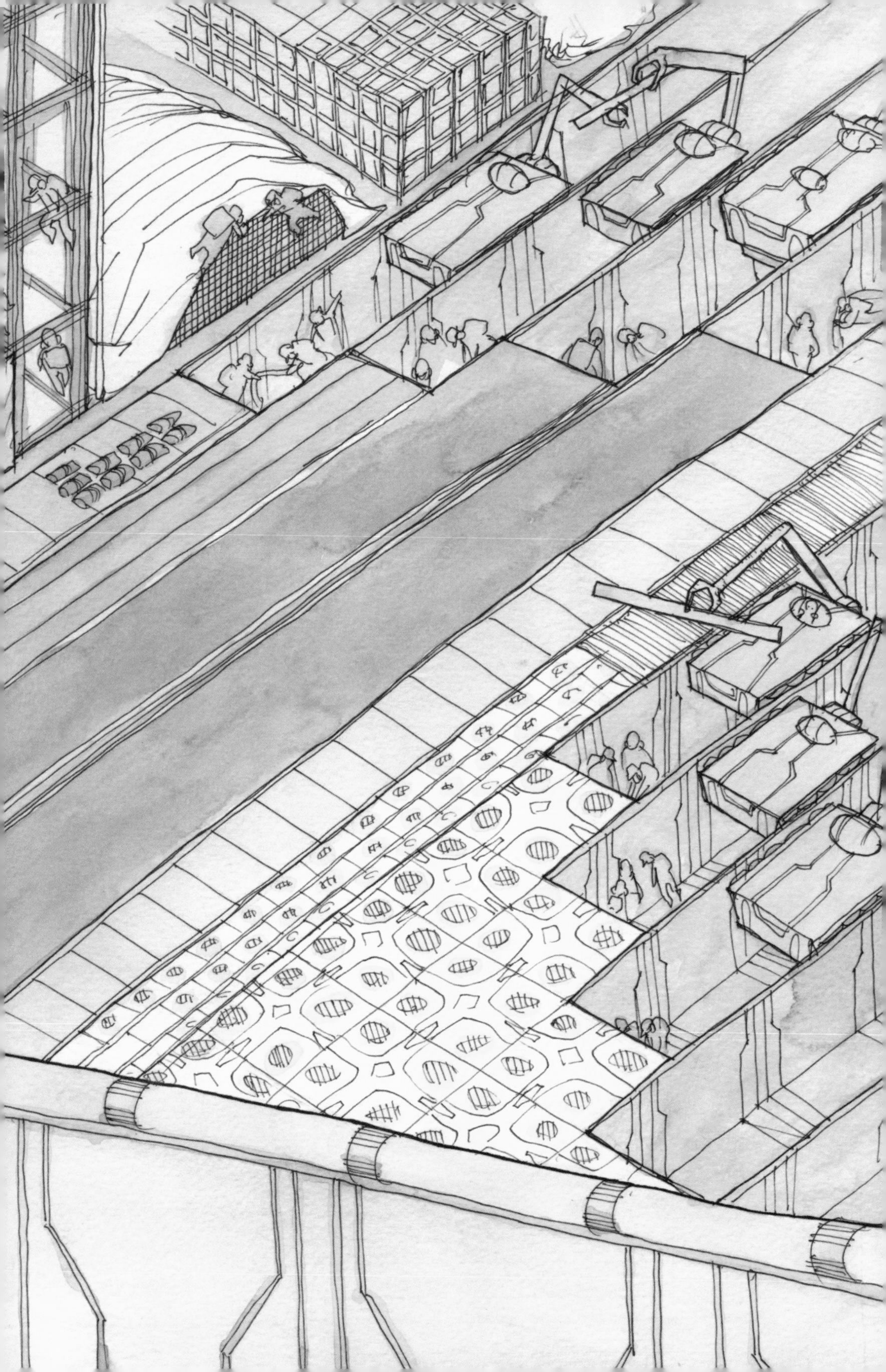

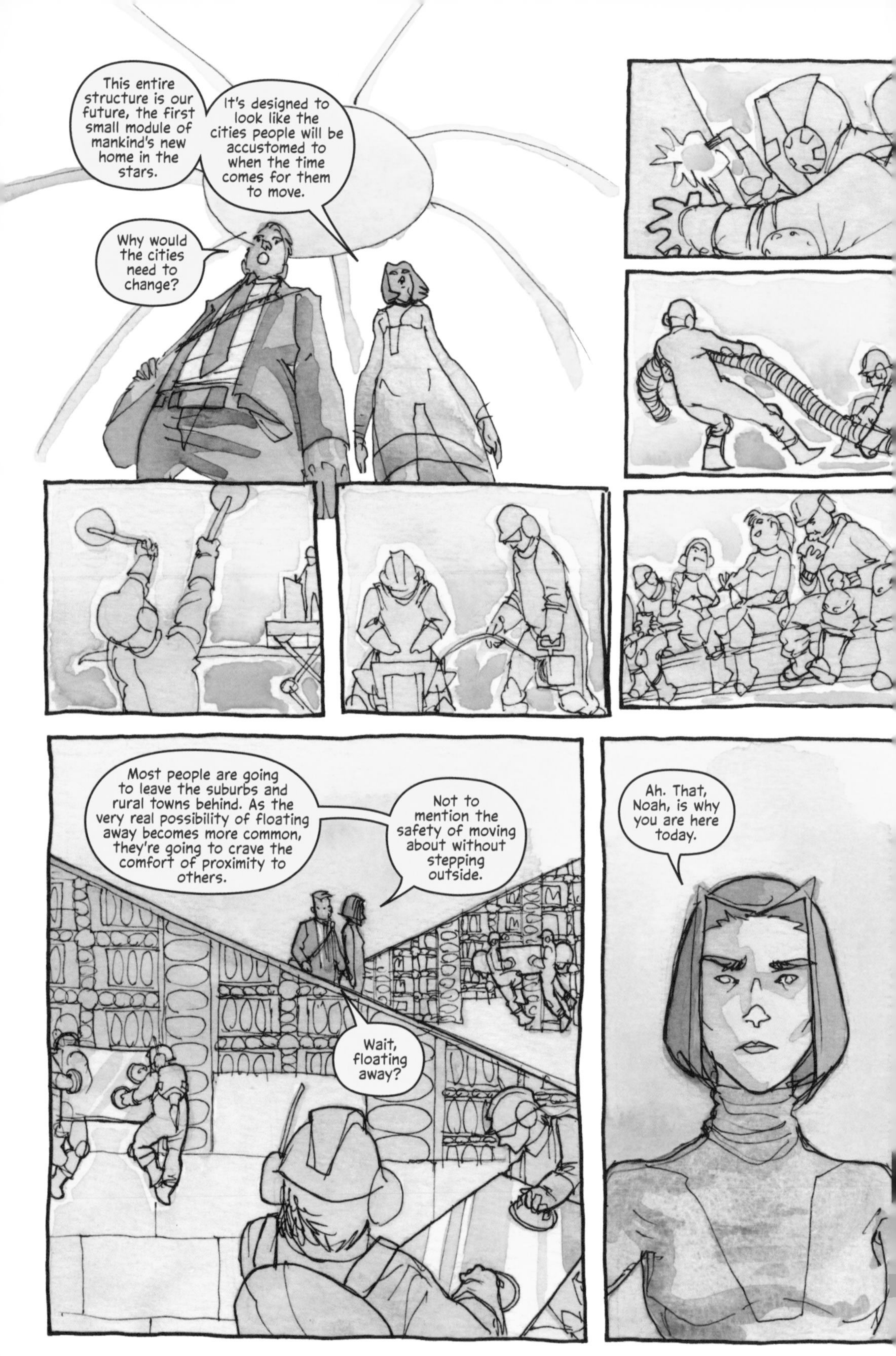
This entire structure is our future, the first small module of mankind's new home in the stars.
It's designed to look like the cities people will be accustomed to when the time comes for them to move.
Why would the cities need to change?
Most people are going to leave the suburbs and rural towns behind. As the very real possibility of floating away becomes more common, they're going to crave the comfort of proximity to others.
Not to mention the safety of moving about without stepping outside.
Wait, floating away?
Ah. That, Noah, is why you are here today.

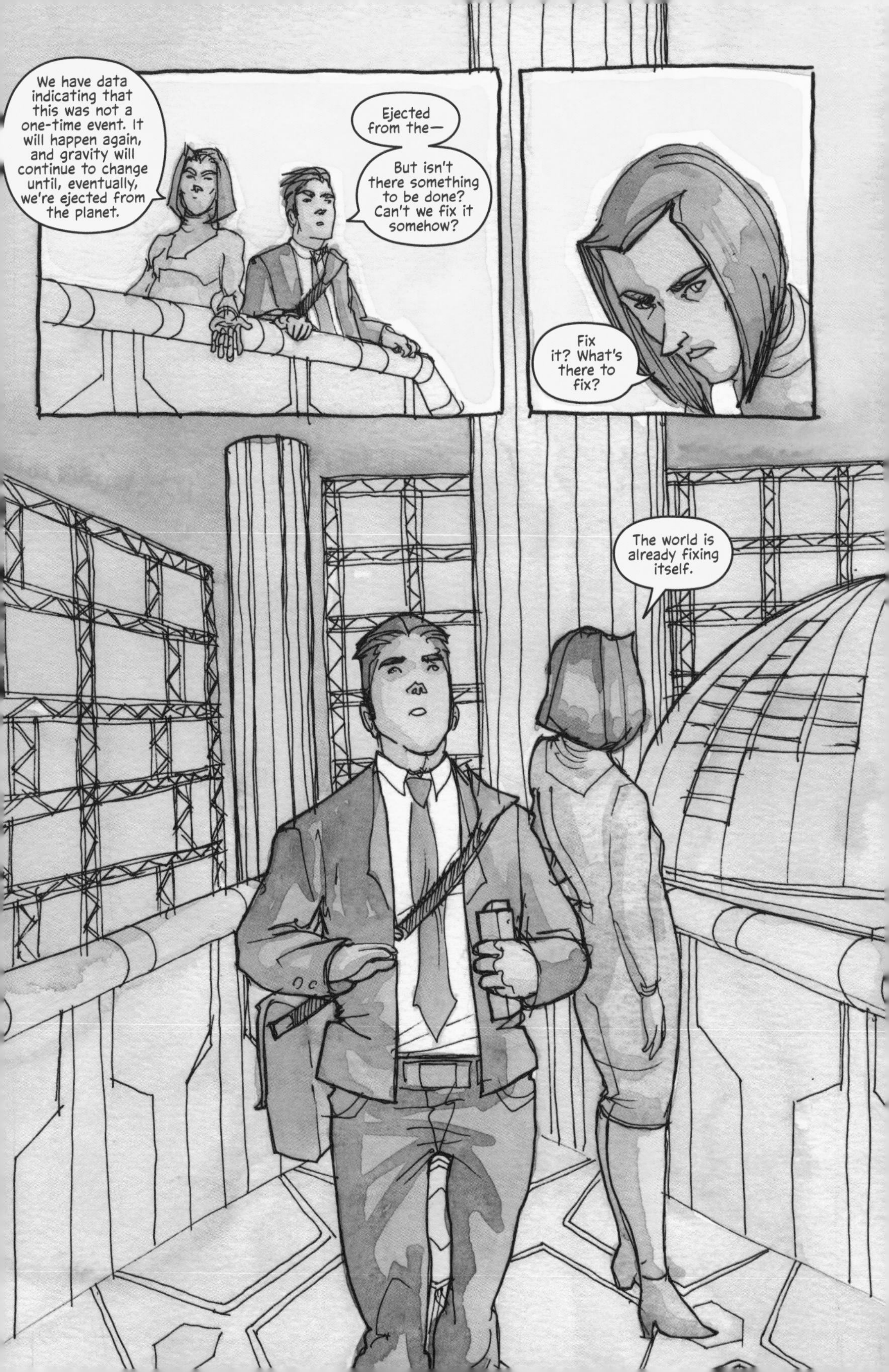
We have data indicating that this was not a one-time event. It will happen again, and gravity will continue to change until, eventually, we're ejected from the planet.
Ejected from the—
But isn't there something to be done? Can't we fix it somehow?
Fix it? What's there to fix?
The world is already fixing itself.

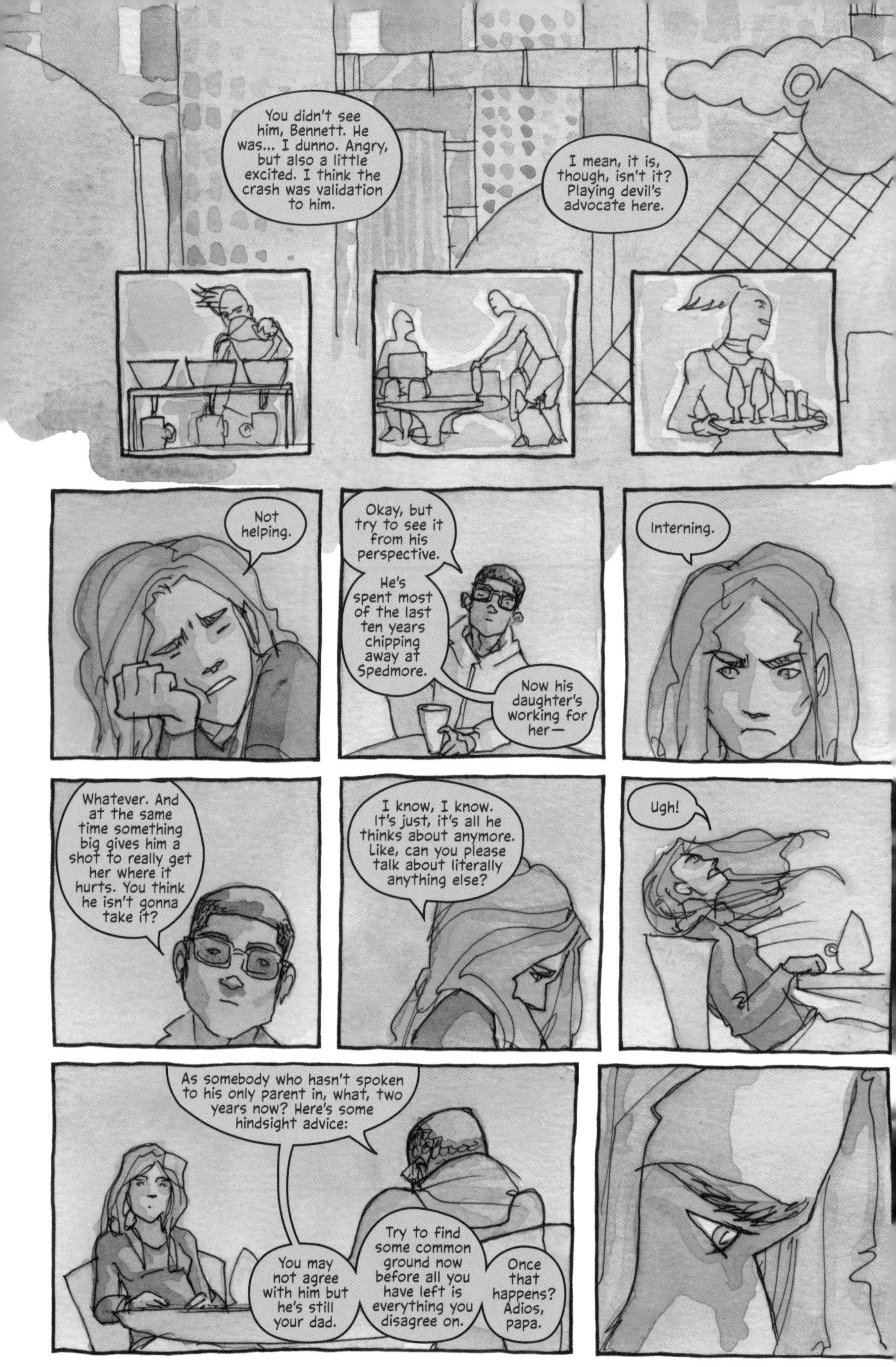
You didn't see him, Bennett. He was... I dunno. Angry, but also a little excited. I think the crash was validation to him.
I mean, it is, though, isn't it? Playing devil's advocate here.
Not helping.
Okay, but try to see it from his perspective.
He's spent most of the last ten years chipping away at Spedmore.
Now his daughter's working for her—
Interning.
Whatever. And at the same time something big gives him a shot to really get her where it hurts. You think he isn't gonna take it?
I know, I know. It's just, it's all he thinks about anymore. Like, can you please talk about literally anything else?
Ugh!
As somebody who hasn't spoken to his only parent in, what, two years now? Here's some hindsight advice:
You may not agree with him but he's still your dad.
Try to find some common ground now before all you have left is everything you disagree on.
Once that happens? Adios, papa.

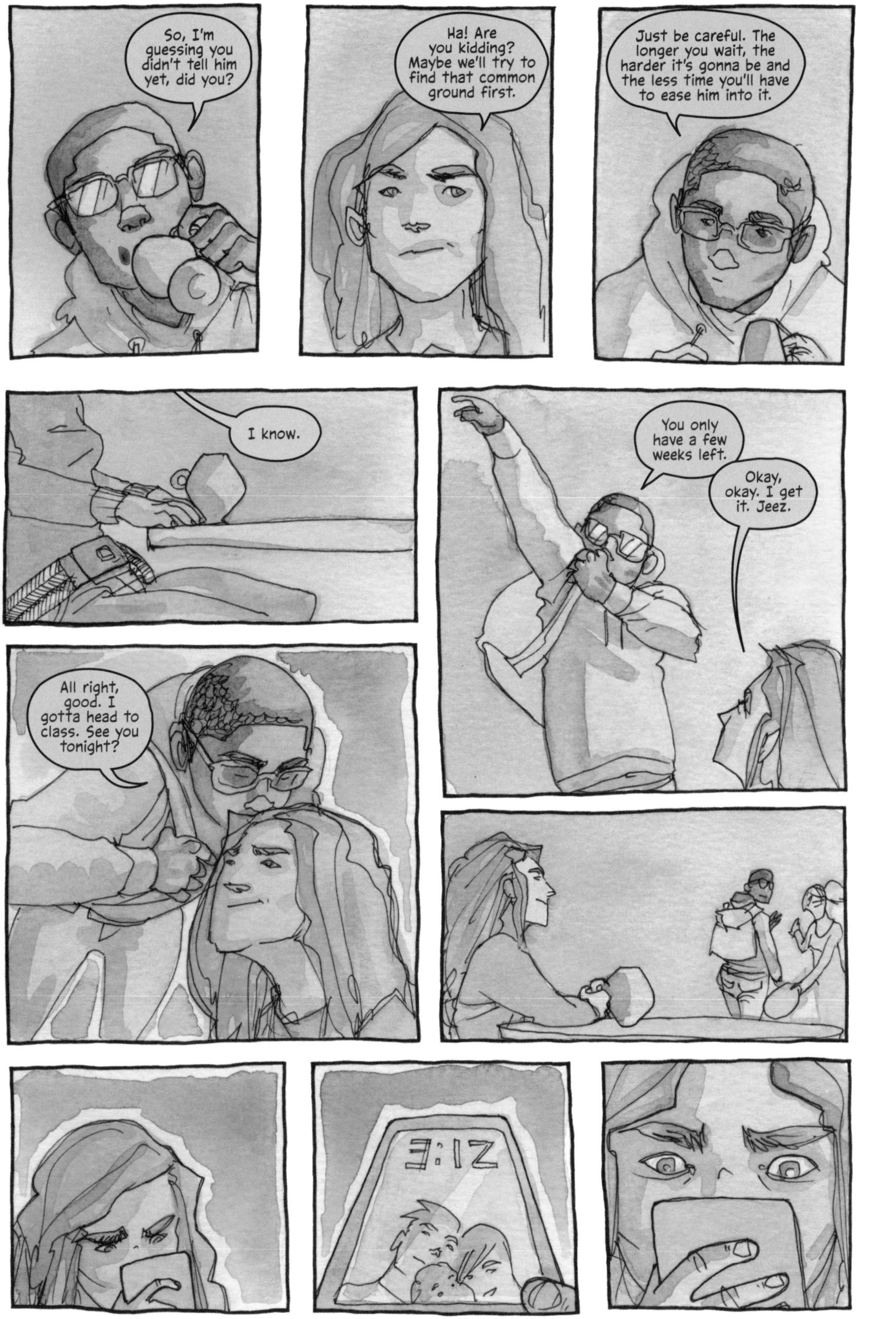
So, I'm guessing you didn't tell him yet, did you?
Ha! Are you kidding? Maybe we'll try to find that common ground first.
Just be careful. The longer you wait, the harder it's gonna be and the less time you'll have to ease him into it.
I know.
You only have a few weeks left.
Okay, okay. I get it. Jeez.
All right, good. I gotta head to class. See you tonight?
3:12

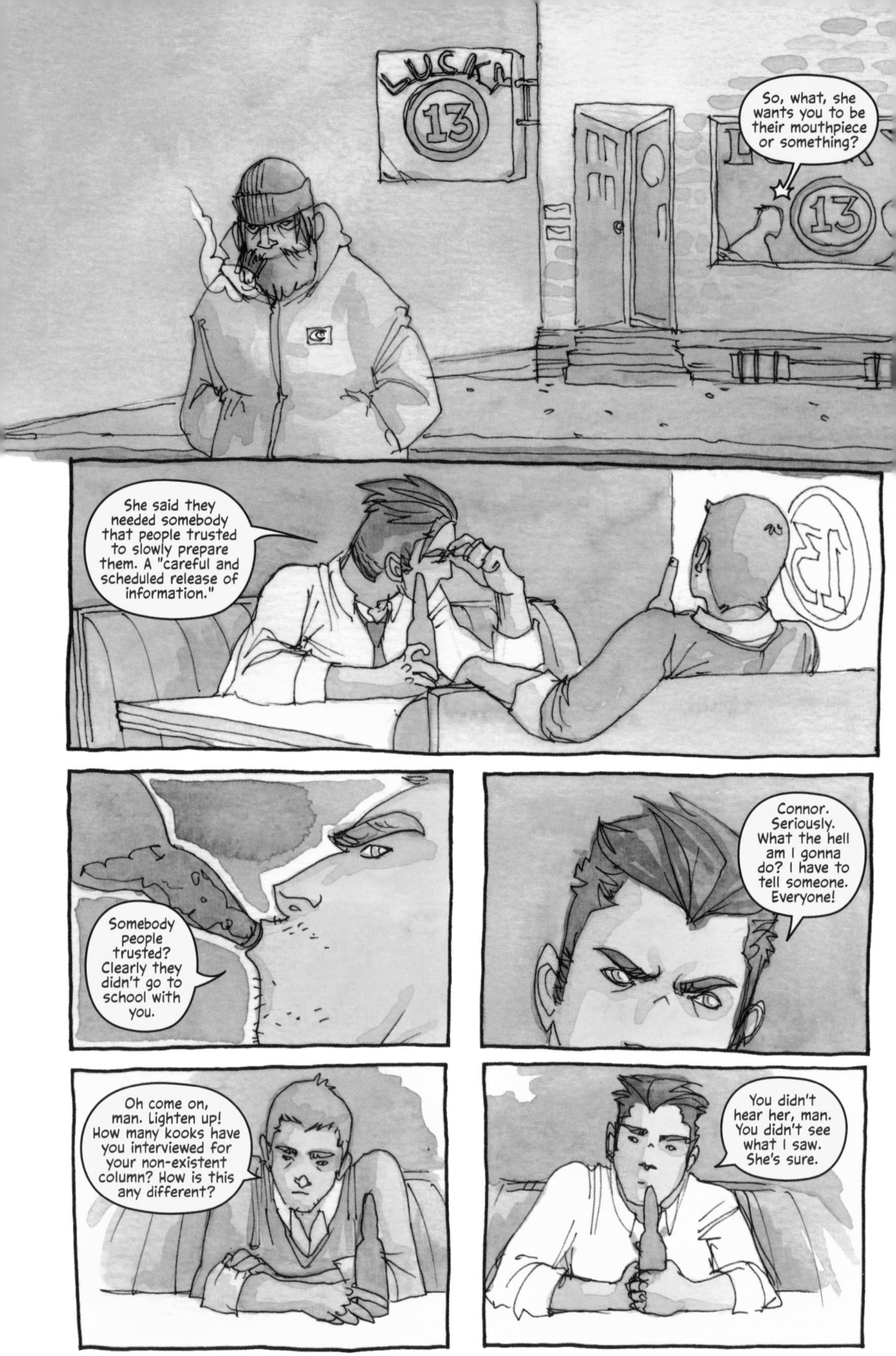
LUCKY
13
So, what, she wants you to be their mouthpiece or something?
She said they needed somebody that people trusted to slowly prepare them. A "careful and scheduled release of information."
Somebody people trusted? Clearly they didn't go to school with you.
Connor. Seriously. What the hell am I gonna do? I have to tell someone. Everyone!
Oh come on, man. Lighten up! How many kooks have you interviewed for your non-existent column? How is this any different?
You didn't hear her, man. You didn't see what I saw. She's sure.

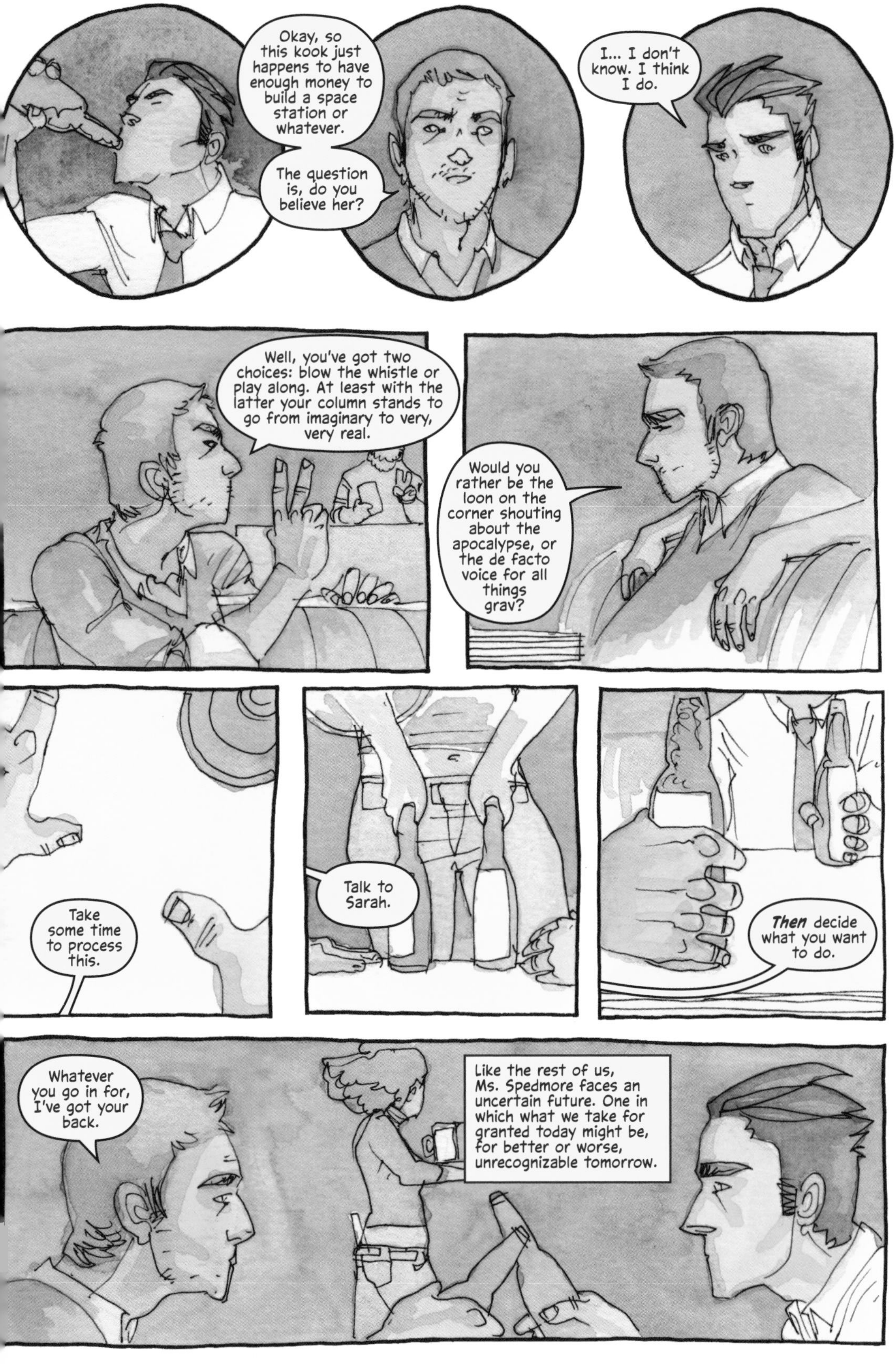

Okay, so this kook just happens to have enough money to build a space station or whatever.
The question is, do you believe her?
I... I don't know. I think I do.
Well, you've got two choices: blow the whistle or play along. At least with the latter your column stands to go from imaginary to very, very real.
Would you rather be the loon on the corner shouting about the apocalypse, or the de facto voice for all things grav?
Take some time to process this.
Talk to Sarah.
Then decide what you want to do.
Whatever you go in for, I've got your back.
Like the rest of us, Ms. Spedmore faces an uncertain future. One in which what we take for granted today might be, for better or worse, unrecognizable tomorrow.

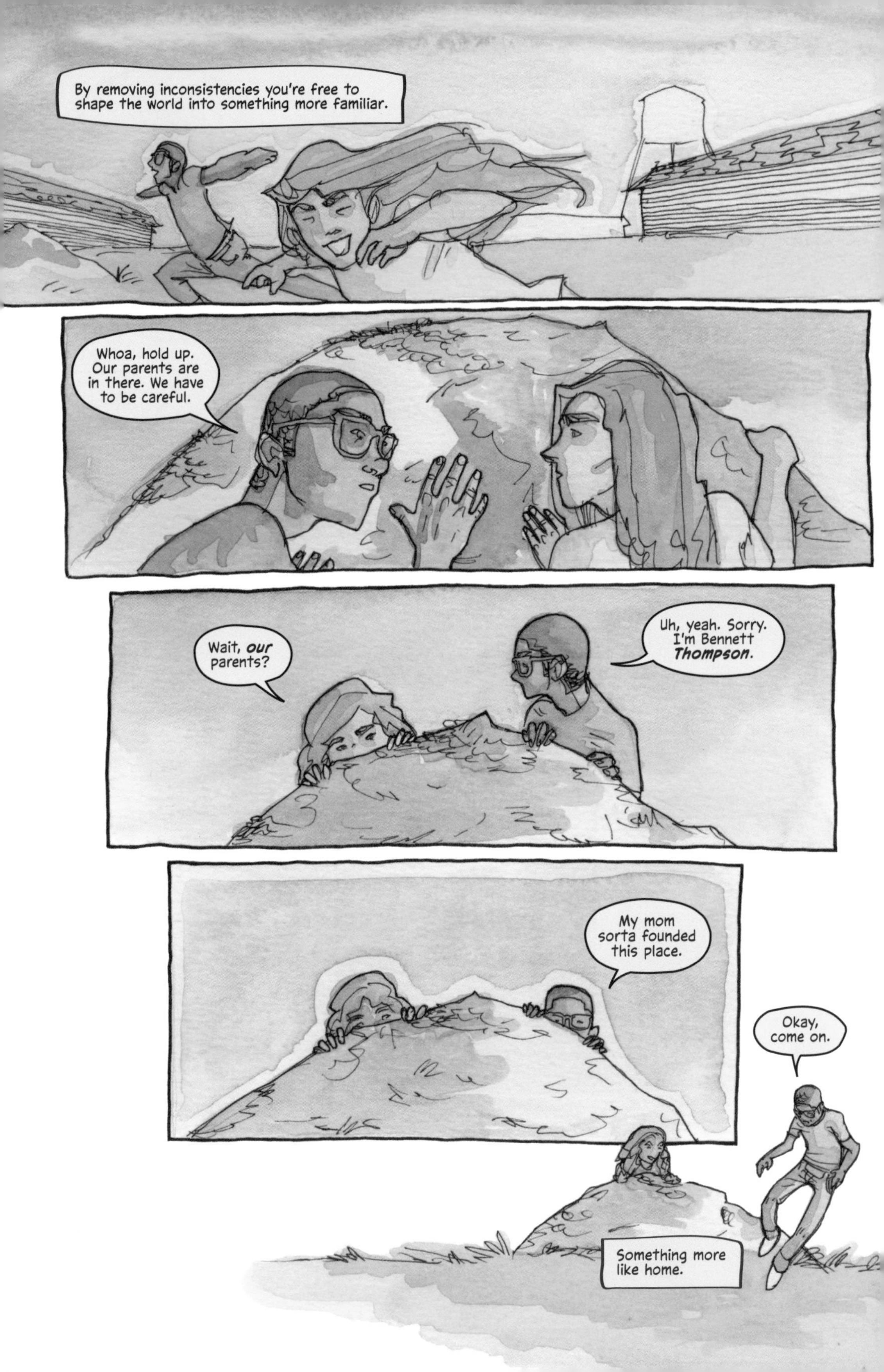

By removing inconsistencies you're free to shape the world into something more familiar.
Whoa, hold up. Our parents are in there. We have to be careful.
Wait, **our** parents?
Uh, yeah. Sorry. I'm Bennett ***Thompson***.
My mom sorta founded this place.
Okay, come on.
Something more like home.

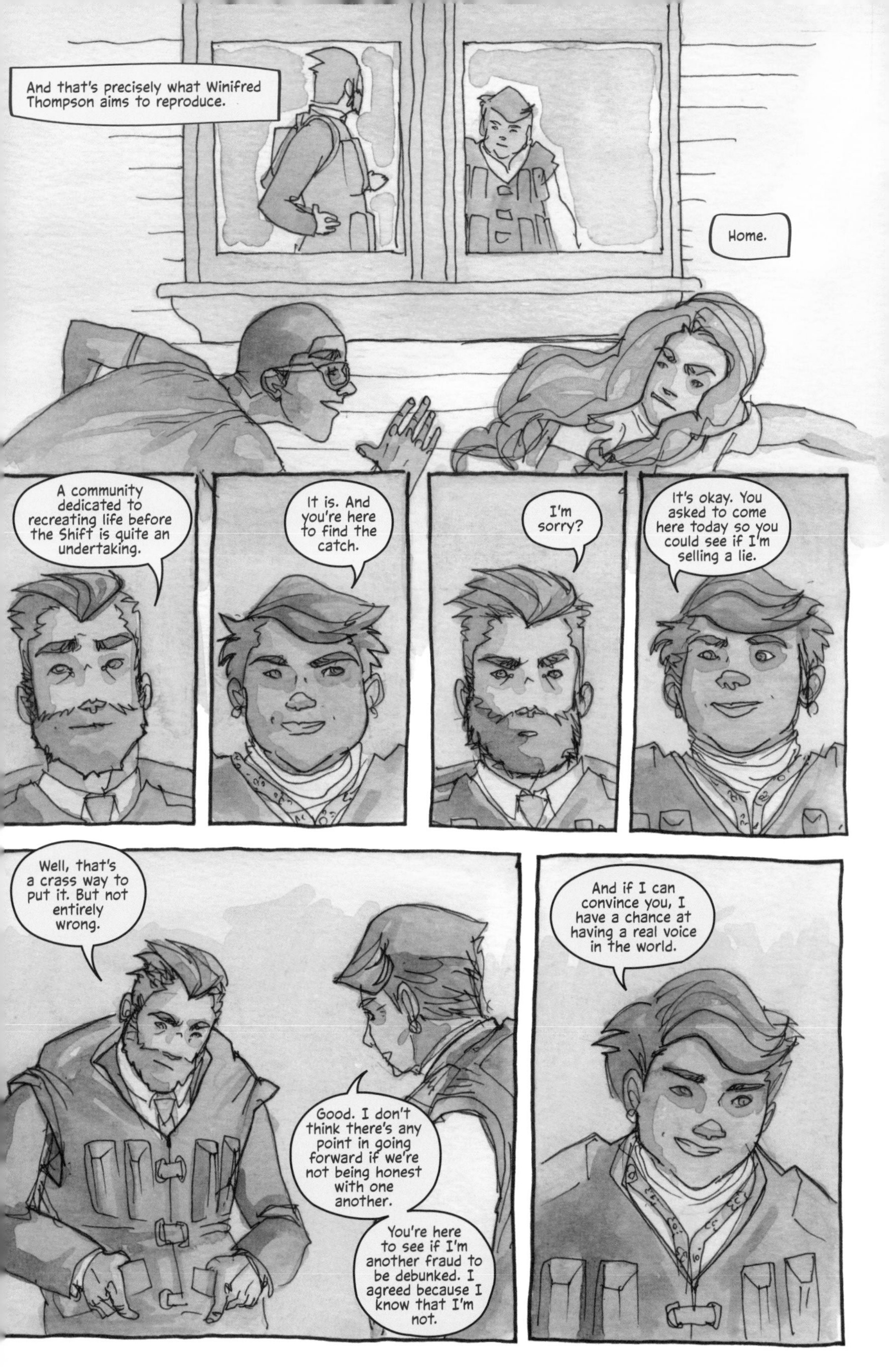

And that's precisely what Winifred Thompson aims to reproduce.
Home.
A community dedicated to recreating life before the Shift is quite an undertaking.
It is. And you're here to find the catch.
I'm sorry?
It's okay. You asked to come here today so you could see if I'm selling a lie.
Well, that's a crass way to put it. But not entirely wrong.
Good. I don't think there's any point in going forward if we're not being honest with one another.
You're here to see if I'm another fraud to be debunked. I agreed because I know that I'm not.
And if I can convince you, I have a chance at having a real voice in the world.

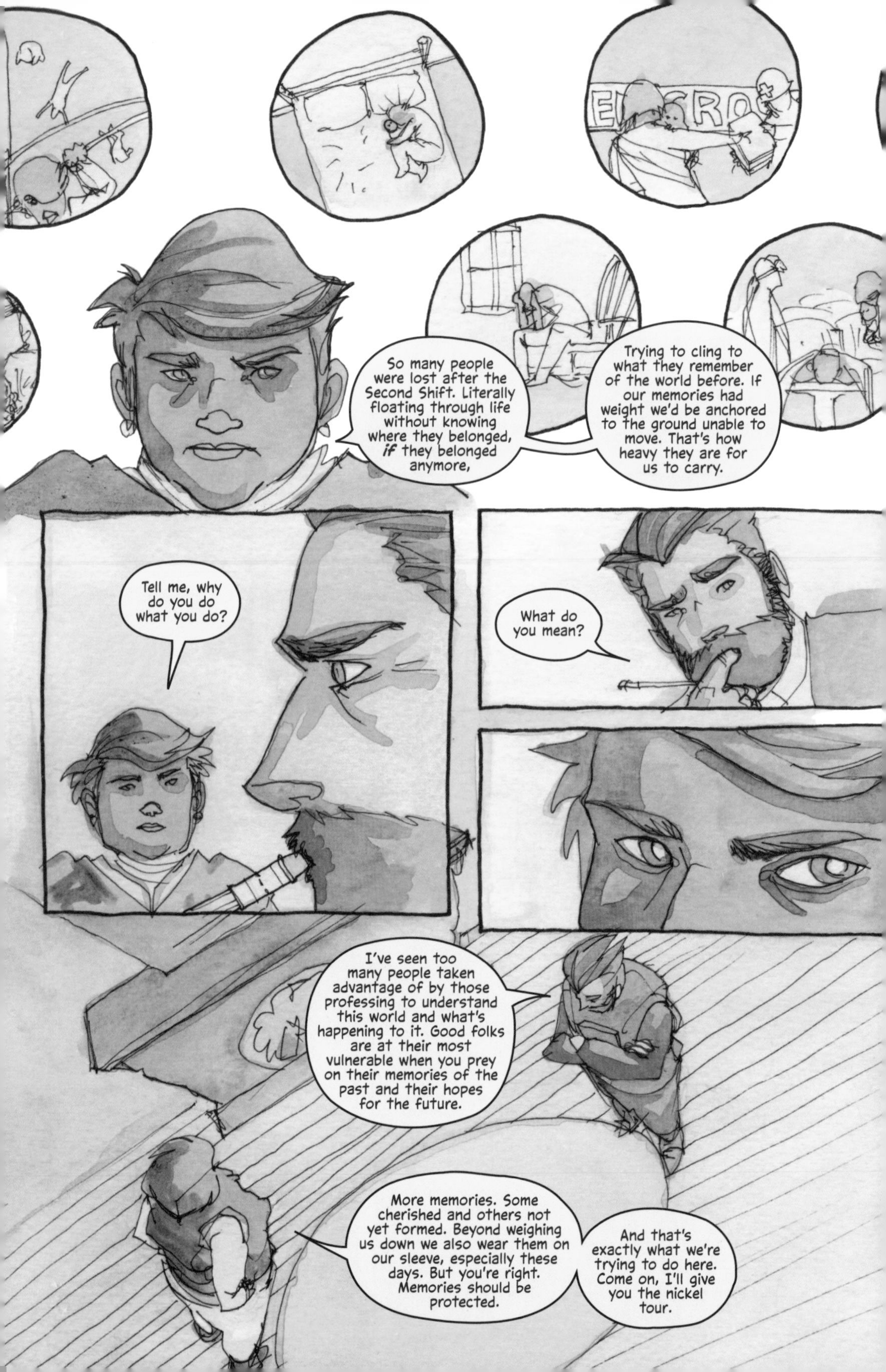
So many people were lost after the Second Shift. Literally floating through life without knowing where they belonged, *if* they belonged anymore,
Trying to cling to what they remember of the world before. If our memories had weight we'd be anchored to the ground unable to move. That's how heavy they are for us to carry.
Tell me, why do you do what you do?
What do you mean?
I've seen too many people taken advantage of by those professing to understand this world and what's happening to it. Good folks are at their most vulnerable when you prey on their memories of the past and their hopes for the future.
More memories. Some cherished and others not yet formed. Beyond weighing us down we also wear them on our sleeve, especially these days. But you're right. Memories should be protected.
And that's exactly what we're trying to do here. Come on, I'll give you the nickel tour.

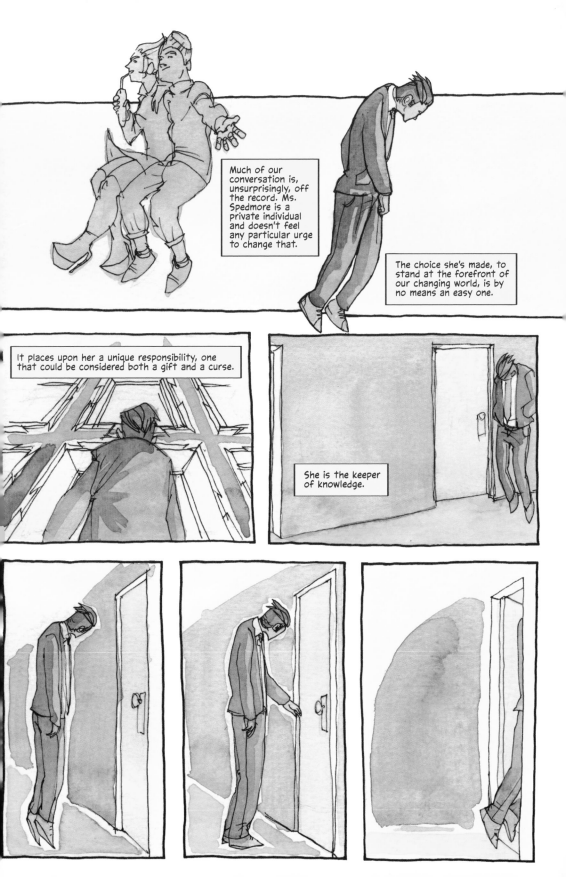

Much of our conversation is, unsurprisingly, off the record. Ms. Spedmore is a private individual and doesn't feel any particular urge to change that.

The choice she's made, to stand at the forefront of our changing world, is by no means an easy one.

It places upon her a unique responsibility, one that could be considered both a gift and a curse.

She is the keeper of knowledge.

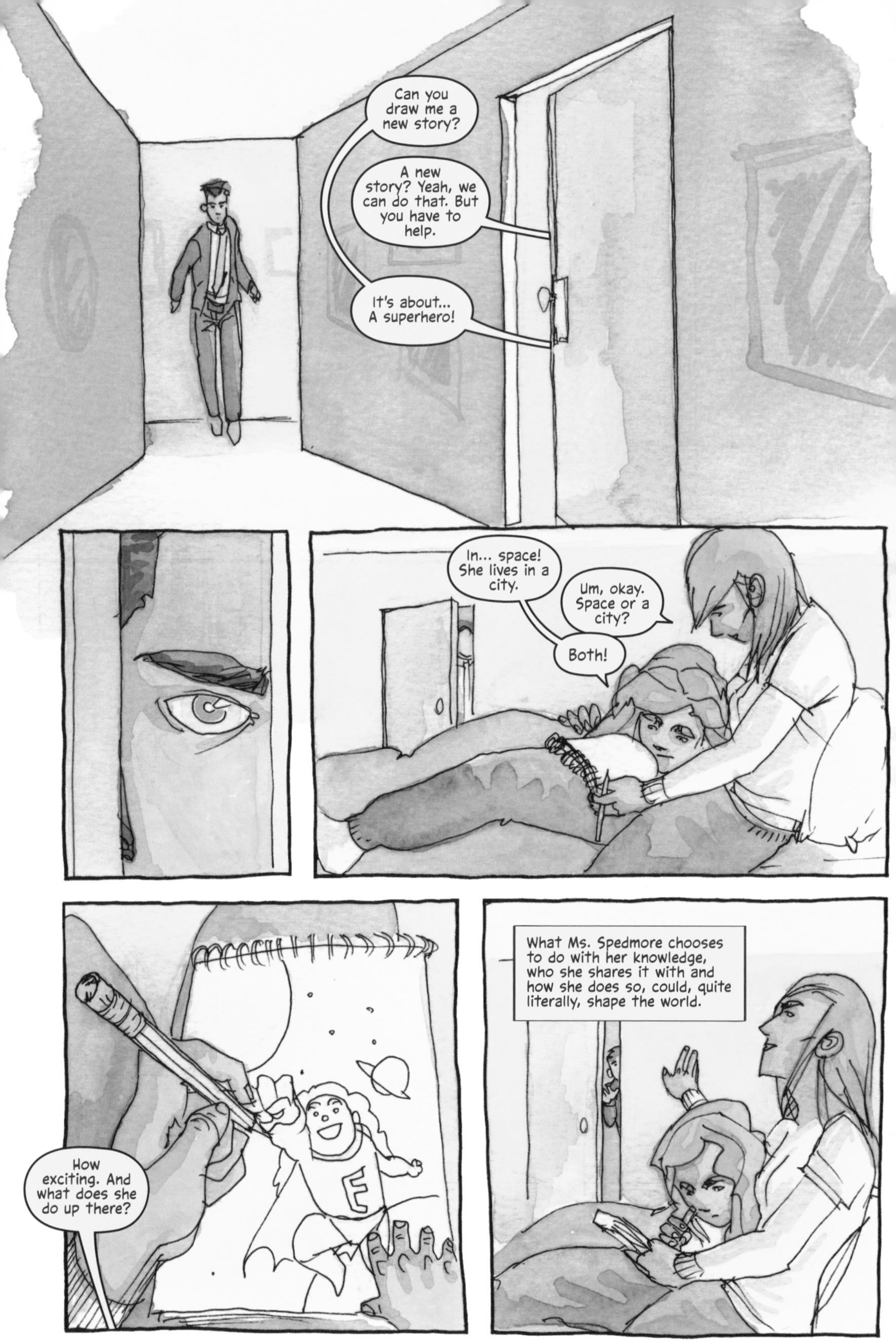

Can you draw me a new story?
A new story? Yeah, we can do that. But you have to help.
It's about... A superhero!
In... space! She lives in a city.
Um, okay. Space or a city?
Both!
How exciting. And what does she do up there?
E
What Ms. Spedmore chooses to do with her knowledge, who she shares it with and how she does so, could, quite literally, shape the world.

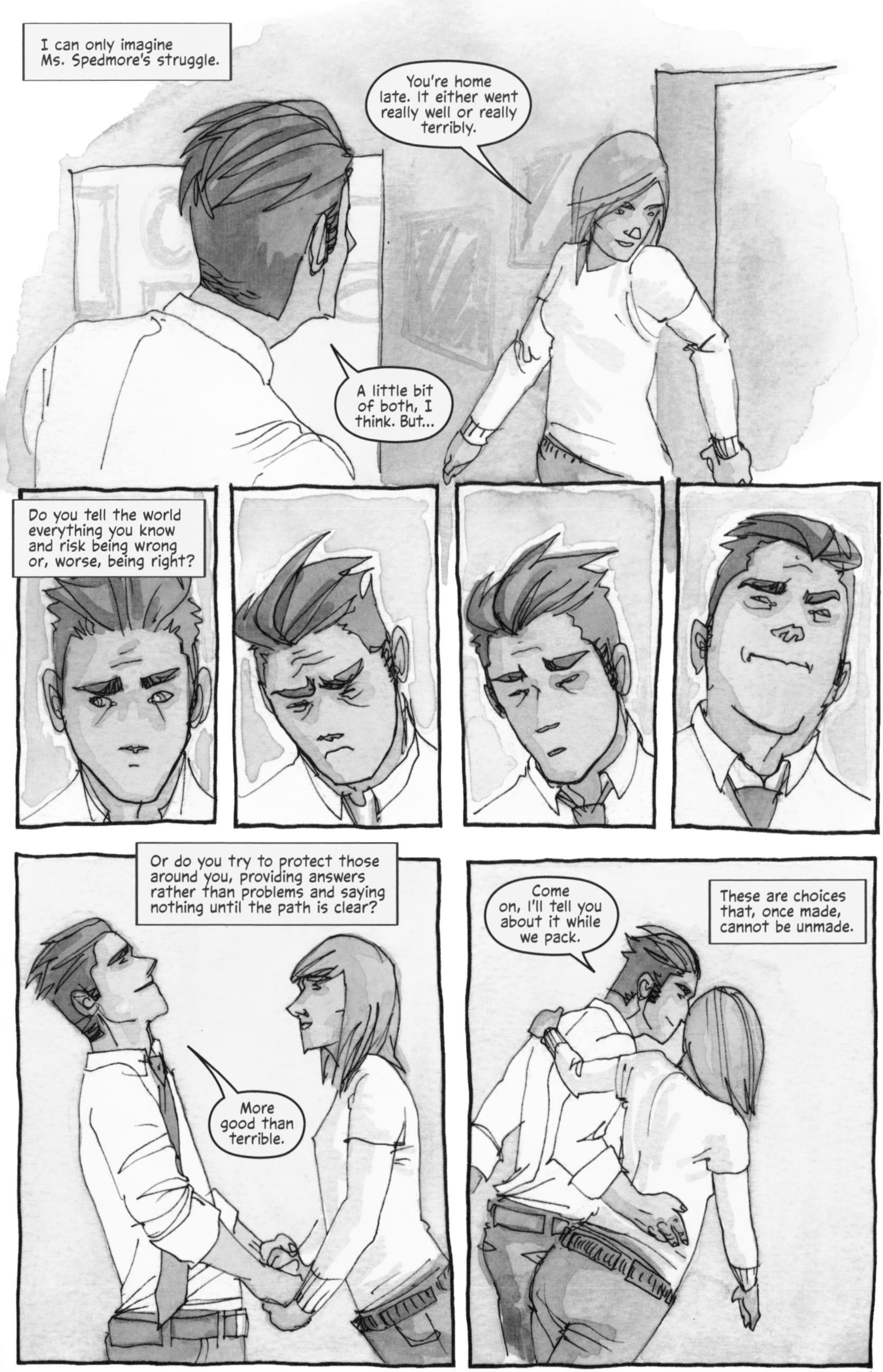
I can only imagine Ms. Spedmore's struggle.
You're home late. It either went really well or really terribly.
A little bit of both, I think. But...
Do you tell the world everything you know and risk being wrong or, worse, being right?
Or do you try to protect those around you, providing answers rather than problems and saying nothing until the path is clear?
More good than terrible.
Come on, I'll tell you about it while we pack.
These are choices that, once made, cannot be unmade.

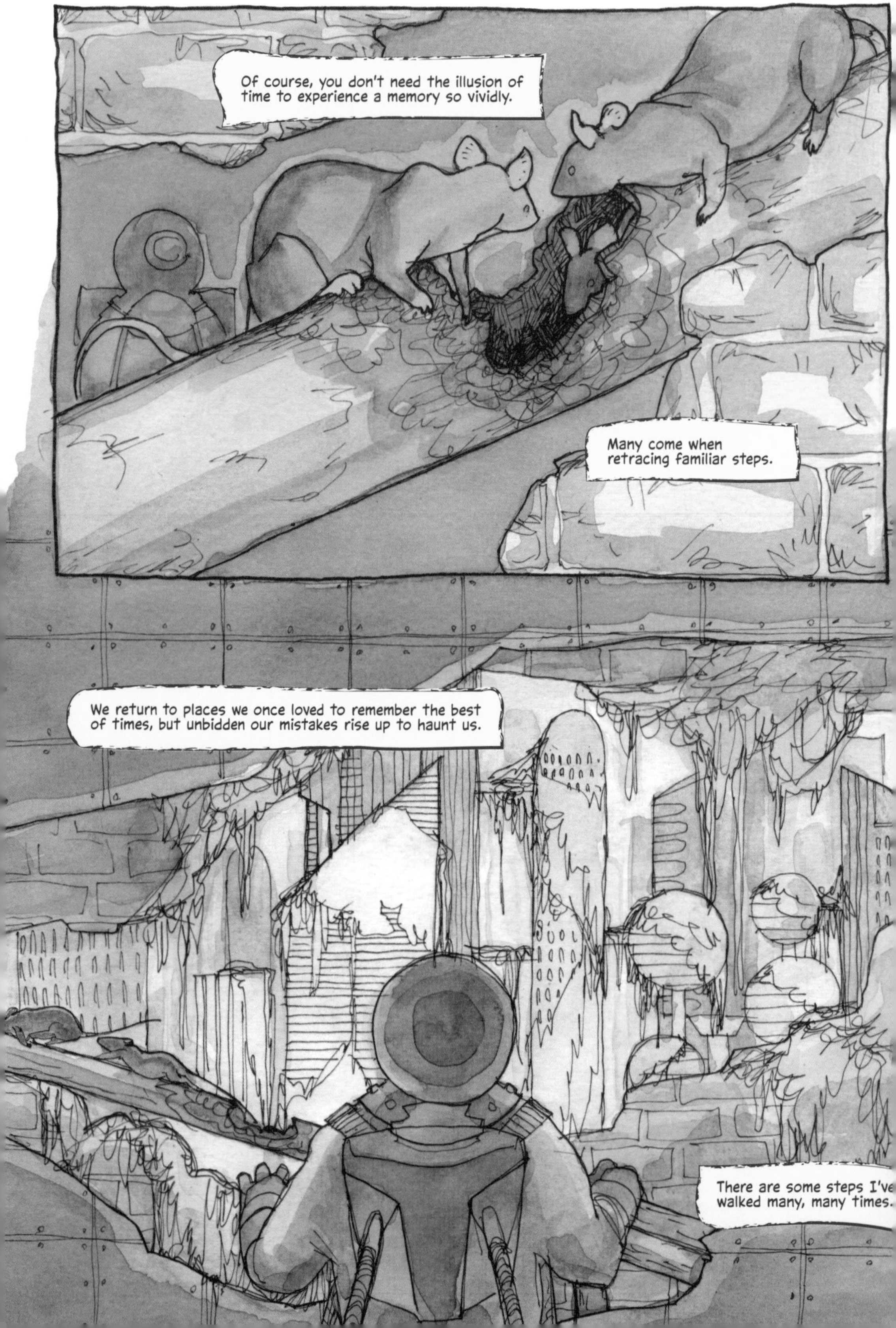
Of course, you don't need the illusion of time to experience a memory so vividly.
Many come when retracing familiar steps.
We return to places we once loved to remember the best of times, but unbidden our mistakes rise up to haunt us.
There are some steps I've walked many, many times.

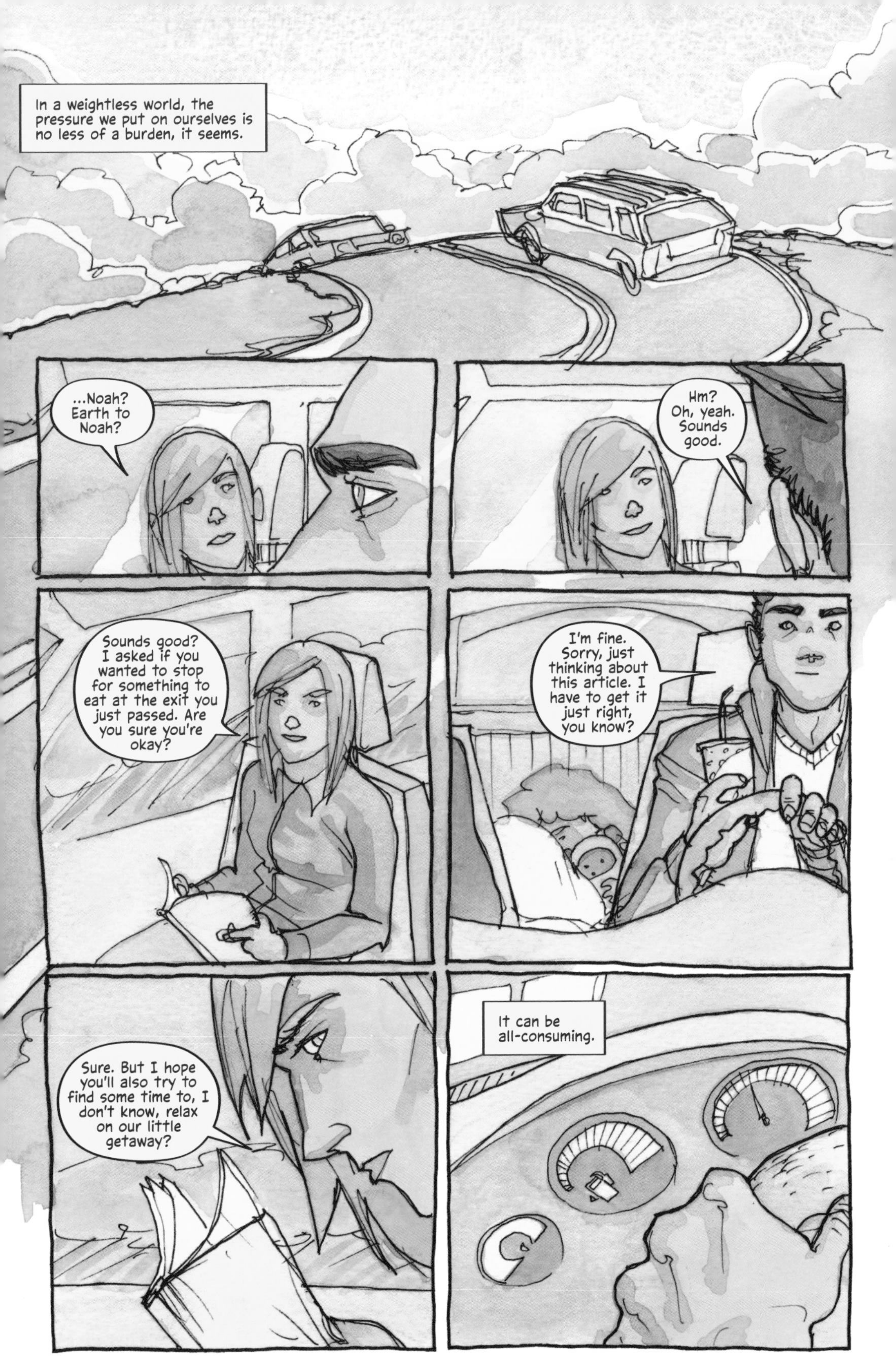
In a weightless world, the pressure we put on ourselves is no less of a burden, it seems.
...Noah? Earth to Noah?
Hm? Oh, yeah. Sounds good.
Sounds good? I asked if you wanted to stop for something to eat at the exit you just passed. Are you sure you're okay?
I'm fine. Sorry, just thinking about this article. I have to get it just right, you know?
Sure. But I hope you'll also try to find some time to, I don't know, relax on our little getaway?
It can be all-consuming.

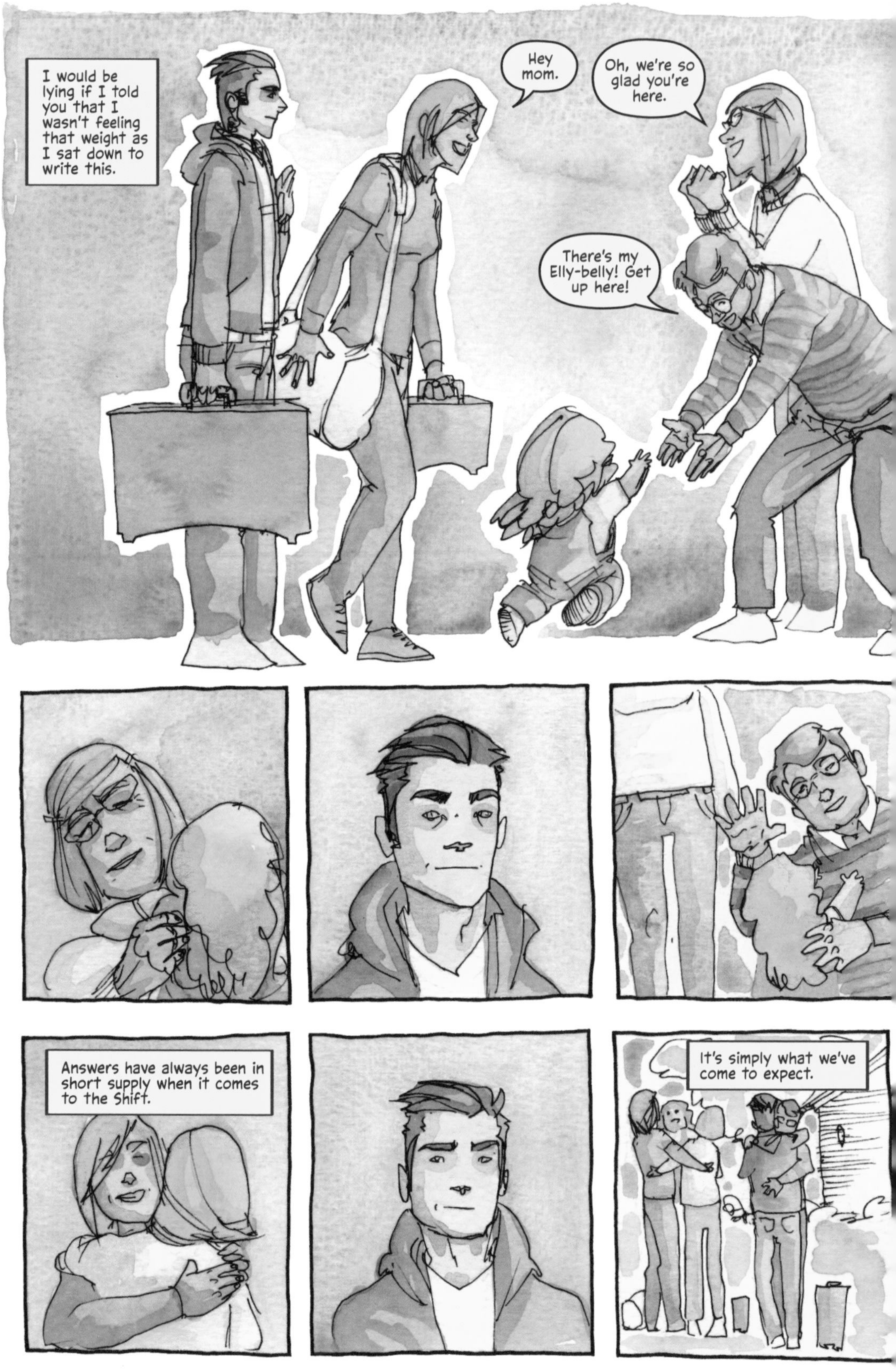
I would be lying if I told you that I wasn't feeling that weight as I sat down to write this.
Hey mom.
Oh, we're so glad you're here.
There's my Elly-belly! Get up here!
Answers have always been in short supply when it comes to the Shift.
It's simply what we've come to expect.

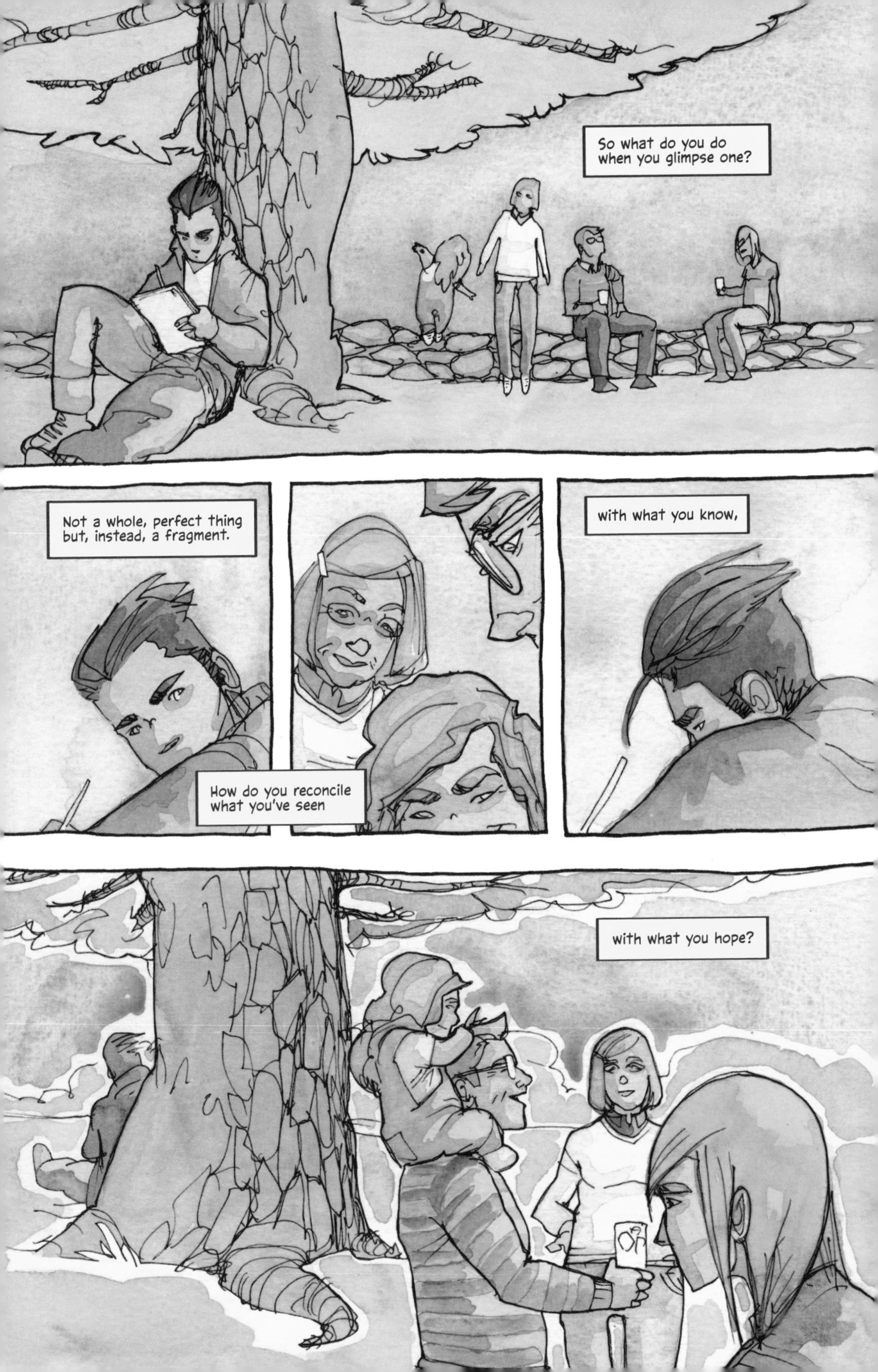
So what do you do when you glimpse one?
Not a whole, perfect thing but, instead, a fragment.
How do you reconcile what you've seen
with what you know,
with what you hope?

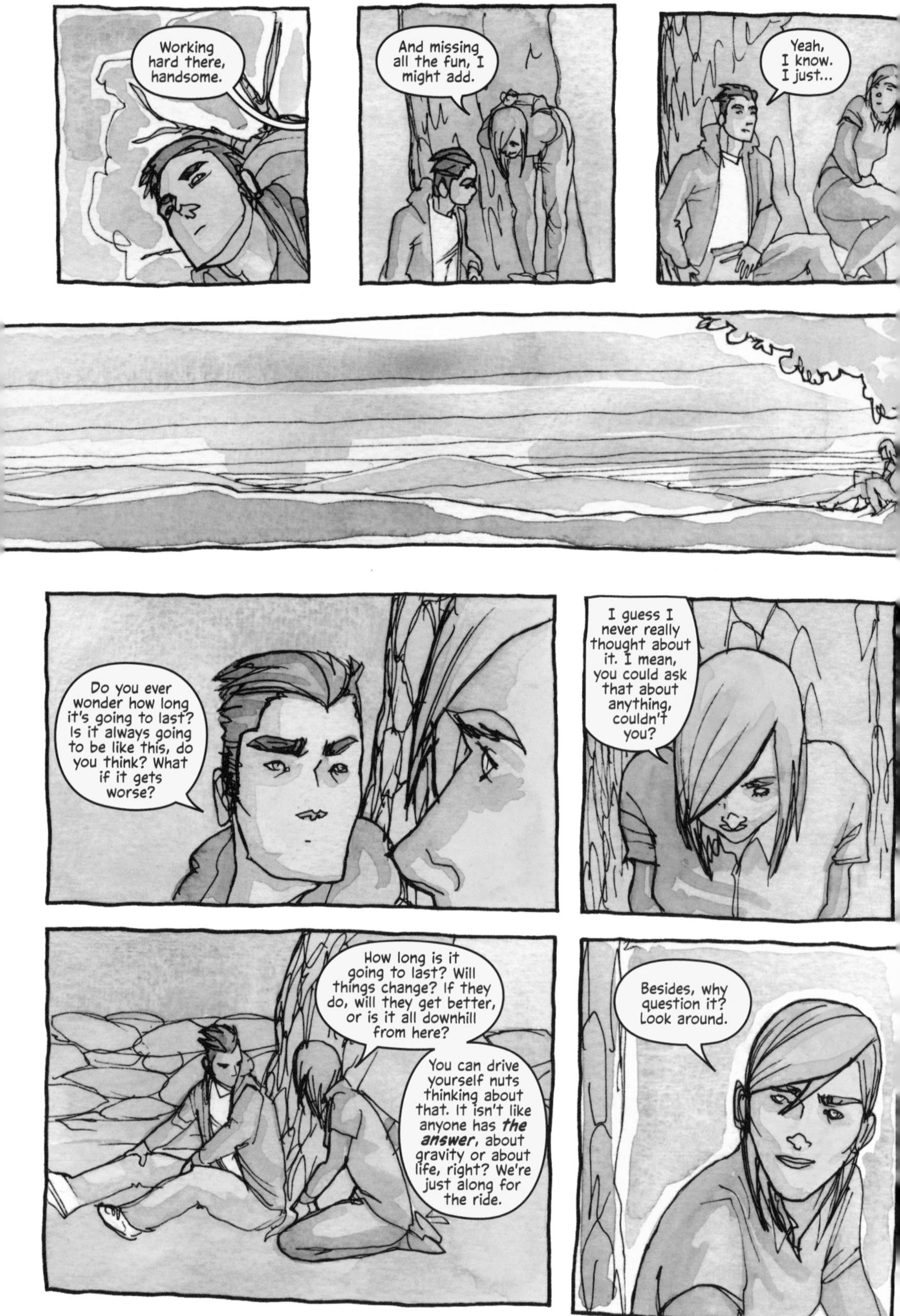
Working hard there, handsome.
And missing all the fun, I might add.
Yeah, I know. I just...
Do you ever wonder how long it's going to last? Is it always going to be like this, do you think? What if it gets worse?
I guess I never really thought about it. I mean, you could ask that about anything, couldn't you?
How long is it going to last? Will things change? If they do, will they get better, or is it all downhill from here?
You can drive yourself nuts thinking about that. It isn't like anyone has ***the answer***, about gravity or about life, right? We're just along for the ride.
Besides, why question it? Look around.

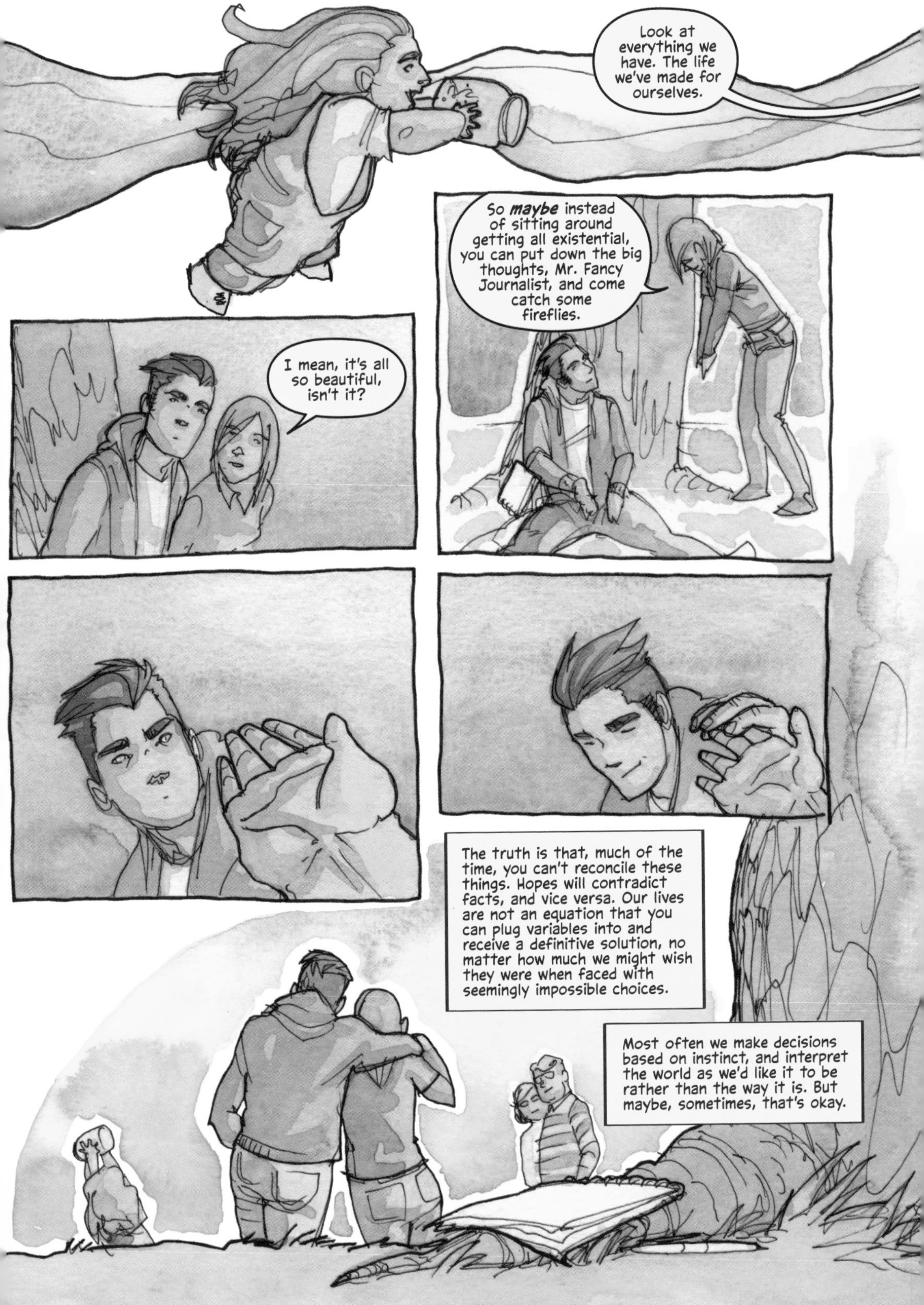
Look at everything we have. The life we've made for ourselves.
So *maybe* instead of sitting around getting all existential, you can put down the big thoughts, Mr. Fancy Journalist, and come catch some fireflies.
I mean, it's all so beautiful, isn't it?
The truth is that, much of the time, you can't reconcile these things. Hopes will contradict facts, and vice versa. Our lives are not an equation that you can plug variables into and receive a definitive solution, no matter how much we might wish they were when faced with seemingly impossible choices.
Most often we make decisions based on instinct, and interpret the world as we'd like it to be rather than the way it is. But maybe, sometimes, that's okay.

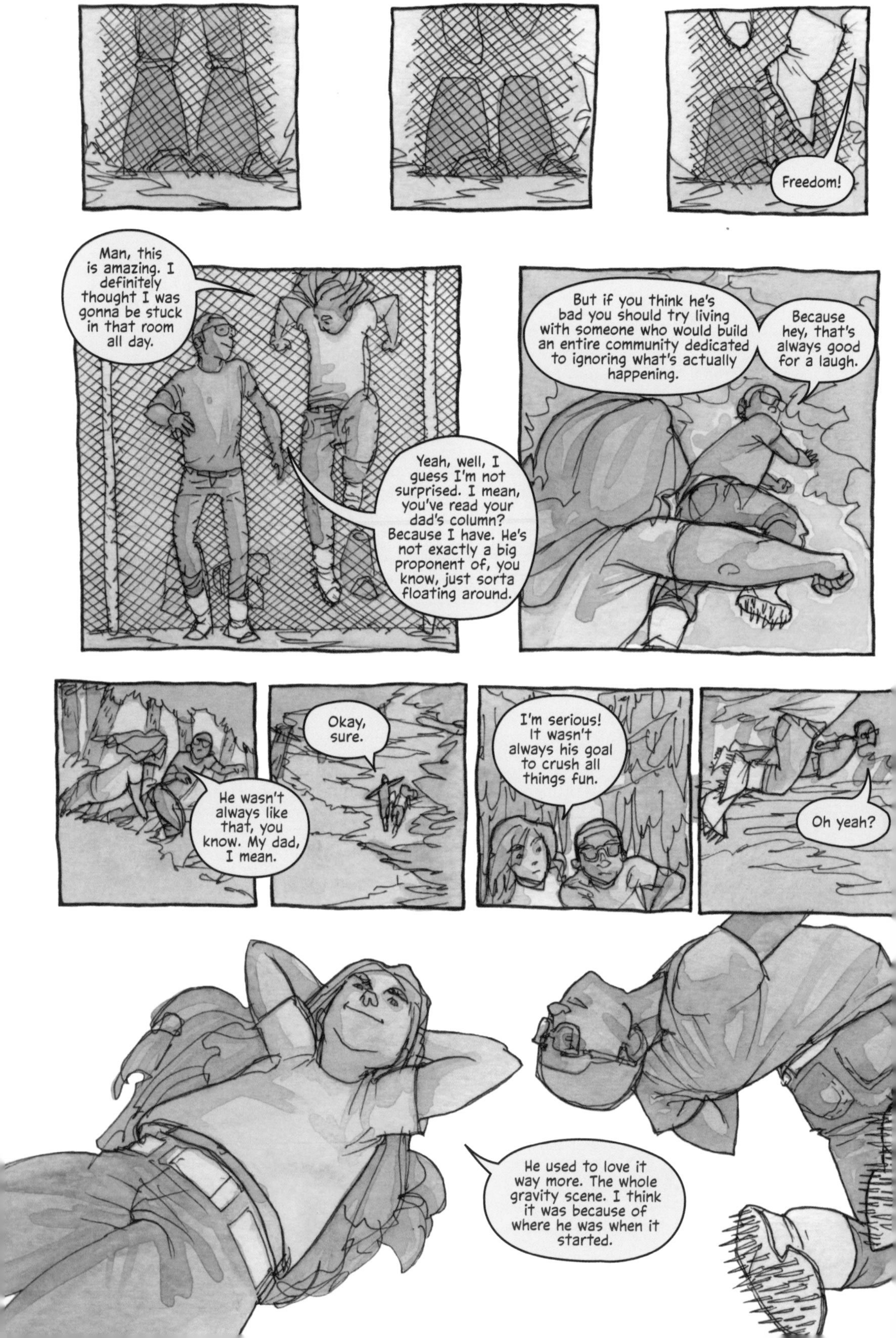

Freedom!
Man, this is amazing. I definitely thought I was gonna be stuck in that room all day.
Yeah, well, I guess I'm not surprised. I mean, you've read your dad's column? Because I have. He's not exactly a big proponent of, you know, just sorta floating around.
But if you think he's bad you should try living with someone who would build an entire community dedicated to ignoring what's actually happening.
Because hey, that's always good for a laugh.
He wasn't always like that, you know. My dad, I mean.
Okay, sure.
I'm serious! It wasn't always his goal to crush all things fun.
Oh yeah?
He used to love it way more. The whole gravity scene. I think it was because of where he was when it started.

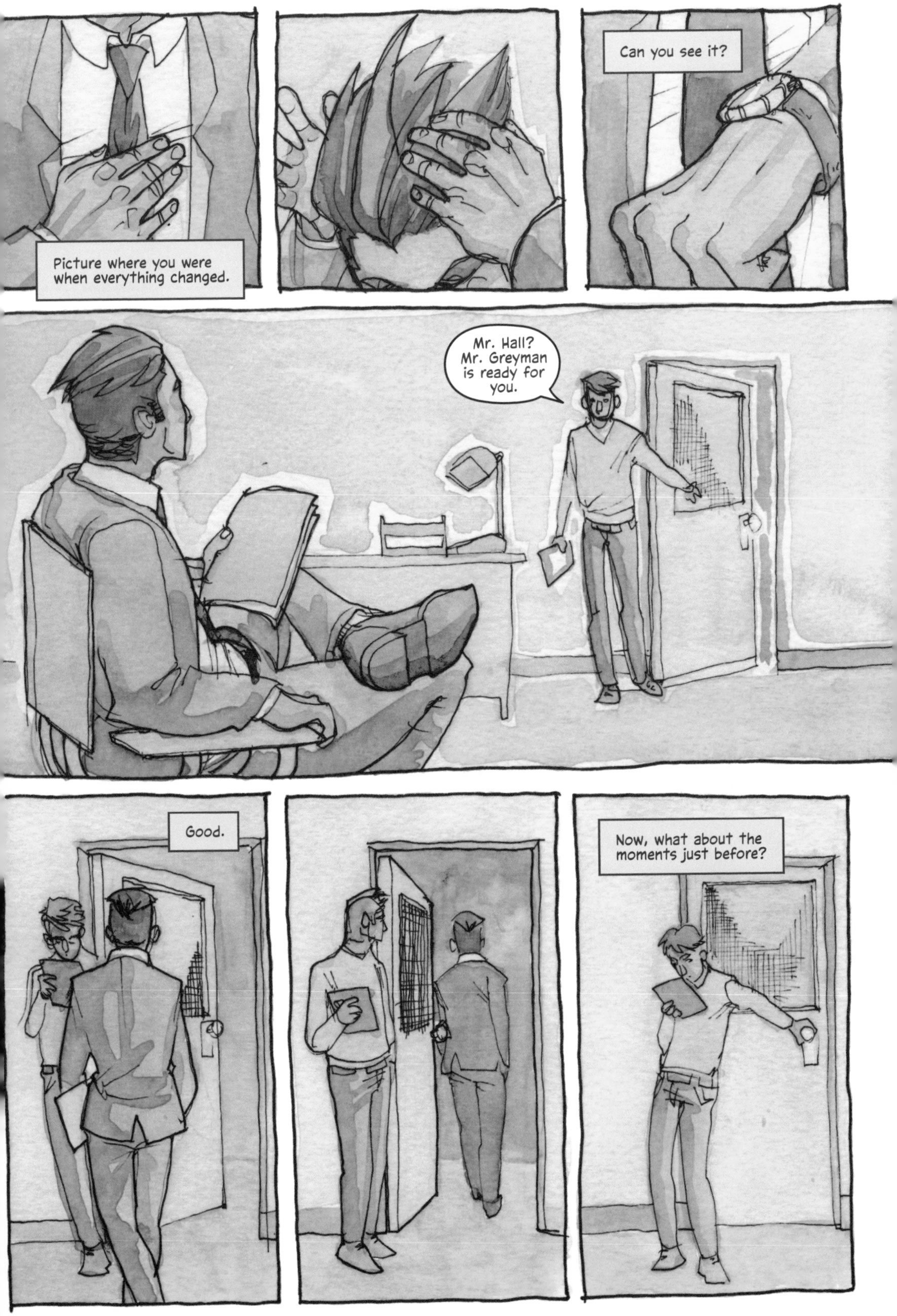
Picture where you were when everything changed.
Can you see it?
Mr. Hall? Mr. Greyman is ready for you.
Good.
Now, what about the moments just before?

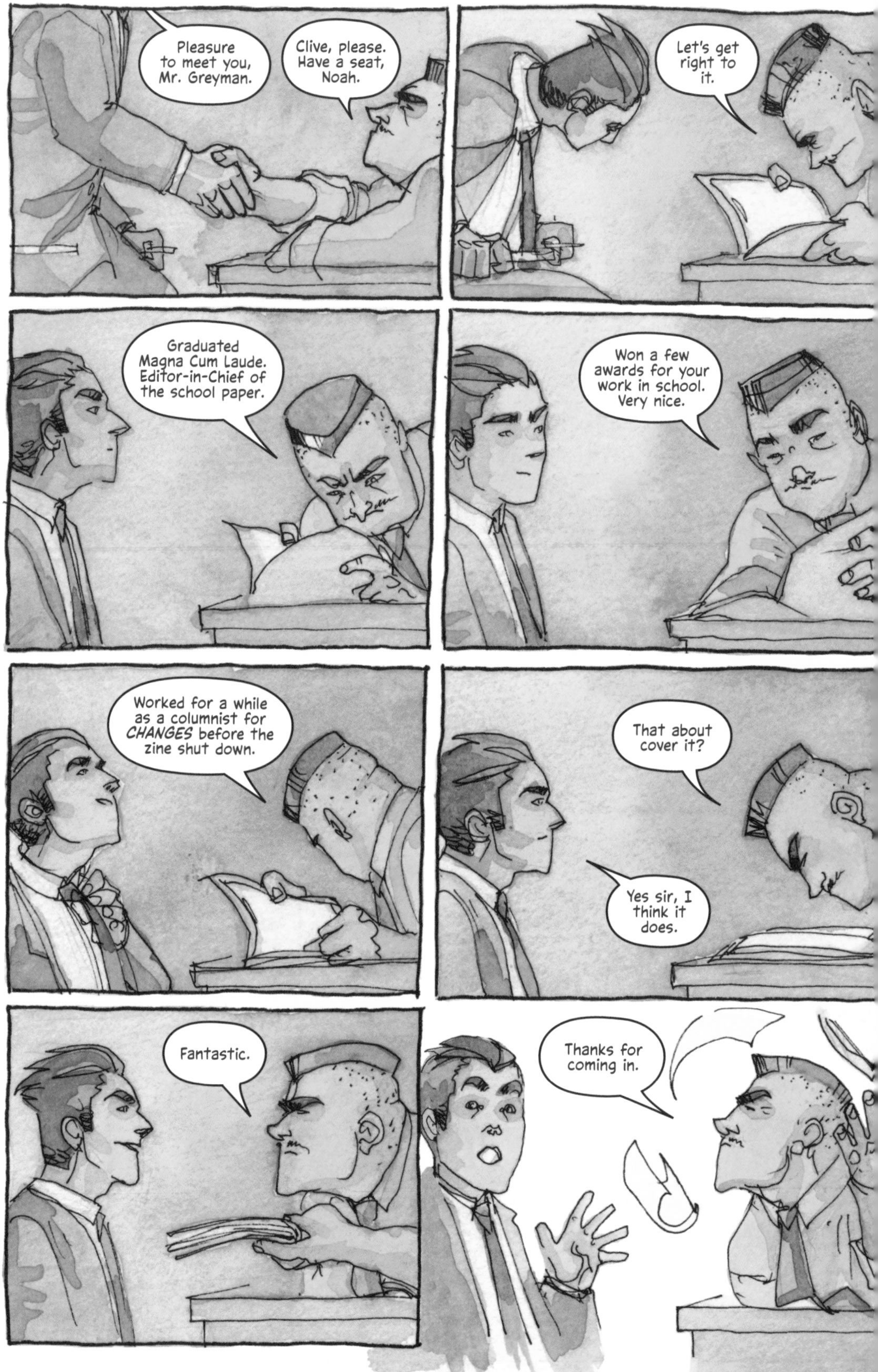
Pleasure to meet you, Mr. Greyman.
Clive, please. Have a seat, Noah.
Let's get right to it.
Graduated Magna Cum Laude. Editor-in-Chief of the school paper.
Won a few awards for your work in school. Very nice.
Worked for a while as a columnist for CHANGES before the zine shut down.
That about cover it?
Yes sir, I think it does.
Fantastic.
Thanks for coming in.

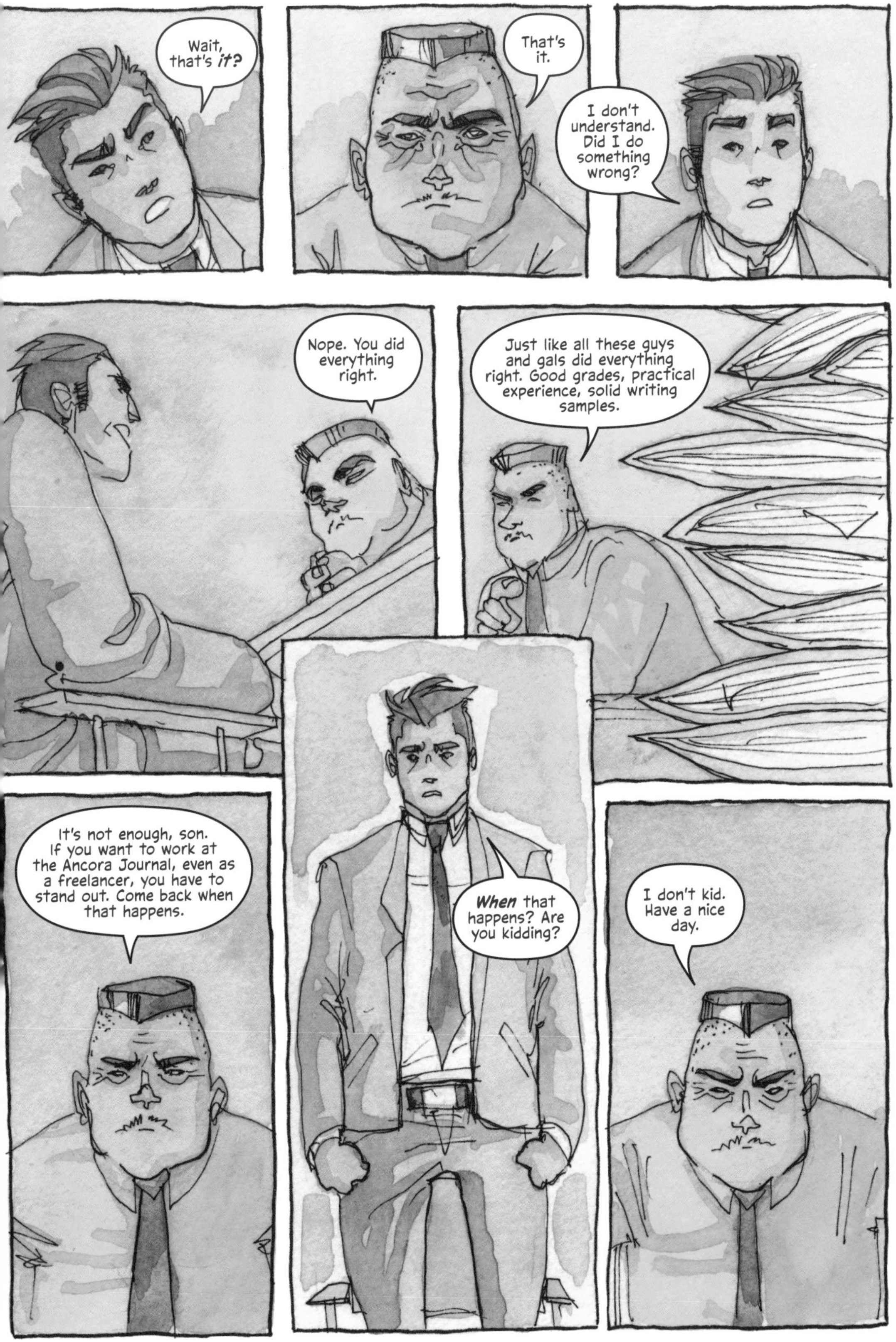
Wait, that's *it?*
That's it.
I don't understand. Did I do something wrong?
Nope. You did everything right.
Just like all these guys and gals did everything right. Good grades, practical experience, solid writing samples.
It's not enough, son. If you want to work at the Ancora Journal, even as a freelancer, you have to stand out. Come back when that happens.
When that happens? Are you kidding?
I don't kid. Have a nice day.

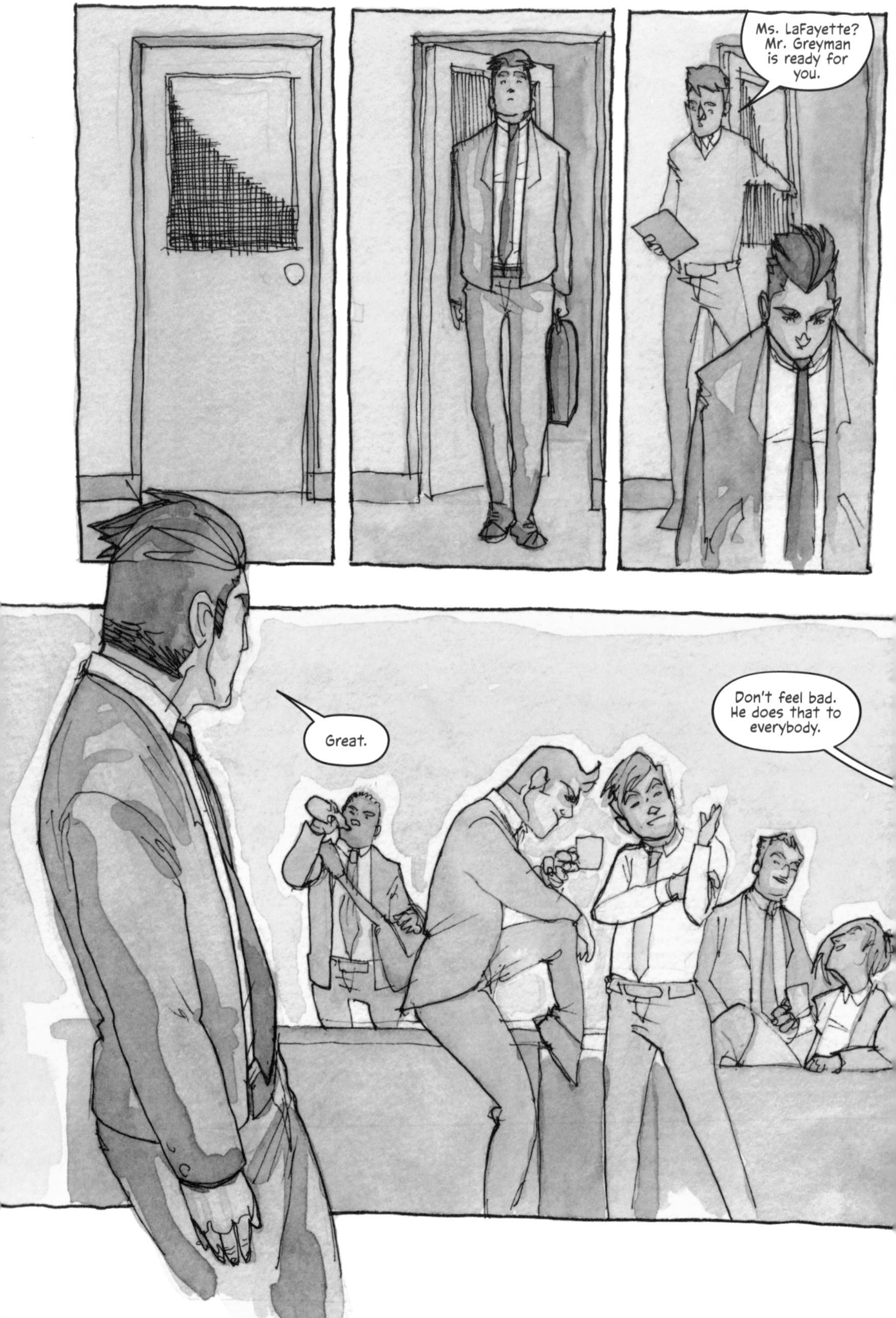
Ms. LaFayette? Mr. Greyman is ready for you.
Great.
Don't feel bad. He does that to everybody.

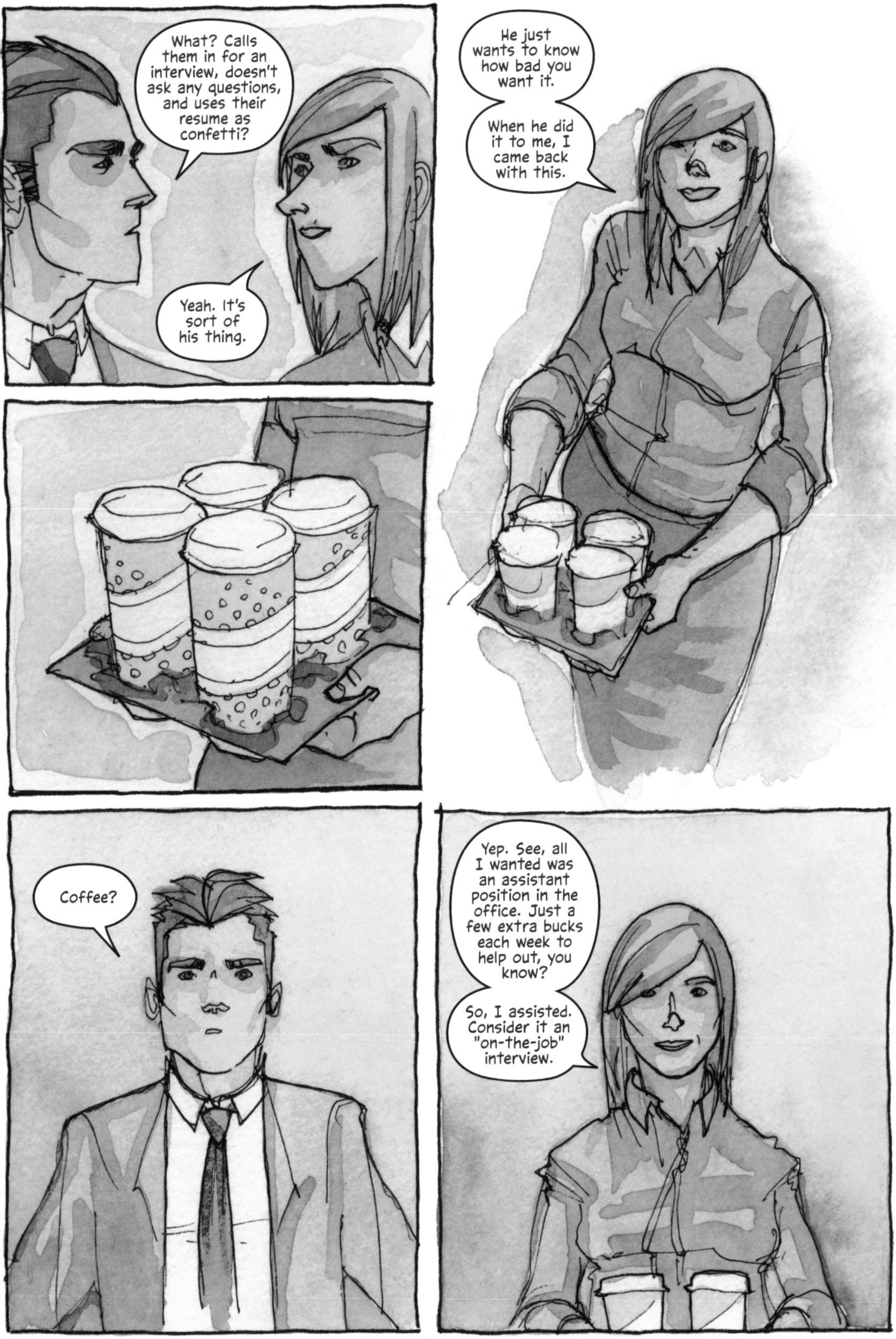
What? Calls them in for an interview, doesn't ask any questions, and uses their resume as confetti?
Yeah. It's sort of his thing.
He just wants to know how bad you want it.
When he did it to me, I came back with this.
Coffee?
Yep. See, all I wanted was an assistant position in the office. Just a few extra bucks each week to help out, you know?
So, I assisted. Consider it an "on-the-job" interview.

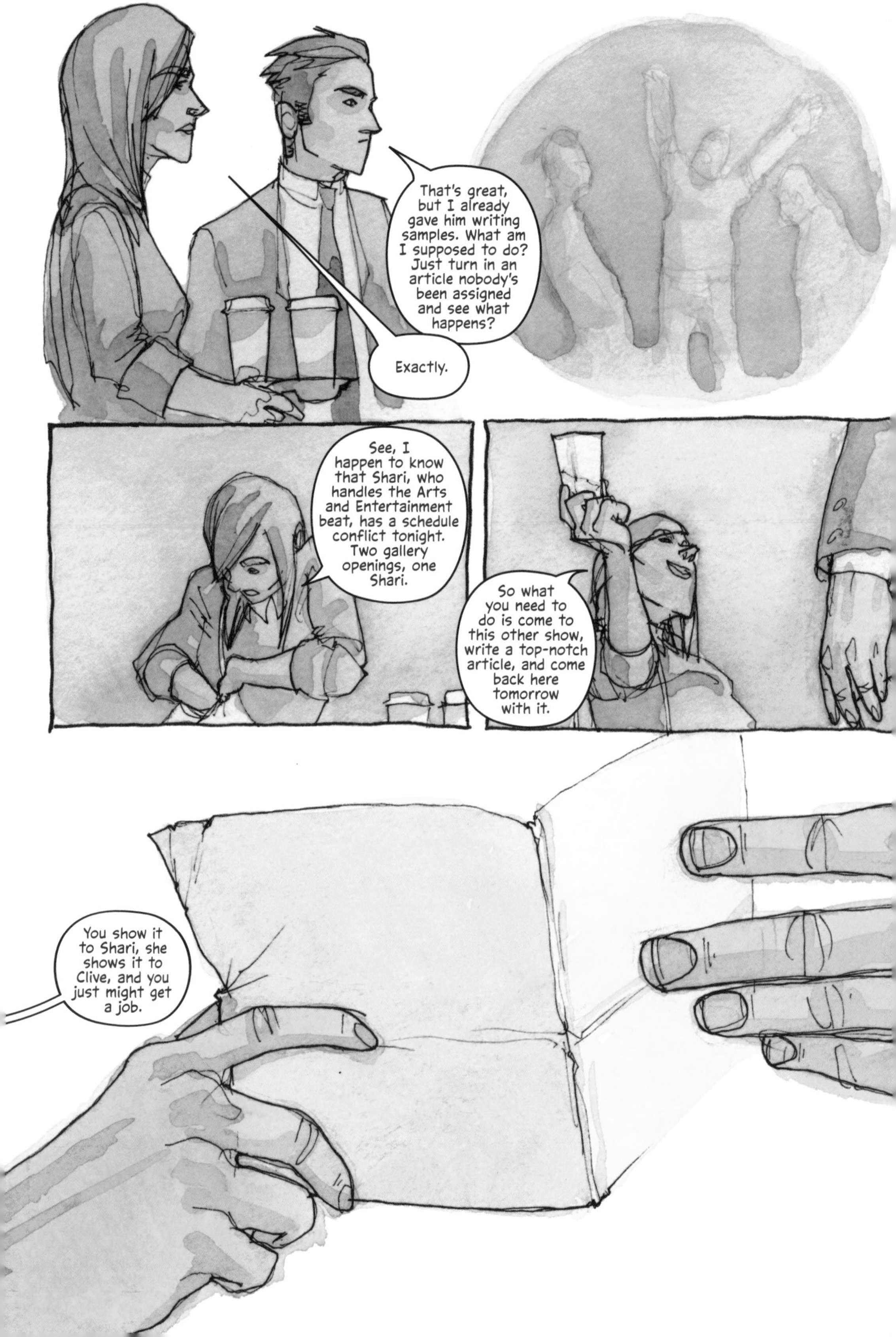
That's great, but I already gave him writing samples. What am I supposed to do? Just turn in an article nobody's been assigned and see what happens?
Exactly.
See, I happen to know that Shari, who handles the Arts and Entertainment beat, has a schedule conflict tonight. Two gallery openings, one Shari.
So what you need to do is come to this other show, write a top-notch article, and come back here tomorrow with it.
You show it to Shari, she shows it to Clive, and you just might get a job.

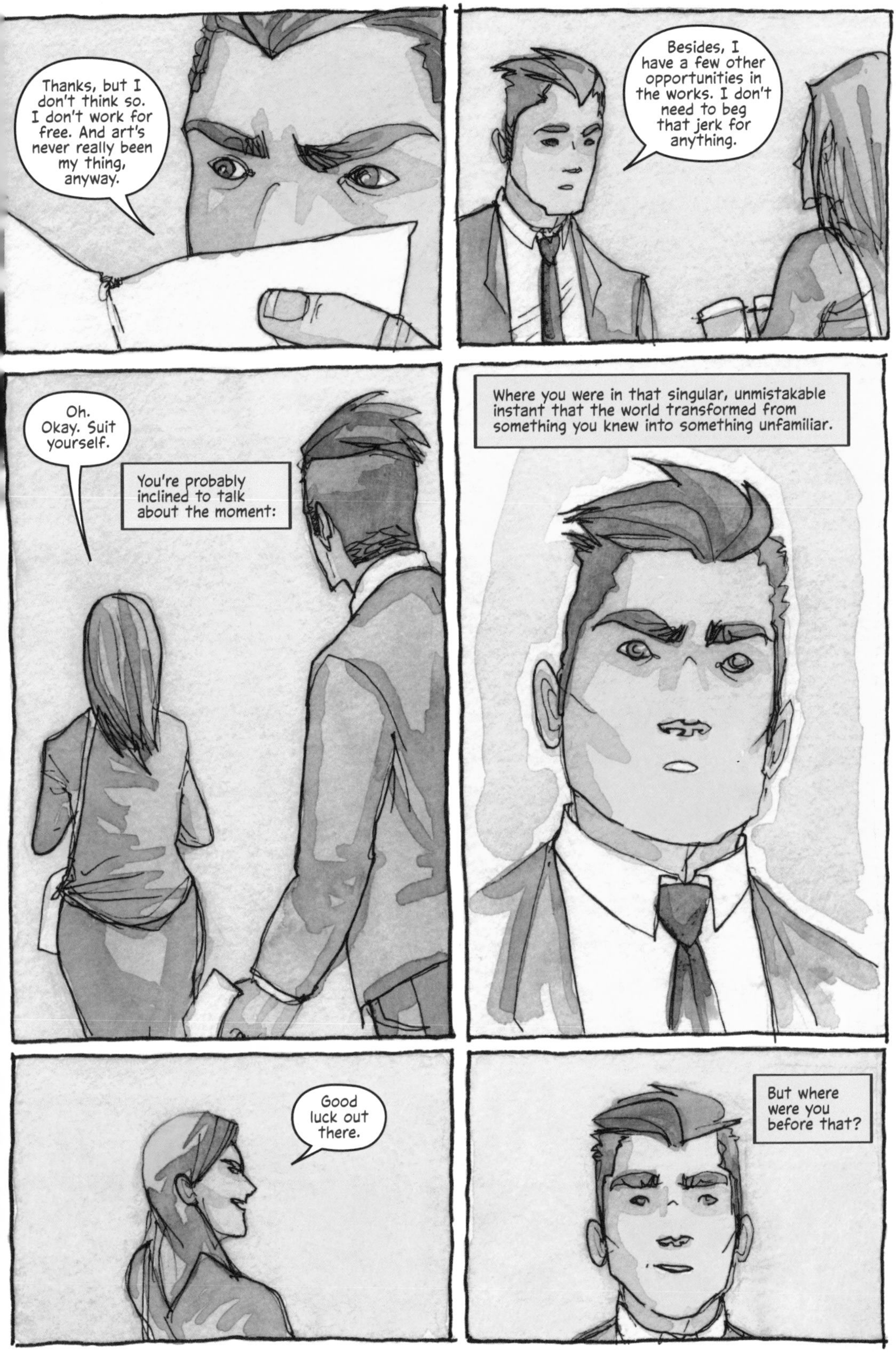
Thanks, but I don't think so. I don't work for free. And art's never really been my thing, anyway.
Besides, I have a few other opportunities in the works. I don't need to beg that jerk for anything.
Oh. Okay. Suit yourself.
You're probably inclined to talk about the moment:
Where you were in that singular, unmistakable instant that the world transformed from something you knew into something unfamiliar.
Good luck out there.
But where were you before that?

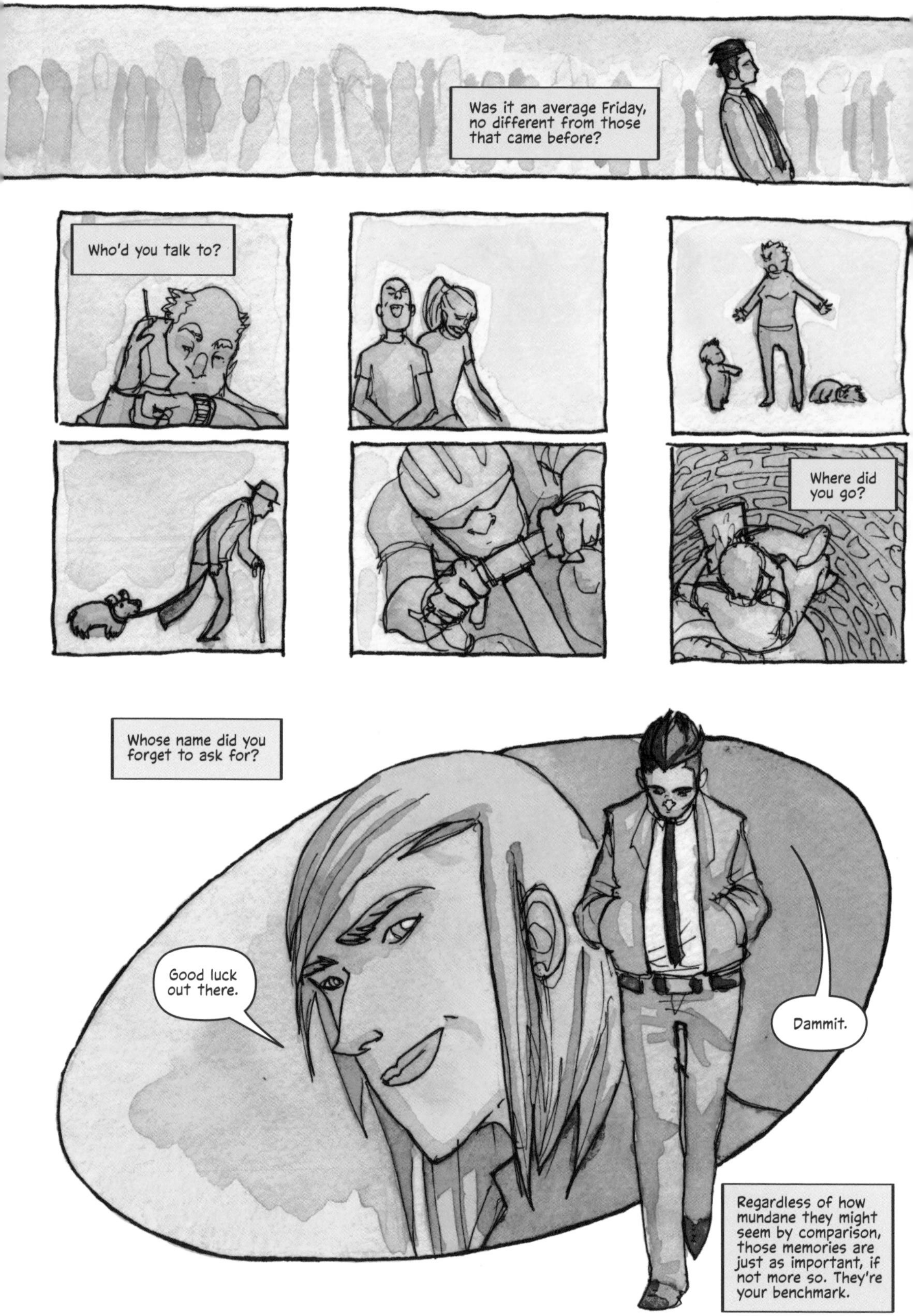
Was it an average Friday, no different from those that came before?
Who'd you talk to?
Where did you go?
Whose name did you forget to ask for?
Good luck out there.
Dammit.
Regardless of how mundane they might seem by comparison, those memories are just as important, if not more so. They're your benchmark.

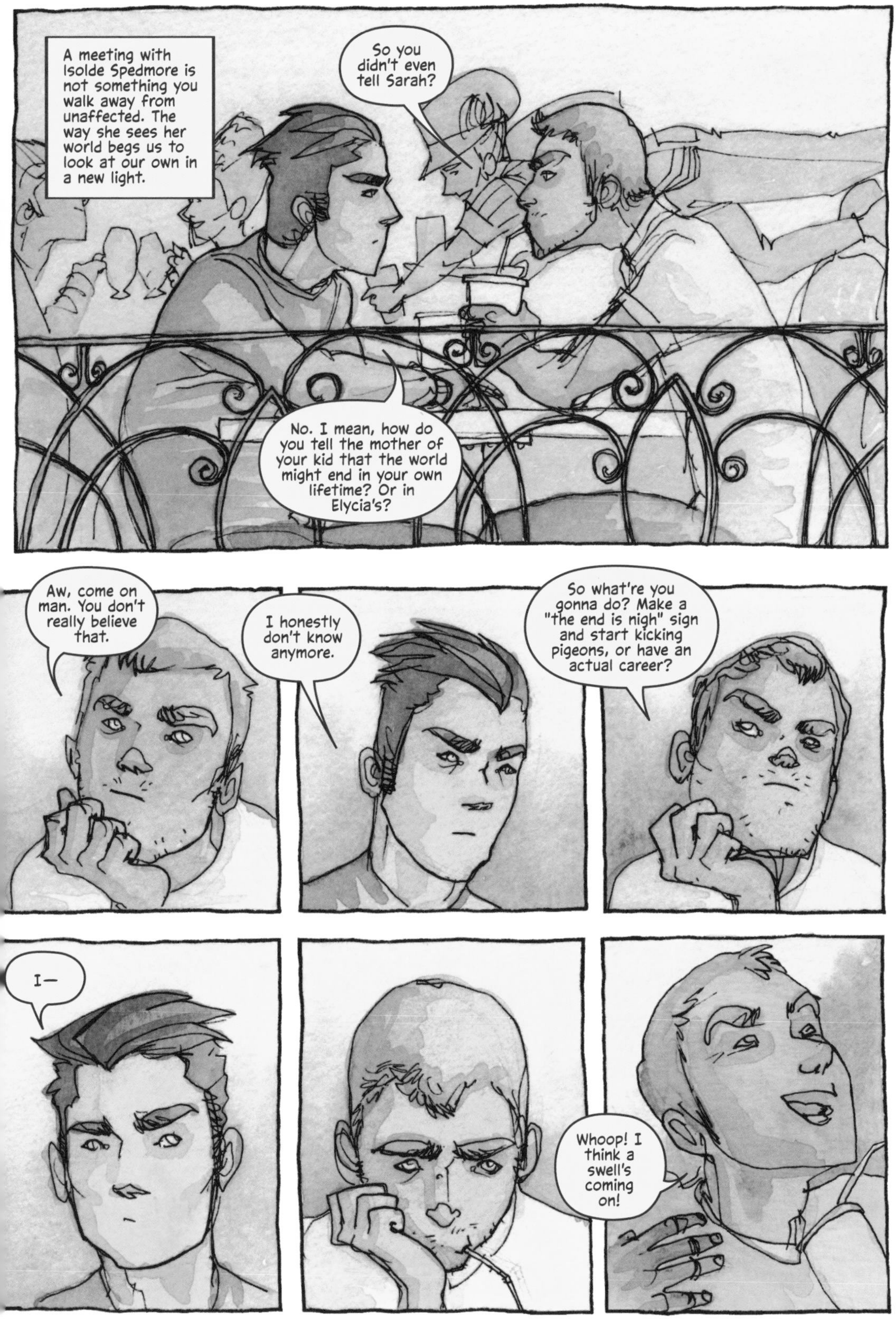

A meeting with Isolde Spedmore is not something you walk away from unaffected. The way she sees her world begs us to look at our own in a new light.
So you didn't even tell Sarah?
No. I mean, how do you tell the mother of your kid that the world might end in your own lifetime? Or in Elycia's?
Aw, come on man. You don't really believe that.
I honestly don't know anymore.
So what're you gonna do? Make a "the end is nigh" sign and start kicking pigeons, or have an actual career?
I—
Whoop! I think a swell's coming on!

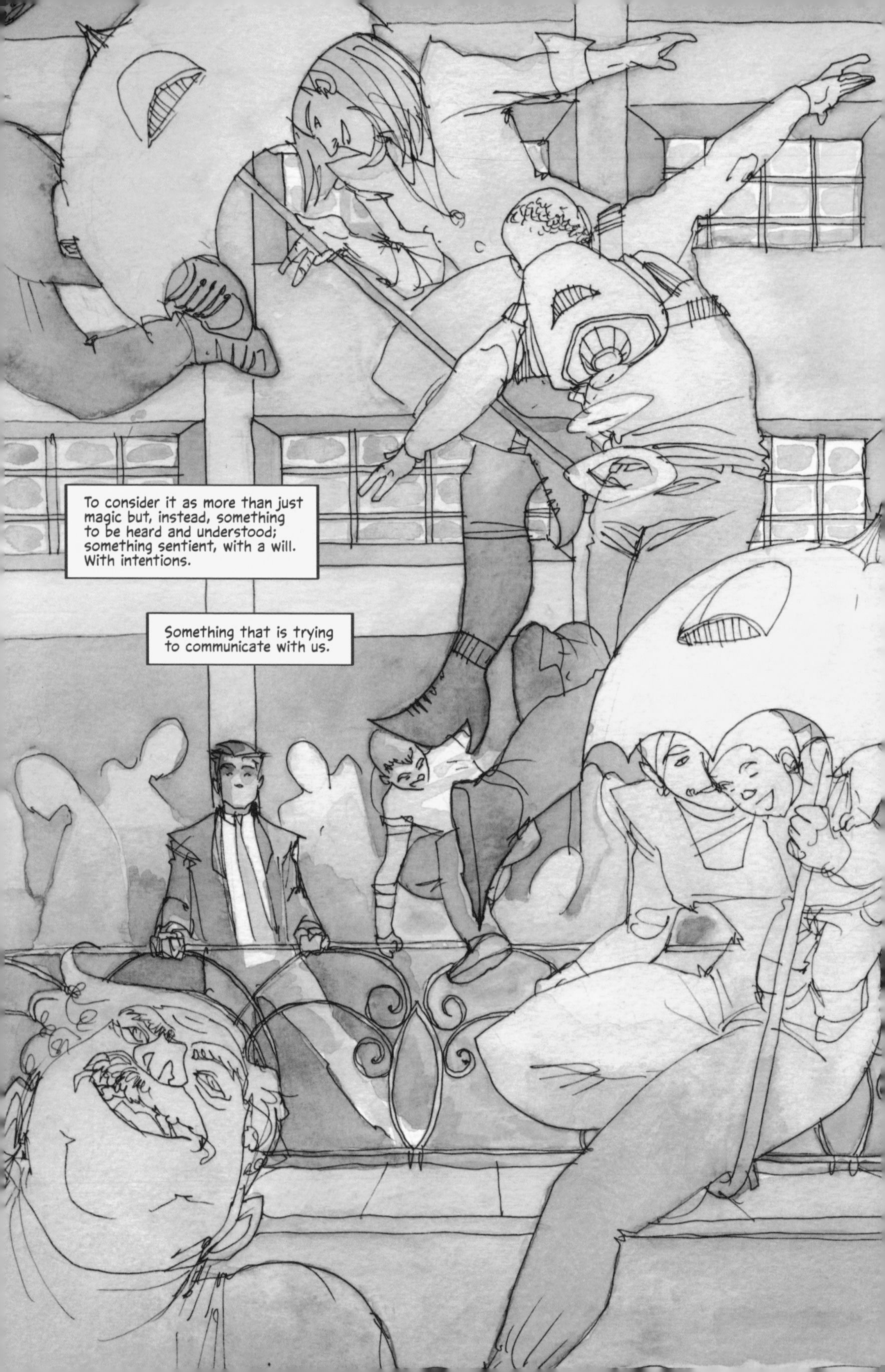
To consider it as more than just magic but, instead, something to be heard and understood; something sentient, with a will. With intentions.
Something that is trying to communicate with us.

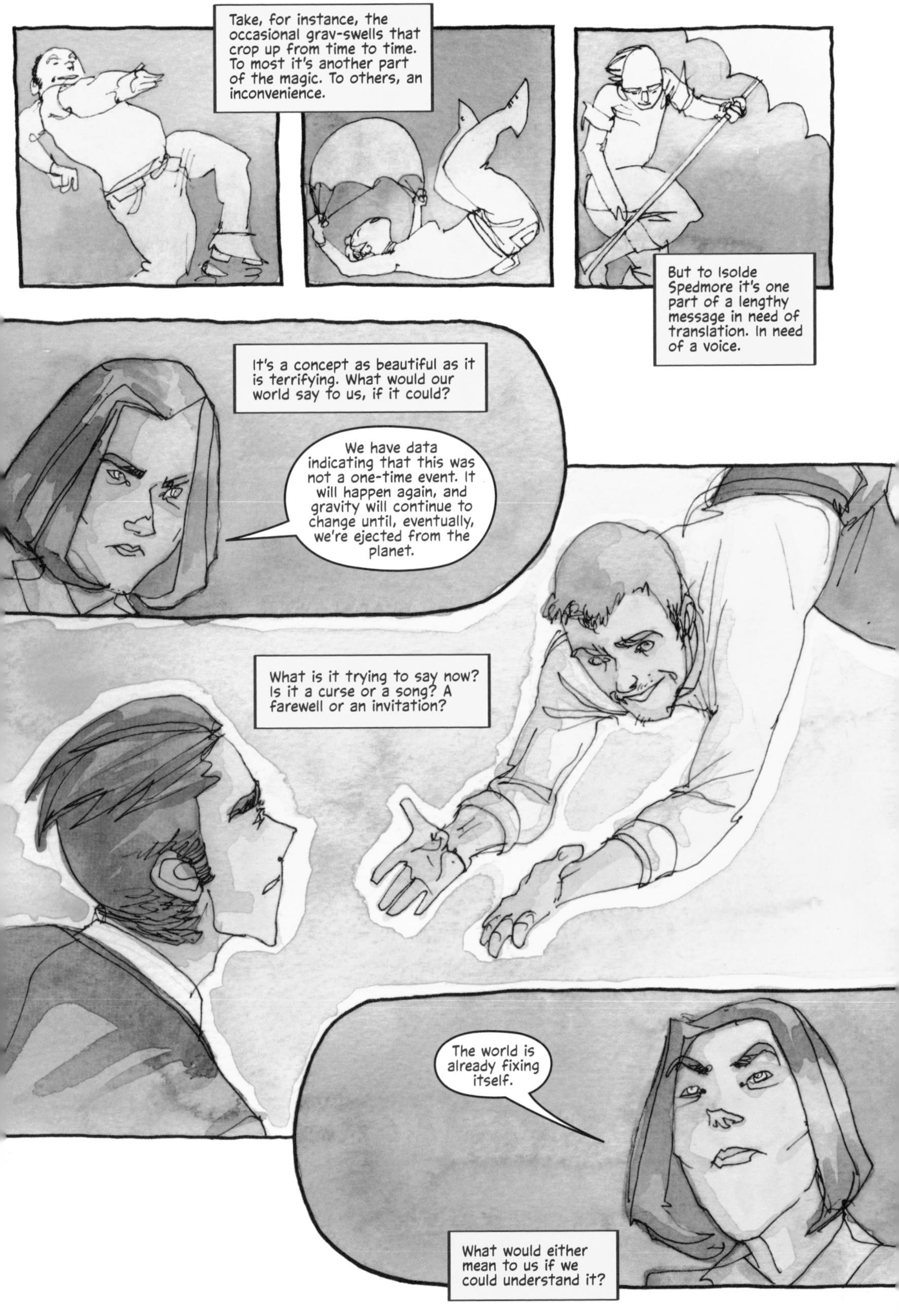
Take, for instance, the occasional grav-swells that crop up from time to time. To most it's another part of the magic. To others, an inconvenience.
But to Isolde Spedmore it's one part of a lengthy message in need of translation. In need of a voice.
It's a concept as beautiful as it is terrifying. What would our world say to us, if it could?
We have data indicating that this was not a one-time event. It will happen again, and gravity will continue to change until, eventually, we're ejected from the planet.
What is it trying to say now? Is it a curse or a song? A farewell or an invitation?
The world is already fixing itself.
What would either mean to us if we could understand it?

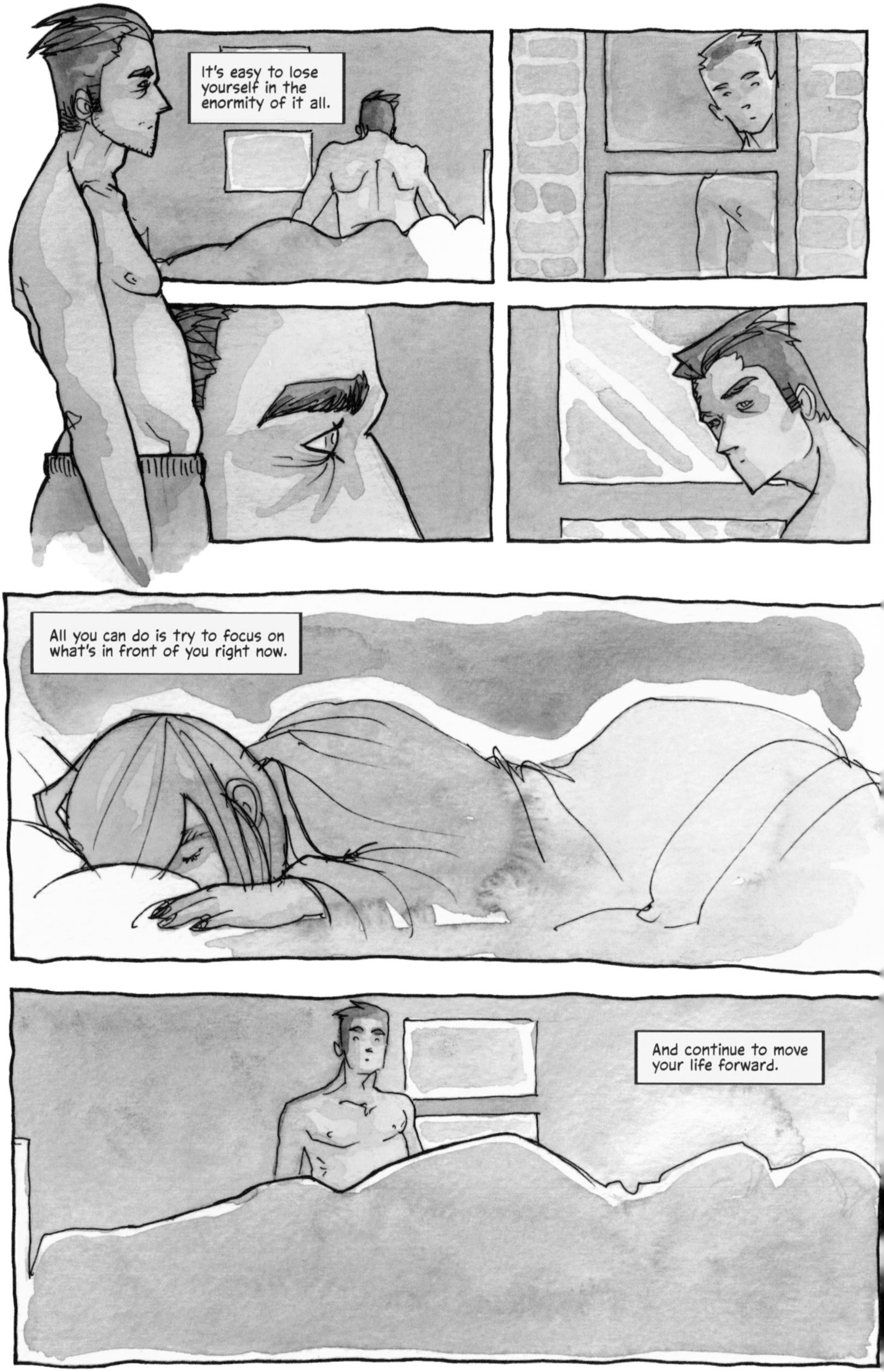
It's easy to lose yourself in the enormity of it all.
All you can do is try to focus on what's in front of you right now.
And continue to move your life forward.

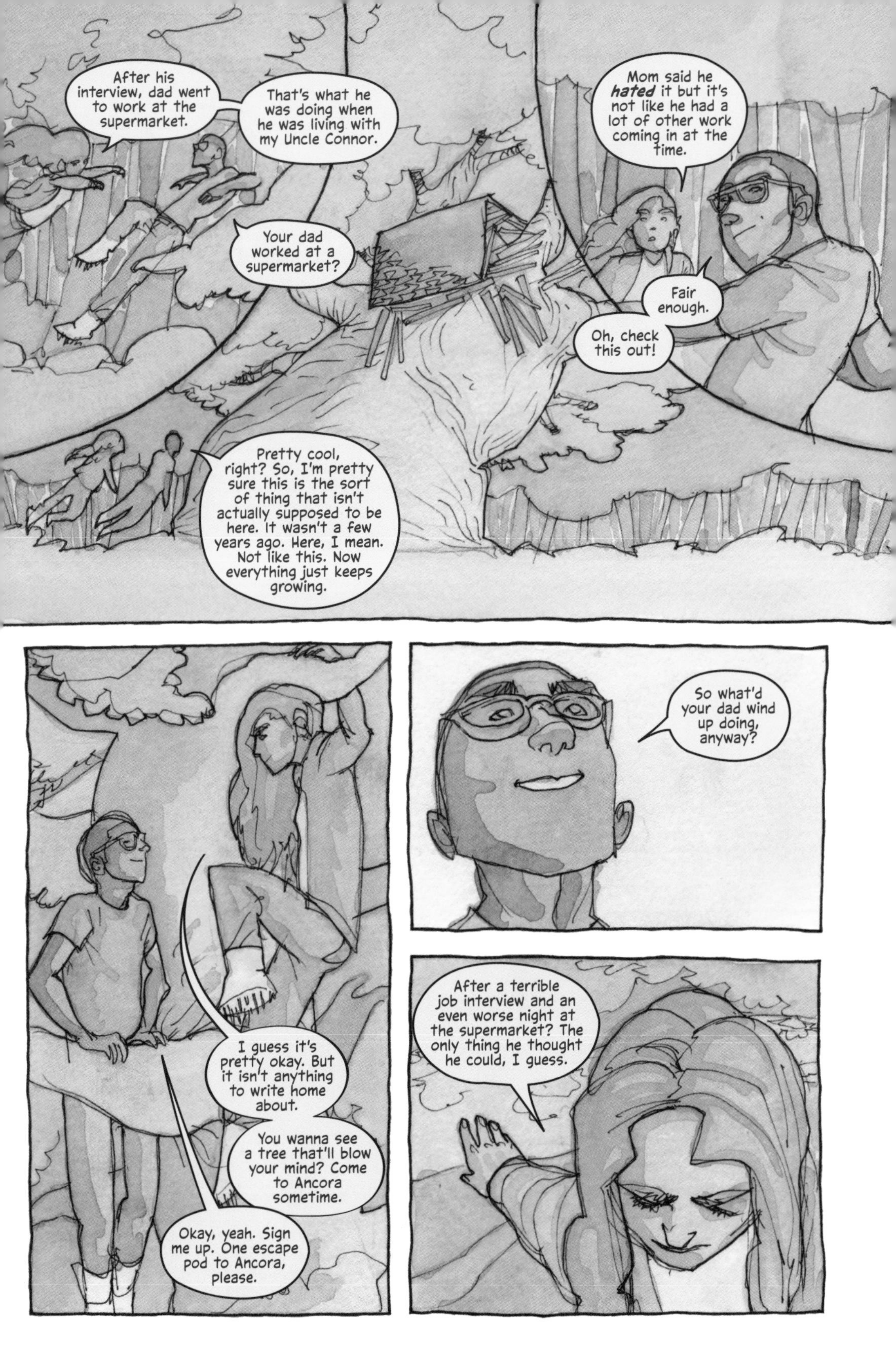

After his interview, dad went to work at the supermarket.
That's what he was doing when he was living with my Uncle Connor.
Your dad worked at a supermarket?
Mom said he **hated** it but it's not like he had a lot of other work coming in at the time.
Fair enough.
Oh, check this out!
Pretty cool, right? So, I'm pretty sure this is the sort of thing that isn't actually supposed to be here. It wasn't a few years ago. Here, I mean. Not like this. Now everything just keeps growing.
I guess it's pretty okay. But it isn't anything to write home about.
You wanna see a tree that'll blow your mind? Come to Ancora sometime.
Okay, yeah. Sign me up. One escape pod to Ancora, please.
So what'd your dad wind up doing, anyway?
After a terrible job interview and an even worse night at the supermarket? The only thing he thought he could, I guess.

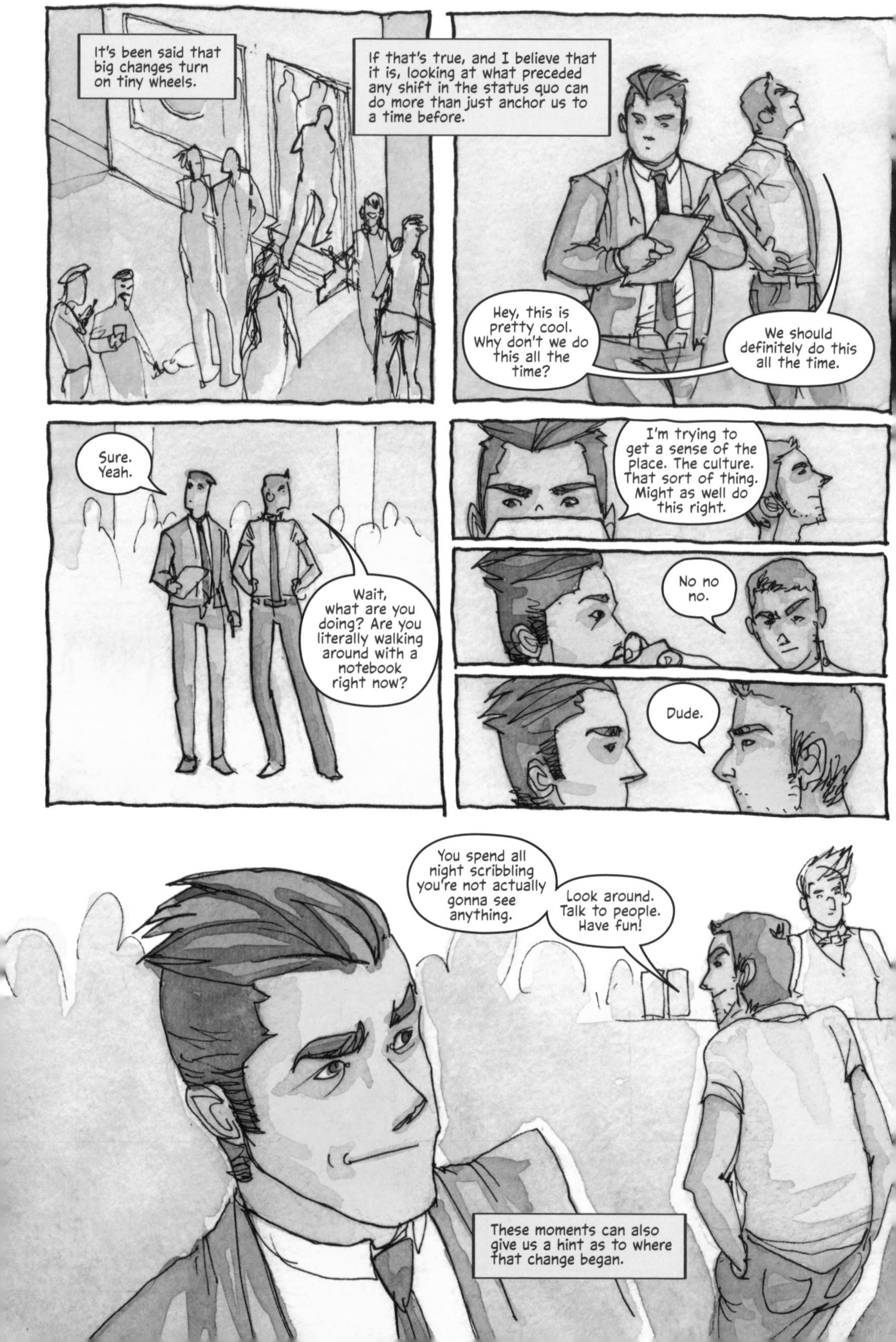
It's been said that big changes turn on tiny wheels.
If that's true, and I believe that it is, looking at what preceded any shift in the status quo can do more than just anchor us to a time before.
Hey, this is pretty cool. Why don't we do this all the time?
We should definitely do this all the time.
Sure. Yeah.
Wait, what are you doing? Are you literally walking around with a notebook right now?
I'm trying to get a sense of the place. The culture. That sort of thing. Might as well do this right.
No no no.
Dude.
You spend all night scribbling you're not actually gonna see anything.
Look around. Talk to people. Have fun!
These moments can also give us a hint as to where that change began.

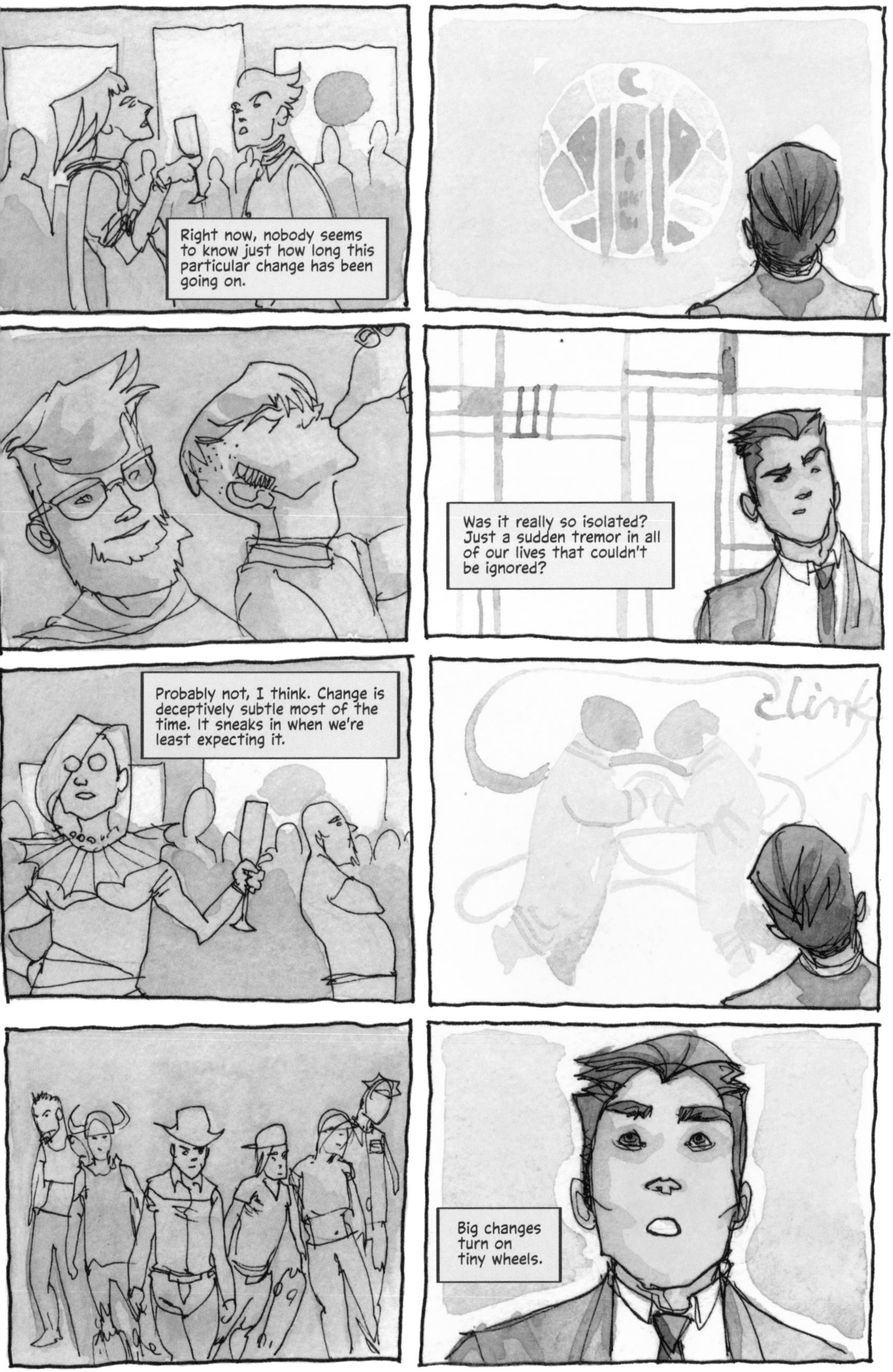
Right now, nobody seems to know just how long this particular change has been going on.
Was it really so isolated? Just a sudden tremor in all of our lives that couldn't be ignored?
Probably not, I think. Change is deceptively subtle most of the time. It sneaks in when we're least expecting it.
clink
Big changes turn on tiny wheels.

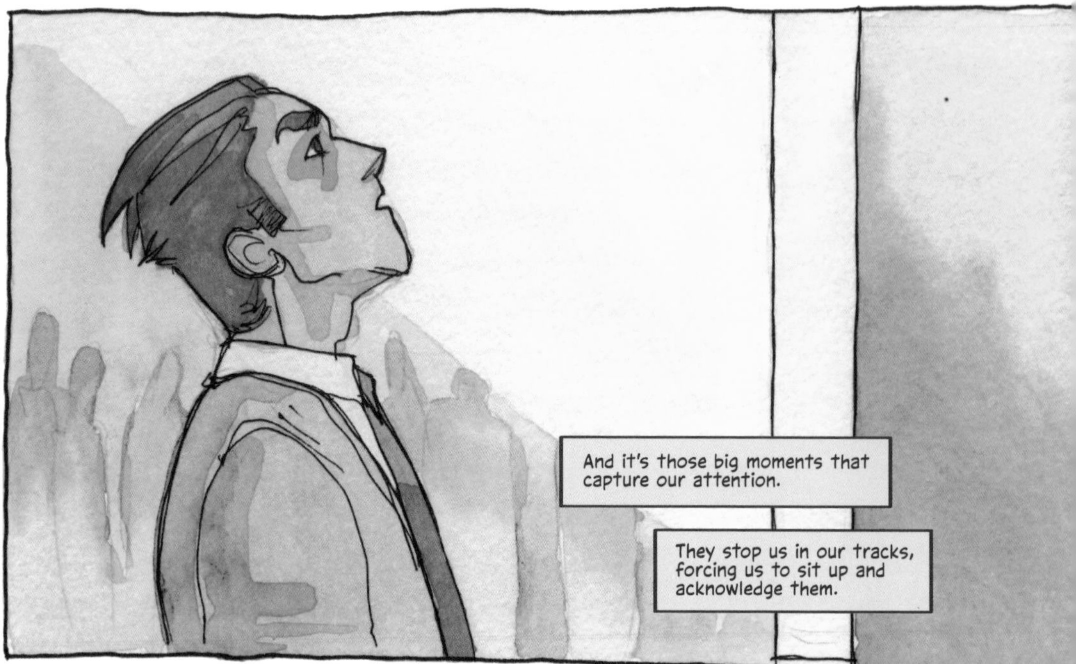
And it's those big moments that capture our attention.
They stop us in our tracks, forcing us to sit up and acknowledge them.

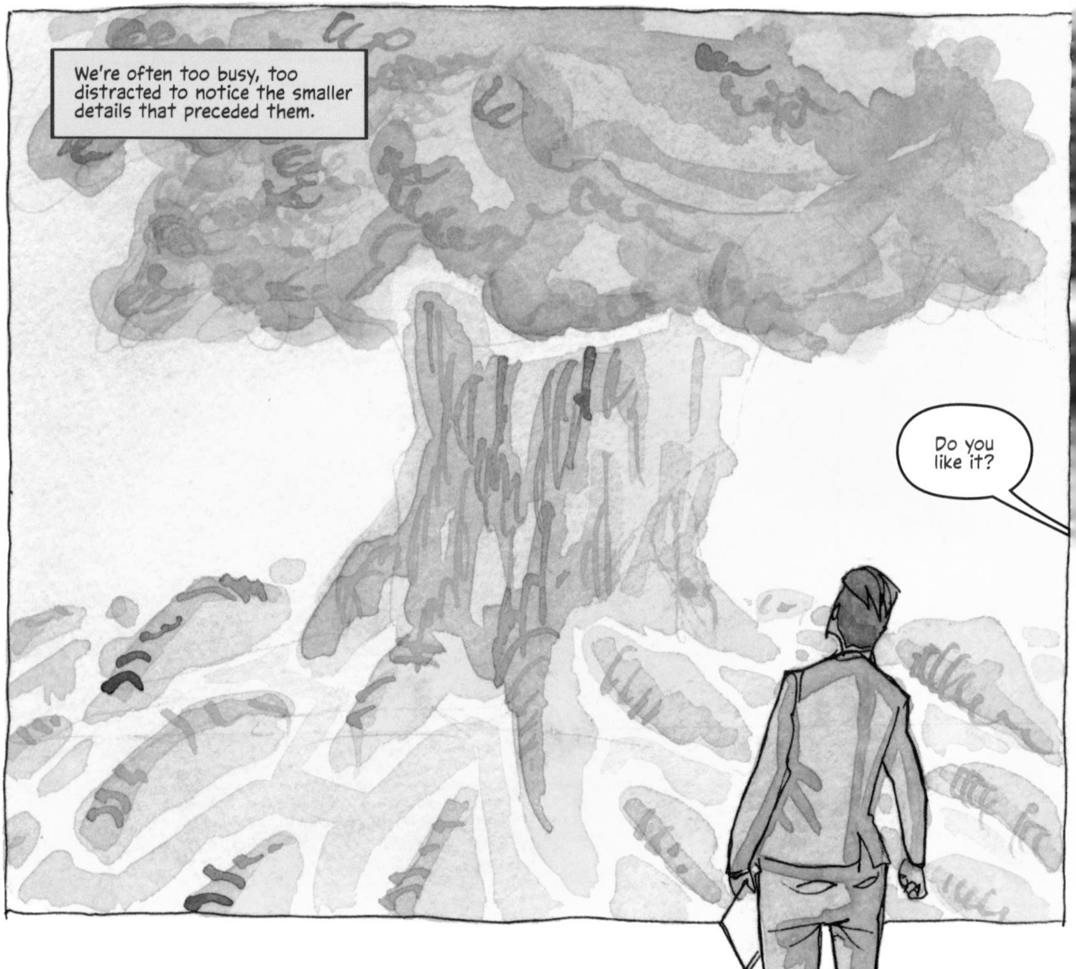
We're often too busy, too distracted to notice the smaller details that preceded them.
Do you like it?

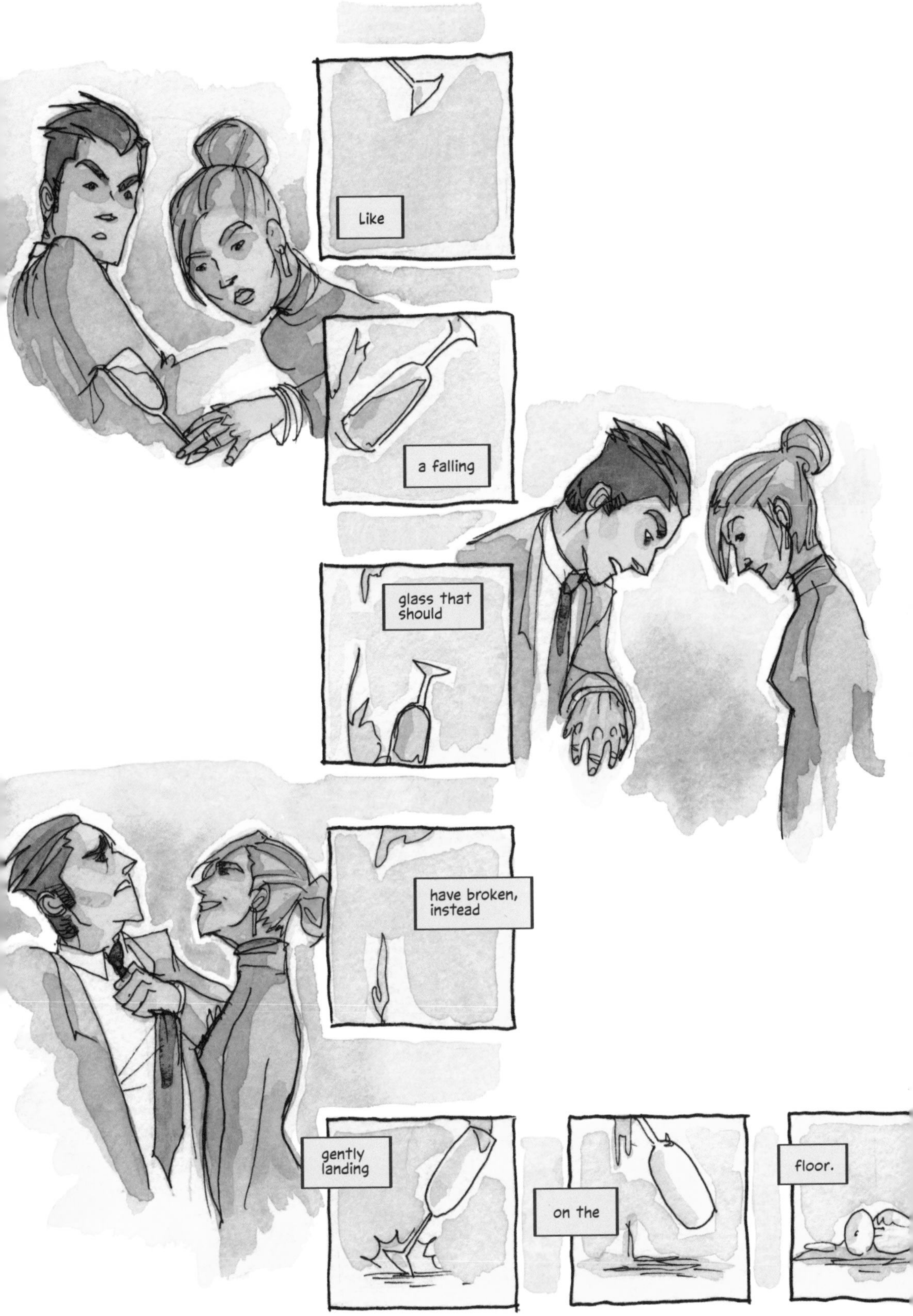
Like
a falling
glass that should
have broken, instead
gently landing
on the
floor.

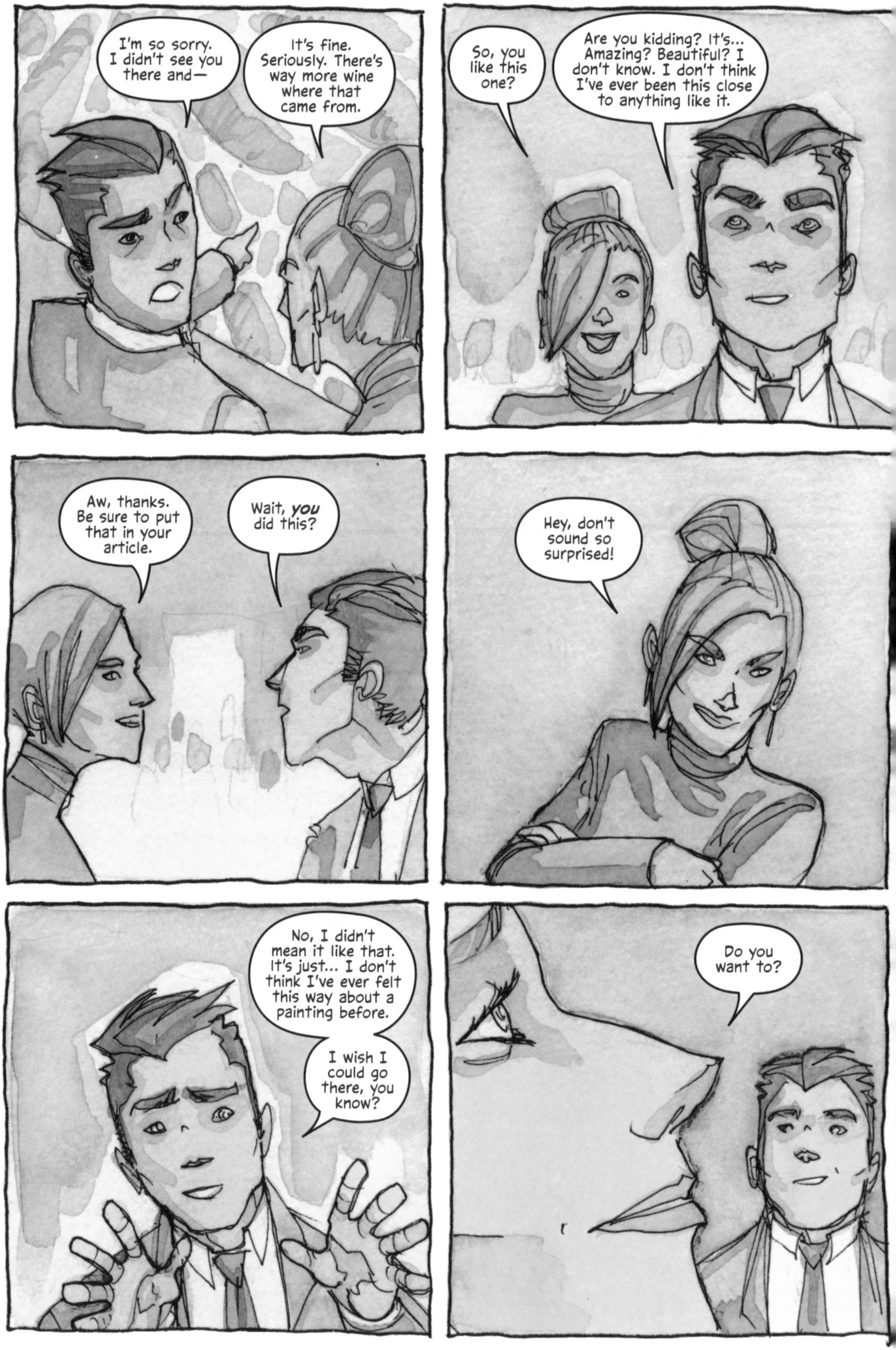
I'm so sorry. I didn't see you there and—
It's fine. Seriously. There's way more wine where that came from.
So, you like this one?
Are you kidding? It's... Amazing? Beautiful? I don't know. I don't think I've ever been this close to anything like it.
Aw, thanks. Be sure to put that in your article.
Wait, *you* did this?
Hey, don't sound so surprised!
No, I didn't mean it like that. It's just... I don't think I've ever felt this way about a painting before.
I wish I could go there, you know?
Do you want to?

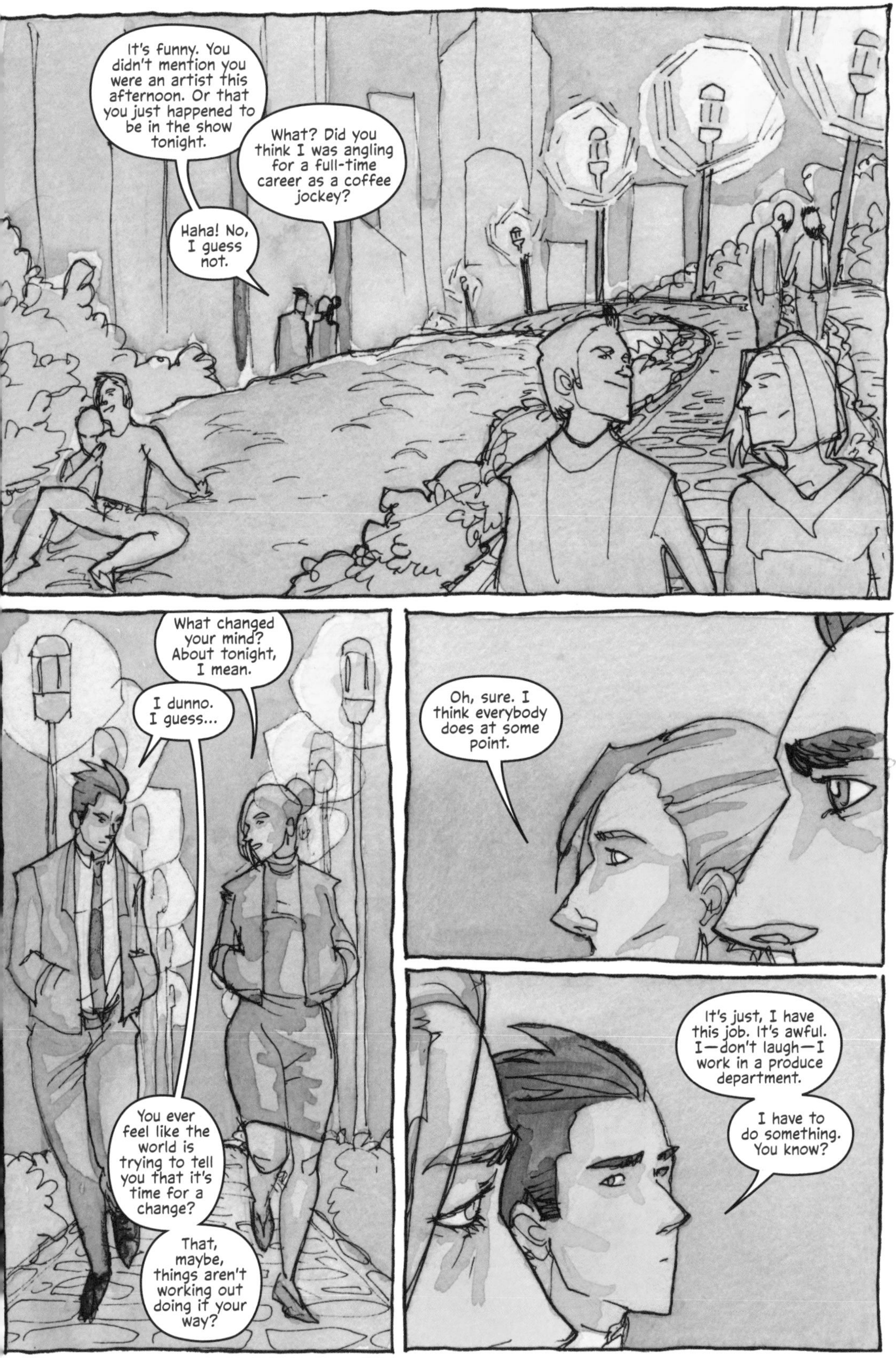
It's funny. You didn't mention you were an artist this afternoon. Or that you just happened to be in the show tonight.
What? Did you think I was angling for a full-time career as a coffee jockey?
Haha! No, I guess not.
What changed your mind? About tonight, I mean.
I dunno. I guess...
You ever feel like the world is trying to tell you that it's time for a change?
That, maybe, things aren't working out doing it your way?
Oh, sure. I think everybody does at some point.
It's just, I have this job. It's awful. I—don't laugh—I work in a produce department.
I have to do something. You know?

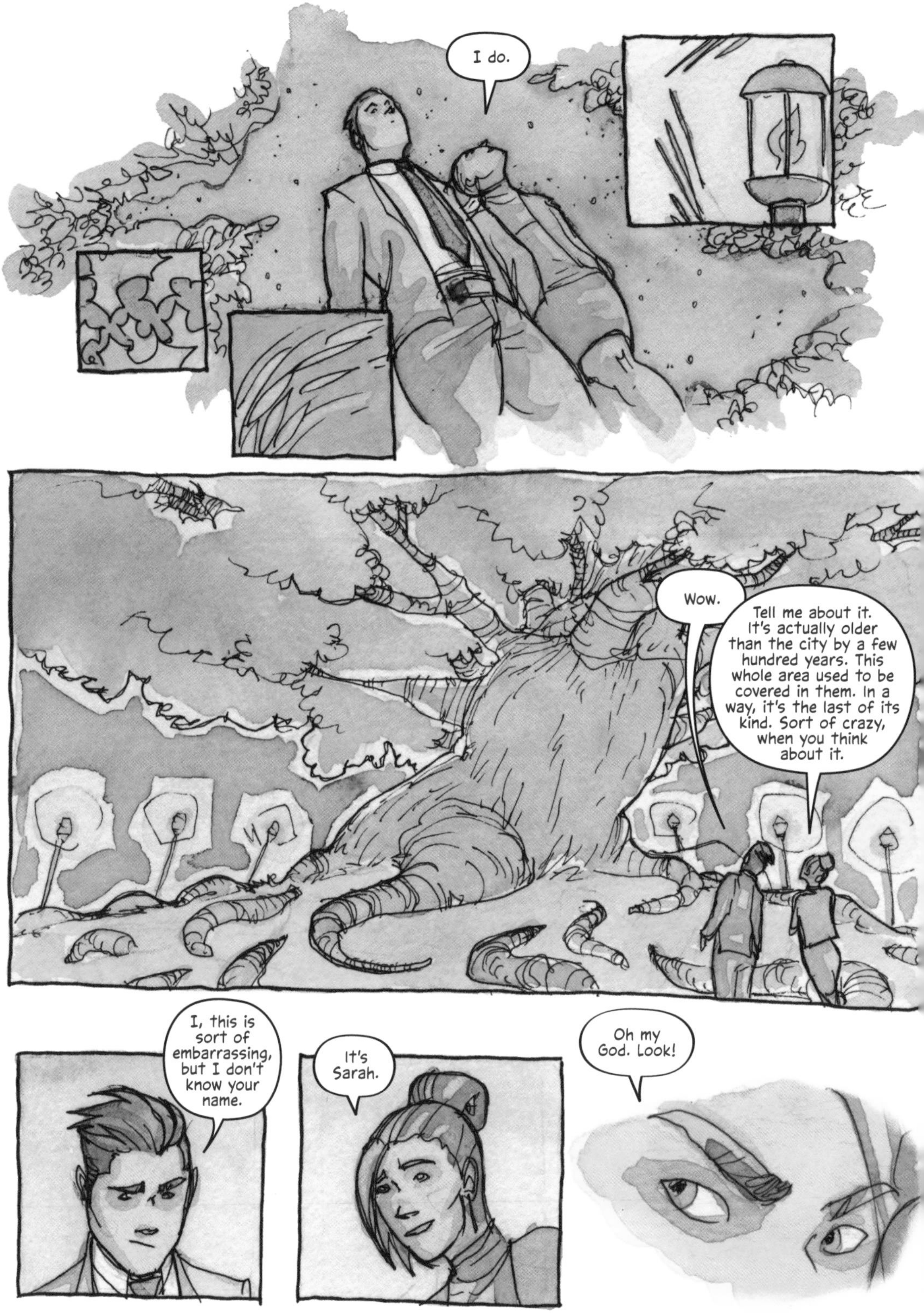
I do.
Wow.
Tell me about it. It's actually older than the city by a few hundred years. This whole area used to be covered in them. In a way, it's the last of its kind. Sort of crazy, when you think about it.
I, this is sort of embarrassing, but I don't know your name.
It's Sarah.
Oh my God. Look!

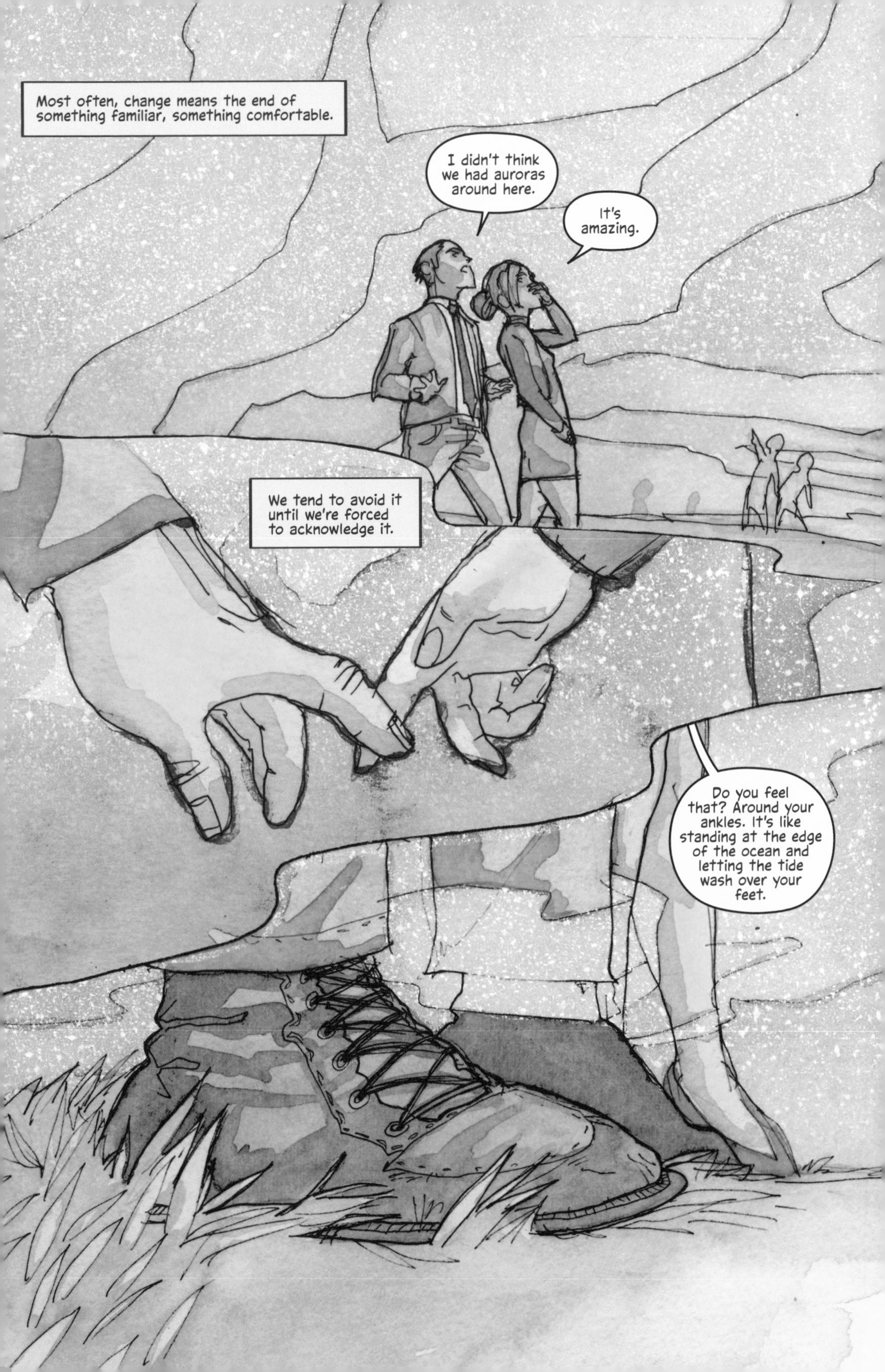
Most often, change means the end of something familiar, something comfortable.
I didn't think we had auroras around here.
It's amazing.
We tend to avoid it until we're forced to acknowledge it.
Do you feel that? Around your ankles. It's like standing at the edge of the ocean and letting the tide wash over your feet.

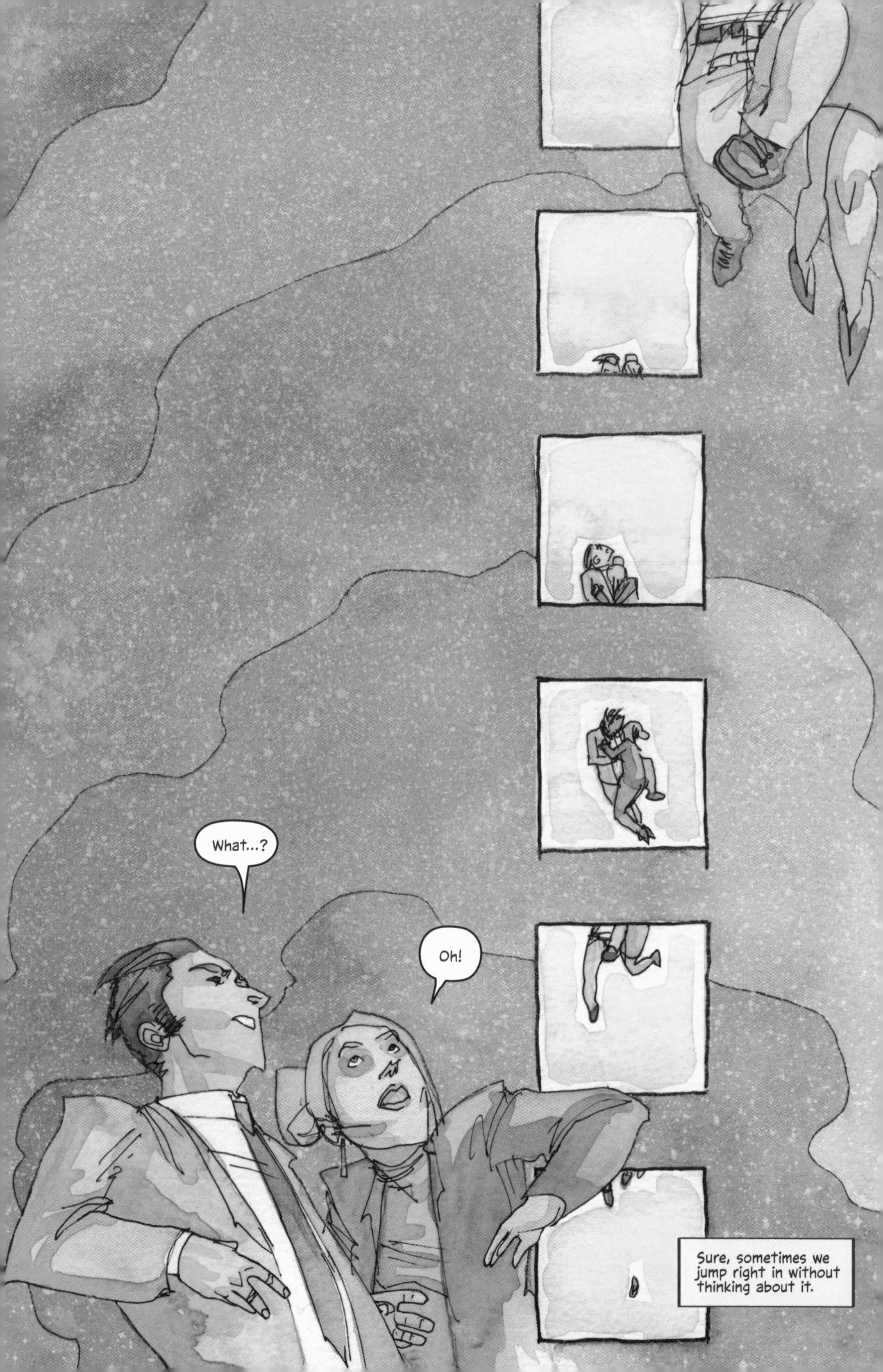
What...?
Oh!
Sure, sometimes we jump right in without thinking about it.

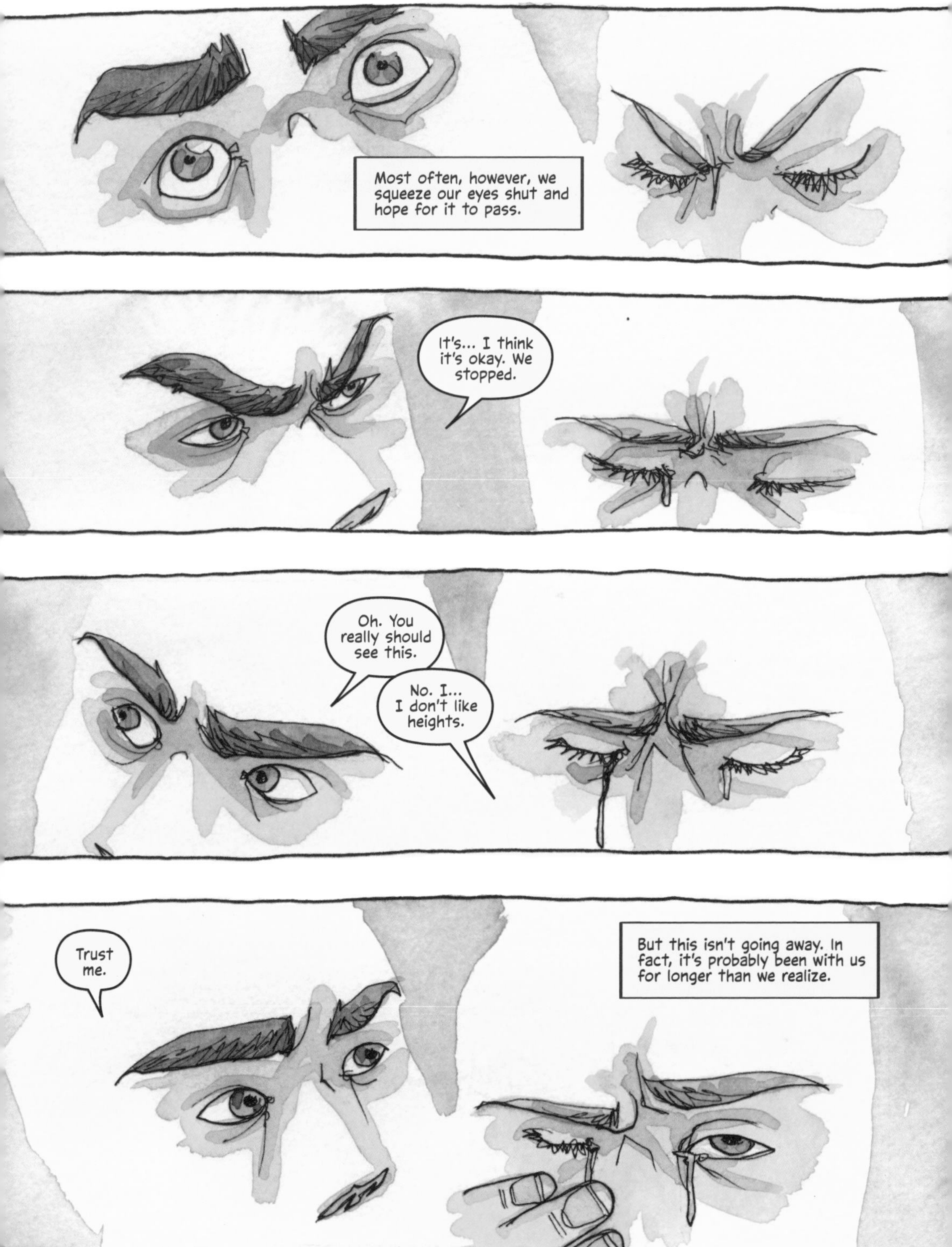
Most often, however, we squeeze our eyes shut and hope for it to pass.
It's... I think it's okay. We stopped.
Oh. You really should see this.
No. I... I don't like heights.
Trust me.
But this isn't going away. In fact, it's probably been with us for longer than we realize.

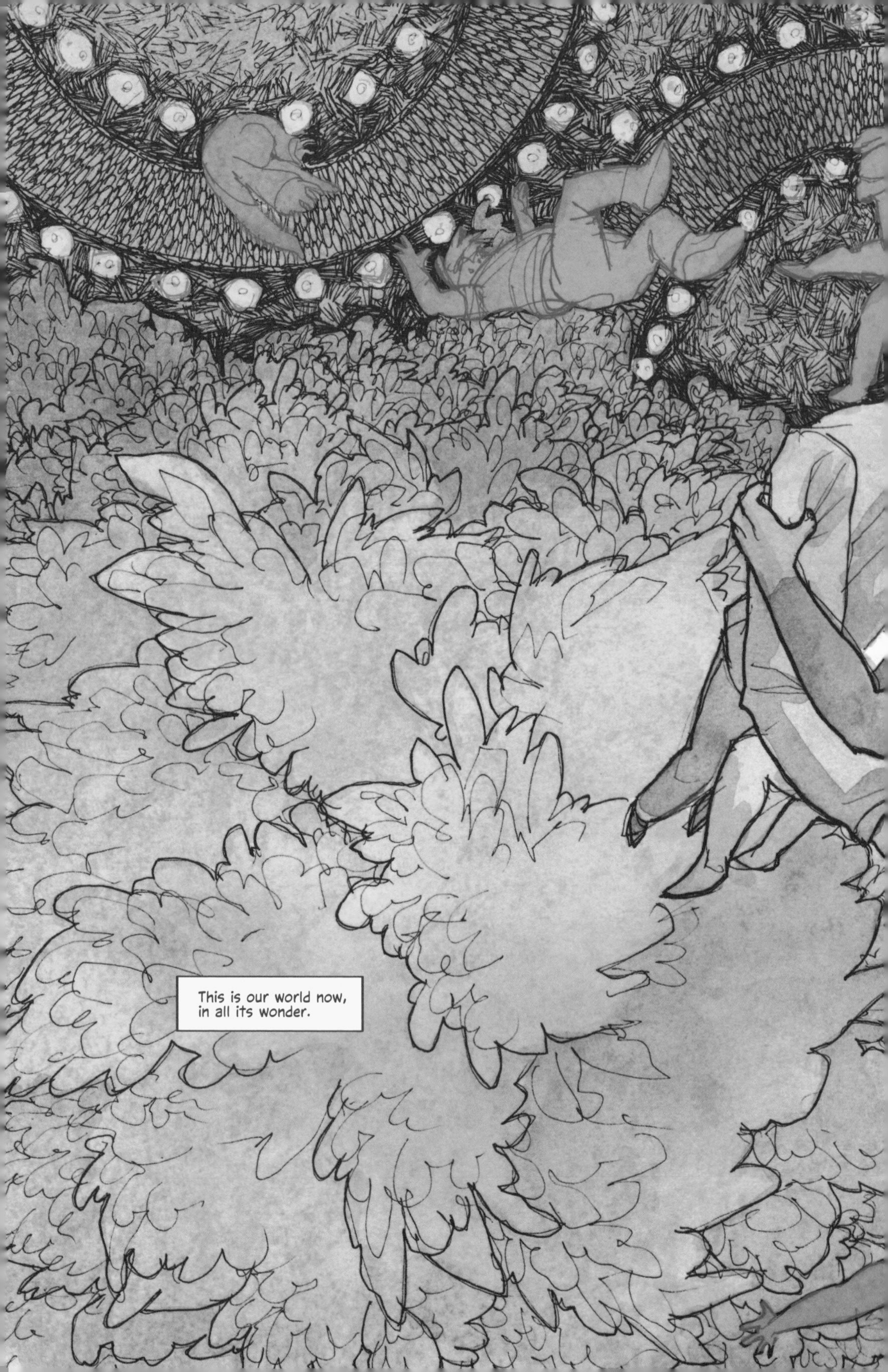
This is our world now, in all its wonder.

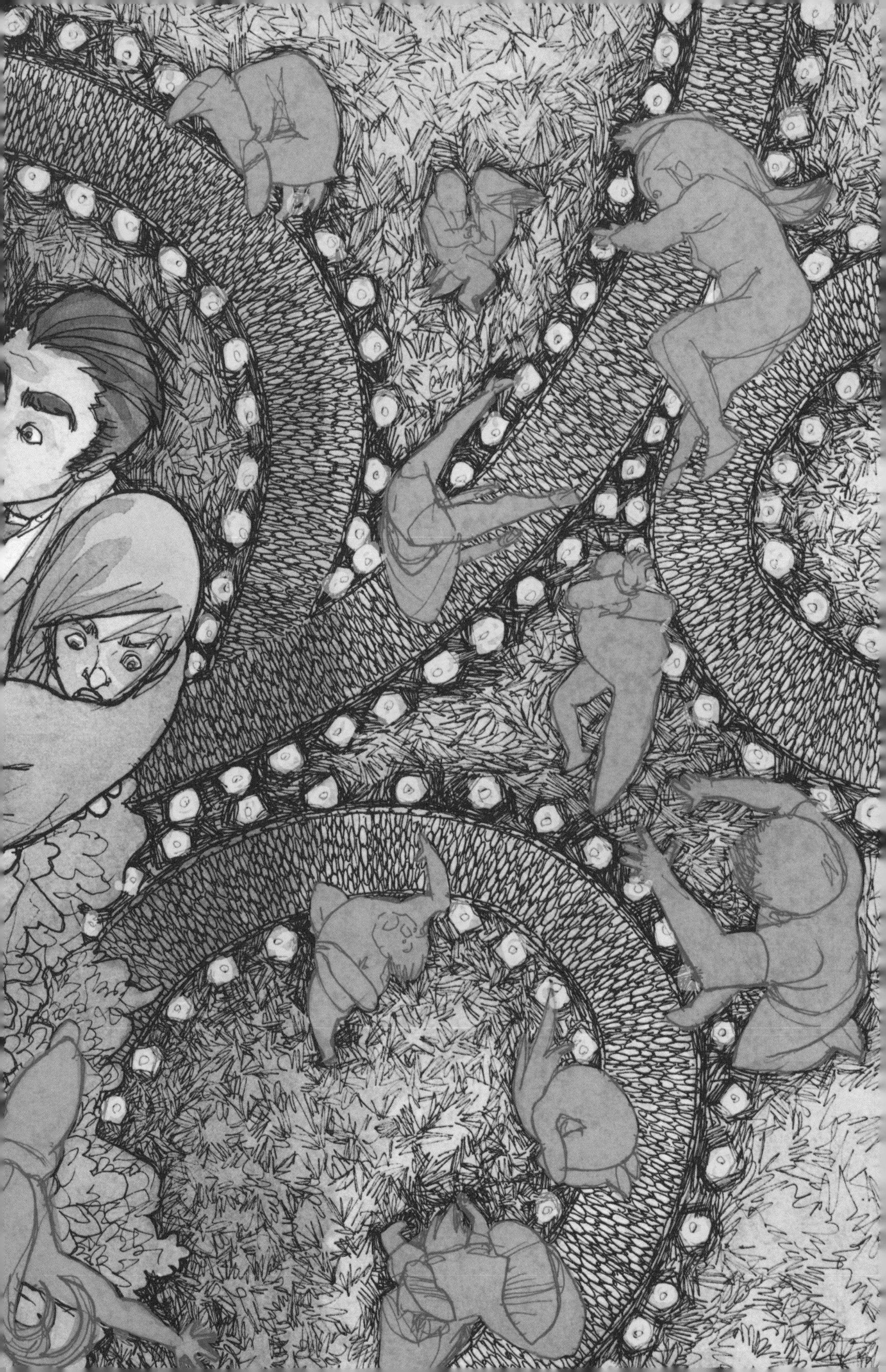

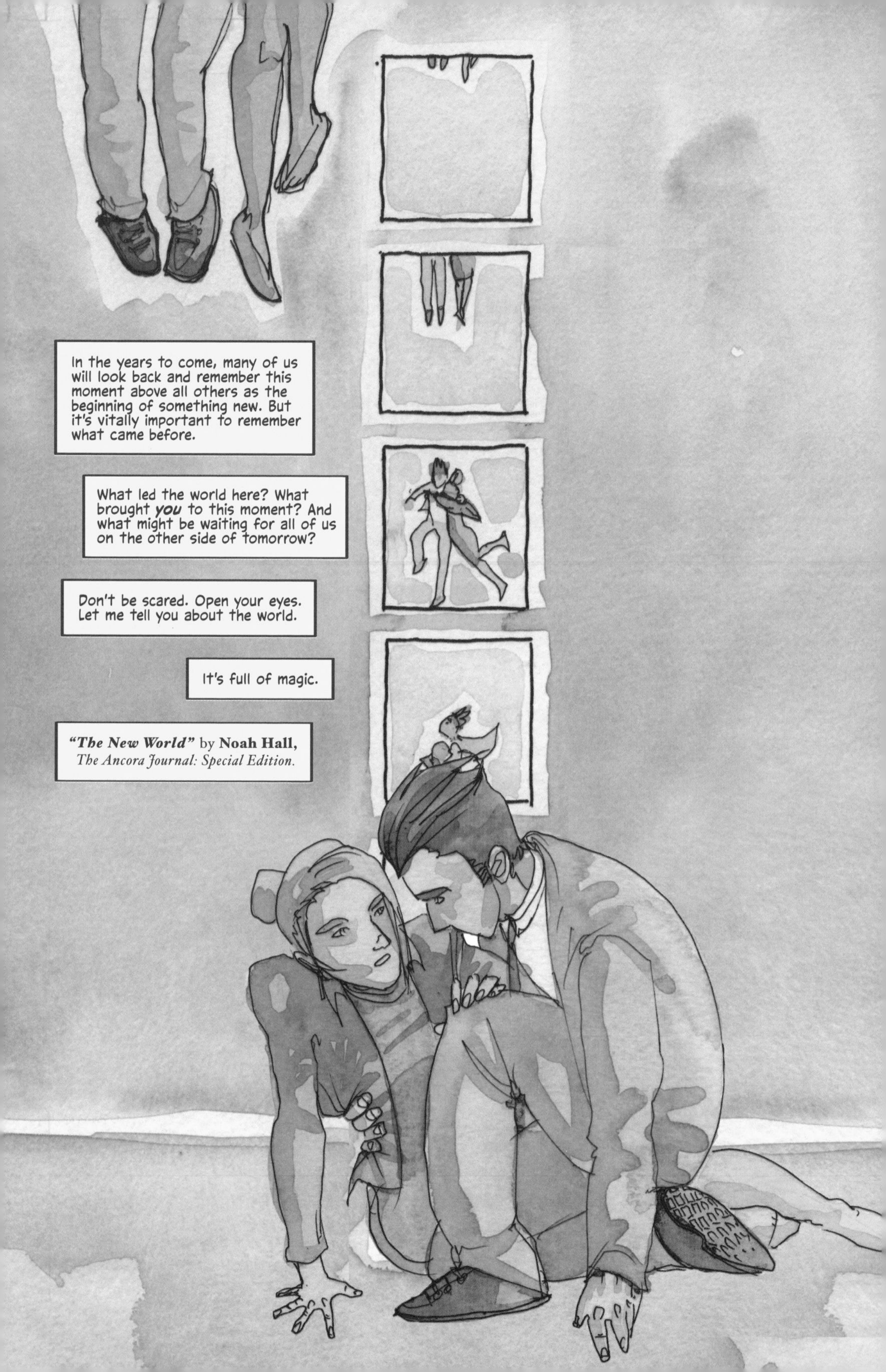

In the years to come, many of us will look back and remember this moment above all others as the beginning of something new. But it's vitally important to remember what came before.
What led the world here? What brought ***you*** to this moment? And what might be waiting for all of us on the other side of tomorrow?
Don't be scared. Open your eyes. Let me tell you about the world.
It's full of magic.
"The New World" by **Noah Hall,** *The Ancora Journal: Special Edition.*

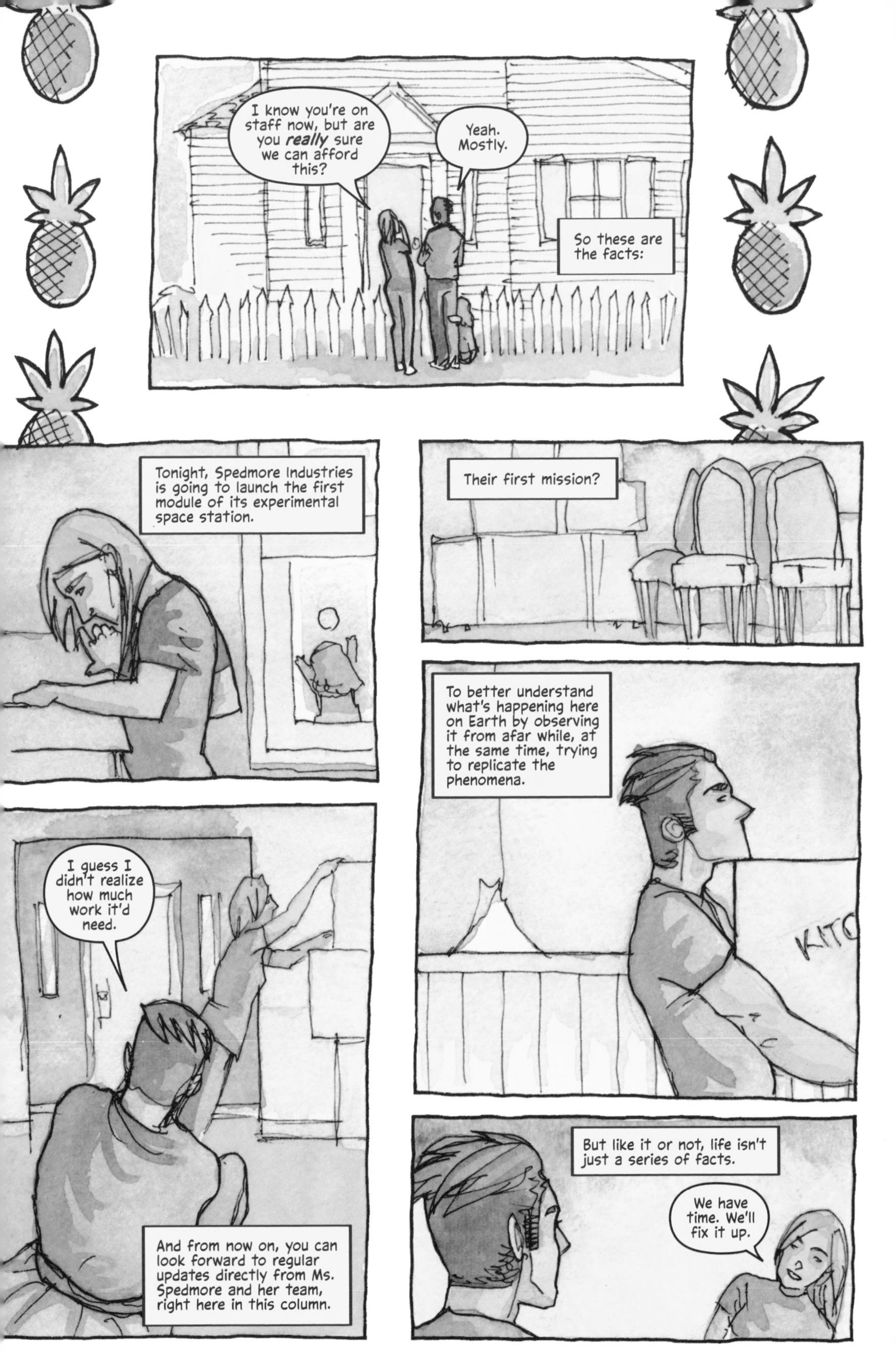
I know you're on staff now, but are you *really* sure we can afford this?
Yeah. Mostly.
So these are the facts:
Tonight, Spedmore Industries is going to launch the first module of its experimental space station.
Their first mission?
To better understand what's happening here on Earth by observing it from afar while, at the same time, trying to replicate the phenomena.
I guess I didn't realize how much work it'd need.
And from now on, you can look forward to regular updates directly from Ms. Spedmore and her team, right here in this column.
But like it or not, life isn't just a series of facts.
We have time. We'll fix it up.

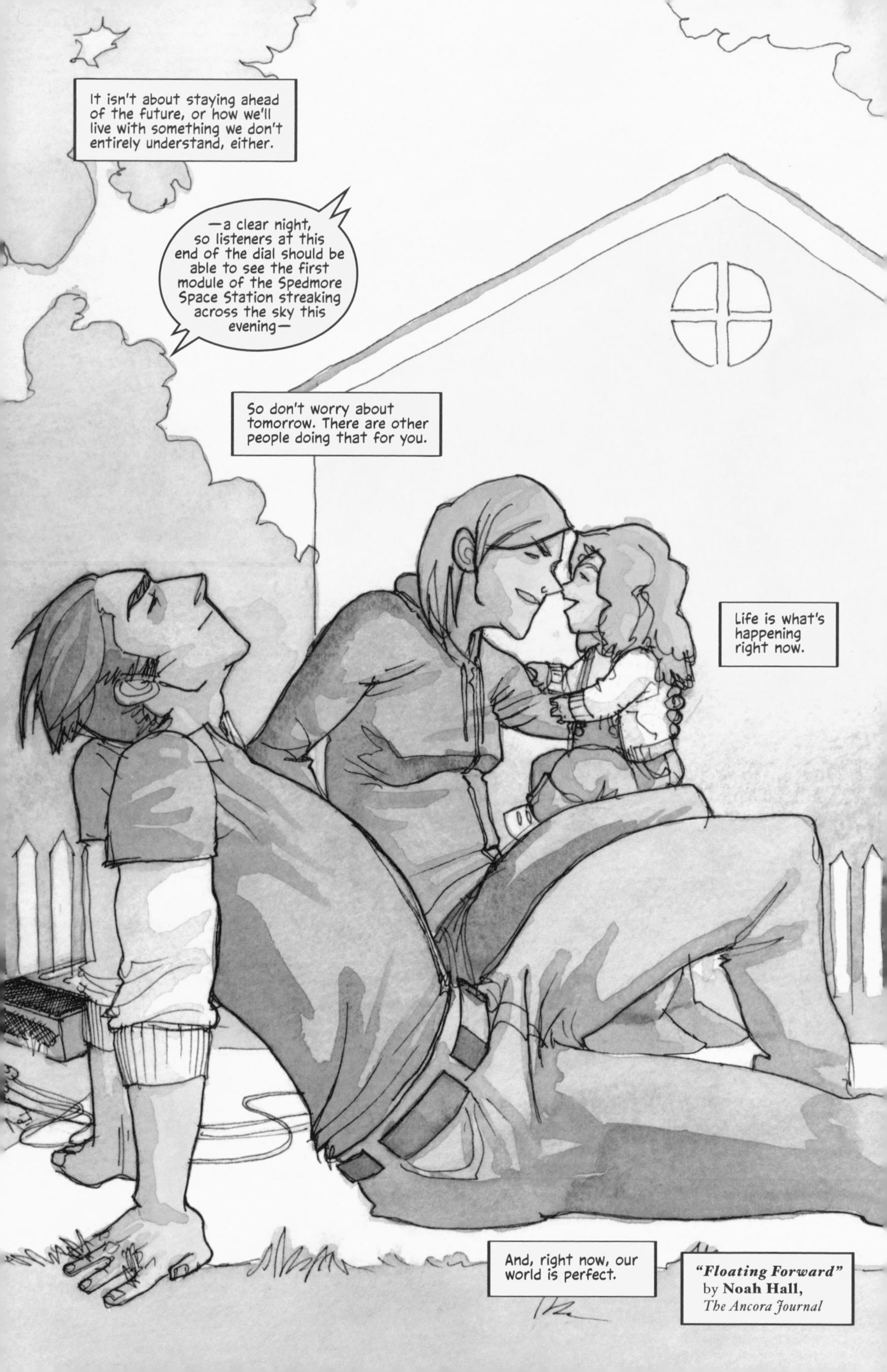
It isn't about staying ahead of the future, or how we'll live with something we don't entirely understand, either.
—a clear night, so listeners at this end of the dial should be able to see the first module of the Spedmore Space Station streaking across the sky this evening—
So don't worry about tomorrow. There are other people doing that for you.
Life is what's happening right now.
And, right now, our world is perfect.
"Floating Forward" by Noah Hall, The Ancora Journal

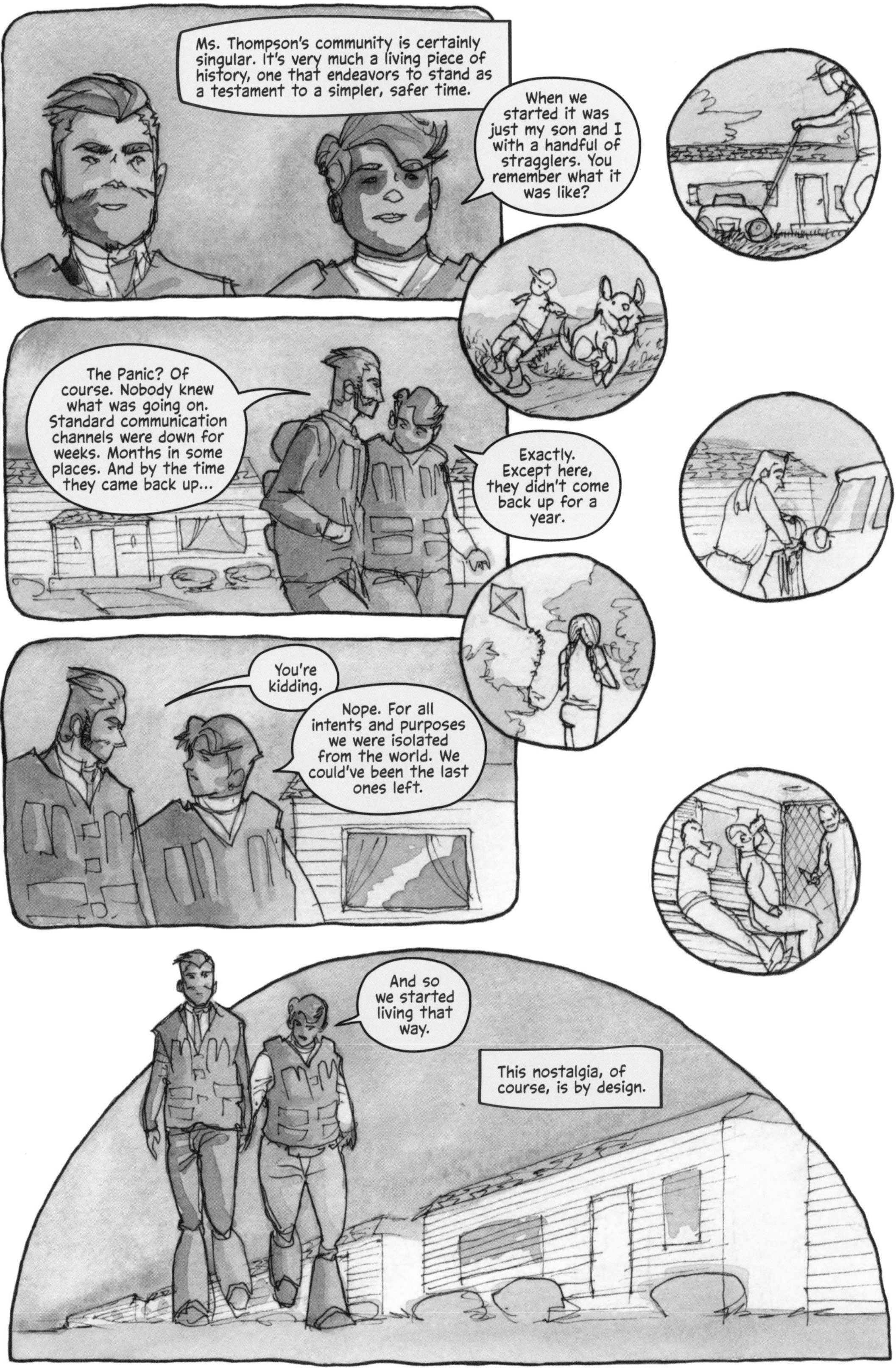
Ms. Thompson's community is certainly singular. It's very much a living piece of history, one that endeavors to stand as a testament to a simpler, safer time.
When we started it was just my son and I with a handful of stragglers. You remember what it was like?
The Panic? Of course. Nobody knew what was going on. Standard communication channels were down for weeks. Months in some places. And by the time they came back up...
Exactly. Except here, they didn't come back up for a year.
You're kidding.
Nope. For all intents and purposes we were isolated from the world. We could've been the last ones left.
And so we started living that way.
This nostalgia, of course, is by design.

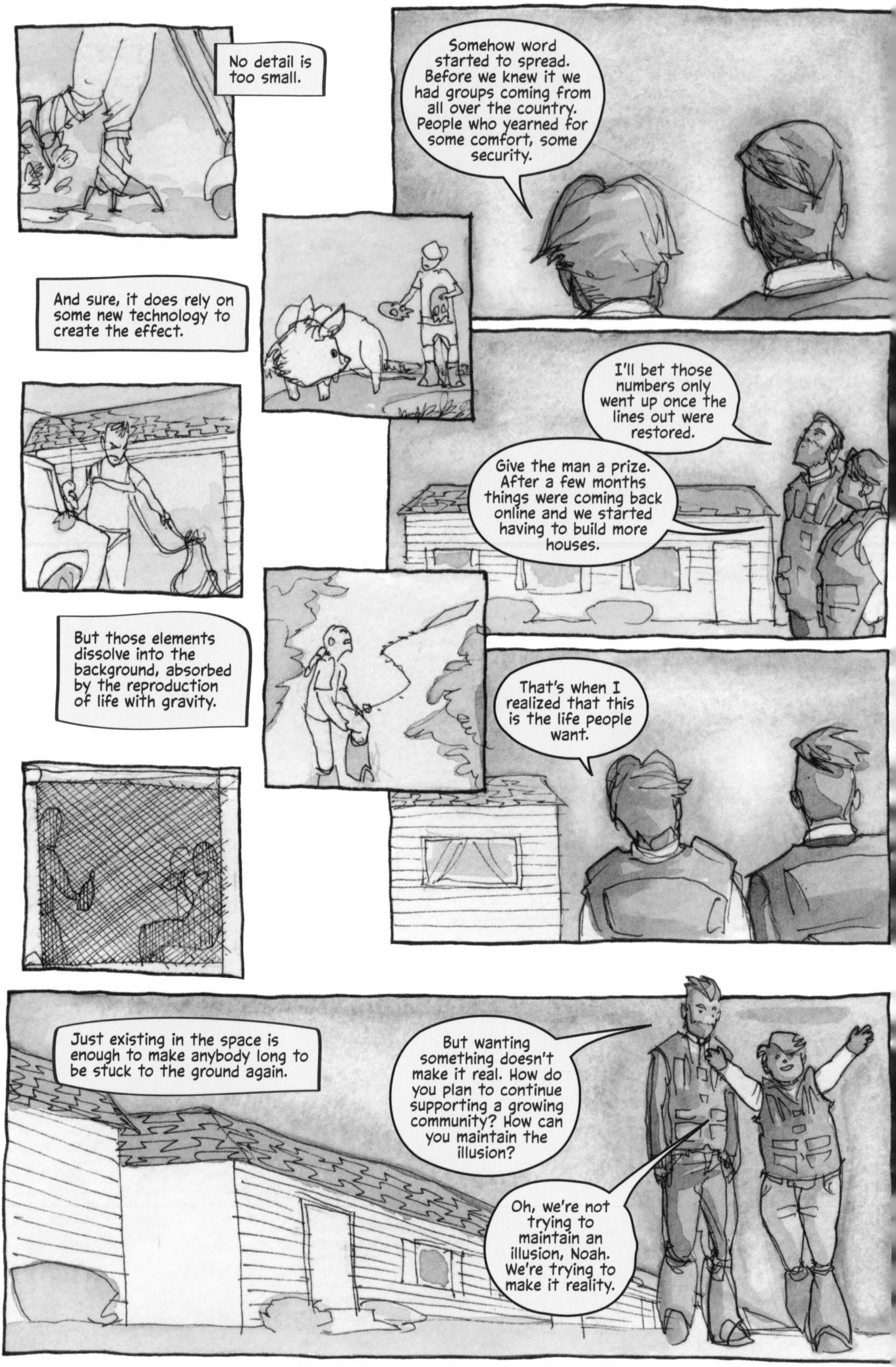
No detail is too small.
Somehow word started to spread. Before we knew it we had groups coming from all over the country. People who yearned for some comfort, some security.
And sure, it does rely on some new technology to create the effect.
I'll bet those numbers only went up once the lines out were restored.
Give the man a prize. After a few months things were coming back online and we started having to build more houses.
But those elements dissolve into the background, absorbed by the reproduction of life with gravity.
That's when I realized that this is the life people want.
Just existing in the space is enough to make anybody long to be stuck to the ground again.
But wanting something doesn't make it real. How do you plan to continue supporting a growing community? How can you maintain the illusion?
Oh, we're not trying to maintain an illusion, Noah. We're trying to make it reality.

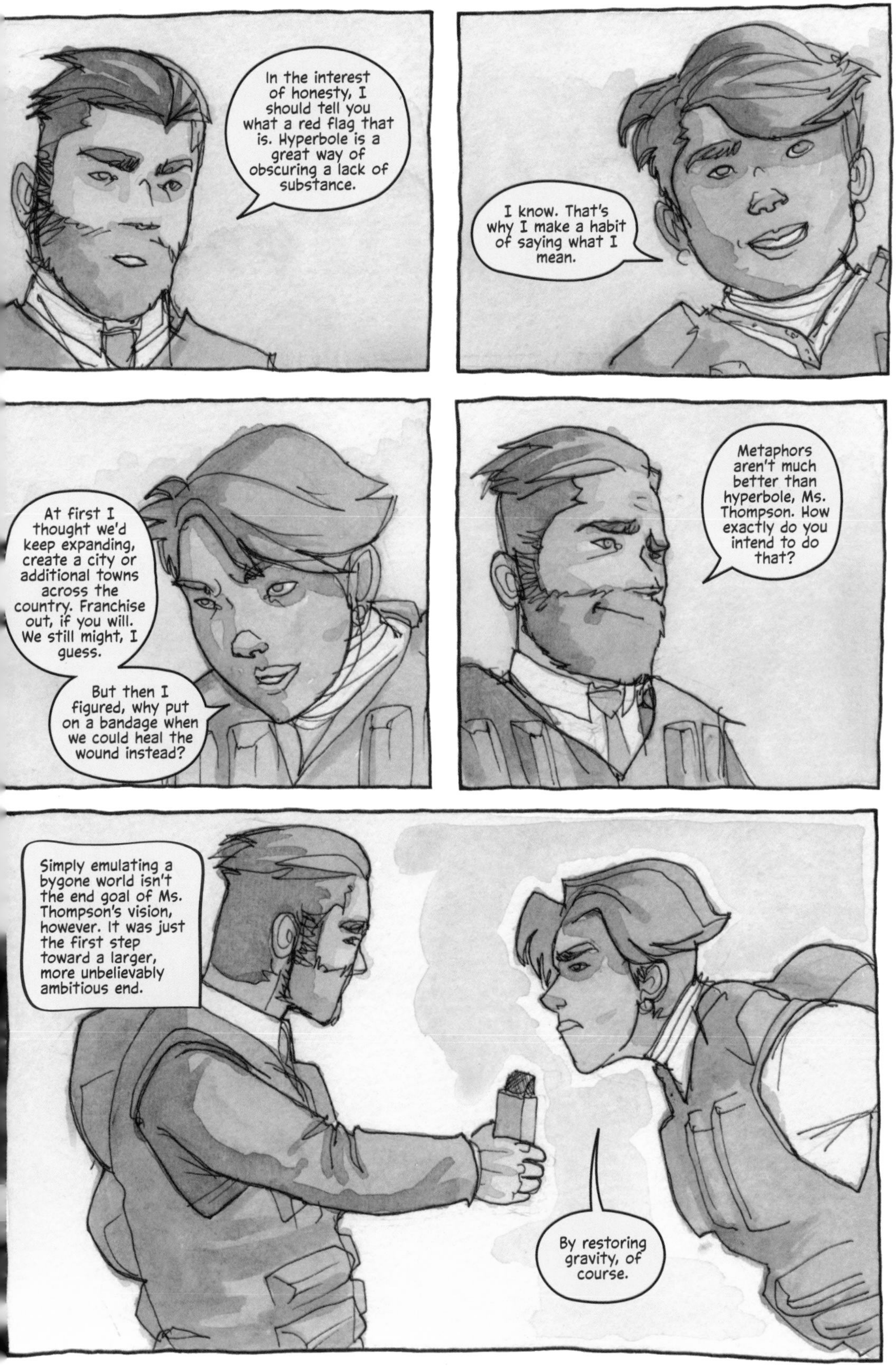
In the interest of honesty, I should tell you what a red flag that is. Hyperbole is a great way of obscuring a lack of substance.
I know. That's why I make a habit of saying what I mean.
At first I thought we'd keep expanding, create a city or additional towns across the country. Franchise out, if you will. We still might, I guess.
But then I figured, why put on a bandage when we could heal the wound instead?
Metaphors aren't much better than hyperbole, Ms. Thompson. How exactly do you intend to do that?
Simply emulating a bygone world isn't the end goal of Ms. Thompson's vision, however. It was just the first step toward a larger, more unbelievably ambitious end.
By restoring gravity, of course.

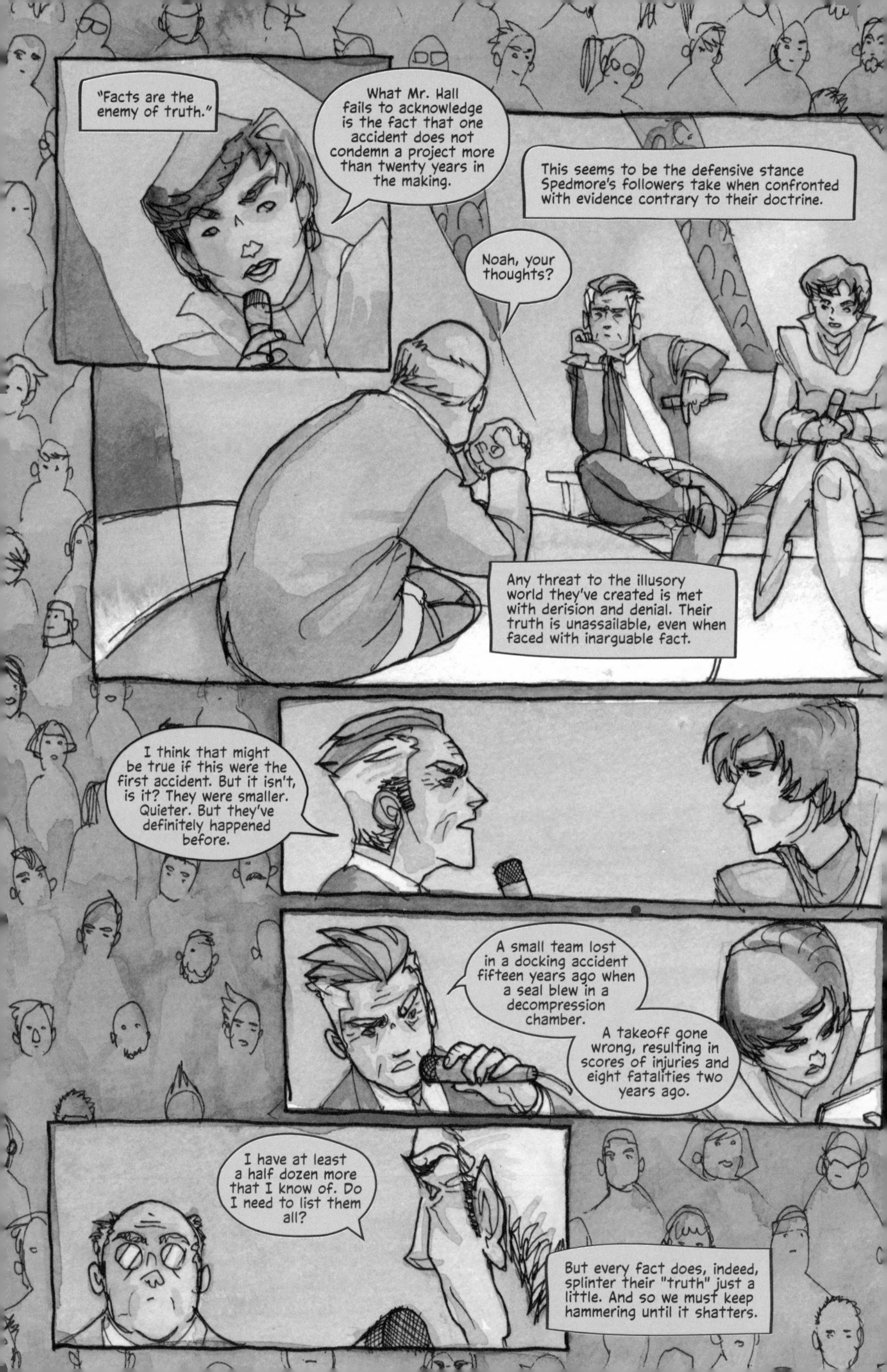
"Facts are the enemy of truth."
What Mr. Hall fails to acknowledge is the fact that one accident does not condemn a project more than twenty years in the making.
This seems to be the defensive stance Spedmore's followers take when confronted with evidence contrary to their doctrine.
Noah, your thoughts?
Any threat to the illusory world they've created is met with derision and denial. Their truth is unassailable, even when faced with inarguable fact.
I think that might be true if this were the first accident. But it isn't, is it? They were smaller. Quieter. But they've definitely happened before.
A small team lost in a docking accident fifteen years ago when a seal blew in a decompression chamber.
A takeoff gone wrong, resulting in scores of injuries and eight fatalities two years ago.
I have at least a half dozen more that I know of. Do I need to list them all?
But every fact does, indeed, splinter their "truth" just a little. And so we must keep hammering until it shatters.

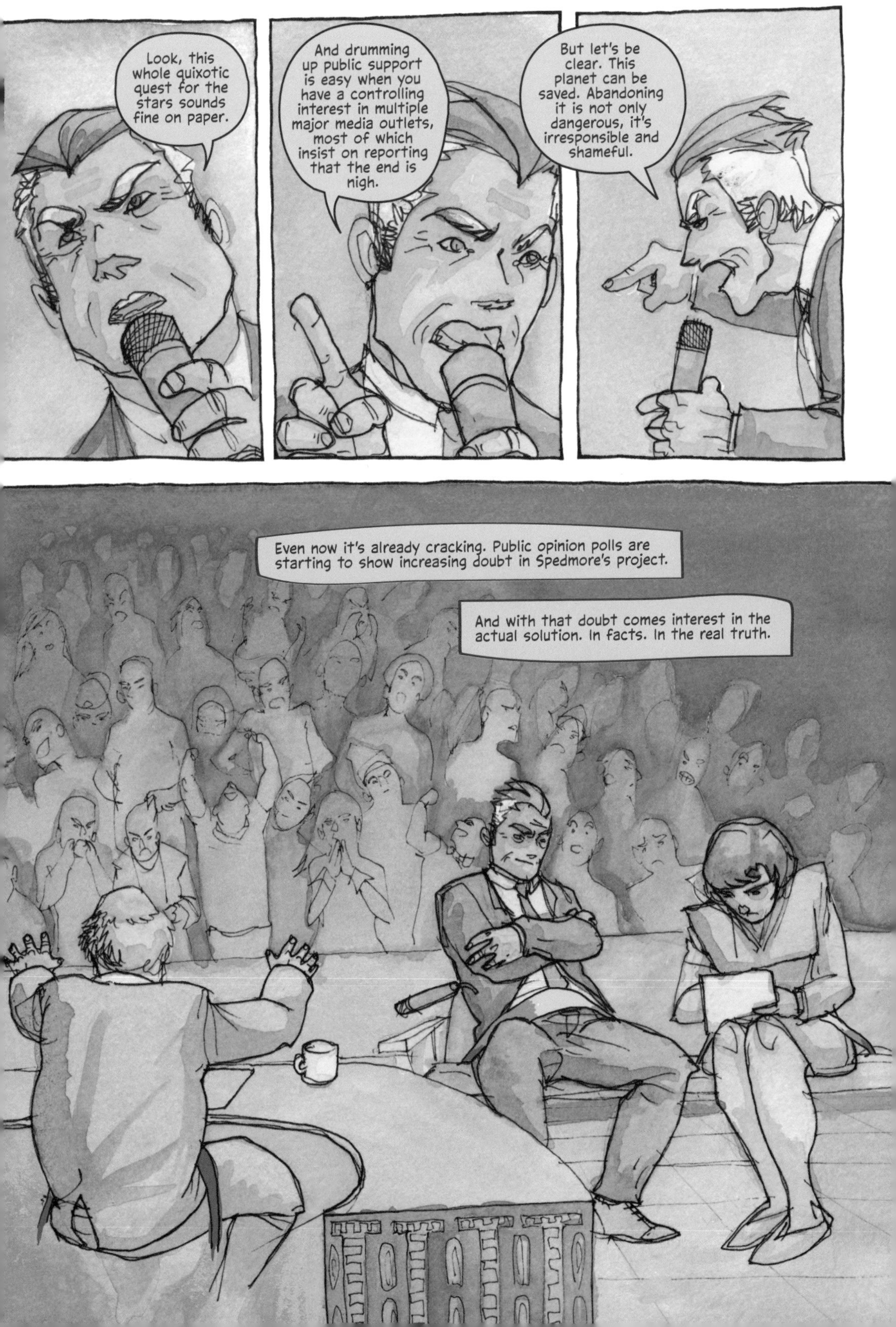

Look, this whole quixotic quest for the stars sounds fine on paper.
And drumming up public support is easy when you have a controlling interest in multiple major media outlets, most of which insist on reporting that the end is nigh.
But let's be clear. This planet can be saved. Abandoning it is not only dangerous, it's irresponsible and shameful.
Even now it's already cracking. Public opinion polls are starting to show increasing doubt in Spedmore's project.
And with that doubt comes interest in the actual solution. In facts. In the real truth.

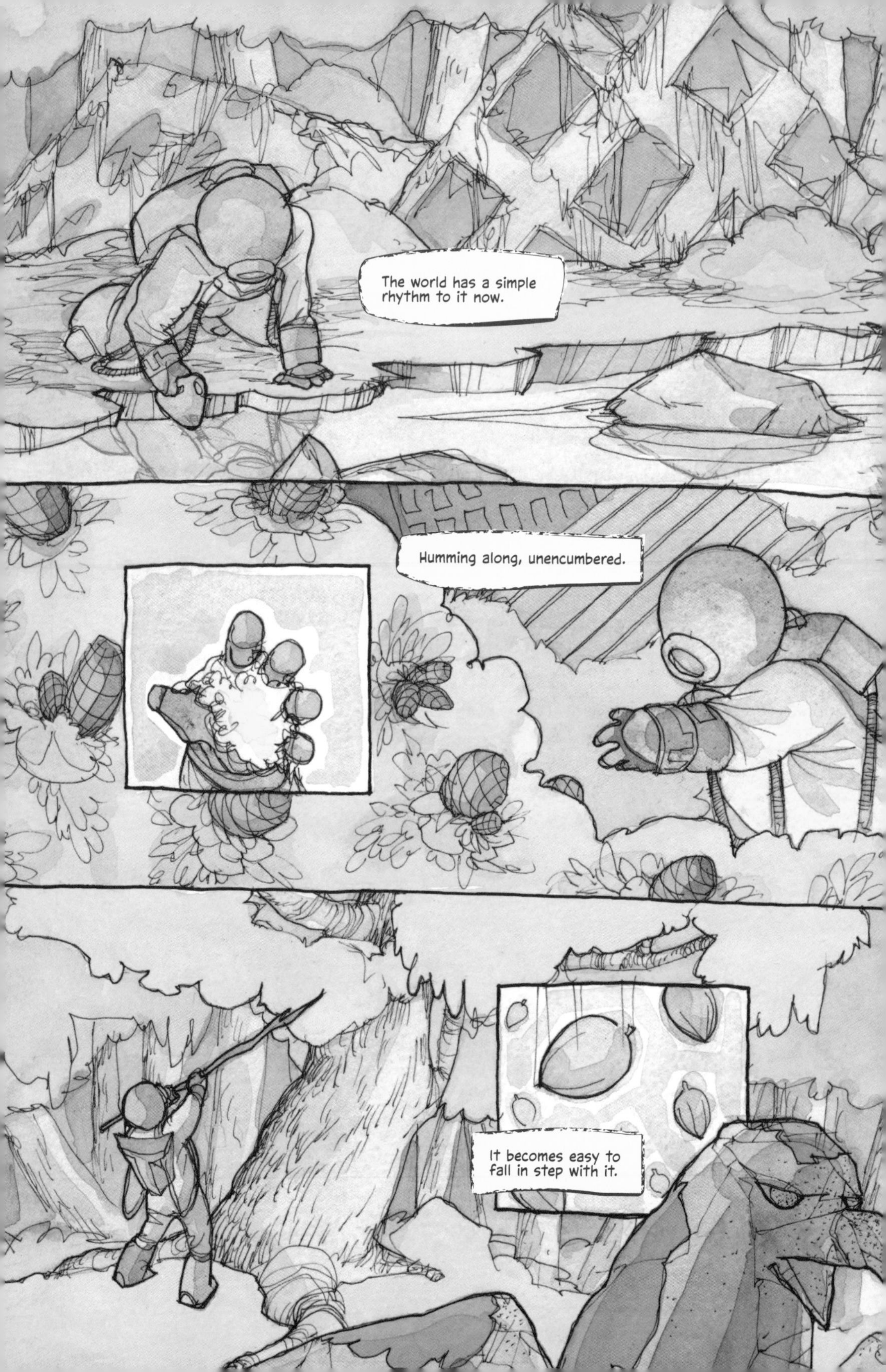
The world has a simple rhythm to it now.
Humming along, unencumbered.
It becomes easy to fall in step with it.

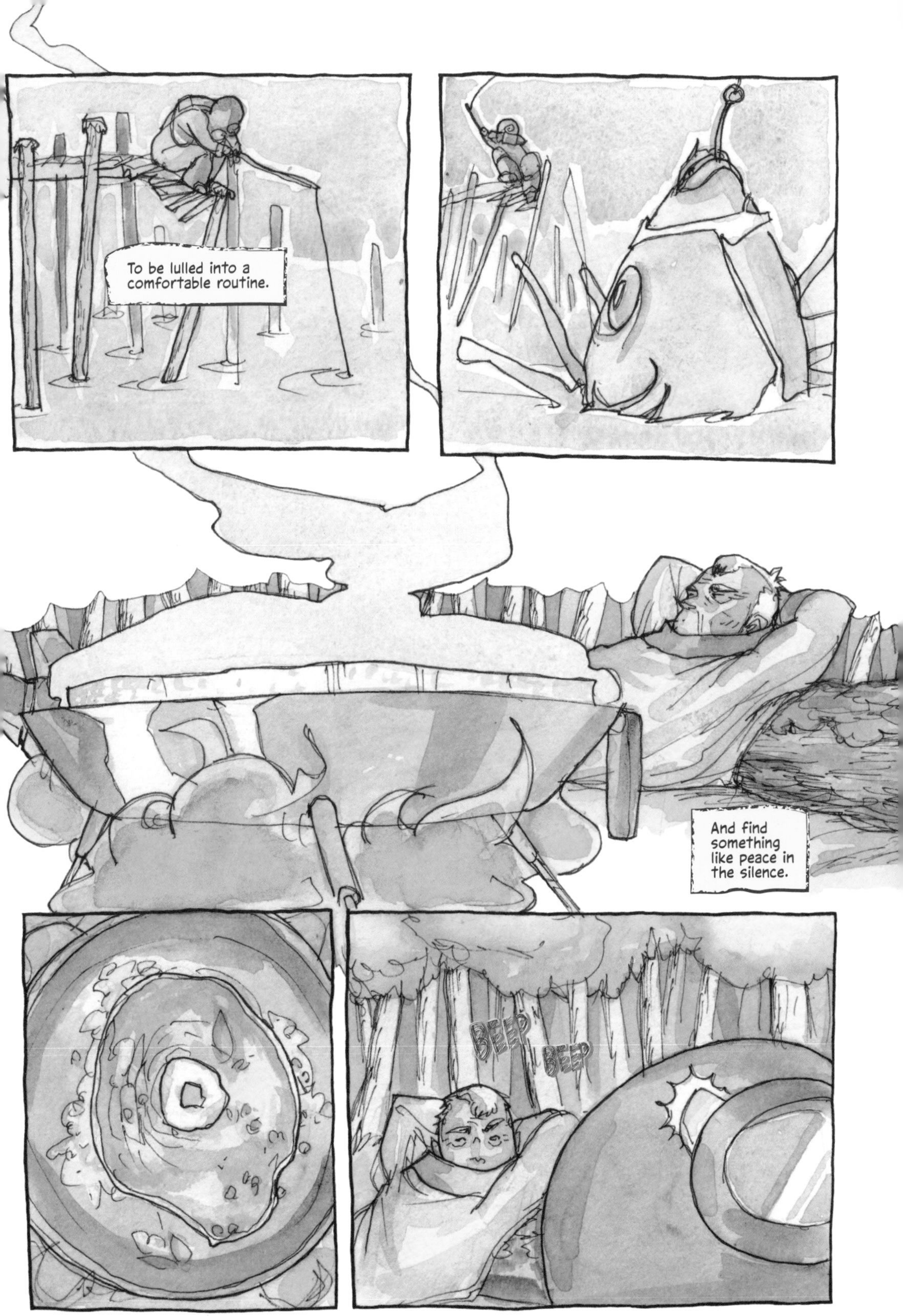
To be lulled into a comfortable routine.
And find something like peace in the silence.
BEEP
BEEP

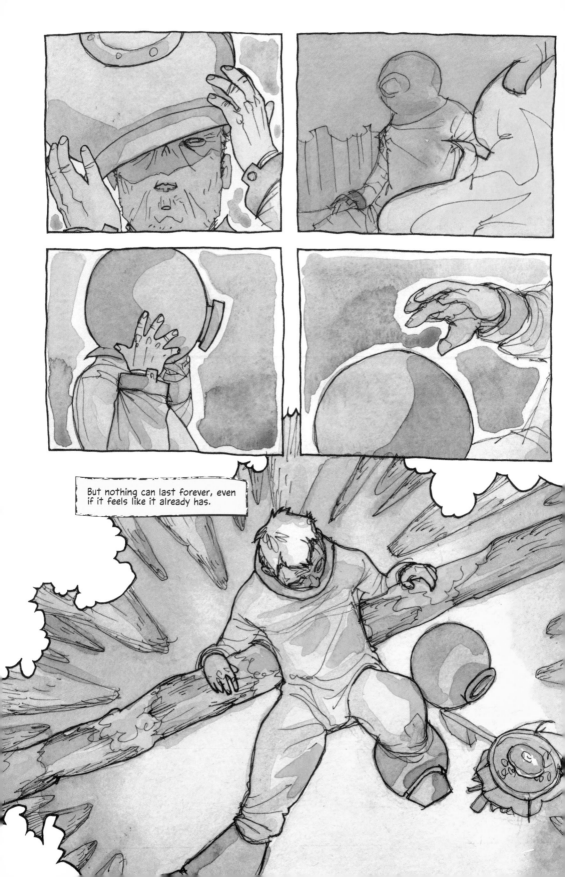

But nothing can last forever, even if it feels like it already has.

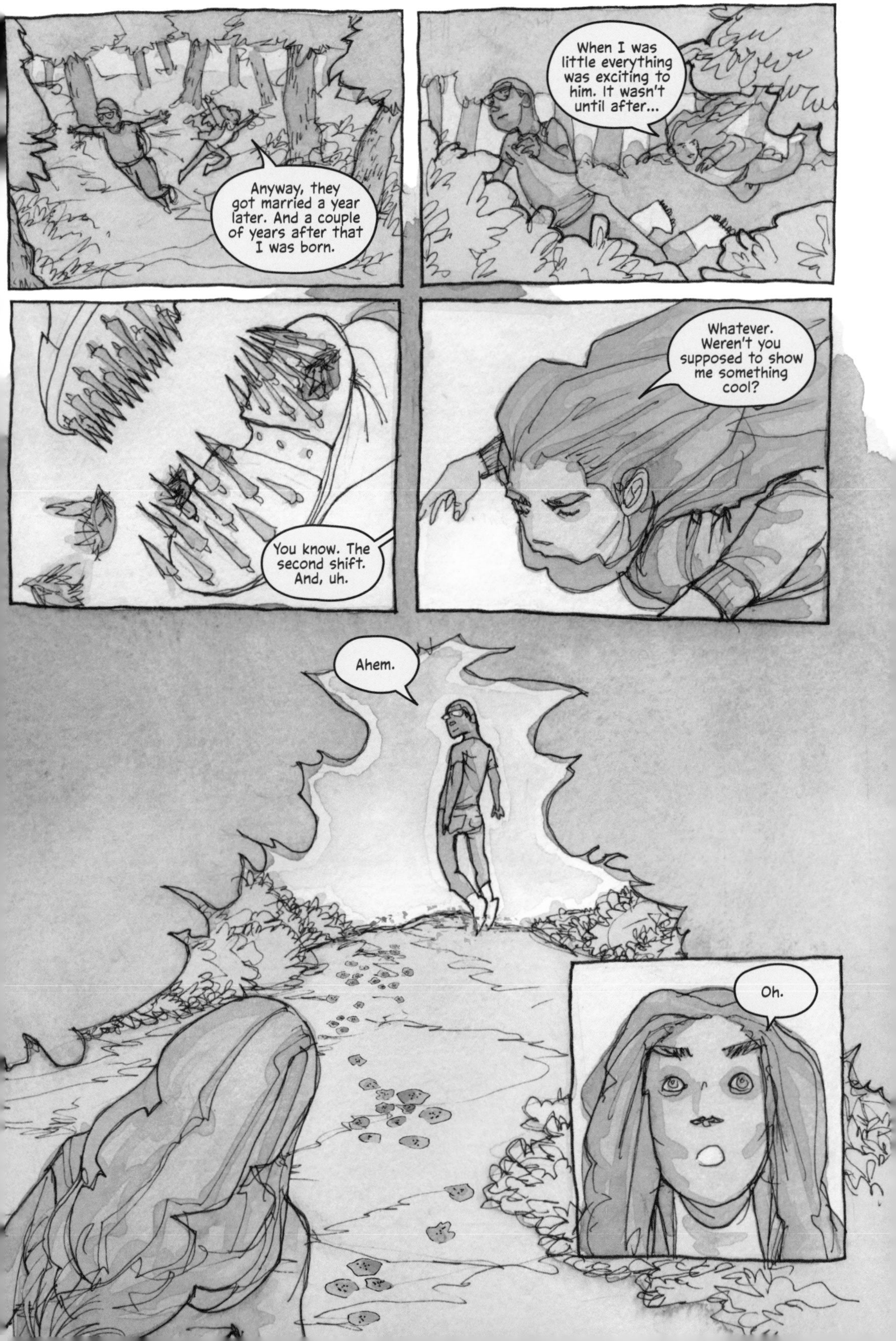
Anyway, they got married a year later. And a couple of years after that I was born.
When I was little everything was exciting to him. It wasn't until after...
You know. The second shift. And, uh.
Whatever. Weren't you supposed to show me something cool?
Ahem.
Oh.

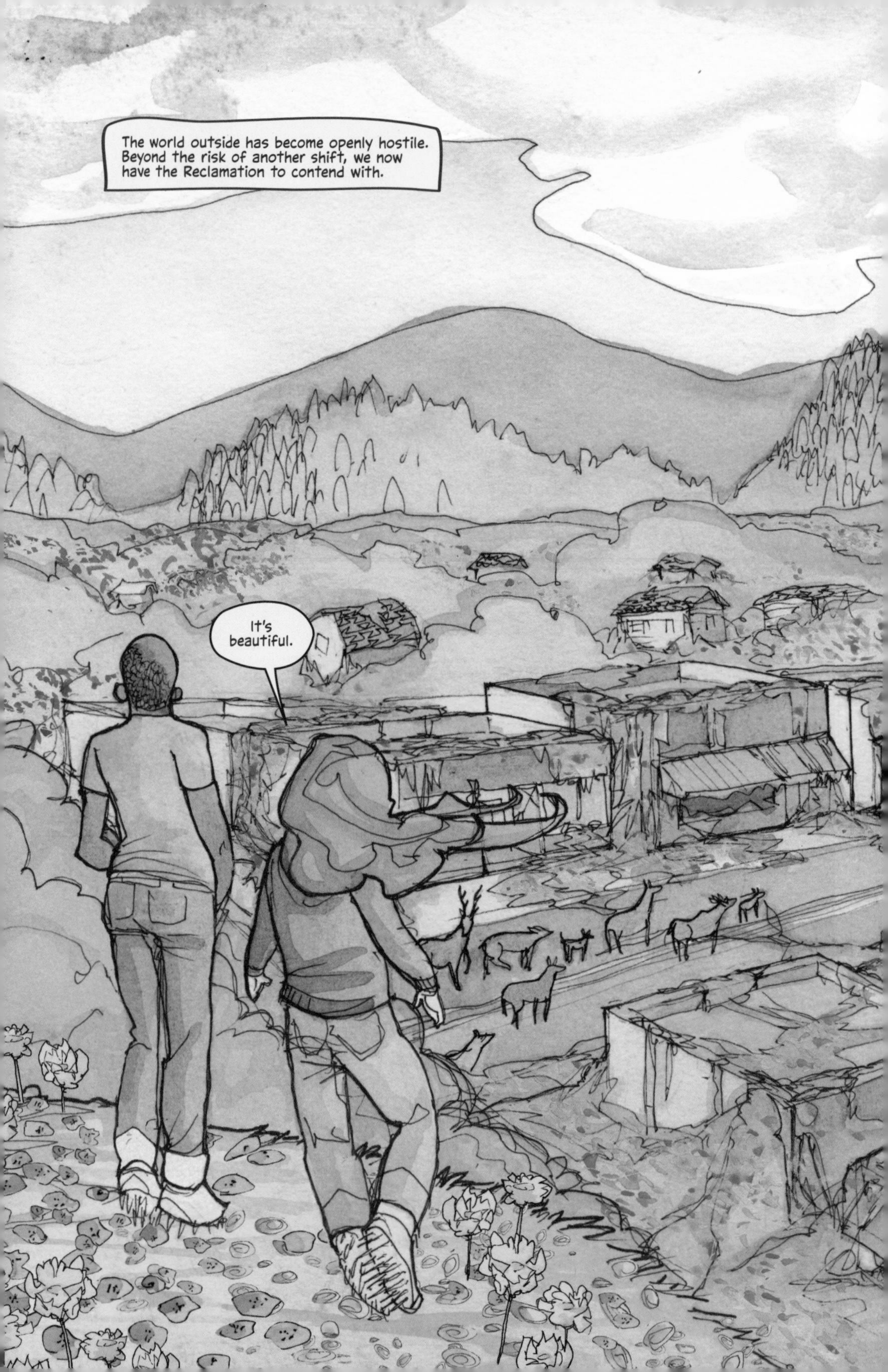
The world outside has become openly hostile. Beyond the risk of another shift, we now have the Reclamation to contend with.
It's beautiful.

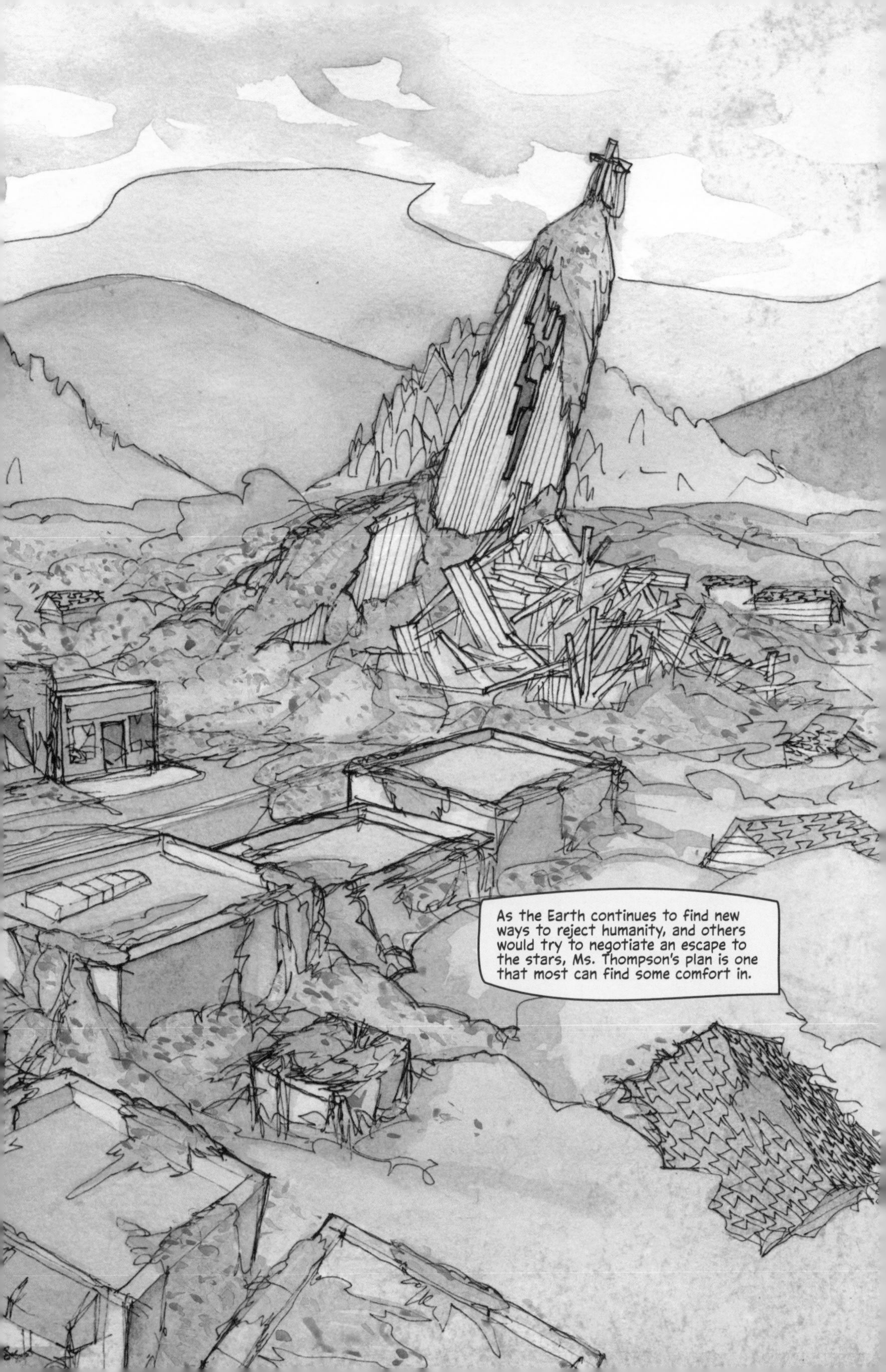
As the Earth continues to find new ways to reject humanity, and others would try to negotiate an escape to the stars, Ms. Thompson's plan is one that most can find some comfort in.

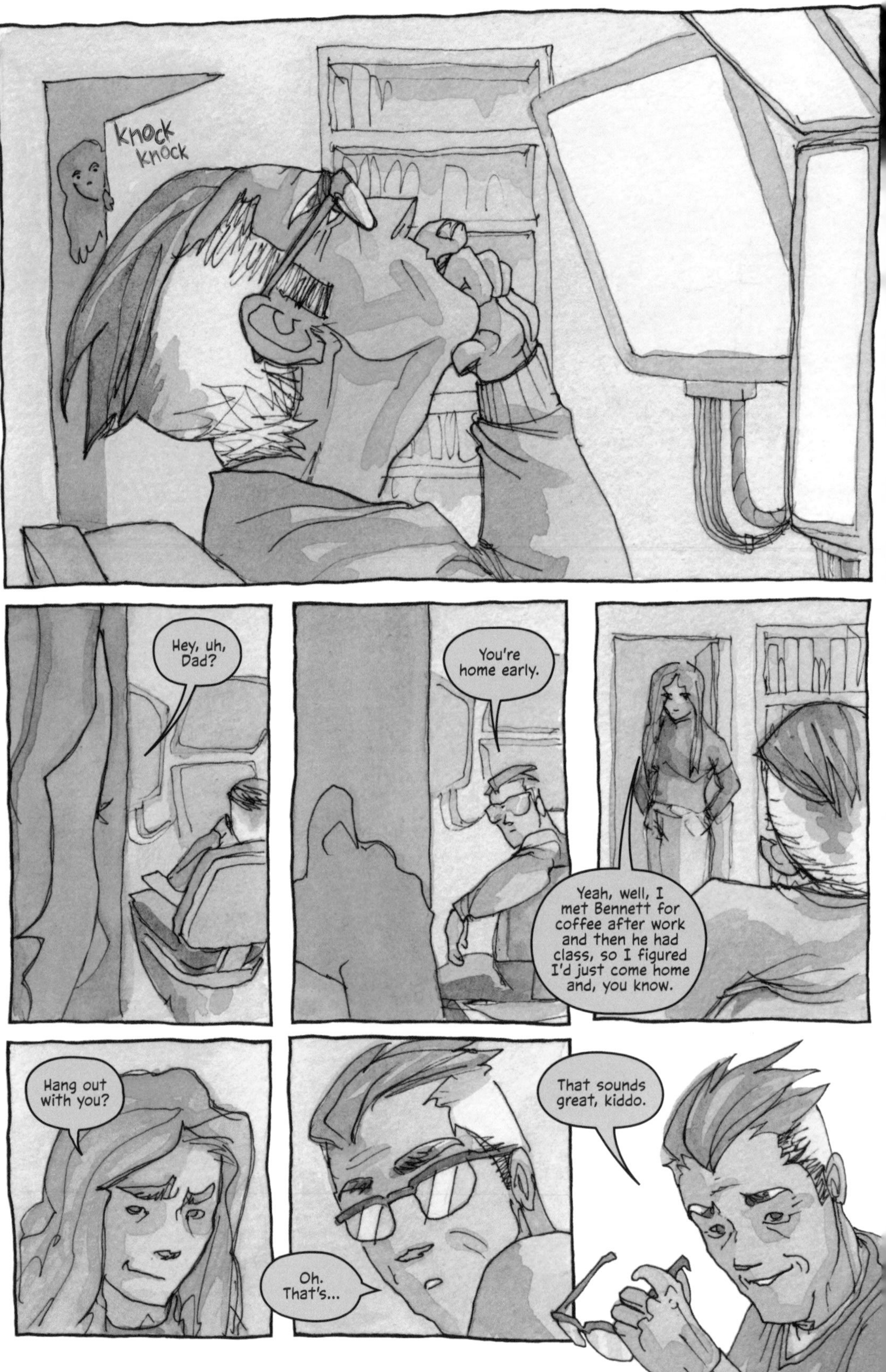
knock
knock
Hey, uh, Dad?
You're home early.
Yeah, well, I met Bennett for coffee after work and then he had class, so I figured I'd just come home and, you know.
Hang out with you?
Oh. That's...
That sounds great, kiddo.

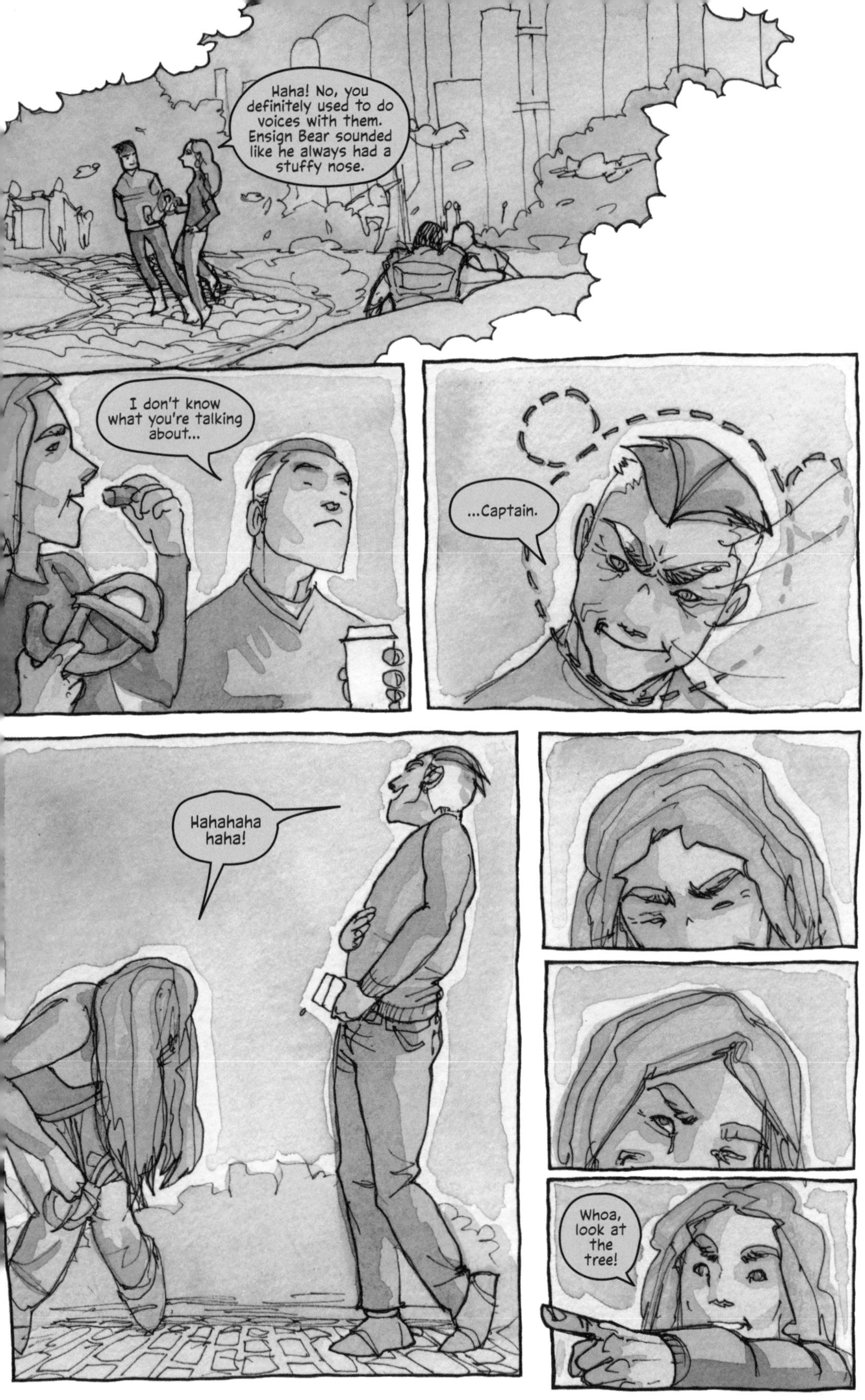
Haha! No, you definitely used to do voices with them. Ensign Bear sounded like he always had a stuffy nose.
I don't know what you're talking about...
...Captain.
Hahahaha haha!
Whoa, look at the tree!

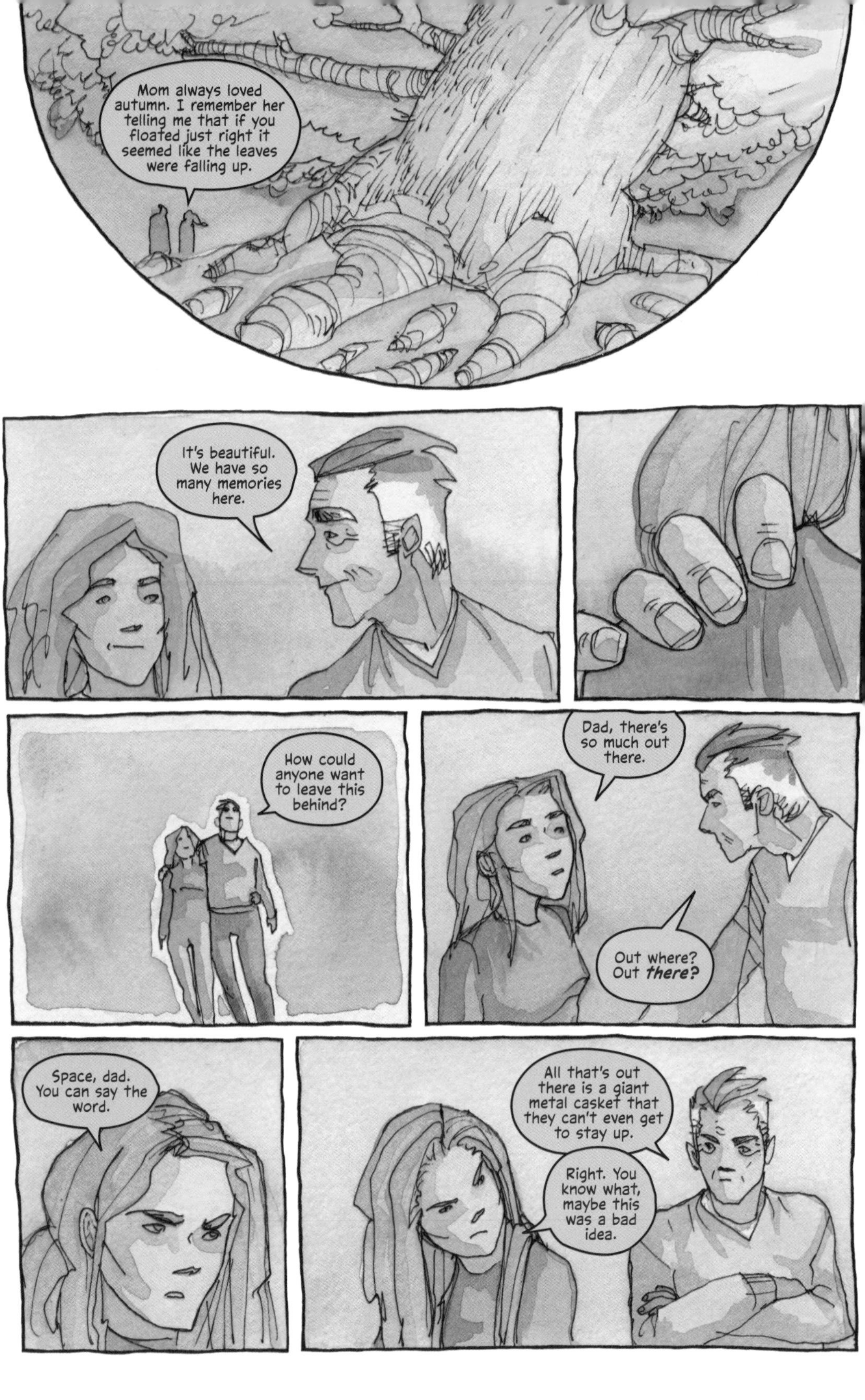

Mom always loved autumn. I remember her telling me that if you floated just right it seemed like the leaves were falling up.
It's beautiful. We have so many memories here.
How could anyone want to leave this behind?
Dad, there's so much out there.
Out where? Out *there?*
Space, dad. You can say the word.
All that's out there is a giant metal casket that they can't even get to stay up.
Right. You know what, maybe this was a bad idea.

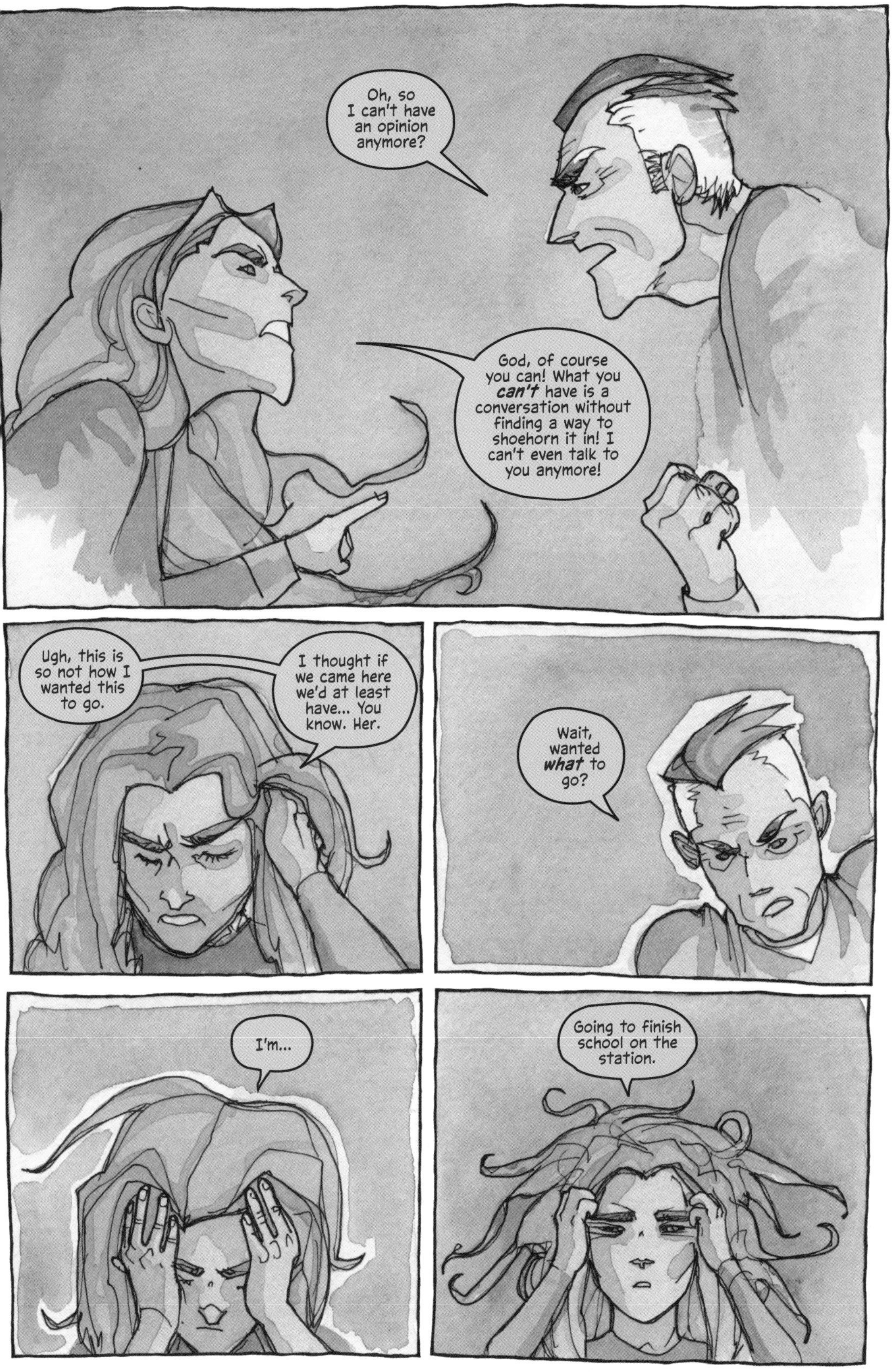
Oh, so I can't have an opinion anymore?
God, of course you can! What you *can't* have is a conversation without finding a way to shoehorn it in! I can't even talk to you anymore!
Ugh, this is so not how I wanted this to go.
I thought if we came here we'd at least have... You know. Her.
Wait, wanted *what* to go?
I'm...
Going to finish school on the station.

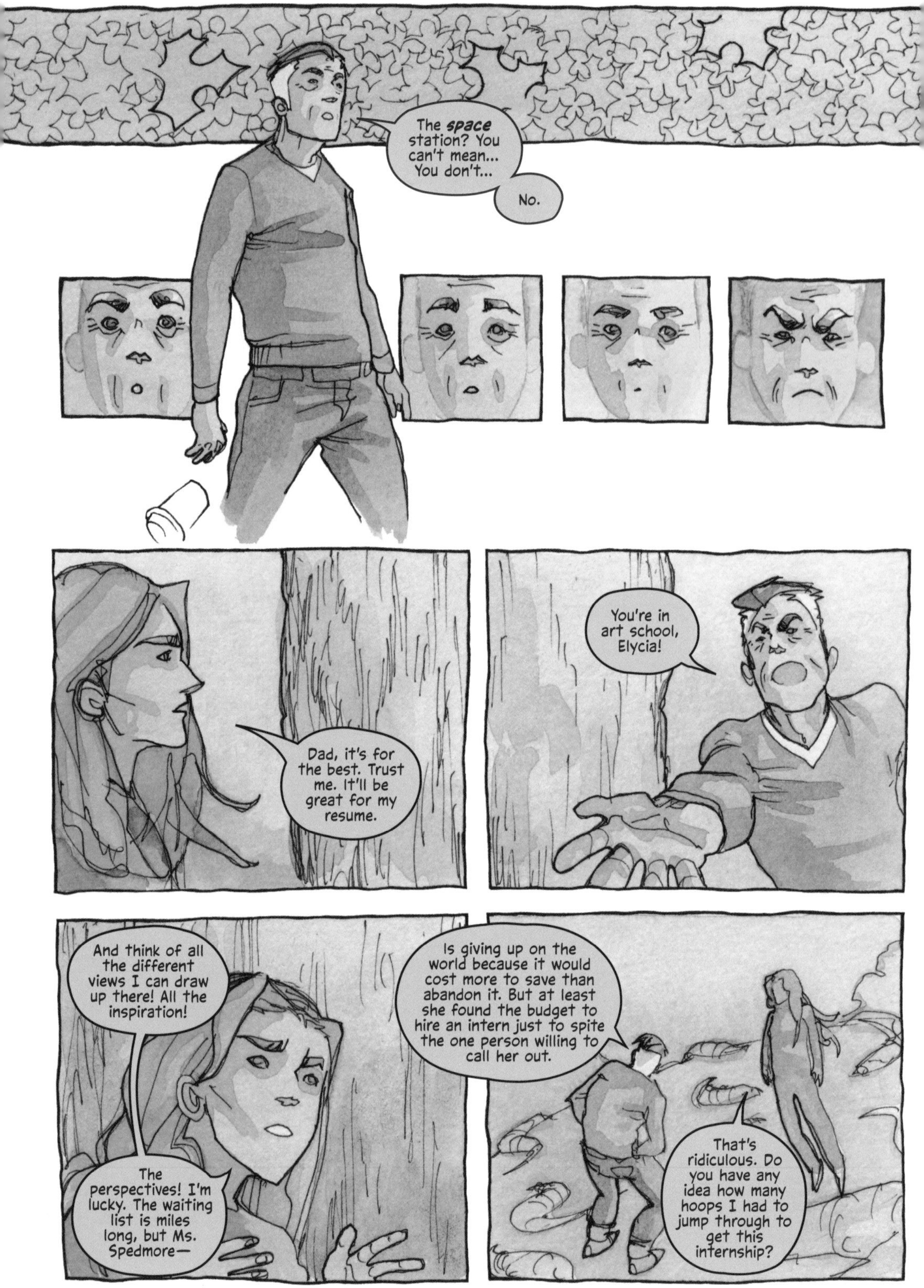
The *space* station? You can't mean... You don't...
No.
Dad, it's for the best. Trust me. It'll be great for my resume.
You're in art school, Elycia!
And think of all the different views I can draw up there! All the inspiration!
The perspectives! I'm lucky. The waiting list is miles long, but Ms. Spedmore—
Is giving up on the world because it would cost more to save than abandon it. But at least she found the budget to hire an intern just to spite the one person willing to call her out.
That's ridiculous. Do you have any idea how many hoops I had to jump through to get this internship?

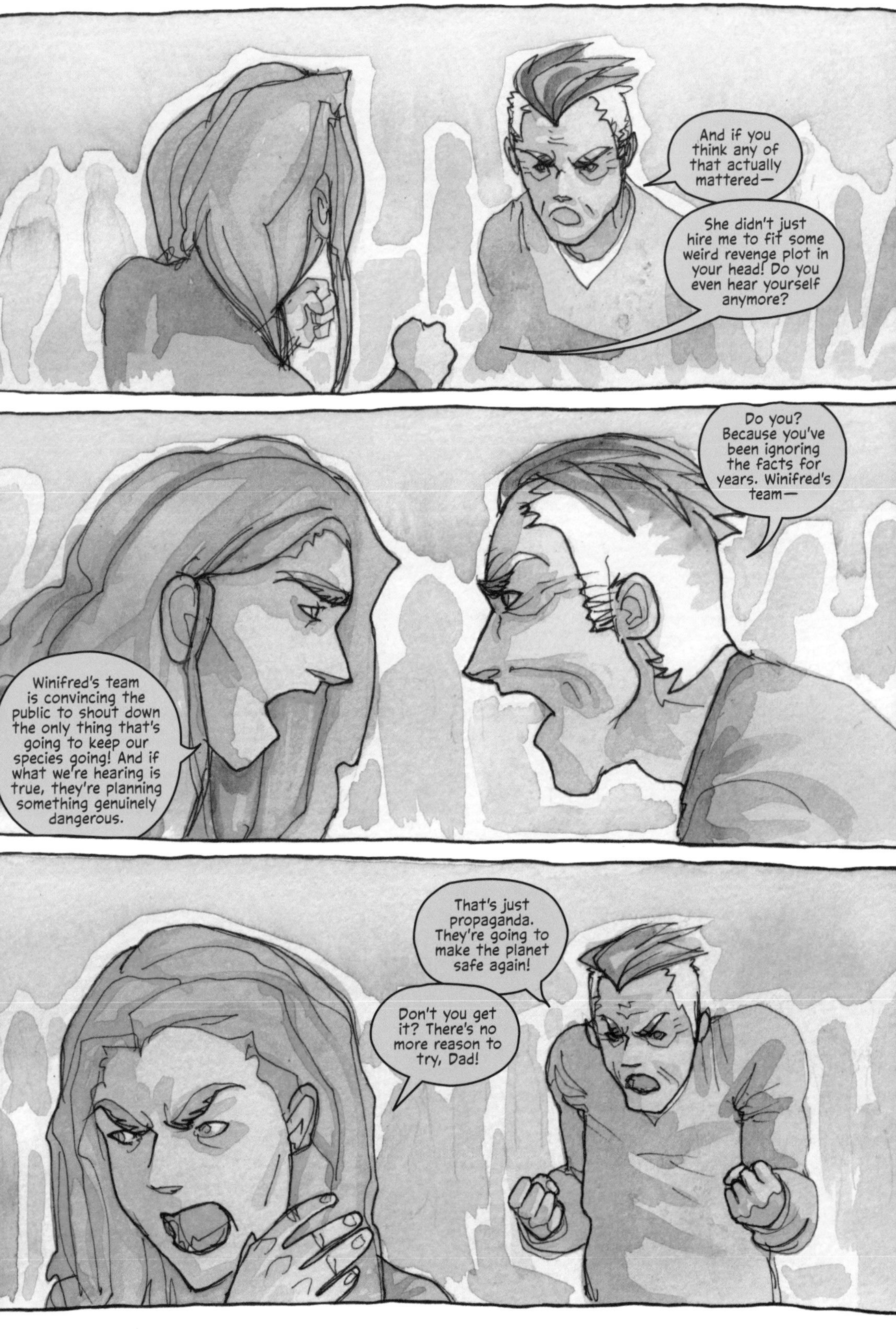
And if you think any of that actually mattered—
She didn't just hire me to fit some weird revenge plot in your head! Do you even hear yourself anymore?
Do you? Because you've been ignoring the facts for years. Winifred's team—
Winifred's team is convincing the public to shout down the only thing that's going to keep our species going! And if what we're hearing is true, they're planning something genuinely dangerous.
That's just propaganda. They're going to make the planet safe again!
Don't you get it? There's no more reason to try, Dad!

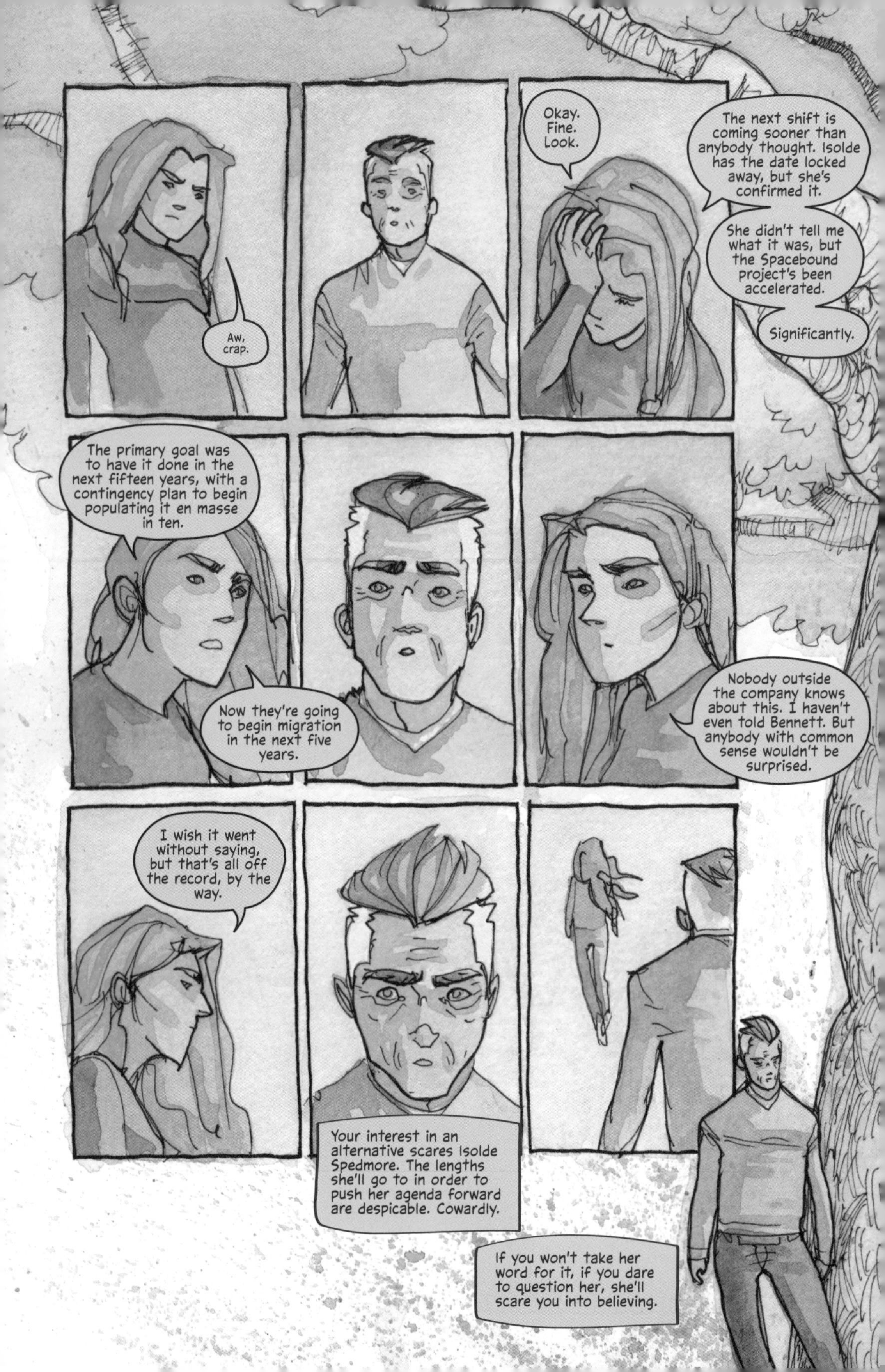
Aw, crap.
Okay. Fine. Look.
The next shift is coming sooner than anybody thought. Isolde has the date locked away, but she's confirmed it.
She didn't tell me what it was, but the Spacebound project's been accelerated.
Significantly.
The primary goal was to have it done in the next fifteen years, with a contingency plan to begin populating it en masse in ten.
Now they're going to begin migration in the next five years.
Nobody outside the company knows about this. I haven't even told Bennett. But anybody with common sense wouldn't be surprised.
I wish it went without saying, but that's all off the record, by the way.
Your interest in an alternative scares Isolde Spedmore. The lengths she'll go to in order to push her agenda forward are despicable. Cowardly.
If you won't take her word for it, if you dare to question her, she'll scare you into believing.

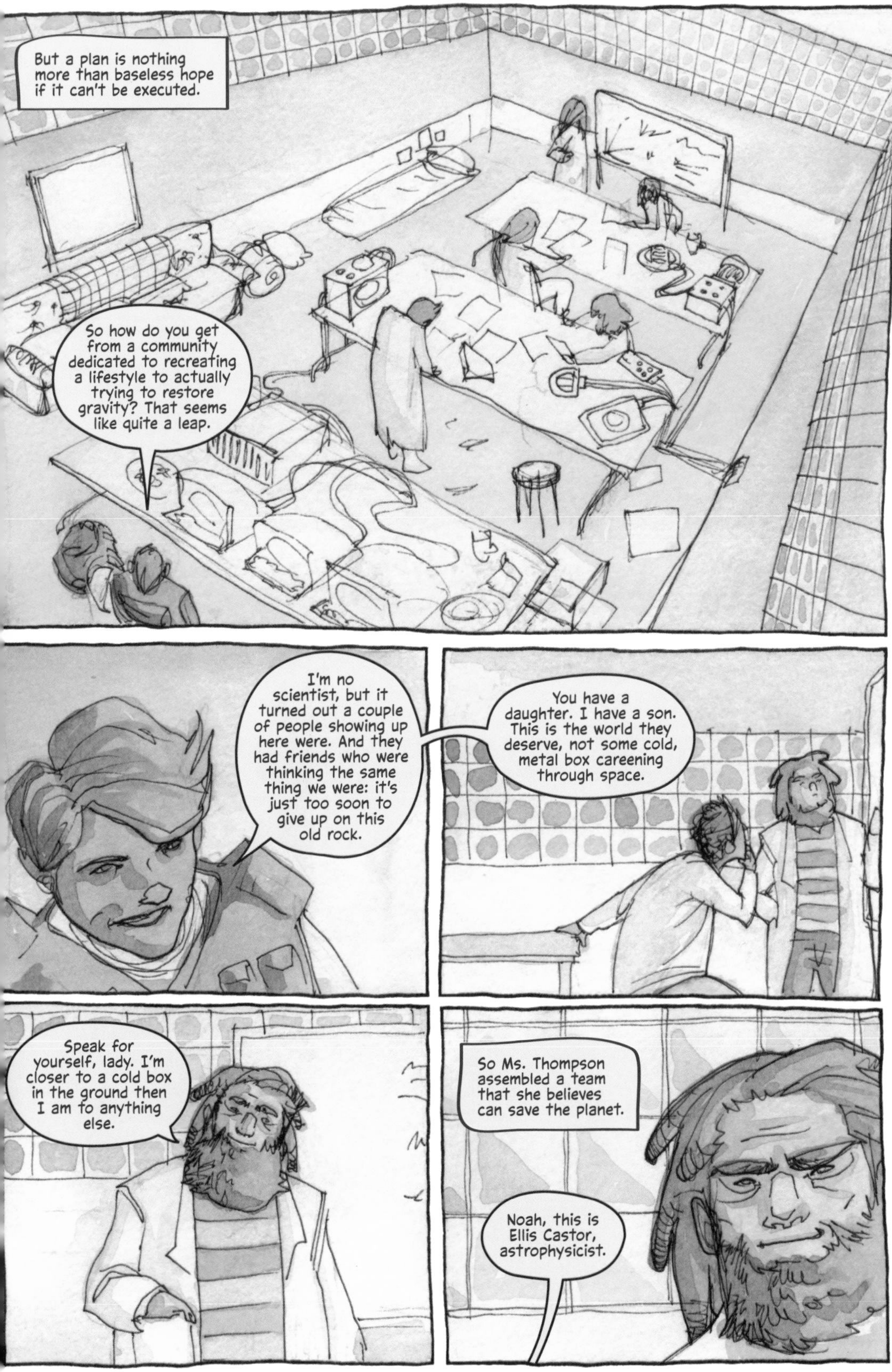

But a plan is nothing more than baseless hope if it can't be executed.
So how do you get from a community dedicated to recreating a lifestyle to actually trying to restore gravity? That seems like quite a leap.
I'm no scientist, but it turned out a couple of people showing up here were. And they had friends who were thinking the same thing we were: it's just too soon to give up on this old rock.
You have a daughter. I have a son. This is the world they deserve, not some cold, metal box careening through space.
Speak for yourself, lady. I'm closer to a cold box in the ground then I am to anything else.
So Ms. Thompson assembled a team that she believes can save the planet.
Noah, this is Ellis Castor, astrophysicist.

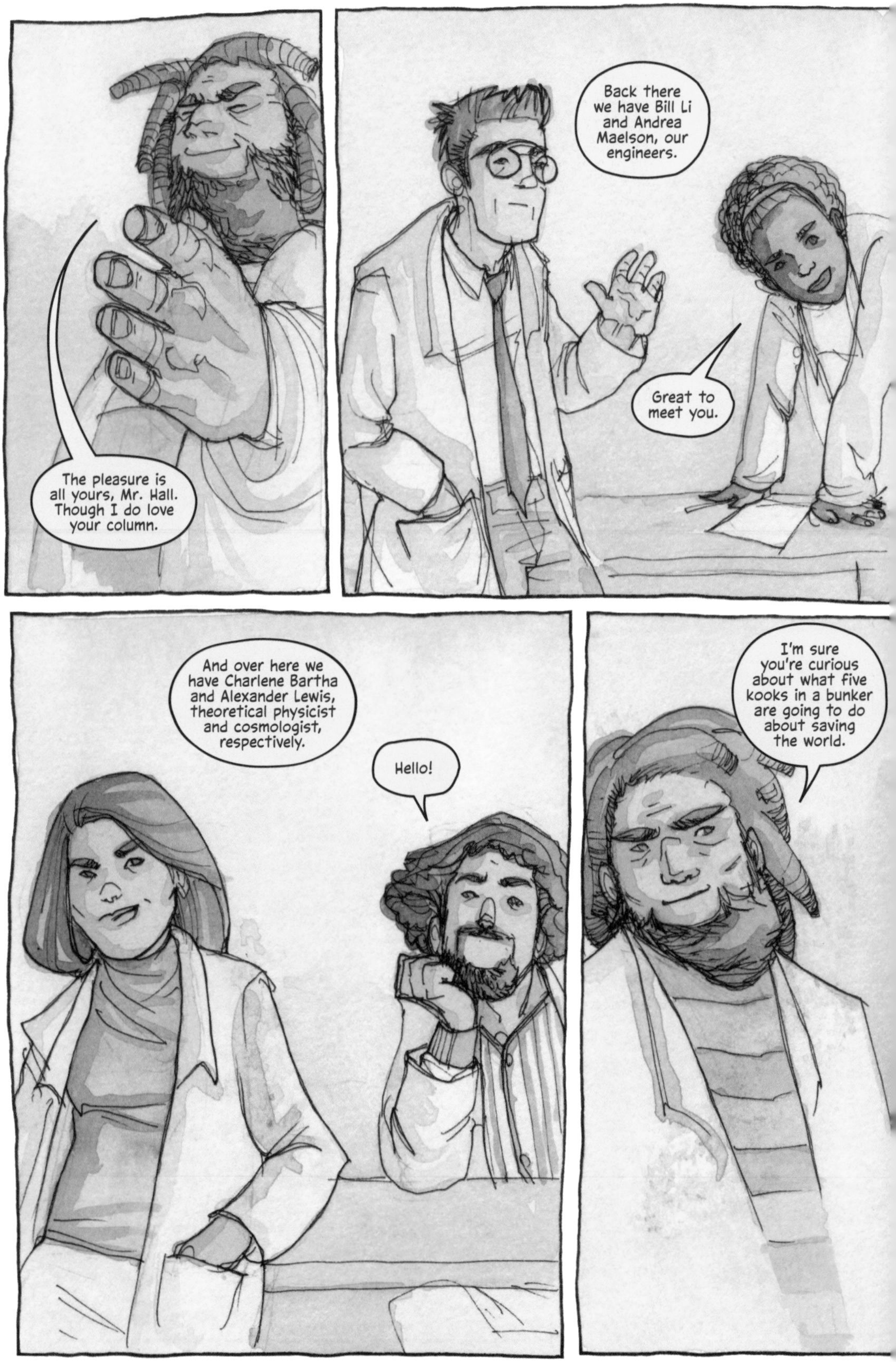
The pleasure is all yours, Mr. Hall. Though I do love your column.
Back there we have Bill Li and Andrea Maelson, our engineers.
Great to meet you.
And over here we have Charlene Bartha and Alexander Lewis, theoretical physicist and cosmologist, respectively.
Hello!
I'm sure you're curious about what five kooks in a bunker are going to do about saving the world.

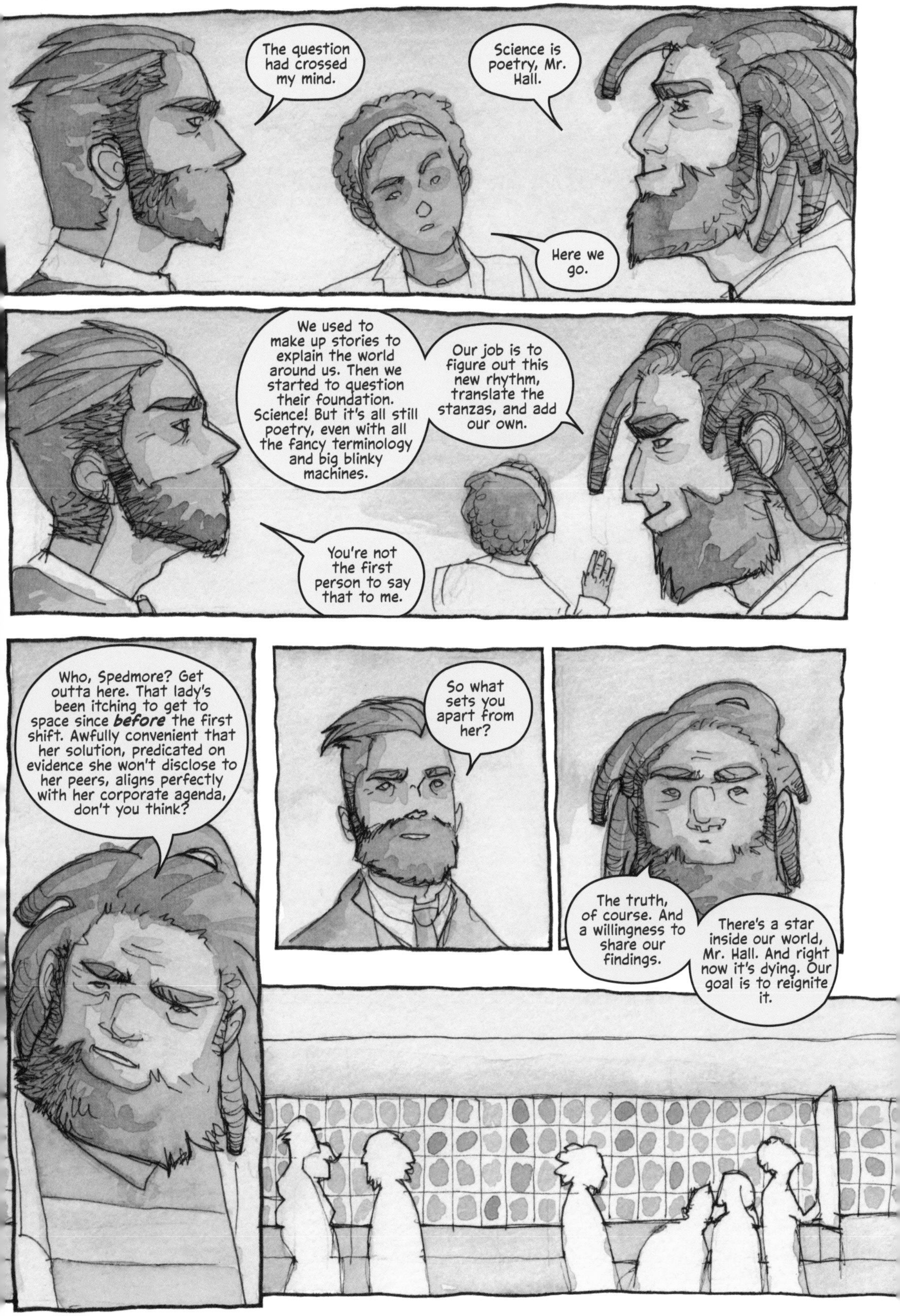
The question had crossed my mind.
Science is poetry, Mr. Hall.
Here we go.
We used to make up stories to explain the world around us. Then we started to question their foundation. Science! But it's all still poetry, even with all the fancy terminology and big blinky machines.
Our job is to figure out this new rhythm, translate the stanzas, and add our own.
You're not the first person to say that to me.
Who, Spedmore? Get outta here. That lady's been itching to get to space since ***before*** the first shift. Awfully convenient that her solution, predicated on evidence she won't disclose to her peers, aligns perfectly with her corporate agenda, don't you think?
So what sets you apart from her?
The truth, of course. And a willingness to share our findings.
There's a star inside our world, Mr. Hall. And right now it's dying. Our goal is to reignite it.

To watch them work, to listen to them speak about the world as though it isn't already a relic of the past, is beyond refreshing.

It's a reminder that our best days may not be behind us.

That we may still have a place on this planet. And we have a responsibility to protect that place.

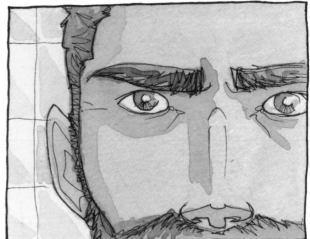

For ourselves, our children, and all of humanity.

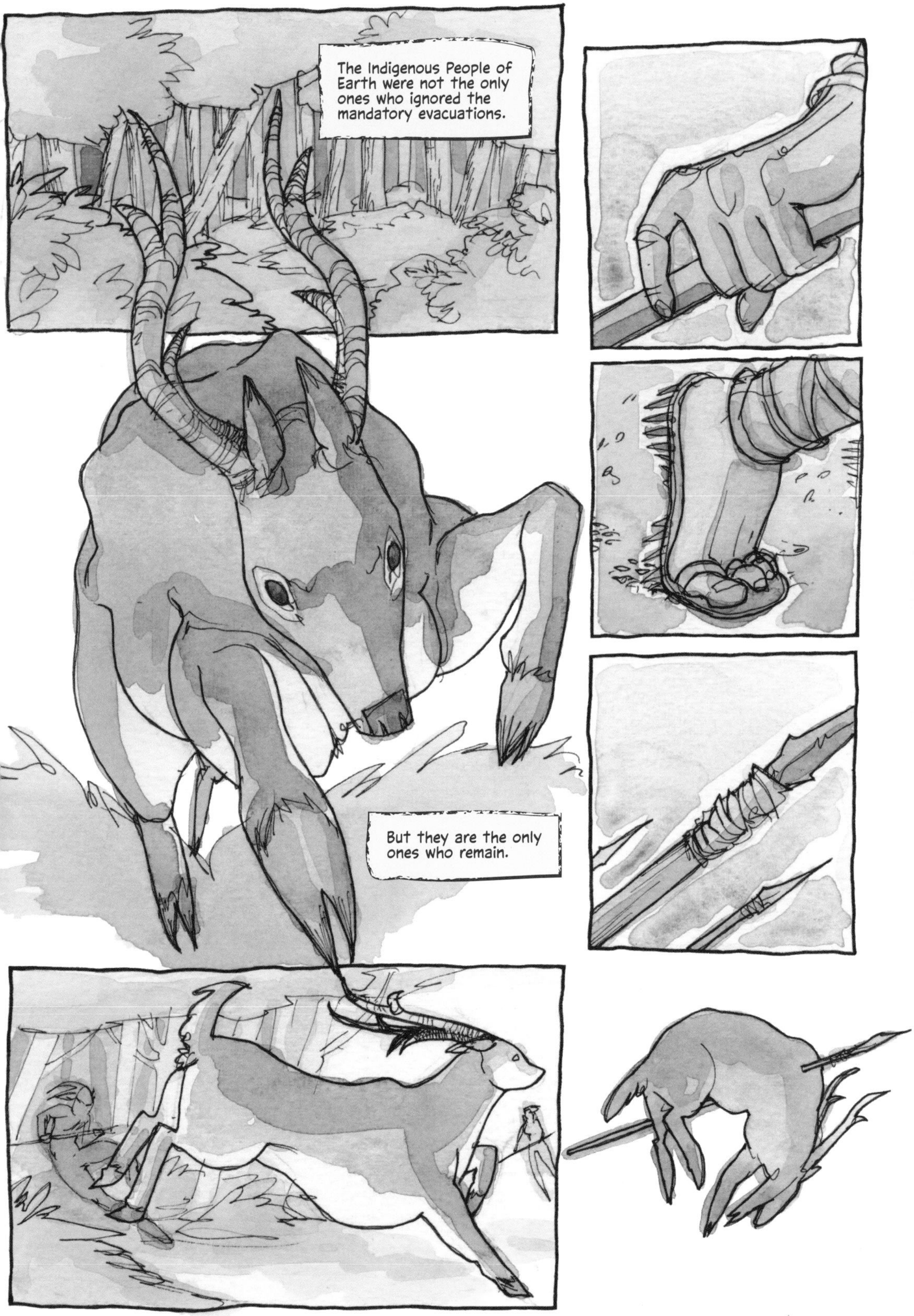
The Indigenous People of Earth were not the only ones who ignored the mandatory evacuations.
But they are the only ones who remain.

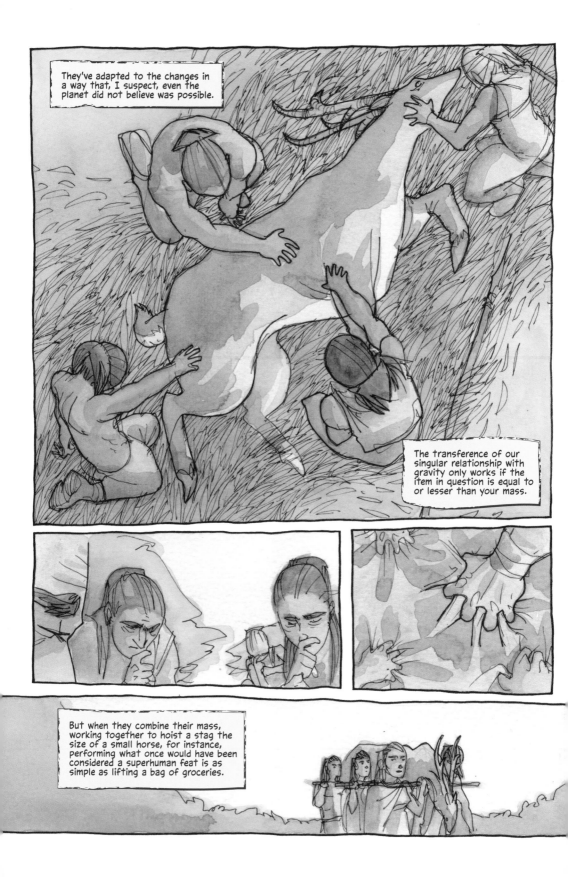

They've adapted to the changes in a way that, I suspect, even the planet did not believe was possible.

The transference of our singular relationship with gravity only works if the item in question is equal to or lesser than your mass.

But when they combine their mass, working together to hoist a stag the size of a small horse, for instance, performing what once would have been considered a superhuman feat is as simple as lifting a bag of groceries.

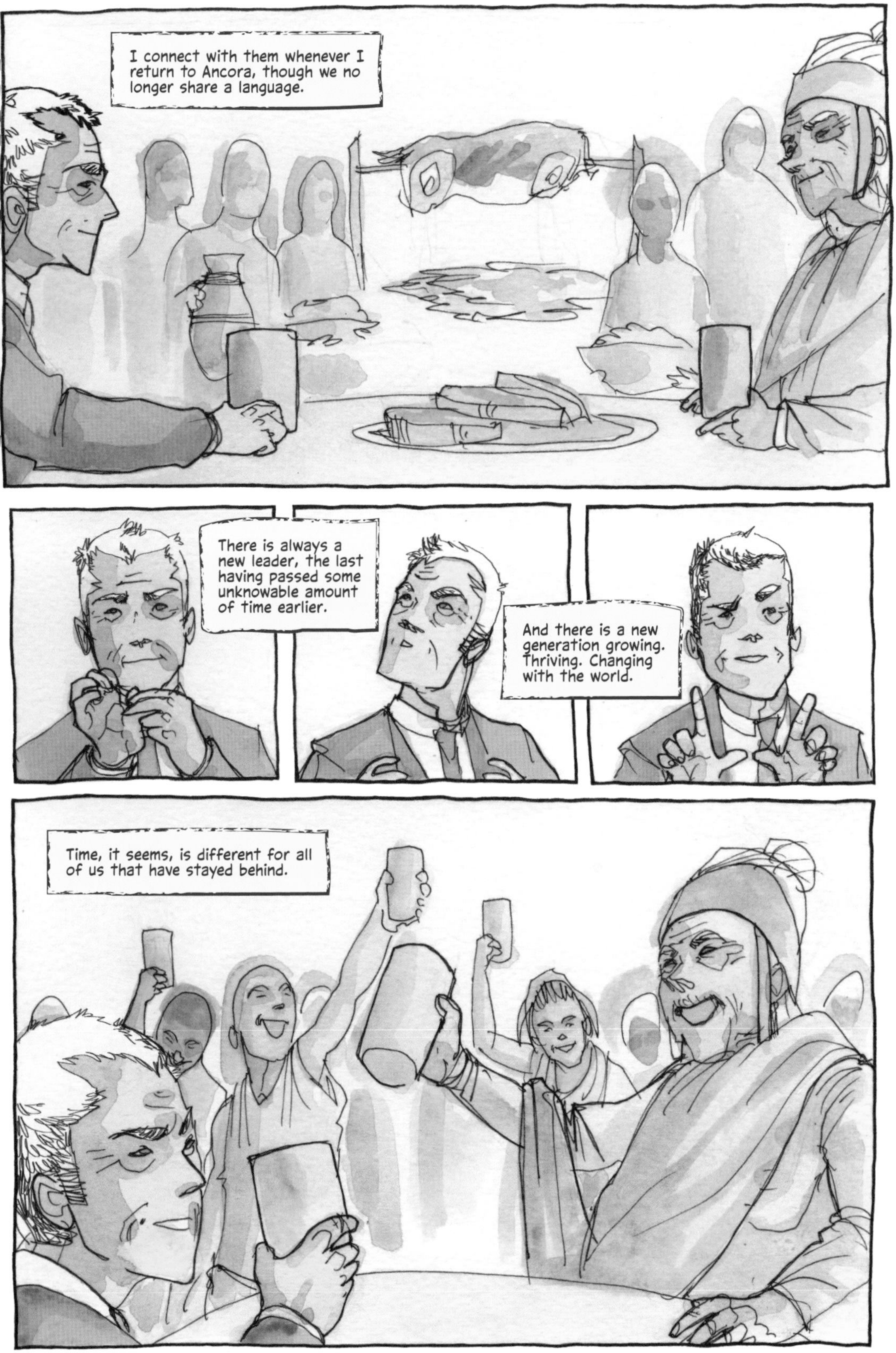
I connect with them whenever I return to Ancora, though we no longer share a language.
There is always a new leader, the last having passed some unknowable amount of time earlier.
And there is a new generation growing. Thriving. Changing with the world.
Time, it seems, is different for all of us that have stayed behind.

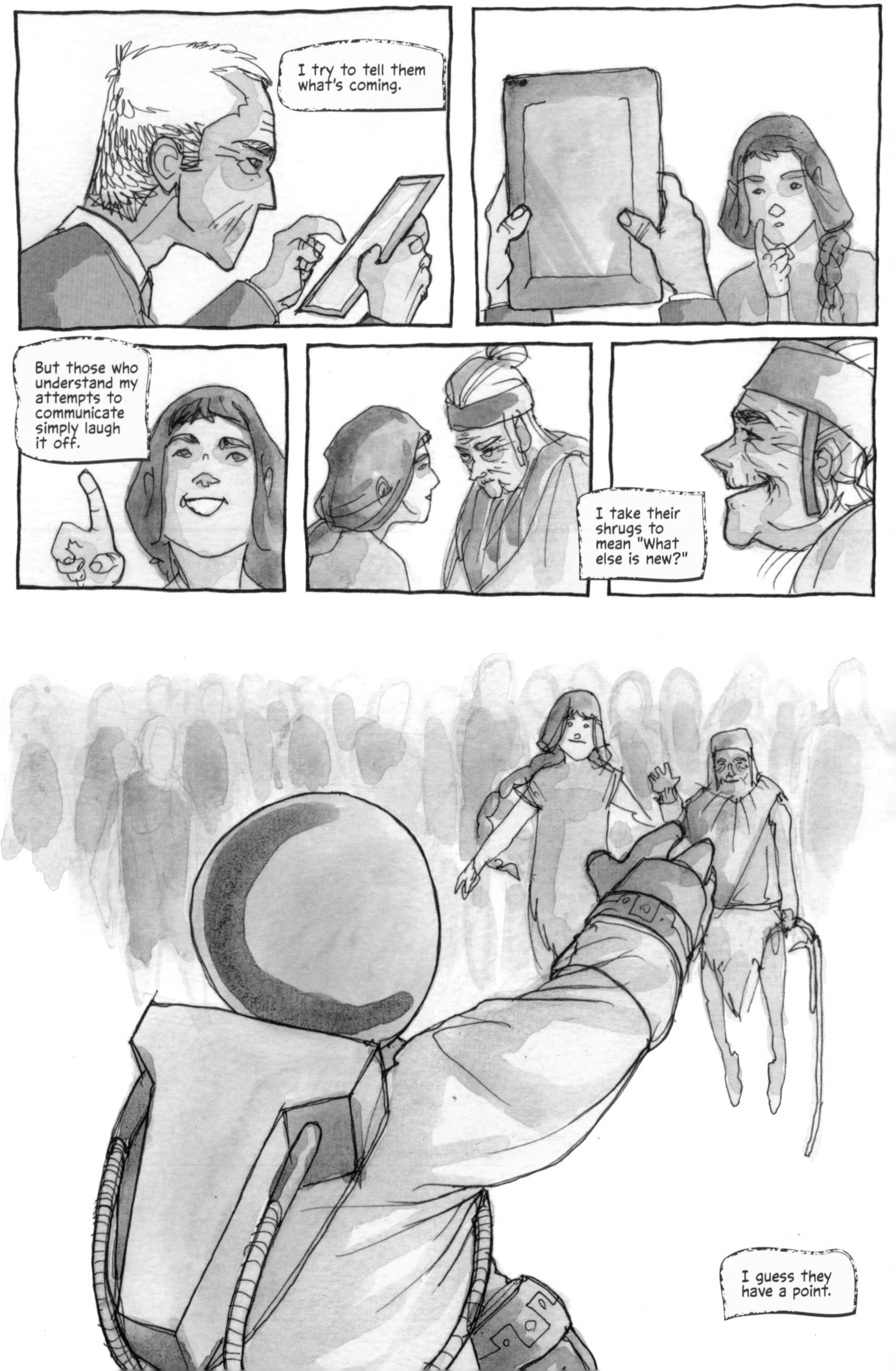
I try to tell them what's coming.
But those who understand my attempts to communicate simply laugh it off.
I take their shrugs to mean "What else is new?"
I guess they have a point.

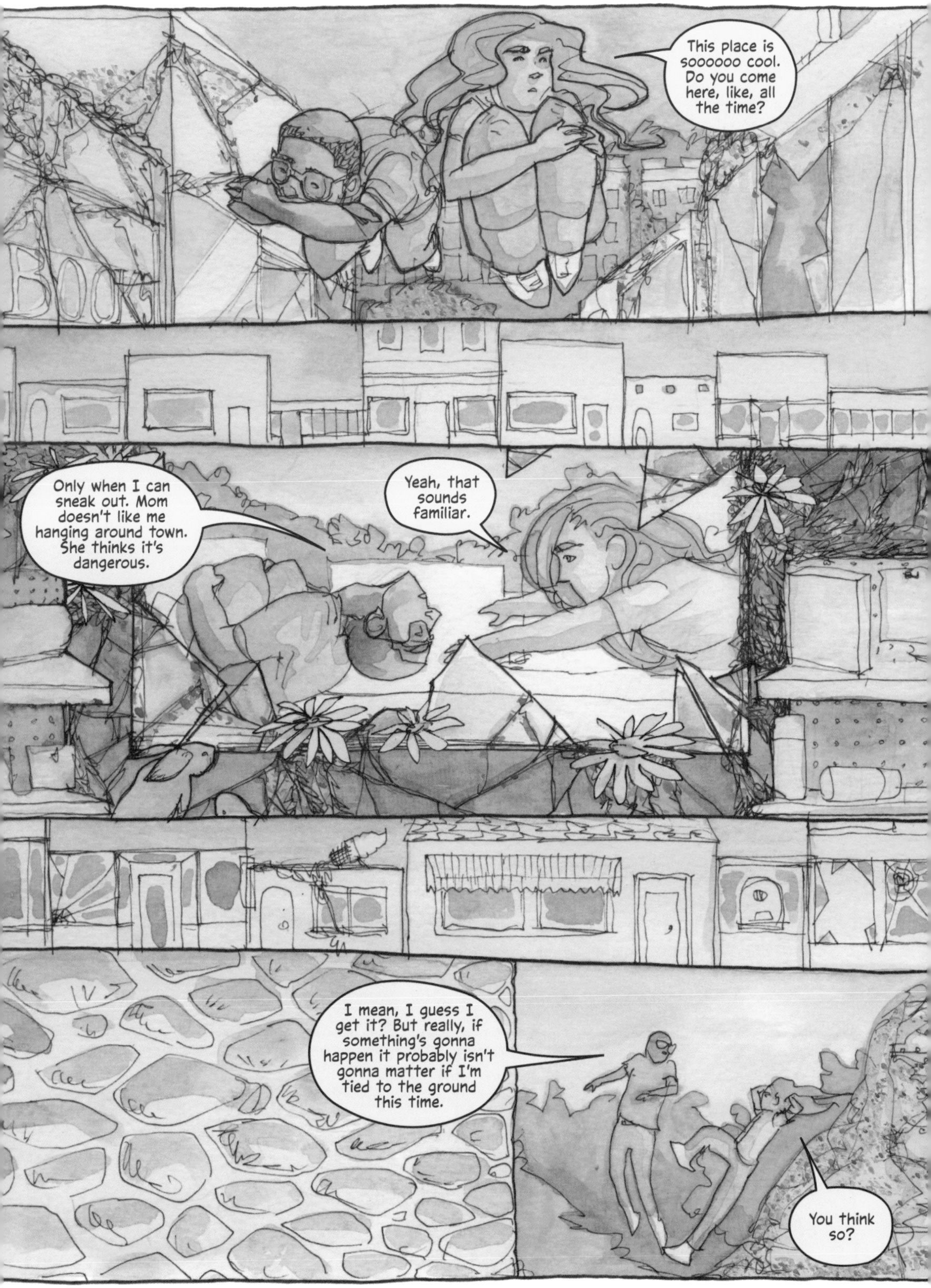
This place is sooooo cool. Do you come here, like, all the time?
Only when I can sneak out. Mom doesn't like me hanging around town. She thinks it's dangerous.
Yeah, that sounds familiar.
I mean, I guess I get it? But really, if something's gonna happen it probably isn't gonna matter if I'm tied to the ground this time.
You think so?

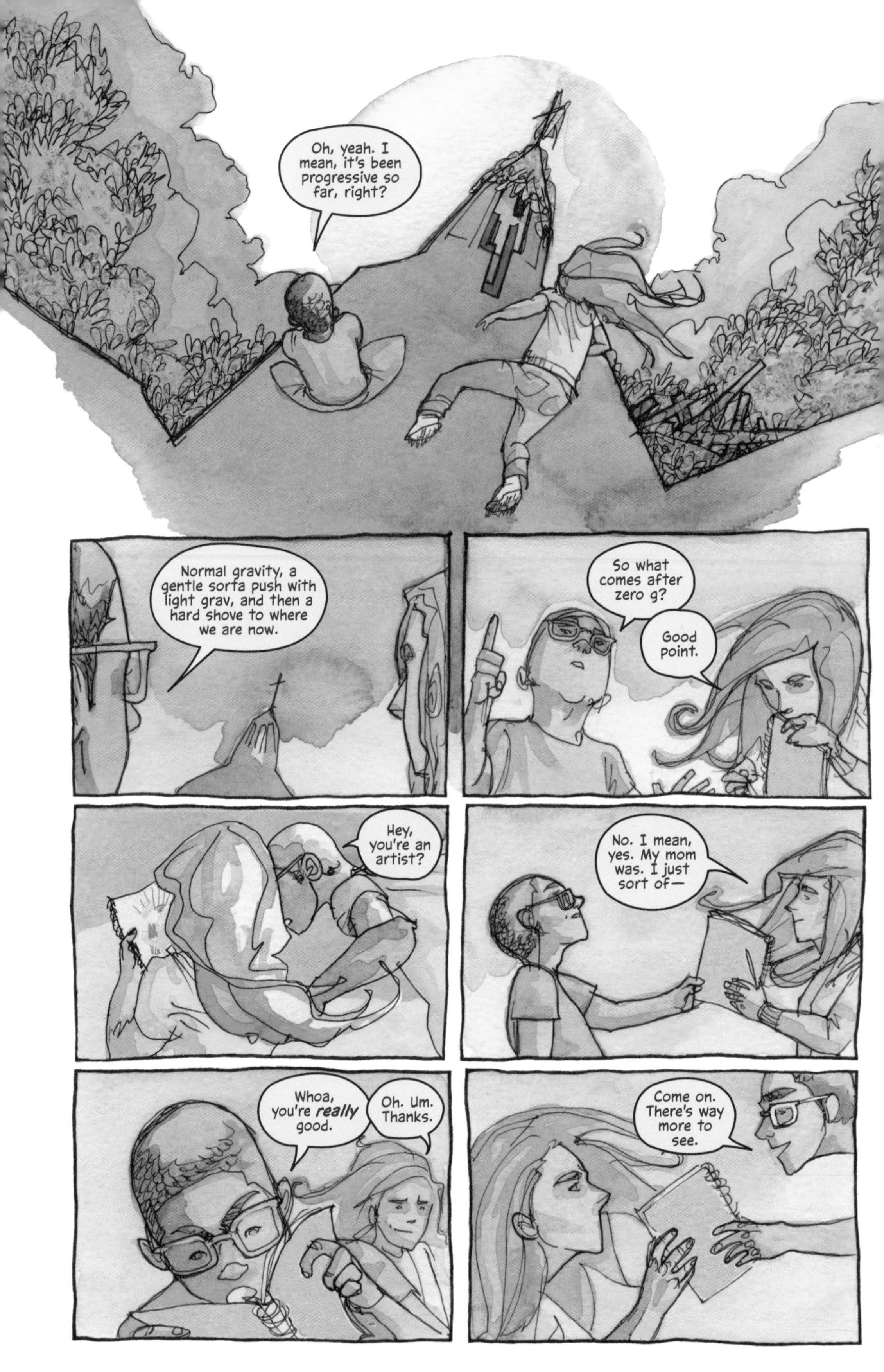
Oh, yeah. I mean, it's been progressive so far, right?
Normal gravity, a gentle sorta push with light grav, and then a hard shove to where we are now.
So what comes after zero g?
Good point.
Hey, you're an artist?
No. I mean, yes. My mom was. I just sort of—
Whoa, you're *really* good.
Oh. Um. Thanks.
Come on. There's way more to see.

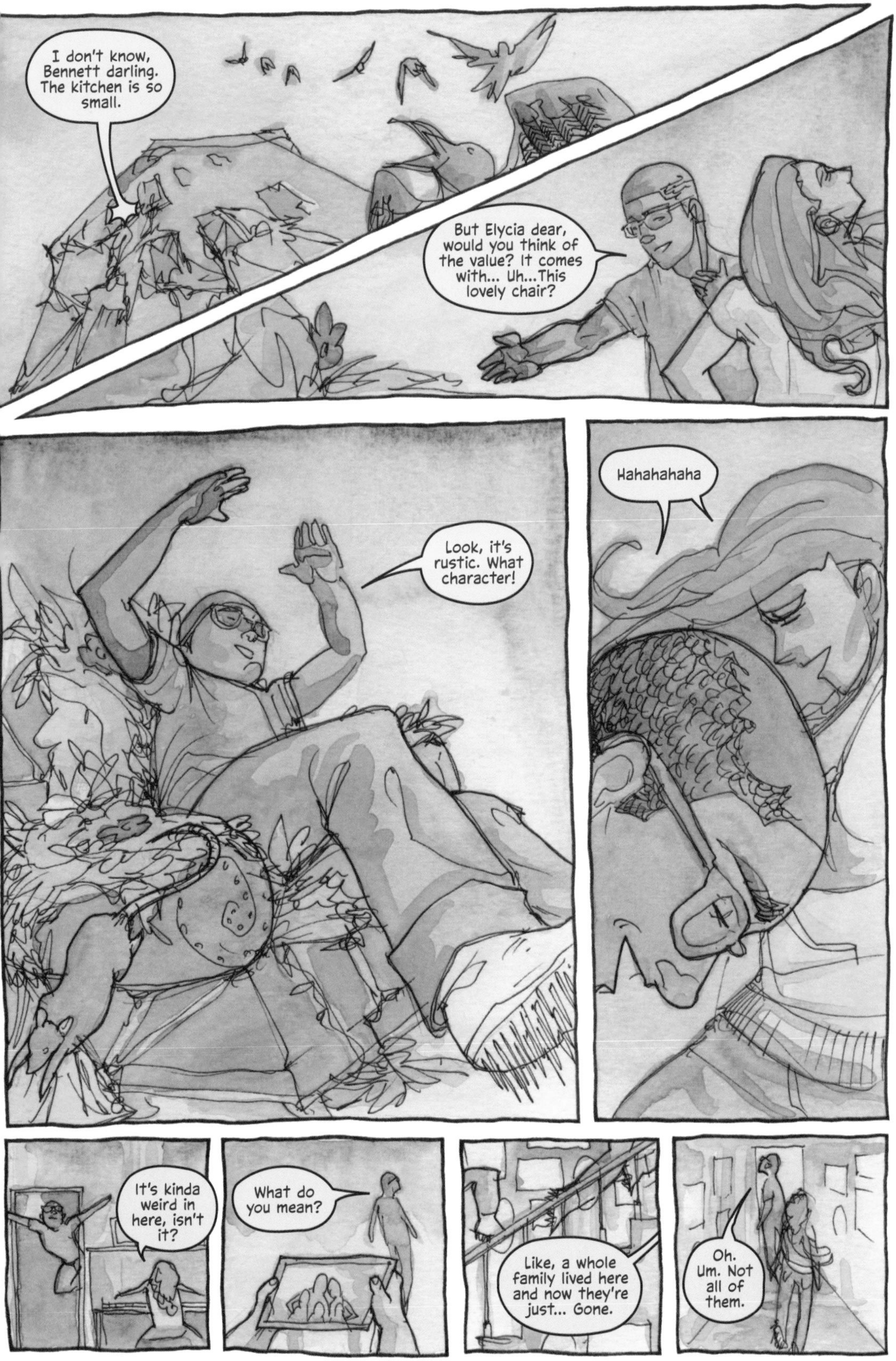
I don't know, Bennett darling. The kitchen is so small.
But Elycia dear, would you think of the value? It comes with... Uh...This lovely chair?
Look, it's rustic. What character!
Hahahahaha
It's kinda weird in here, isn't it?
What do you mean?
Like, a whole family lived here and now they're just... Gone.
Oh. Um. Not all of them.

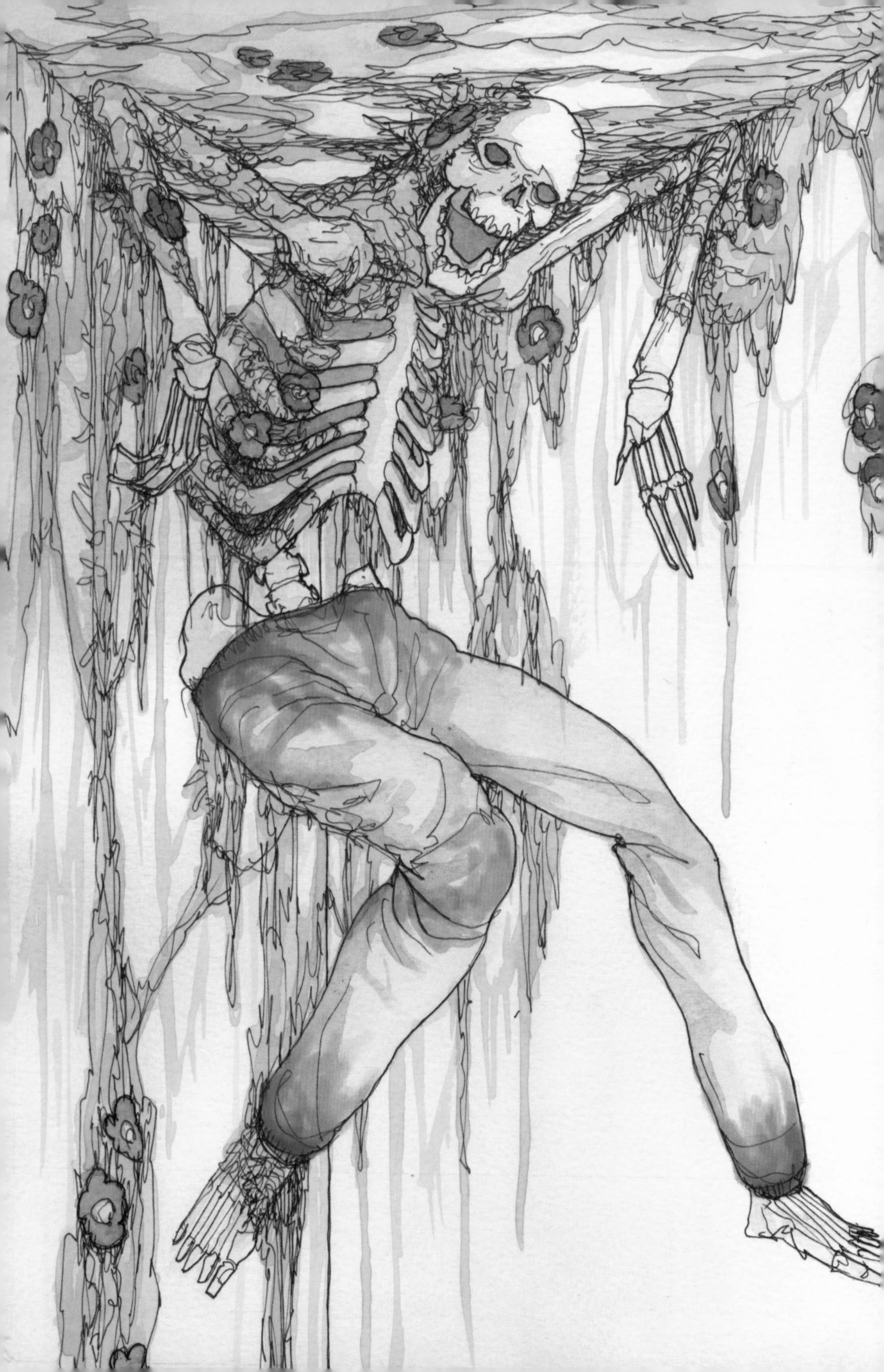

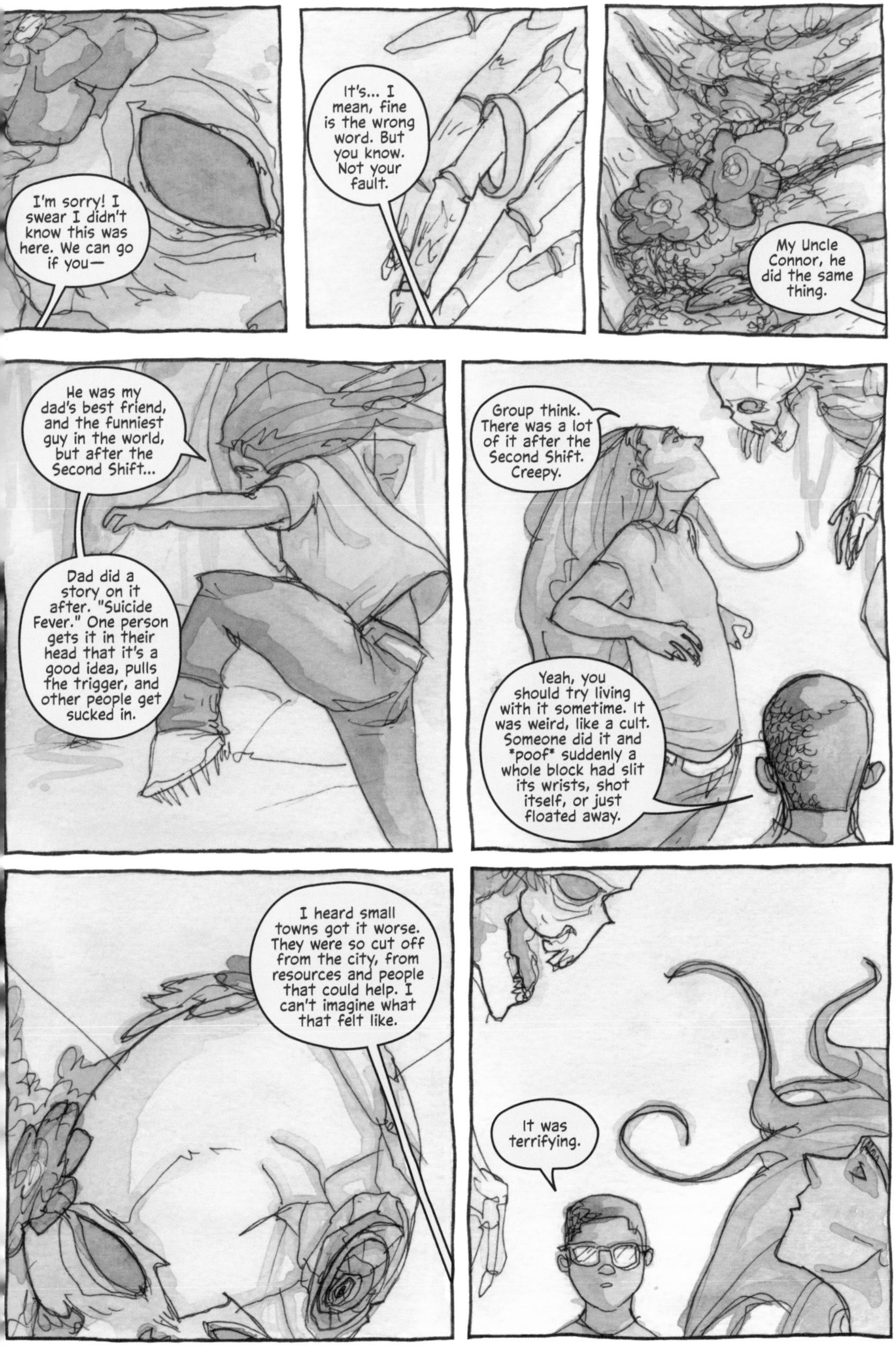
I'm sorry! I swear I didn't know this was here. We can go if you—
It's... I mean, fine is the wrong word. But you know. Not your fault.
My Uncle Connor, he did the same thing.
He was my dad's best friend, and the funniest guy in the world, but after the Second Shift...
Dad did a story on it after. "Suicide Fever." One person gets it in their head that it's a good idea, pulls the trigger, and other people get sucked in.
Group think. There was a lot of it after the Second Shift. Creepy.
Yeah, you should try living with it sometime. It was weird, like a cult. Someone did it and *poof* suddenly a whole block had slit its wrists, shot itself, or just floated away.
I heard small towns got it worse. They were so cut off from the city, from resources and people that could help. I can't imagine what that felt like.
It was terrifying.

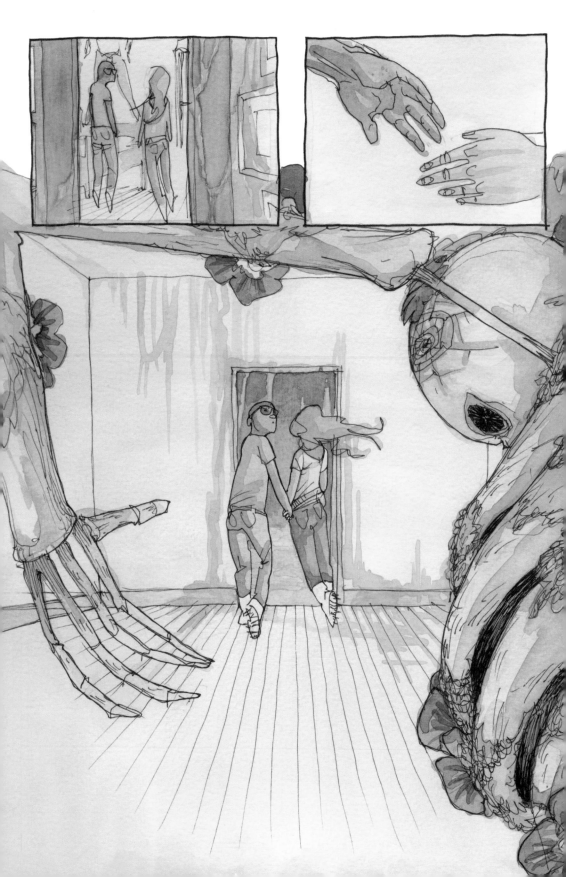

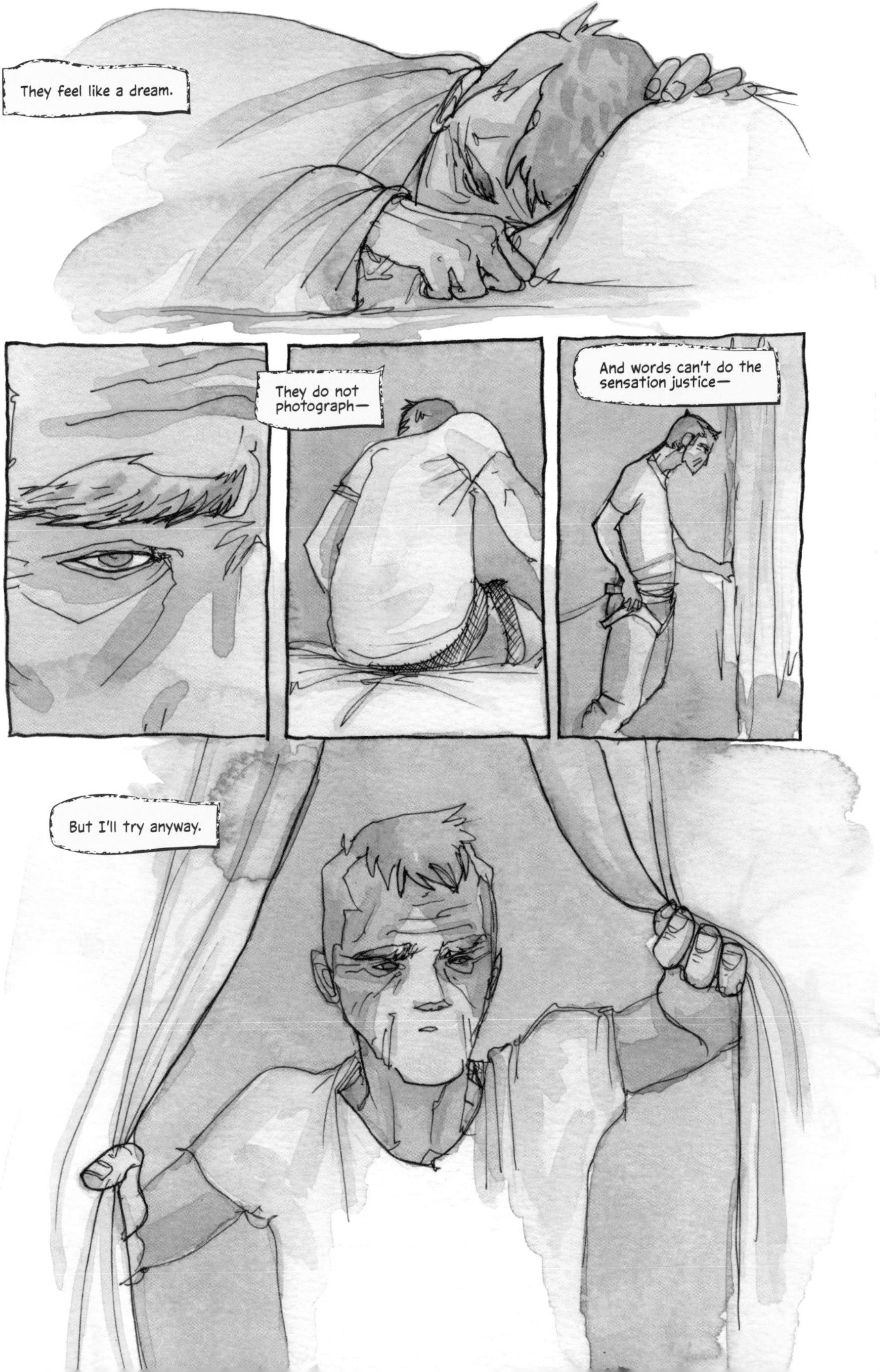
They feel like a dream.
They do not photograph—
And words can't do the sensation justice—
But I'll try anyway.

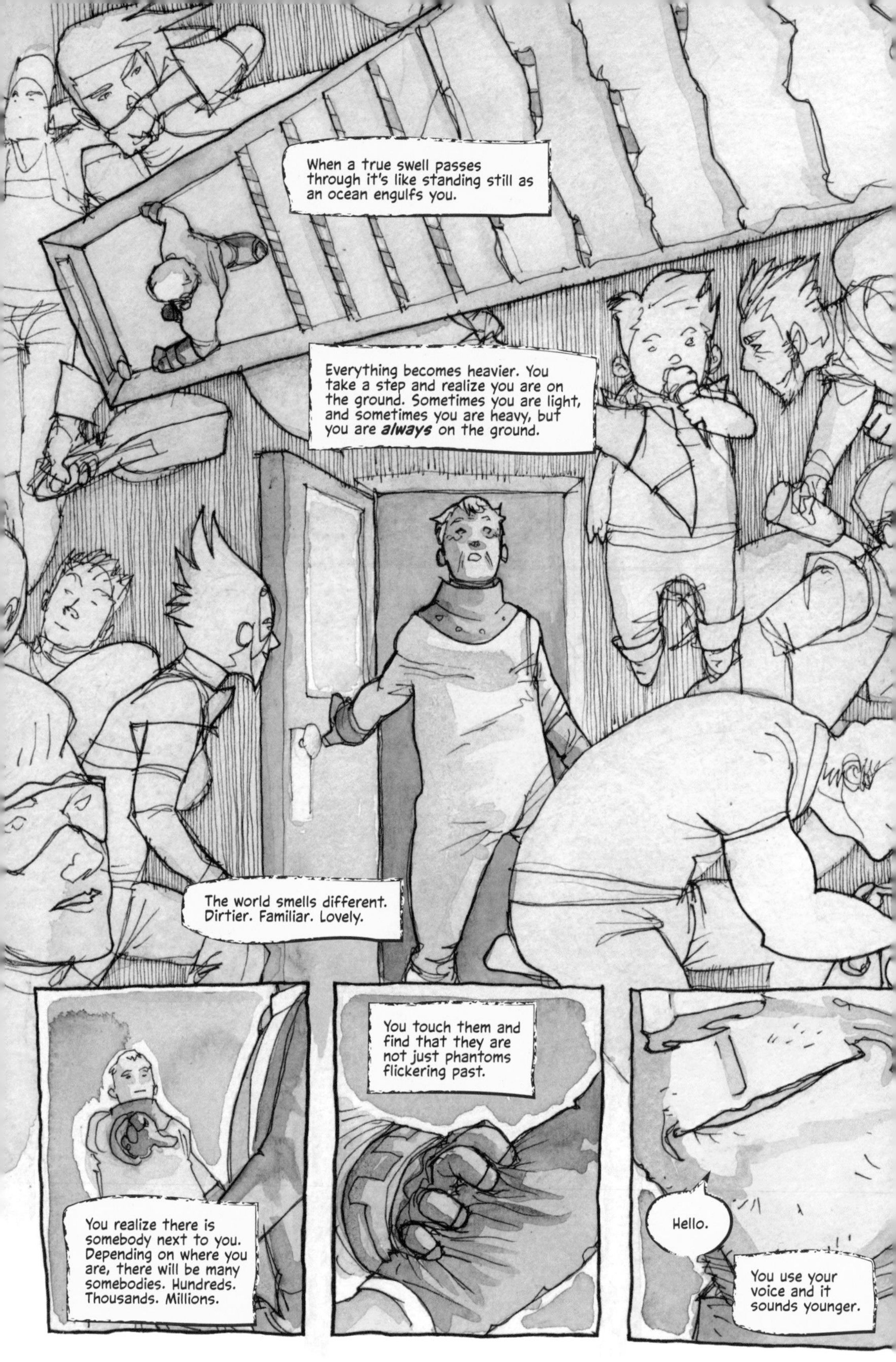
When a true swell passes through it's like standing still as an ocean engulfs you.
Everything becomes heavier. You take a step and realize you are on the ground. Sometimes you are light, and sometimes you are heavy, but you are ***always*** on the ground.
The world smells different. Dirtier. Familiar. Lovely.
You realize there is somebody next to you. Depending on where you are, there will be many somebodies. Hundreds. Thousands. Millions.
You touch them and find that they are not just phantoms flickering past.
Hello.
You use your voice and it sounds younger.

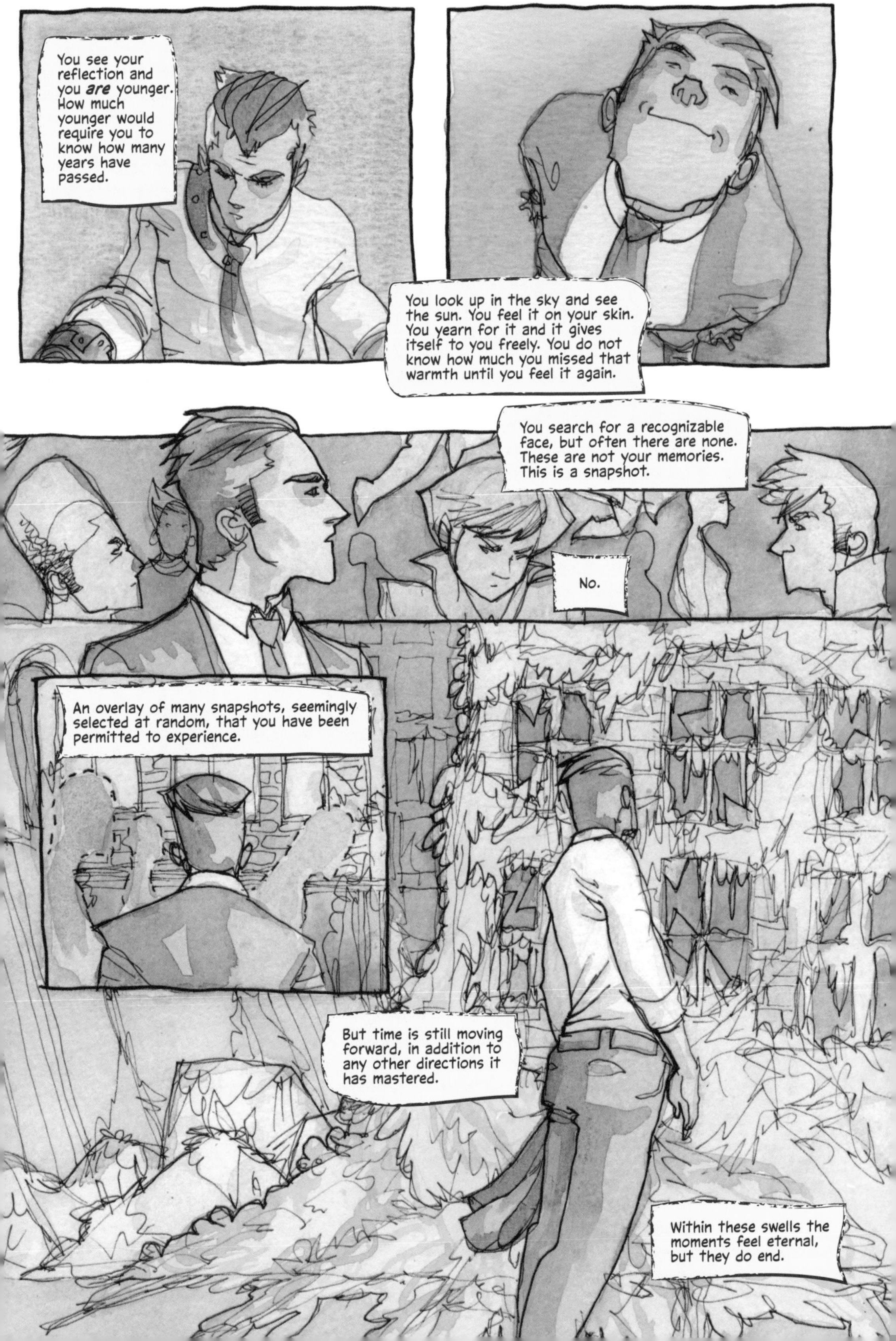
You see your reflection and you *are* younger. How much younger would require you to know how many years have passed.
You look up in the sky and see the sun. You feel it on your skin. You yearn for it and it gives itself to you freely. You do not know how much you missed that warmth until you feel it again.
You search for a recognizable face, but often there are none. These are not your memories. This is a snapshot.
No.
An overlay of many snapshots, seemingly selected at random, that you have been permitted to experience.
But time is still moving forward, in addition to any other directions it has mastered.
Within these swells the moments feel eternal, but they do end.

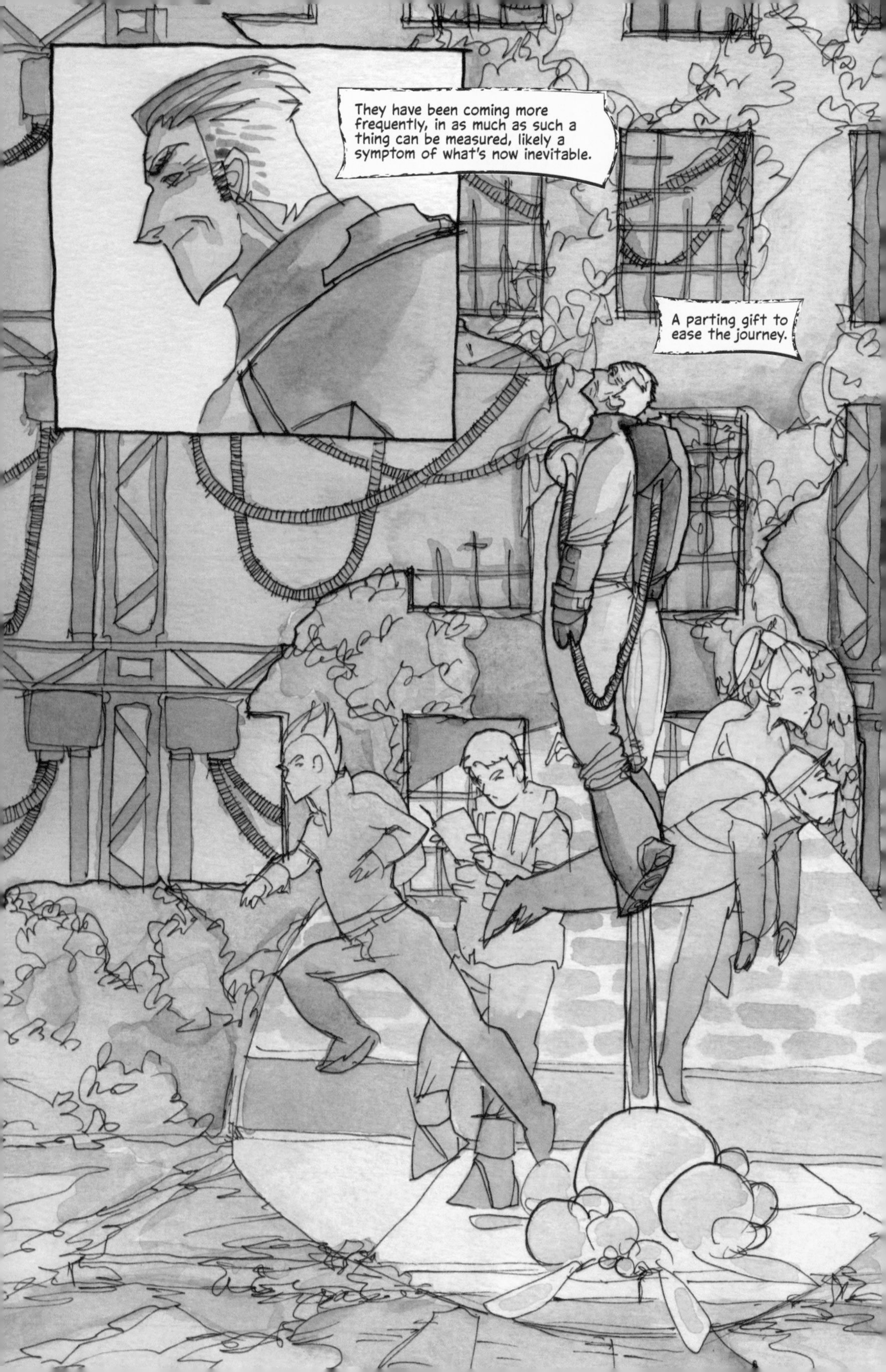
They have been coming more frequently, in as much as such a thing can be measured, likely a symptom of what's now inevitable.
A parting gift to ease the journey.

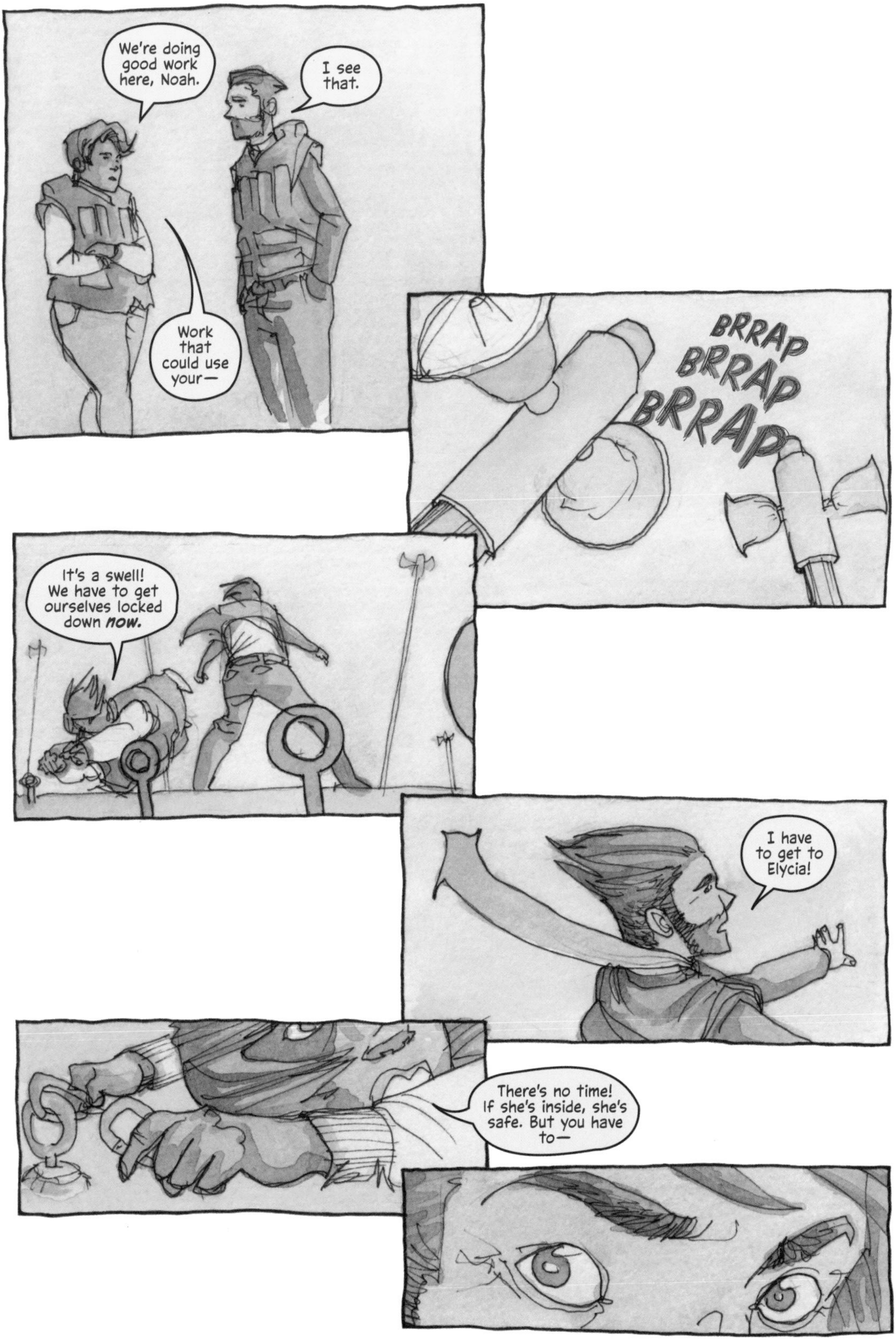
We're doing good work here, Noah.
I see that.
Work that could use your—
BRRAP BRRAP BRRAP
It's a swell! We have to get ourselves locked down *now.*
I have to get to Elycia!
There's no time! If she's inside, she's safe. But you have to—

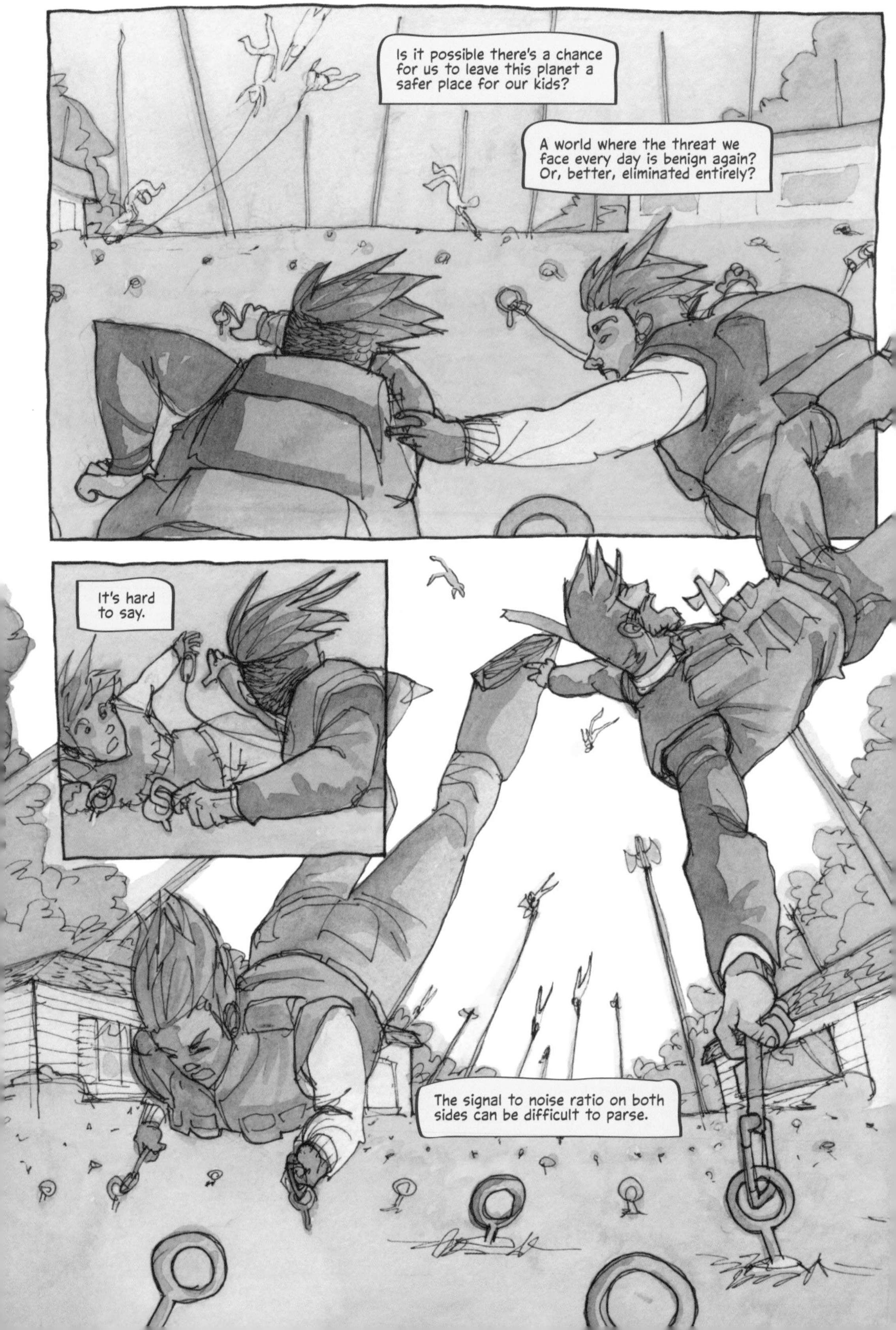
Is it possible there's a chance for us to leave this planet a safer place for our kids?
A world where the threat we face every day is benign again? Or, better, eliminated entirely?
It's hard to say.
The signal to noise ratio on both sides can be difficult to parse.

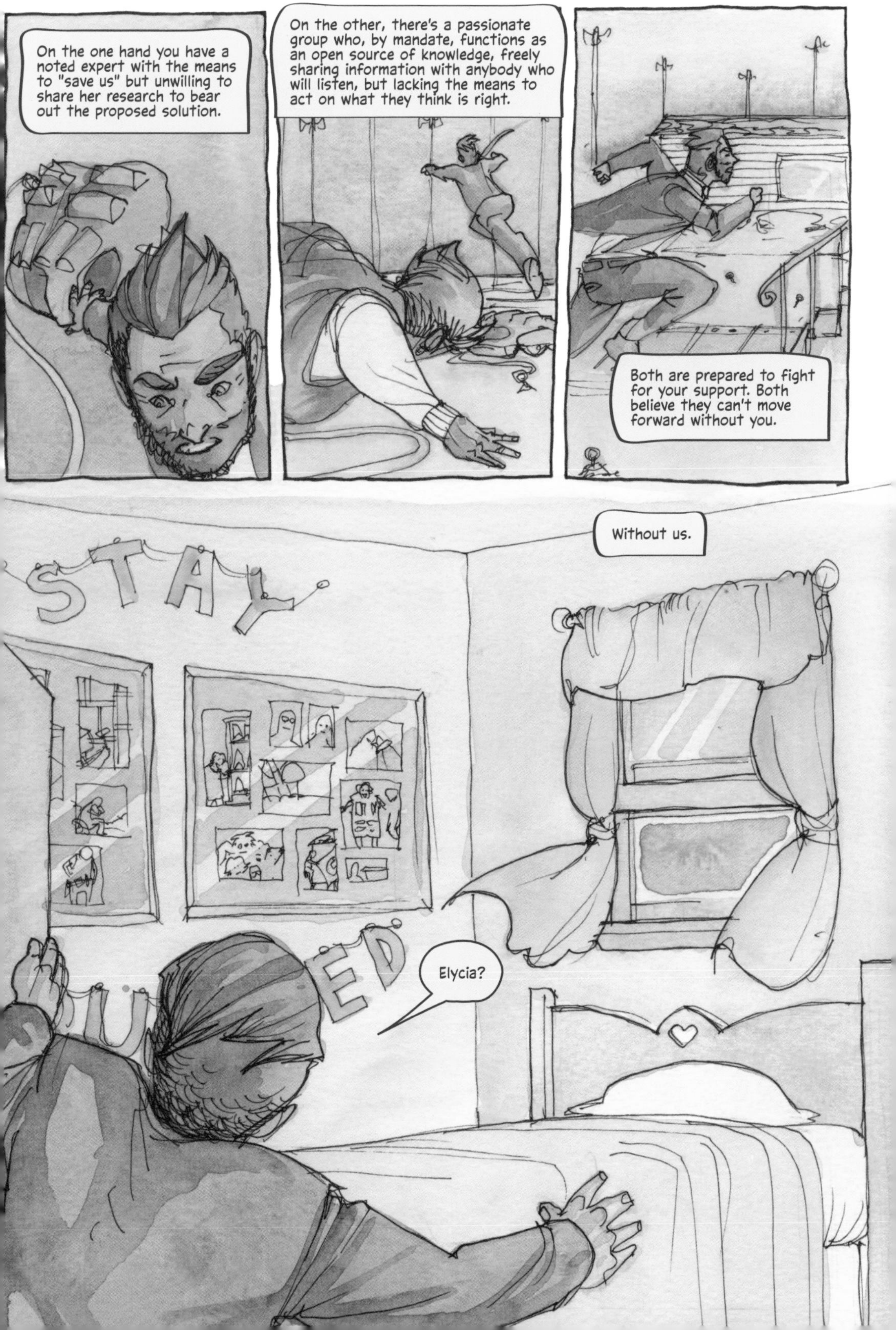
On the one hand you have a noted expert with the means to "save us" but unwilling to share her research to bear out the proposed solution.
On the other, there's a passionate group who, by mandate, functions as an open source of knowledge, freely sharing information with anybody who will listen, but lacking the means to act on what they think is right.
Both are prepared to fight for your support. Both believe they can't move forward without you.
Without us.
STAY
Elycia?

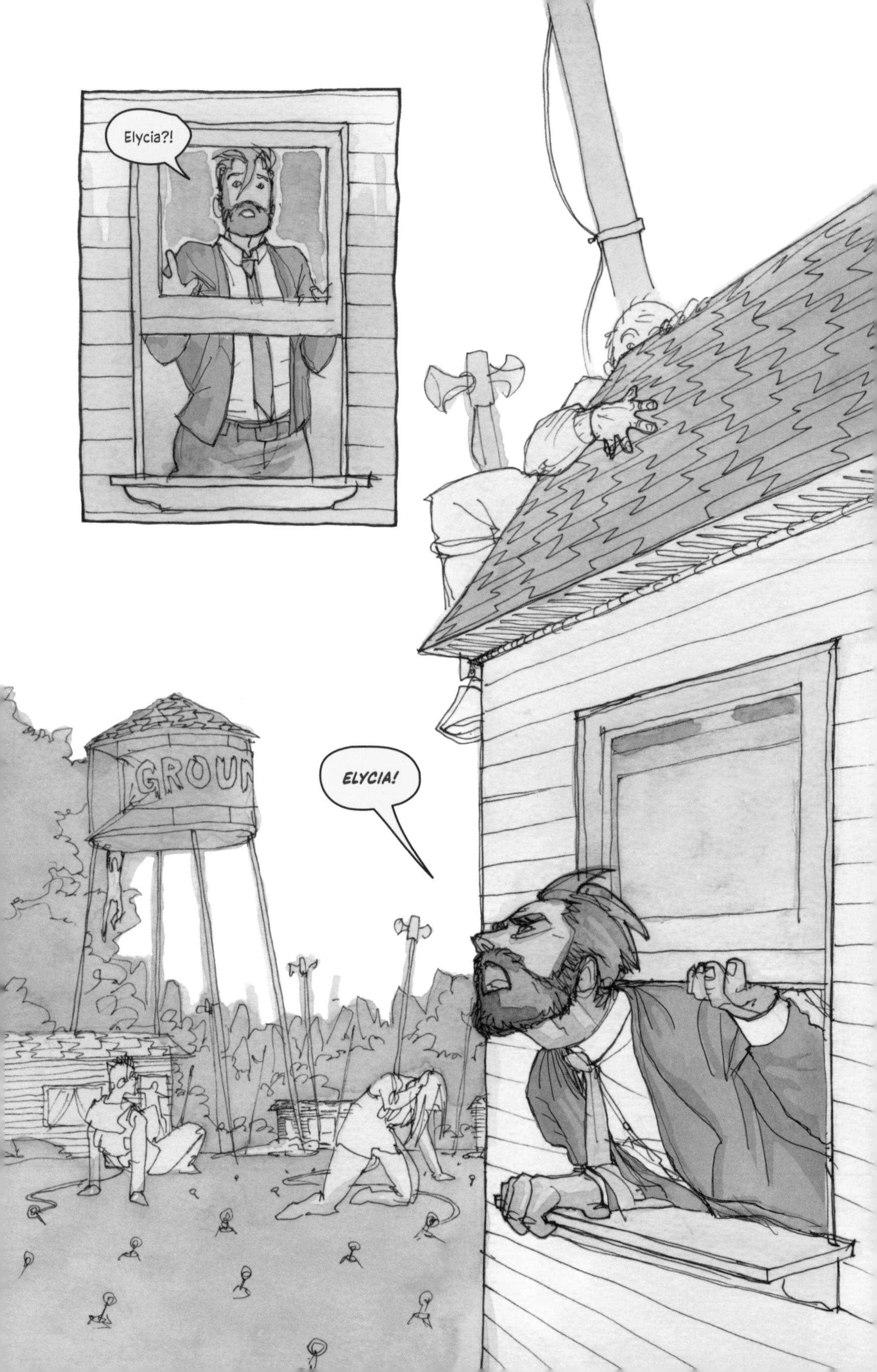
Elycia?!
GROUN
ELYCIA!

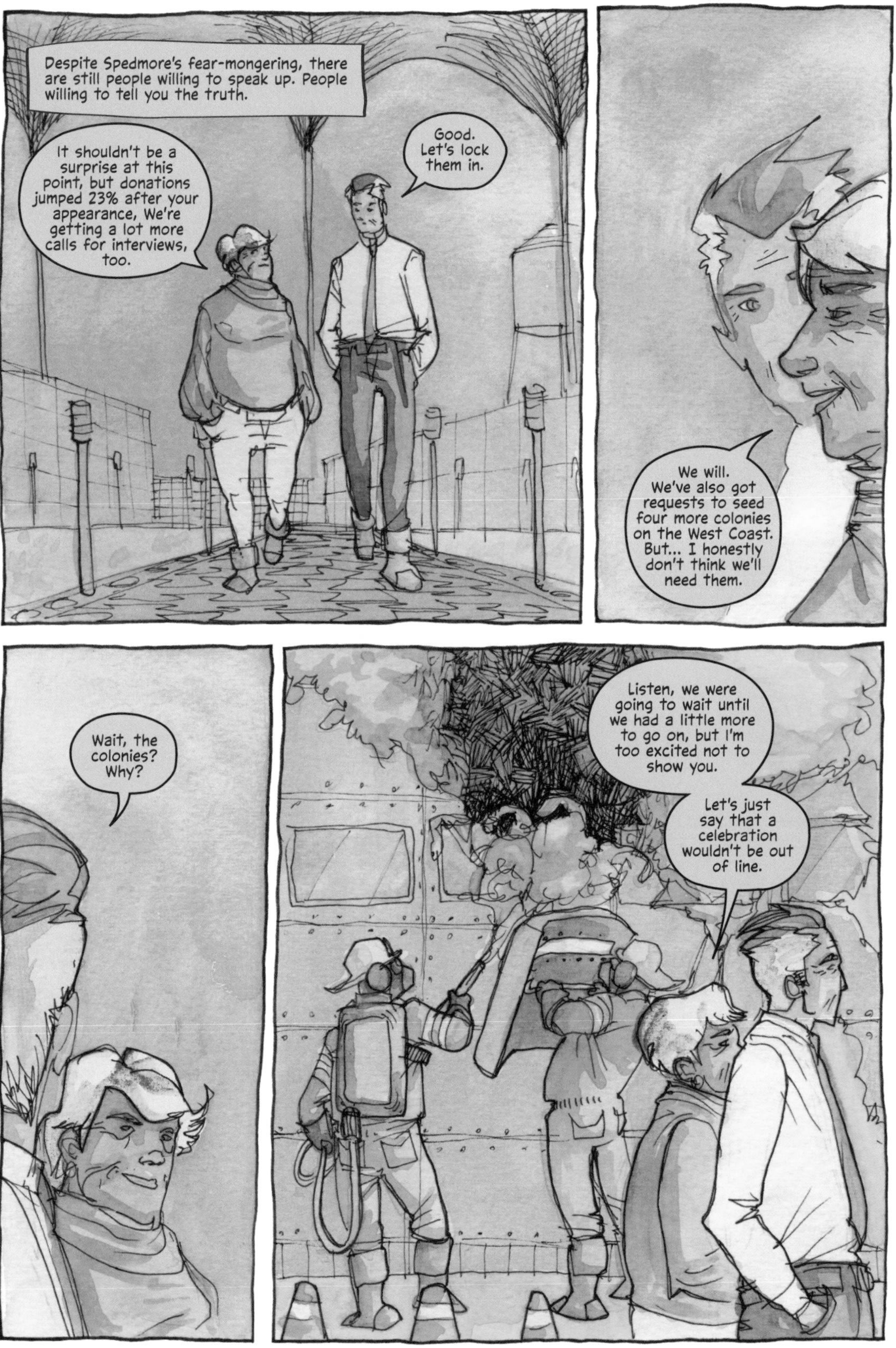
Despite Spedmore's fear-mongering, there are still people willing to speak up. People willing to tell you the truth.
It shouldn't be a surprise at this point, but donations jumped 23% after your appearance, We're getting a lot more calls for interviews, too.
Good. Let's lock them in.
We will. We've also got requests to seed four more colonies on the West Coast. But... I honestly don't think we'll need them.
Wait, the colonies? Why?
Listen, we were going to wait until we had a little more to go on, but I'm too excited not to show you.
Let's just say that a celebration wouldn't be out of line.

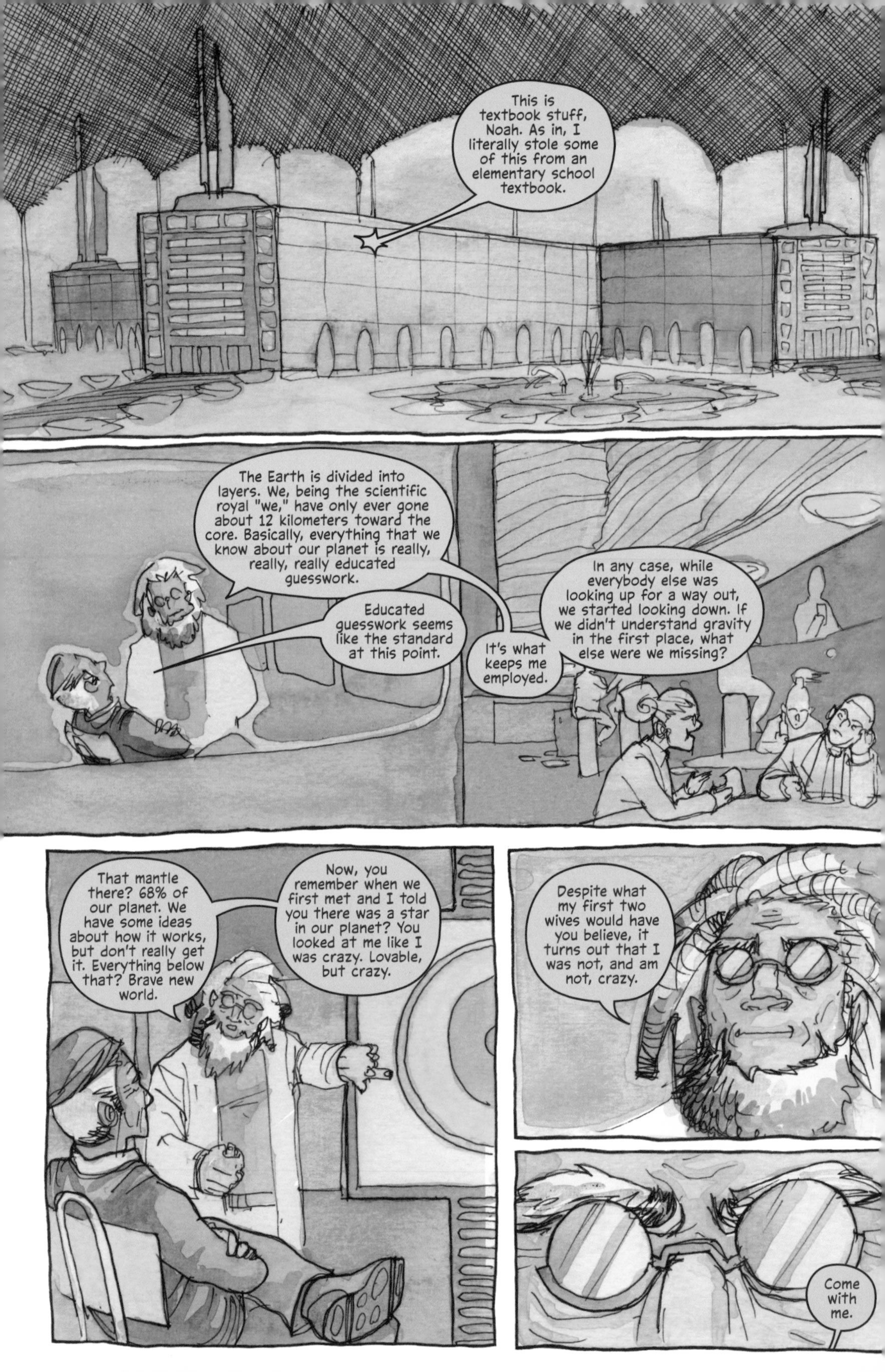
This is textbook stuff, Noah. As in, I literally stole some of this from an elementary school textbook.
The Earth is divided into layers. We, being the scientific royal "we," have only ever gone about 12 kilometers toward the core. Basically, everything that we know about our planet is really, really, really educated guesswork.
Educated guesswork seems like the standard at this point.
It's what keeps me employed.
In any case, while everybody else was looking up for a way out, we started looking down. If we didn't understand gravity in the first place, what else were we missing?
That mantle there? 68% of our planet. We have some ideas about how it works, but don't really get it. Everything below that? Brave new world.
Now, you remember when we first met and I told you there was a star in our planet? You looked at me like I was crazy. Lovable, but crazy.
Despite what my first two wives would have you believe, it turns out that I was not, and am not, crazy.
Come with me.

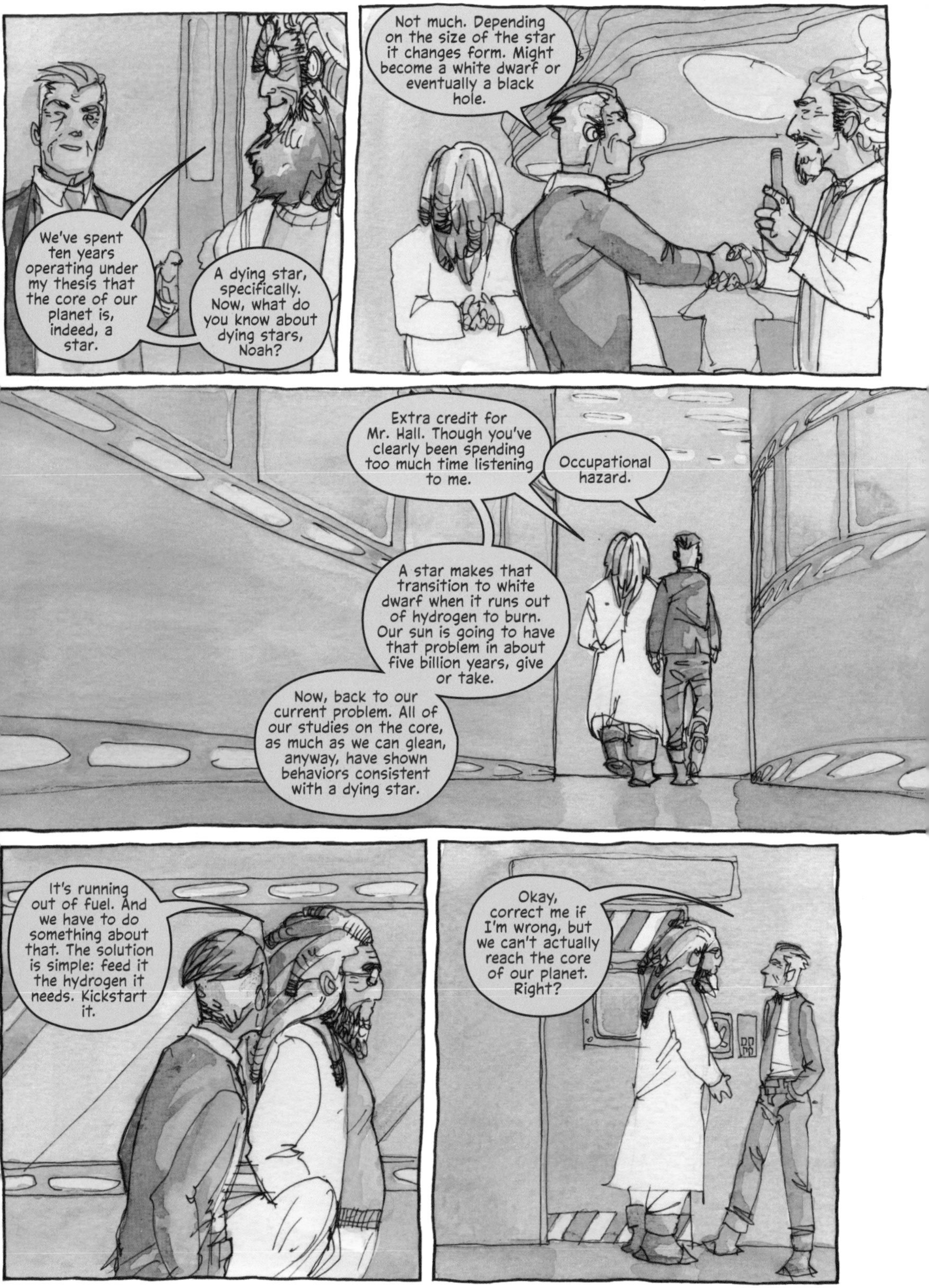
We've spent ten years operating under my thesis that the core of our planet is, indeed, a star.
A dying star, specifically. Now, what do you know about dying stars, Noah?
Not much. Depending on the size of the star it changes form. Might become a white dwarf or eventually a black hole.
Extra credit for Mr. Hall. Though you've clearly been spending too much time listening to me.
Occupational hazard.
A star makes that transition to white dwarf when it runs out of hydrogen to burn. Our sun is going to have that problem in about five billion years, give or take.
Now, back to our current problem. All of our studies on the core, as much as we can glean, anyway, have shown behaviors consistent with a dying star.
It's running out of fuel. And we have to do something about that. The solution is simple: feed it the hydrogen it needs. Kickstart it.
Okay, correct me if I'm wrong, but we can't actually reach the core of our planet. Right?

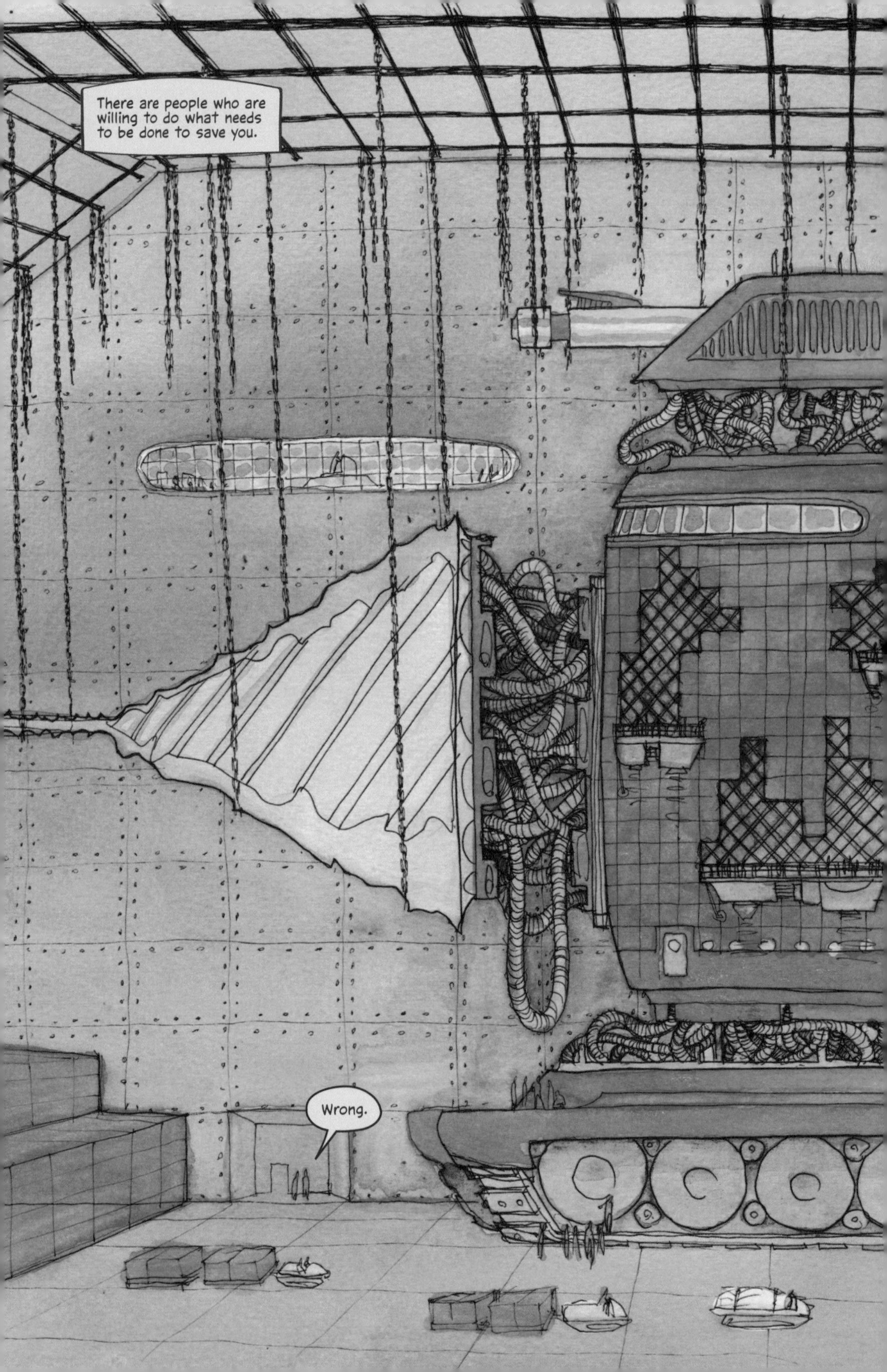
There are people who are willing to do what needs to be done to save you.
Wrong.

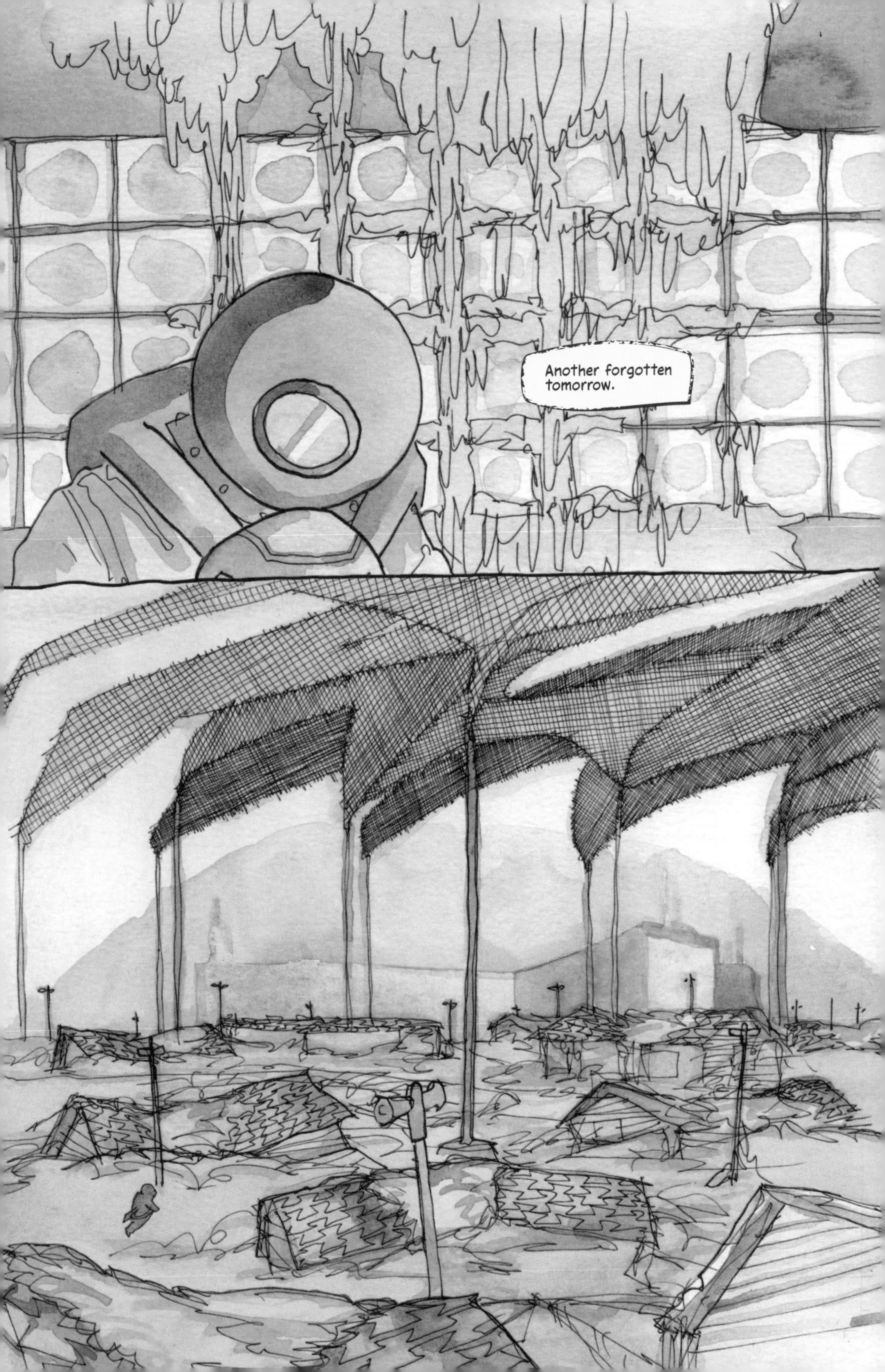
Another forgotten tomorrow.

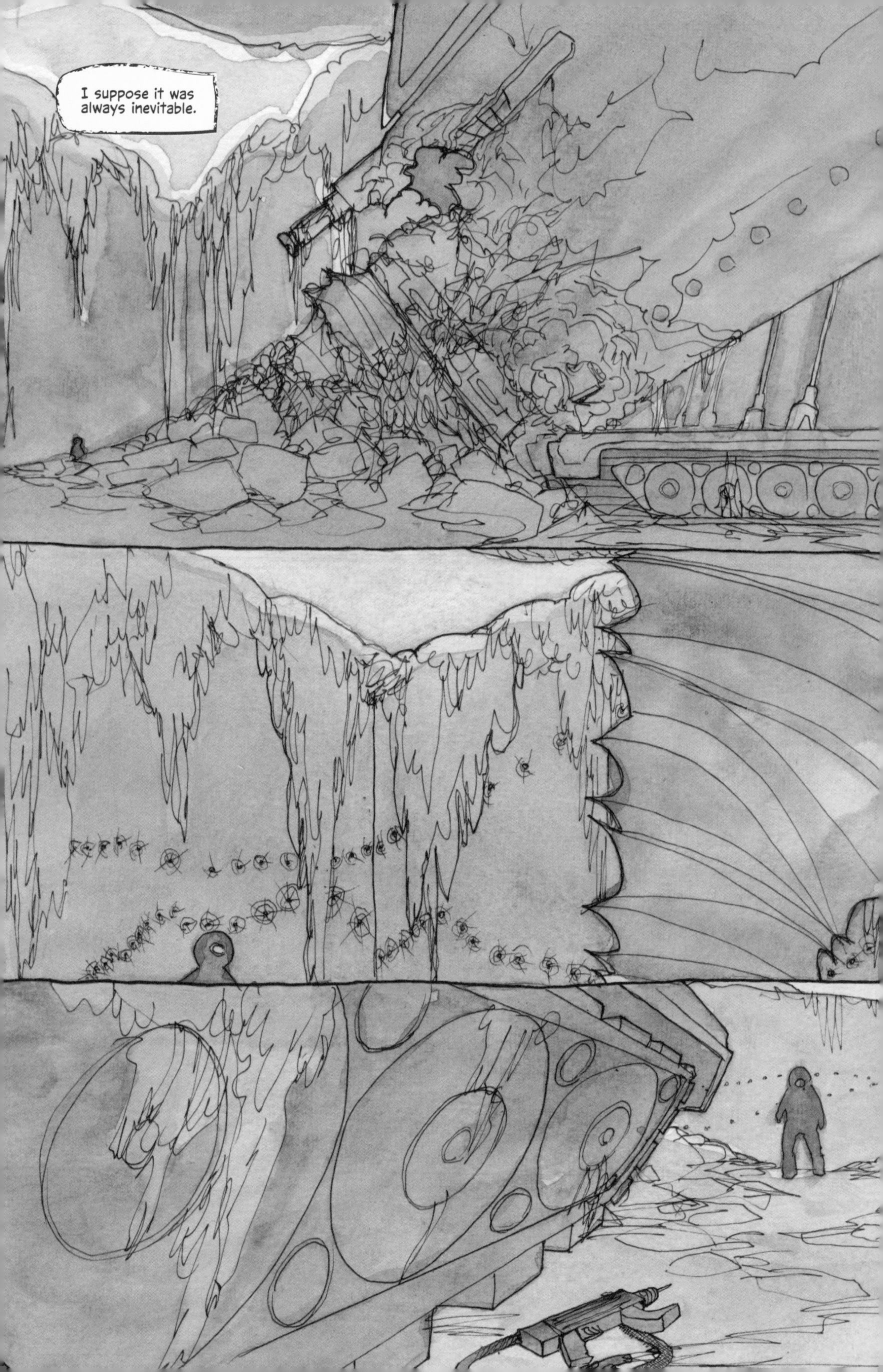
I suppose it was always inevitable.

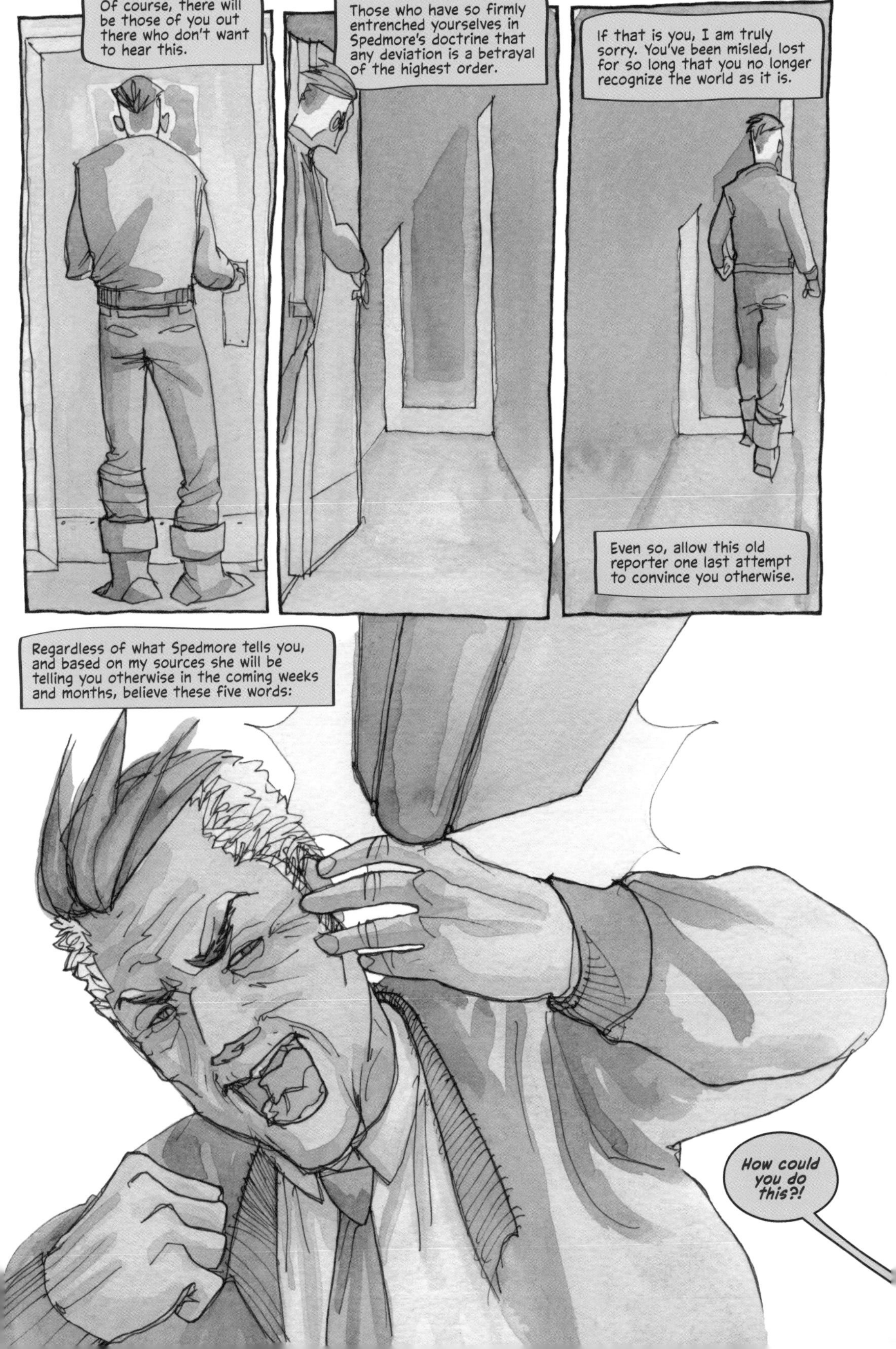
Of course, there will be those of you out there who don't want to hear this.
Those who have so firmly entrenched yourselves in Spedmore's doctrine that any deviation is a betrayal of the highest order.
If that is you, I am truly sorry. You've been misled, lost for so long that you no longer recognize the world as it is.
Even so, allow this old reporter one last attempt to convince you otherwise.
Regardless of what Spedmore tells you, and based on my sources she will be telling you otherwise in the coming weeks and months, believe these five words:
How could you do this?!

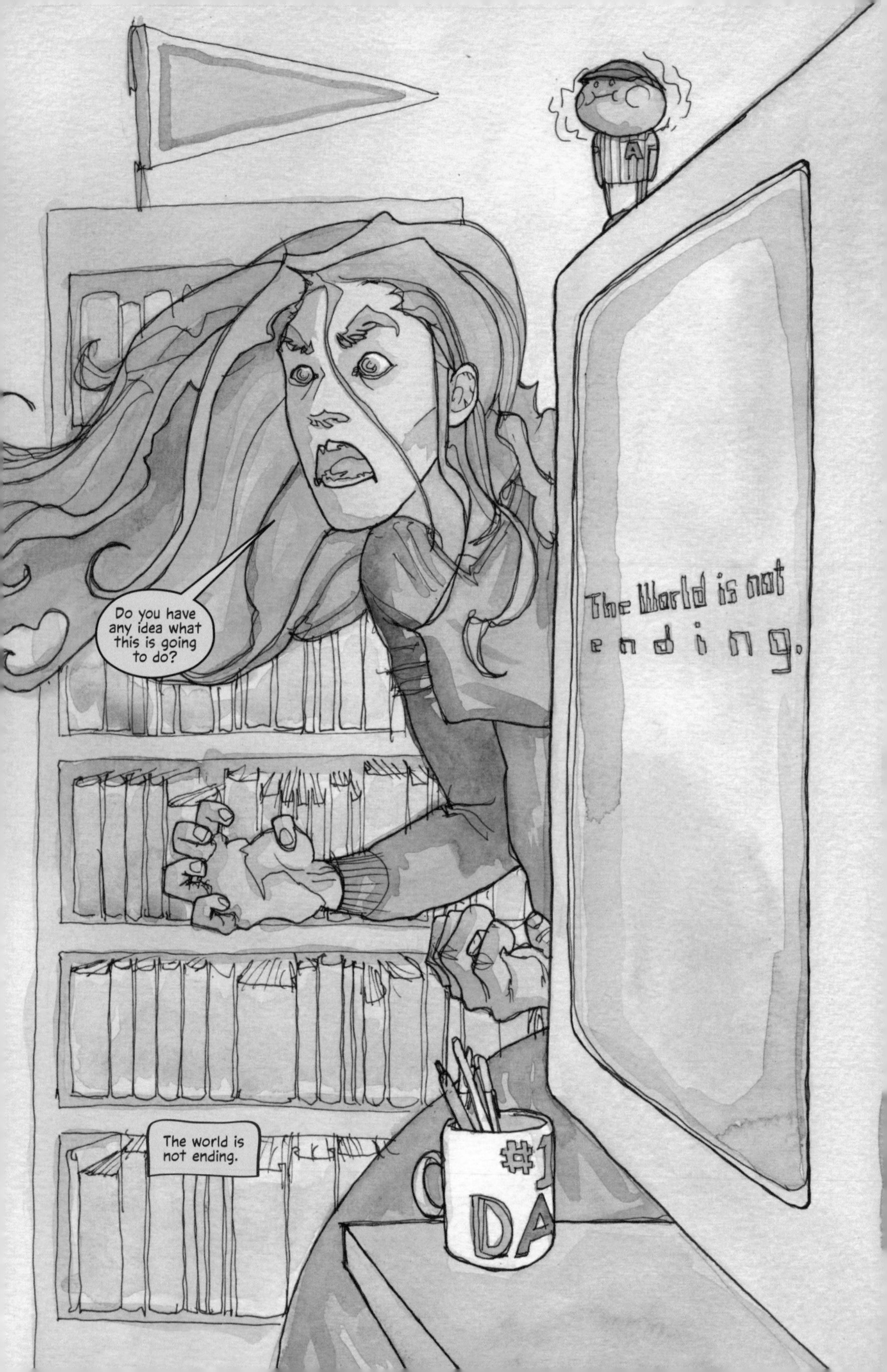
Do you have any idea what this is going to do?
The World is not ending.
The world is not ending.
#1 DA

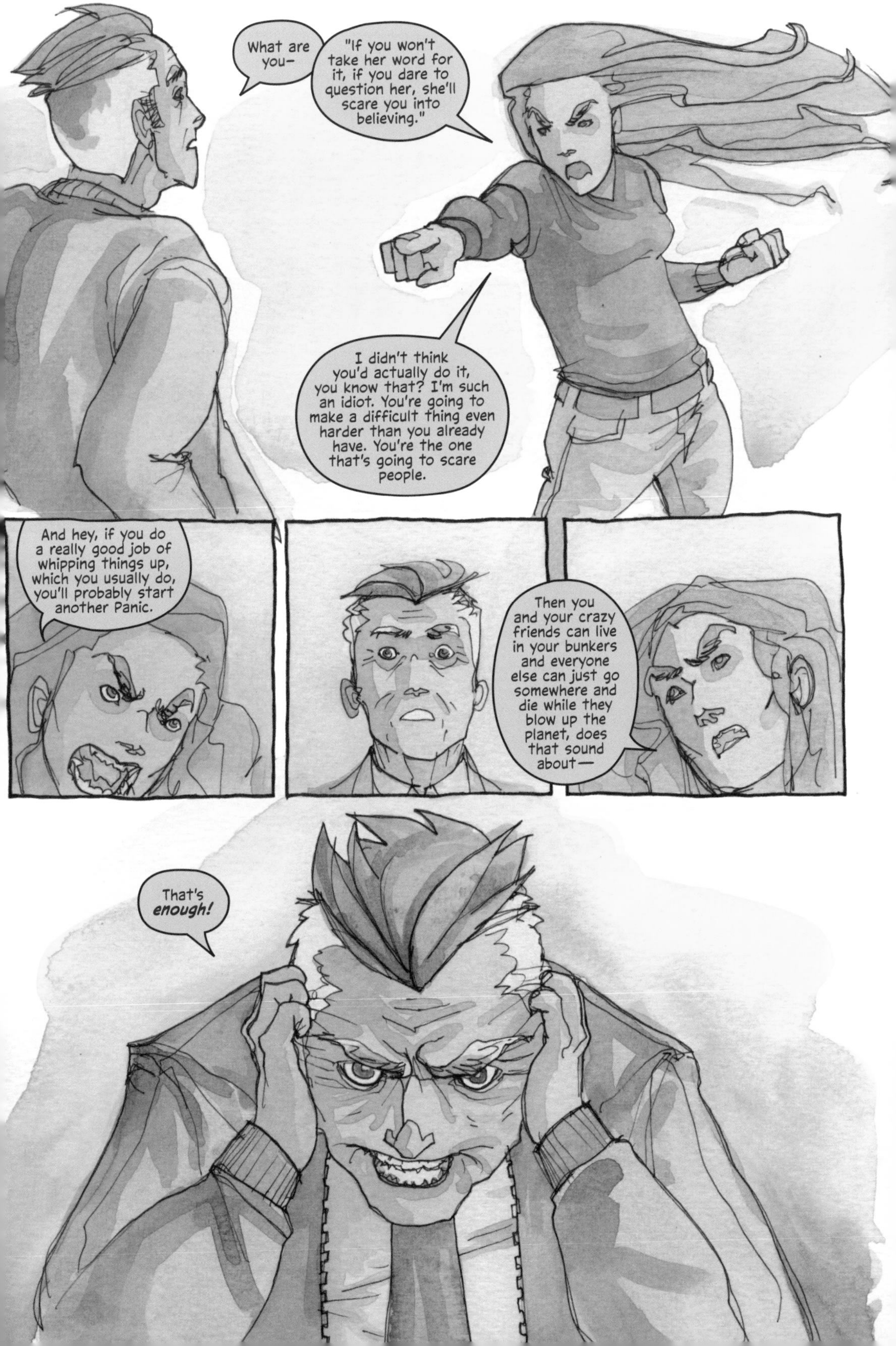
What are you—
"If you won't take her word for it, if you dare to question her, she'll scare you into believing."
I didn't think you'd actually do it, you know that? I'm such an idiot. You're going to make a difficult thing even harder than you already have. You're the one that's going to scare people.
And hey, if you do a really good job of whipping things up, which you usually do, you'll probably start another Panic.
Then you and your crazy friends can live in your bunkers and everyone else can just go somewhere and die while they blow up the planet, does that sound about—
That's *enough!*

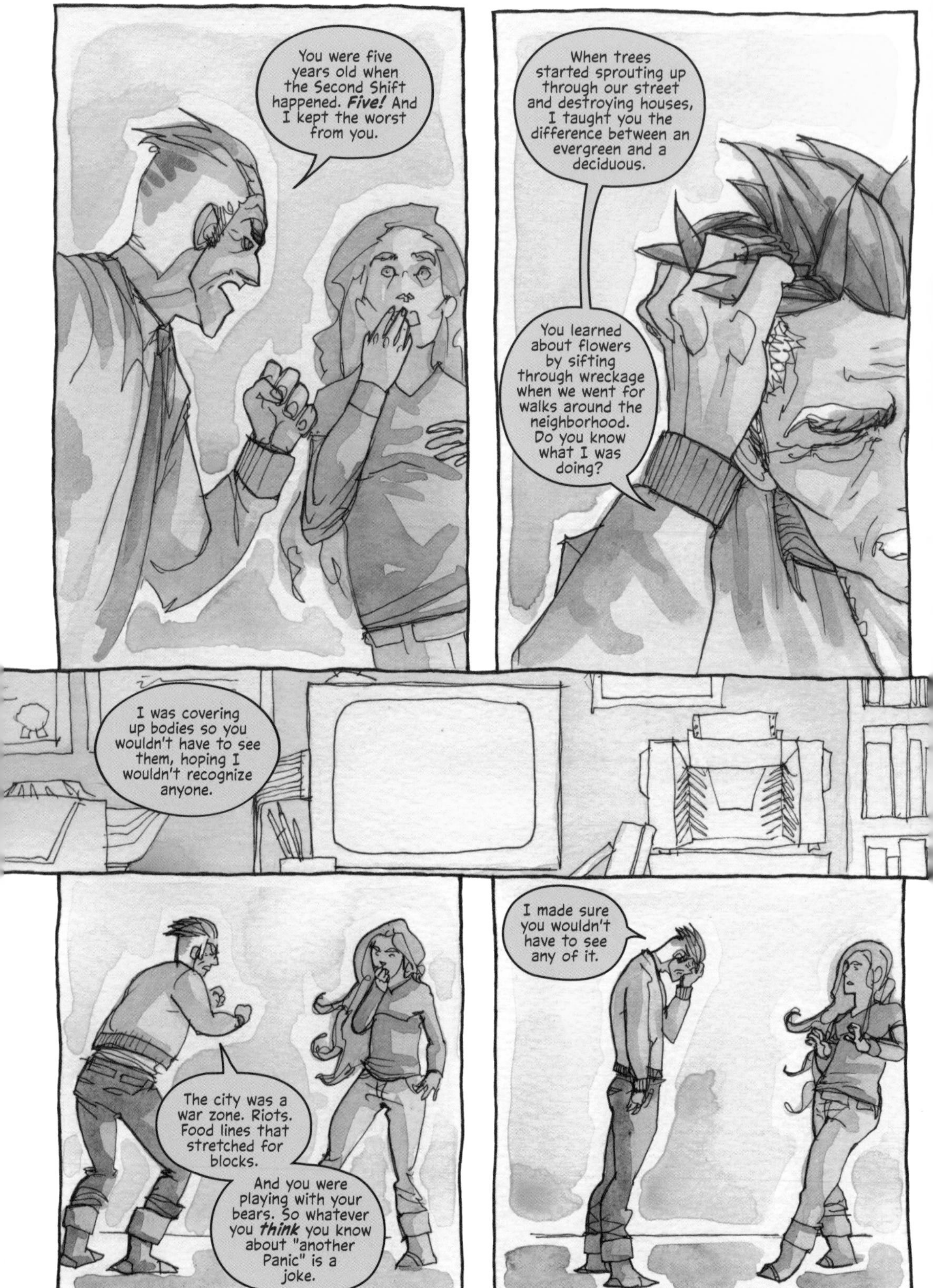
You were five years old when the Second Shift happened. *Five!* And I kept the worst from you.
When trees started sprouting up through our street and destroying houses, I taught you the difference between an evergreen and a deciduous.
You learned about flowers by sifting through wreckage when we went for walks around the neighborhood. Do you know what I was doing?
I was covering up bodies so you wouldn't have to see them, hoping I wouldn't recognize anyone.
The city was a war zone. Riots. Food lines that stretched for blocks.
And you were playing with your bears. So whatever you *think* you know about "another Panic" is a joke.
I made sure you wouldn't have to see any of it.

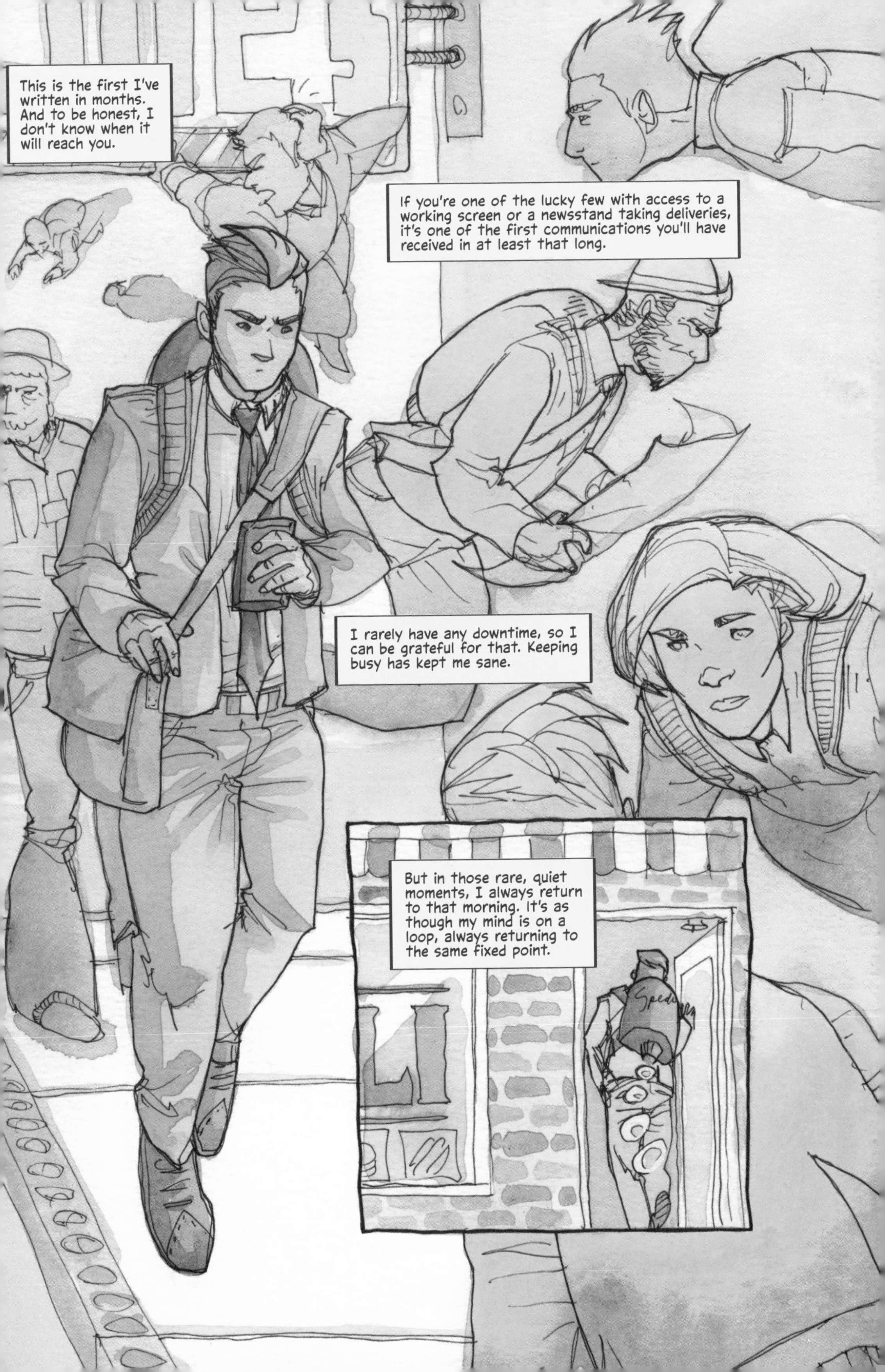
This is the first I've written in months. And to be honest, I don't know when it will reach you.
If you're one of the lucky few with access to a working screen or a newsstand taking deliveries, it's one of the first communications you'll have received in at least that long.
I rarely have any downtime, so I can be grateful for that. Keeping busy has kept me sane.
But in those rare, quiet moments, I always return to that morning. It's as though my mind is on a loop, always returning to the same fixed point.

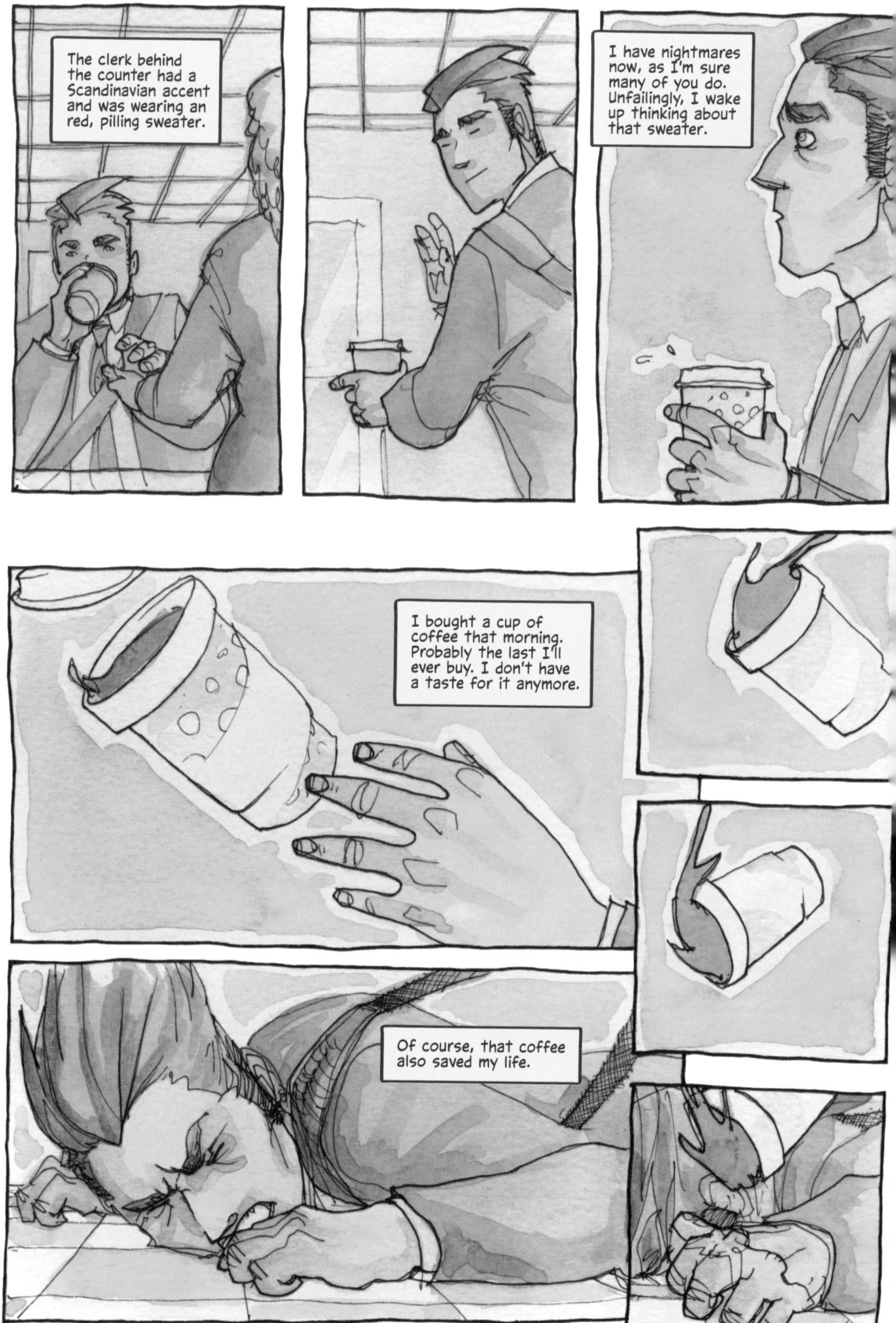

The clerk behind the counter had a Scandinavian accent and was wearing an red, pilling sweater.
I have nightmares now, as I'm sure many of you do. Unfailingly, I wake up thinking about that sweater.
I bought a cup of coffee that morning. Probably the last I'll ever buy. I don't have a taste for it anymore.
Of course, that coffee also saved my life.

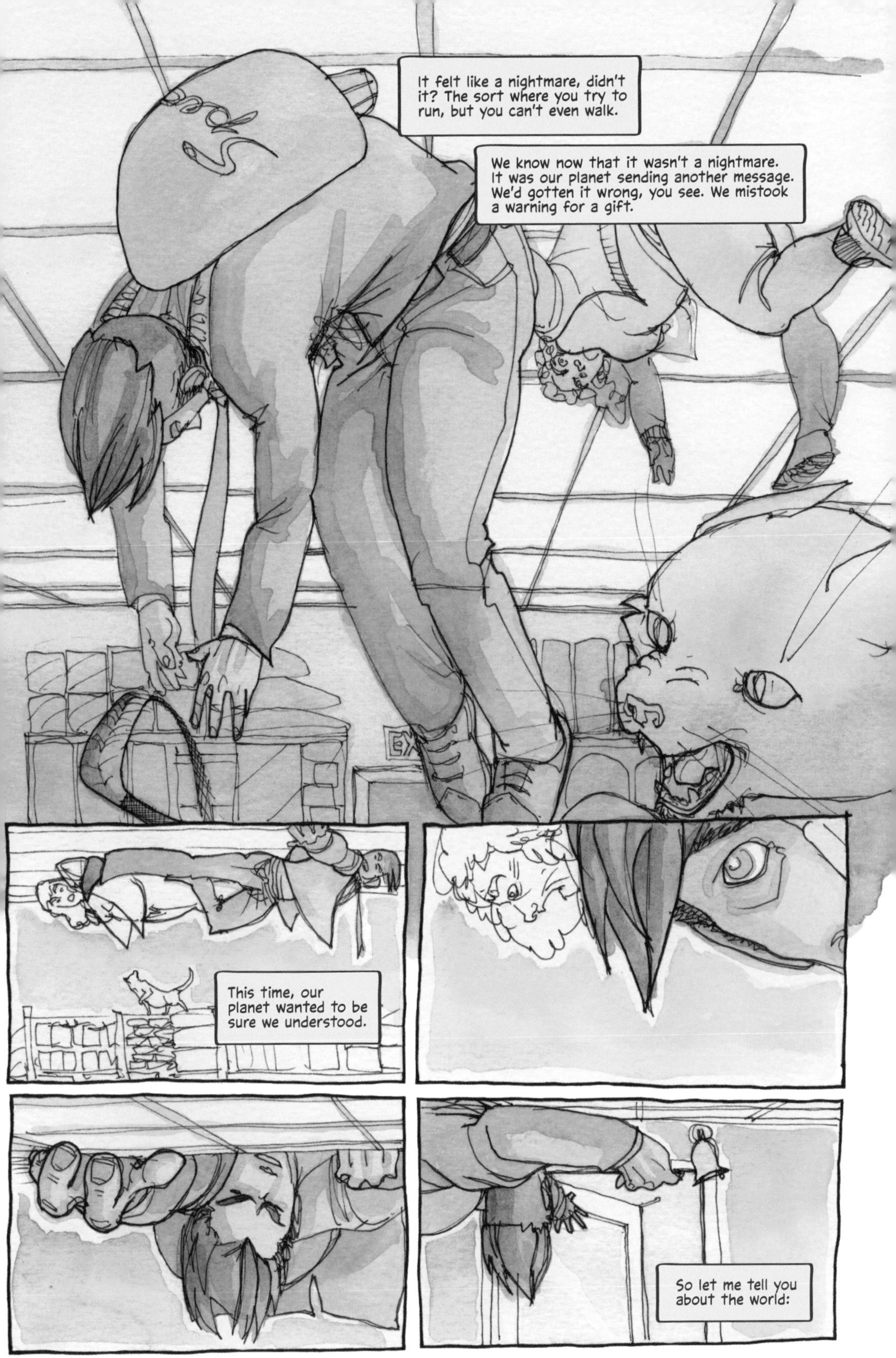
It felt like a nightmare, didn't it? The sort where you try to run, but you can't even walk.
We know now that it wasn't a nightmare. It was our planet sending another message. We'd gotten it wrong, you see. We mistook a warning for a gift.
This time, our planet wanted to be sure we understood.
So let me tell you about the world:

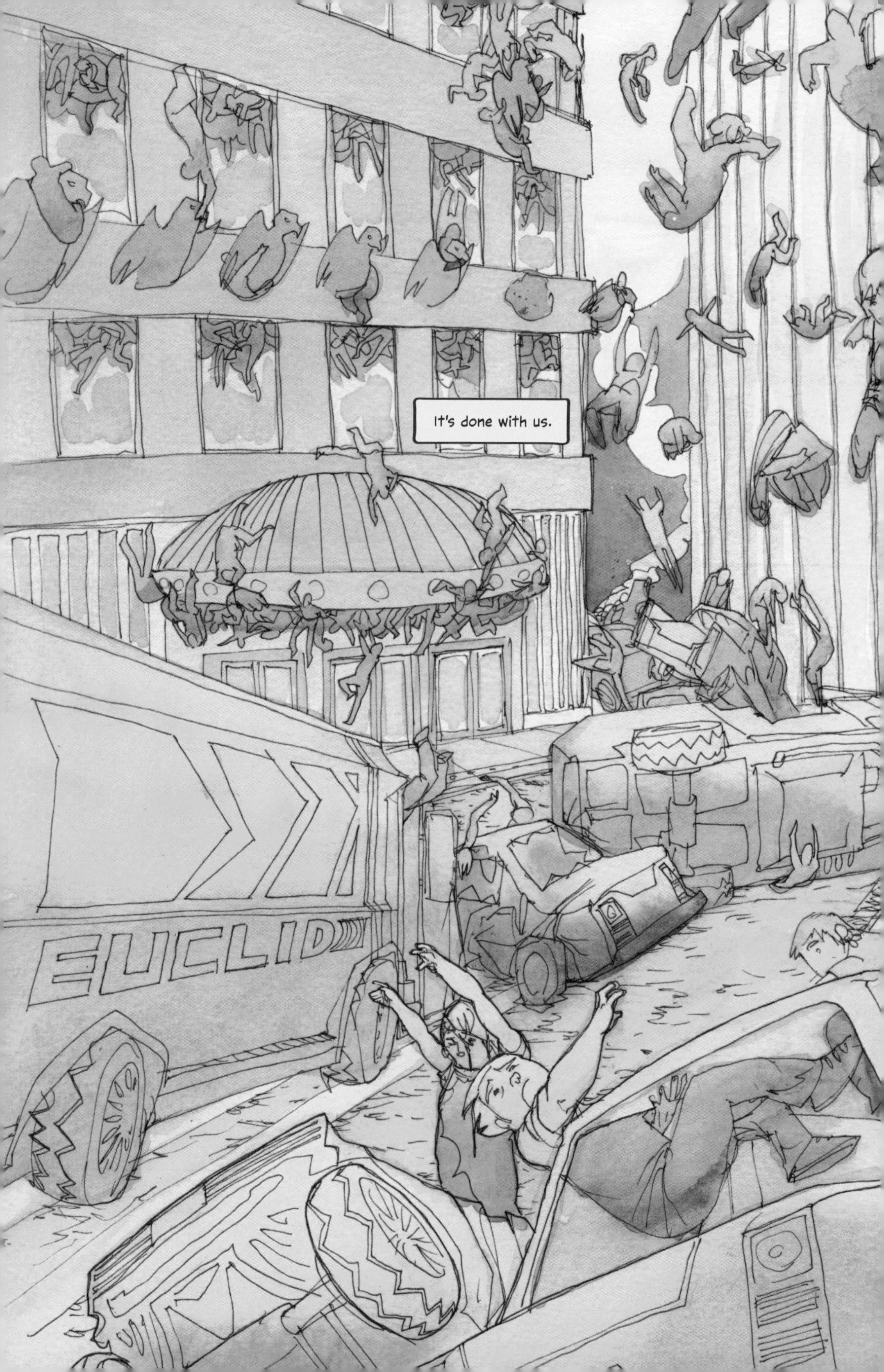
It's done with us.
EUCLID

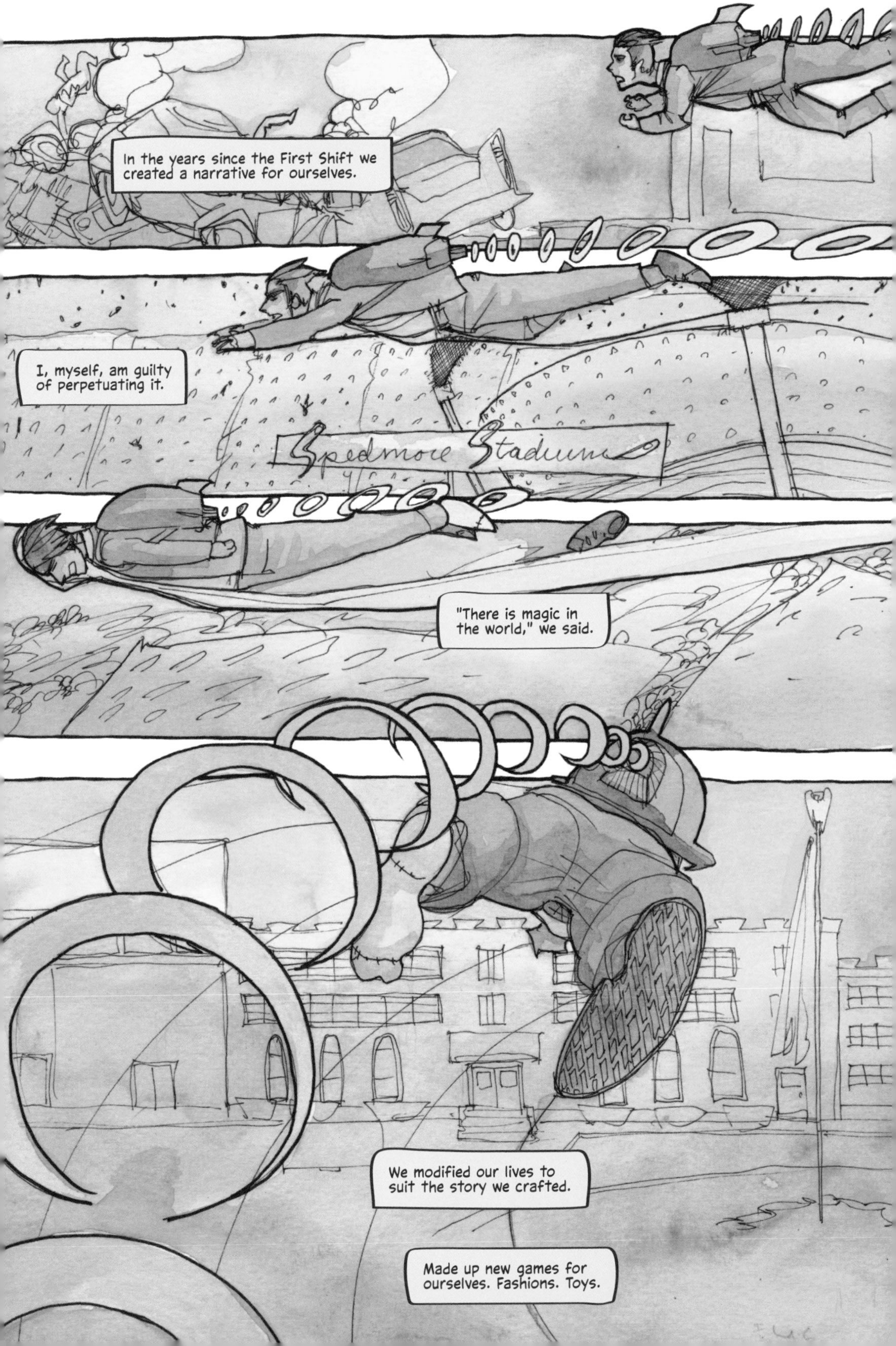

In the years since the First Shift we created a narrative for ourselves.
I, myself, am guilty of perpetuating it.
"There is magic in the world," we said.
We modified our lives to suit the story we crafted.
Made up new games for ourselves. Fashions. Toys.

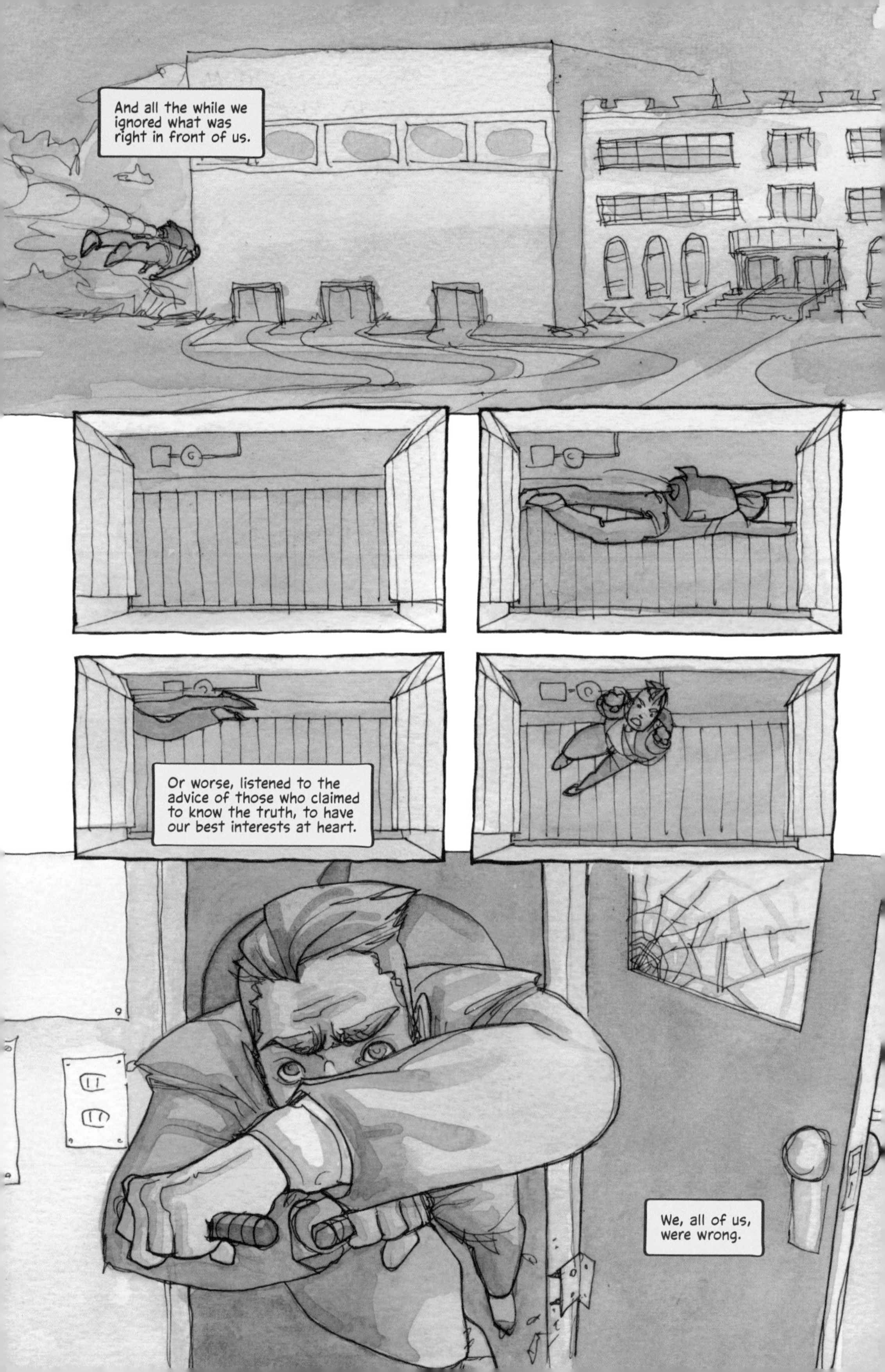
And all the while we ignored what was right in front of us.
Or worse, listened to the advice of those who claimed to know the truth, to have our best interests at heart.
We, all of us, were wrong.

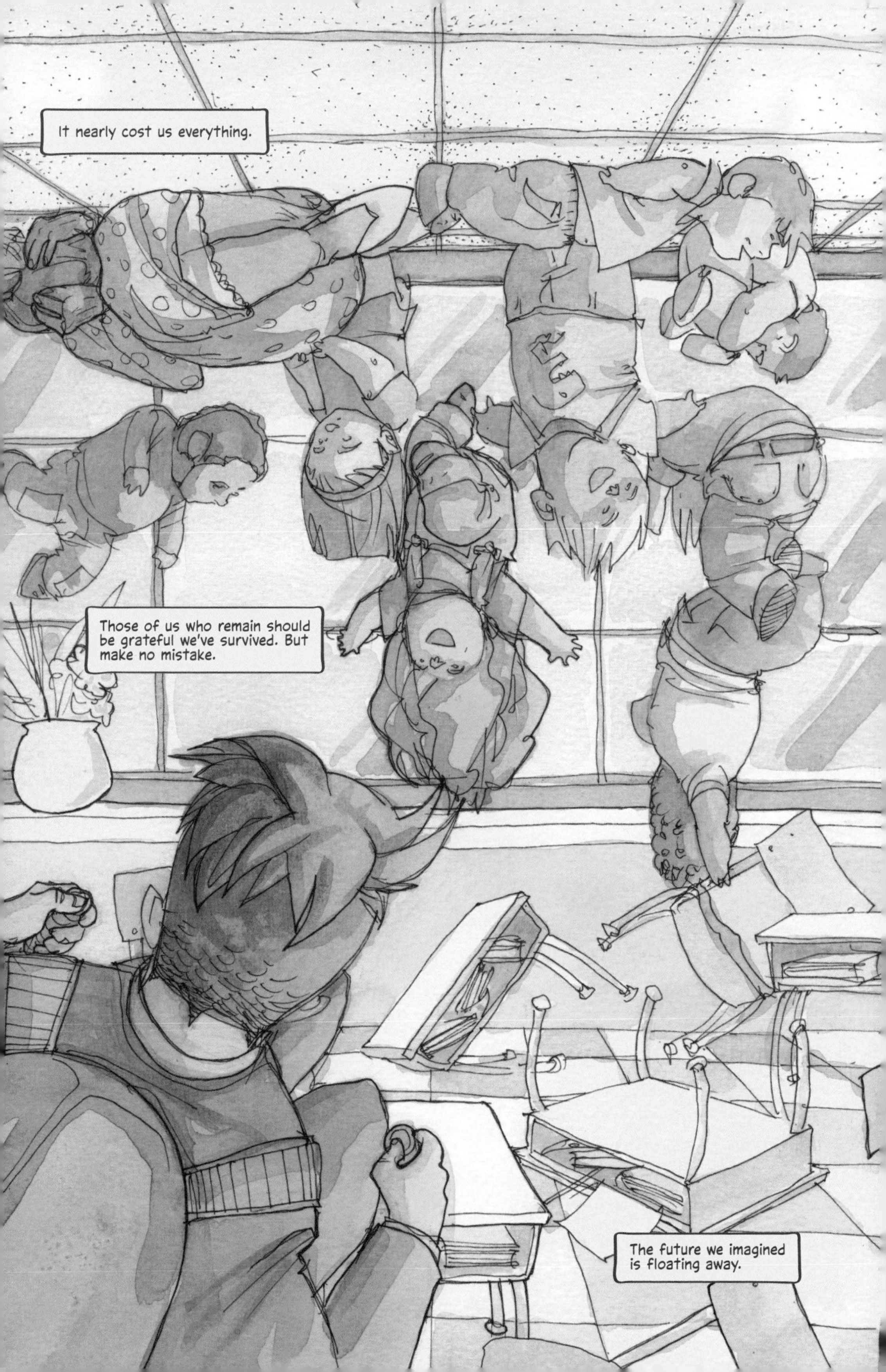
It nearly cost us everything.
Those of us who remain should be grateful we've survived. But make no mistake.
The future we imagined is floating away.

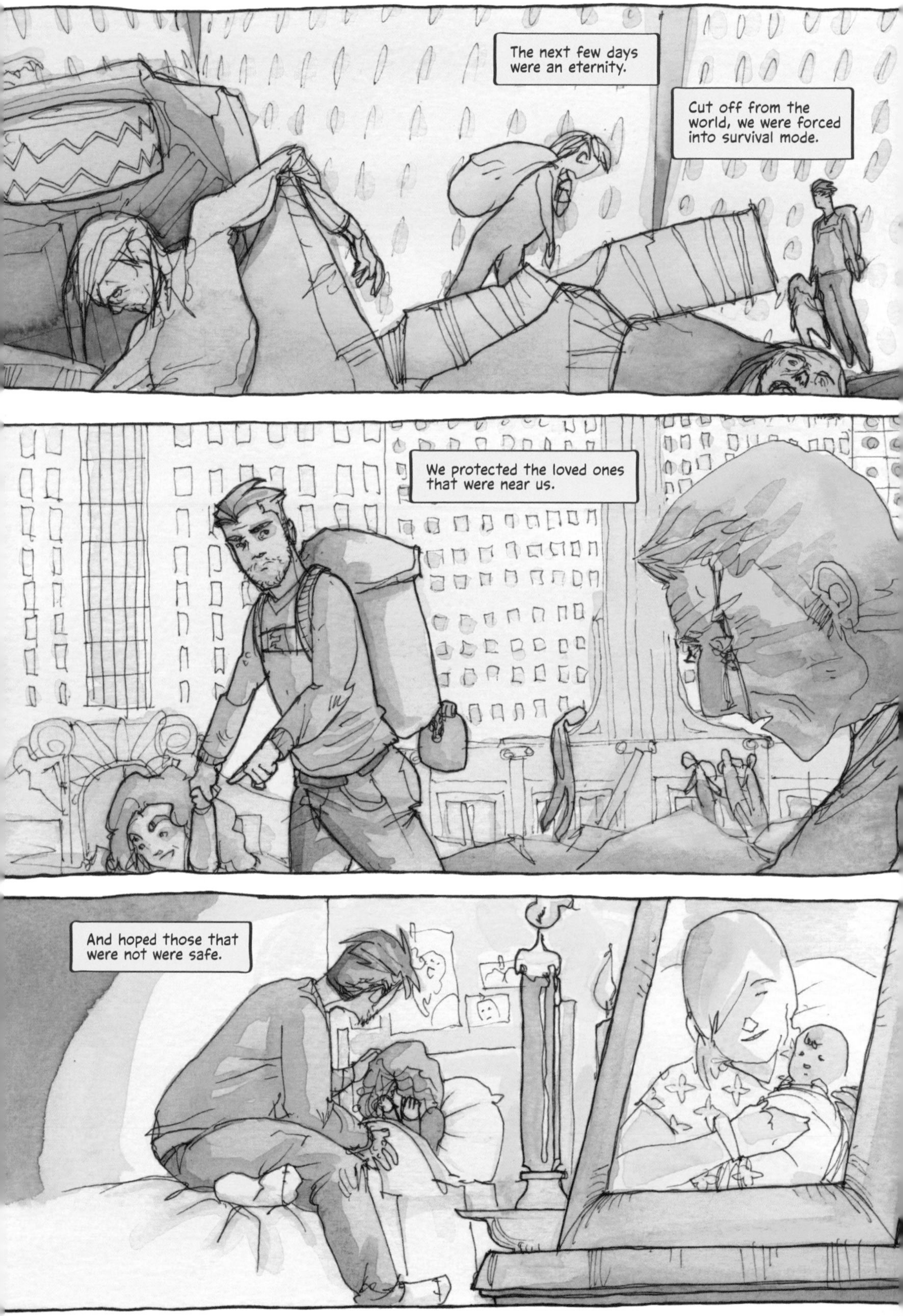
The next few days were an eternity.
Cut off from the world, we were forced into survival mode.
We protected the loved ones that were near us.
And hoped those that were not were safe.

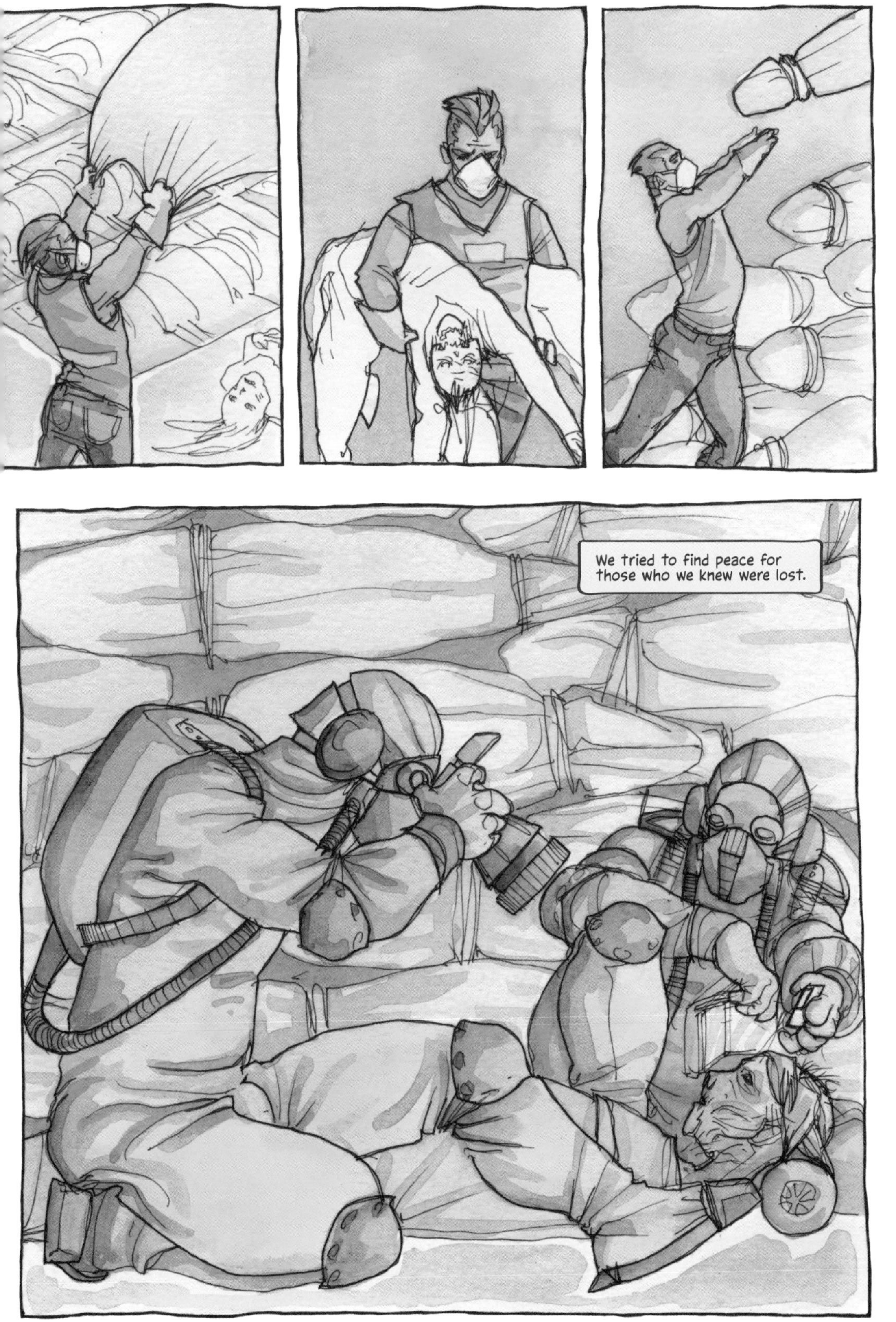
We tried to find peace for those who we knew were lost.

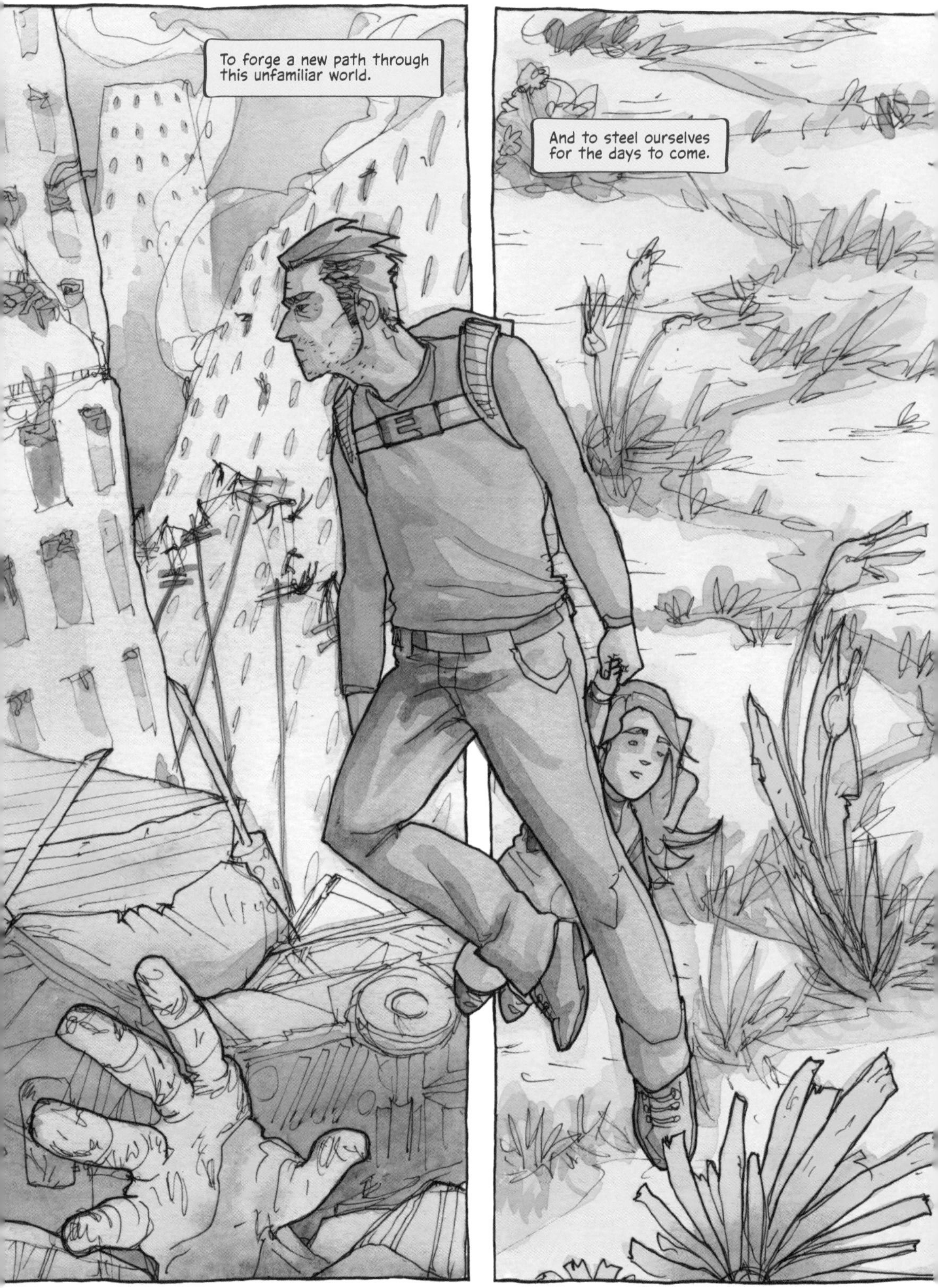
To forge a new path through this unfamiliar world.
And to steel ourselves for the days to come.

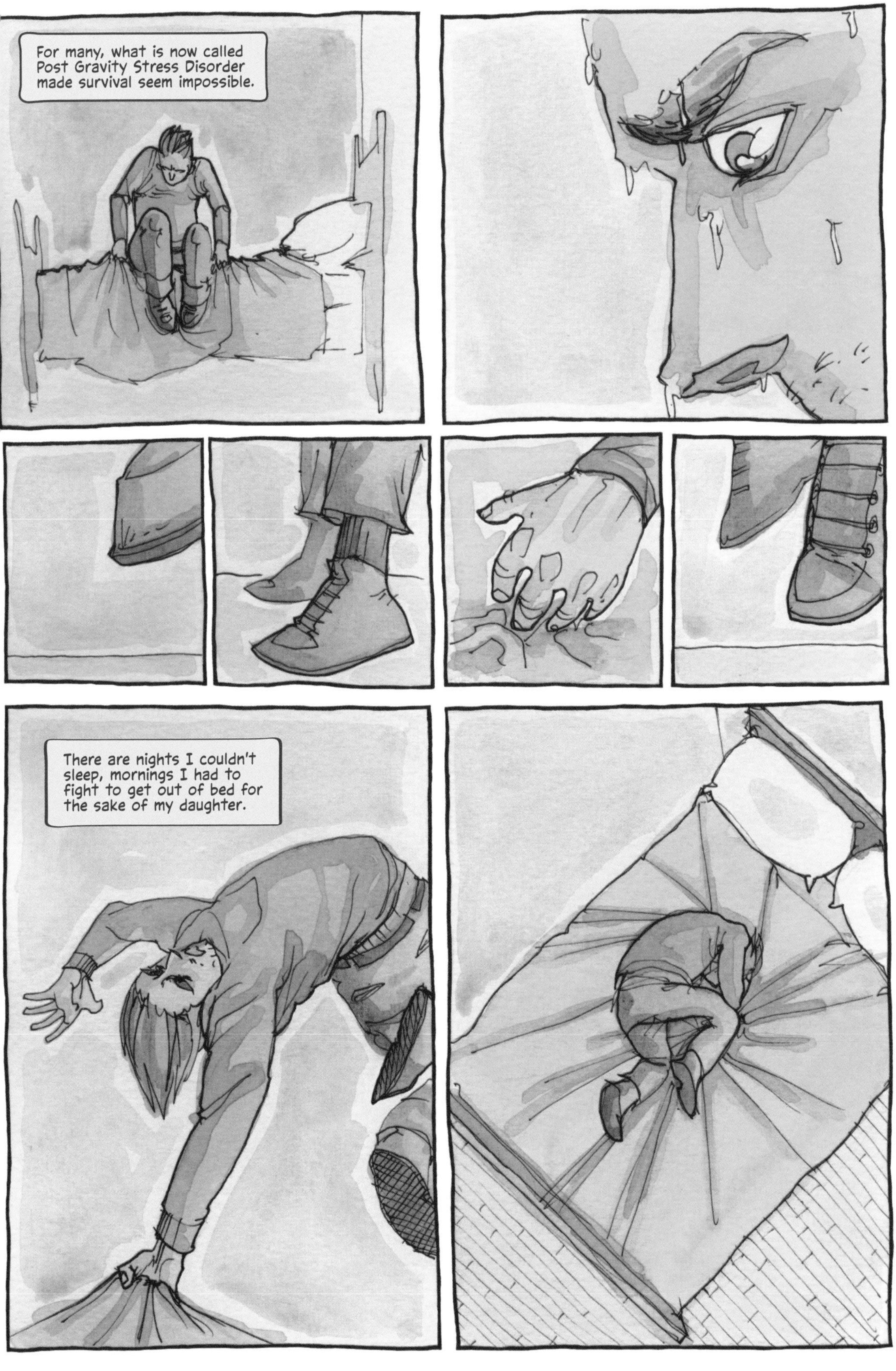
For many, what is now called Post Gravity Stress Disorder made survival seem impossible.
There are nights I couldn't sleep, mornings I had to fight to get out of bed for the sake of my daughter.

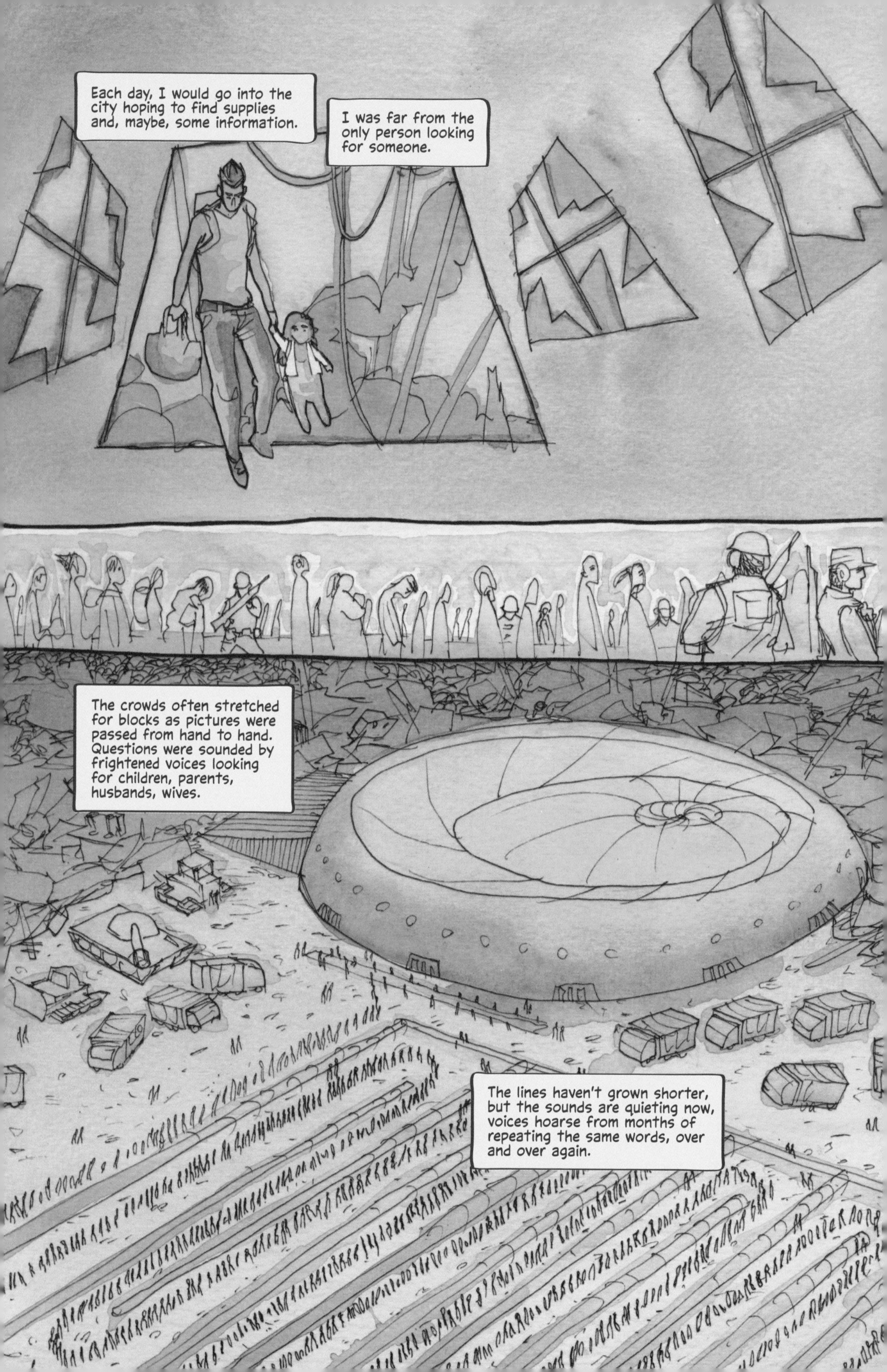

Each day, I would go into the city hoping to find supplies and, maybe, some information.
I was far from the only person looking for someone.
The crowds often stretched for blocks as pictures were passed from hand to hand. Questions were sounded by frightened voices looking for children, parents, husbands, wives.
The lines haven't grown shorter, but the sounds are quieting now, voices hoarse from months of repeating the same words, over and over again.

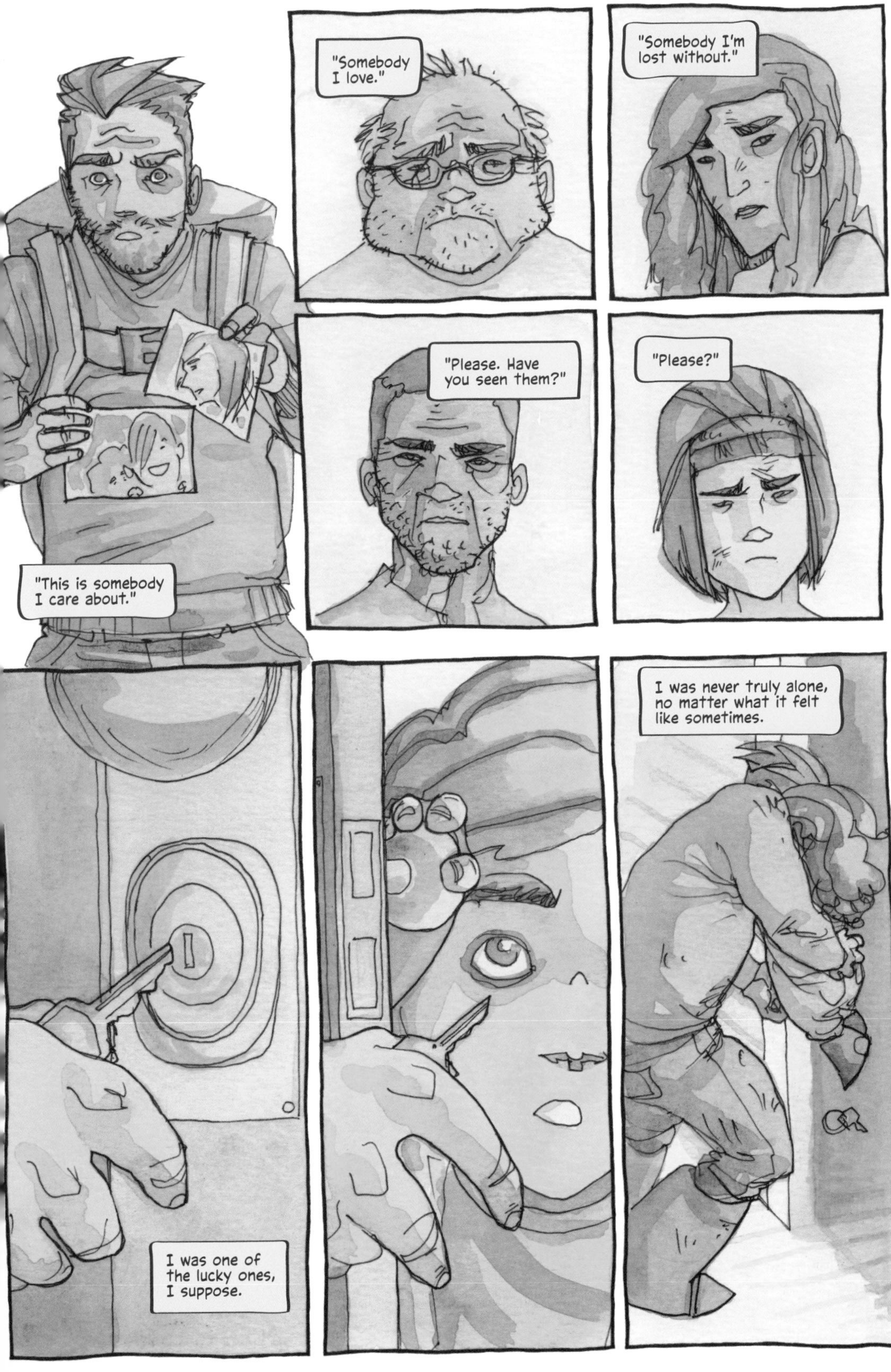
"This is somebody I care about."
"Somebody I love."
"Somebody I'm lost without."
"Please. Have you seen them?"
"Please?"
I was one of the lucky ones, I suppose.
I was never truly alone, no matter what it felt like sometimes.

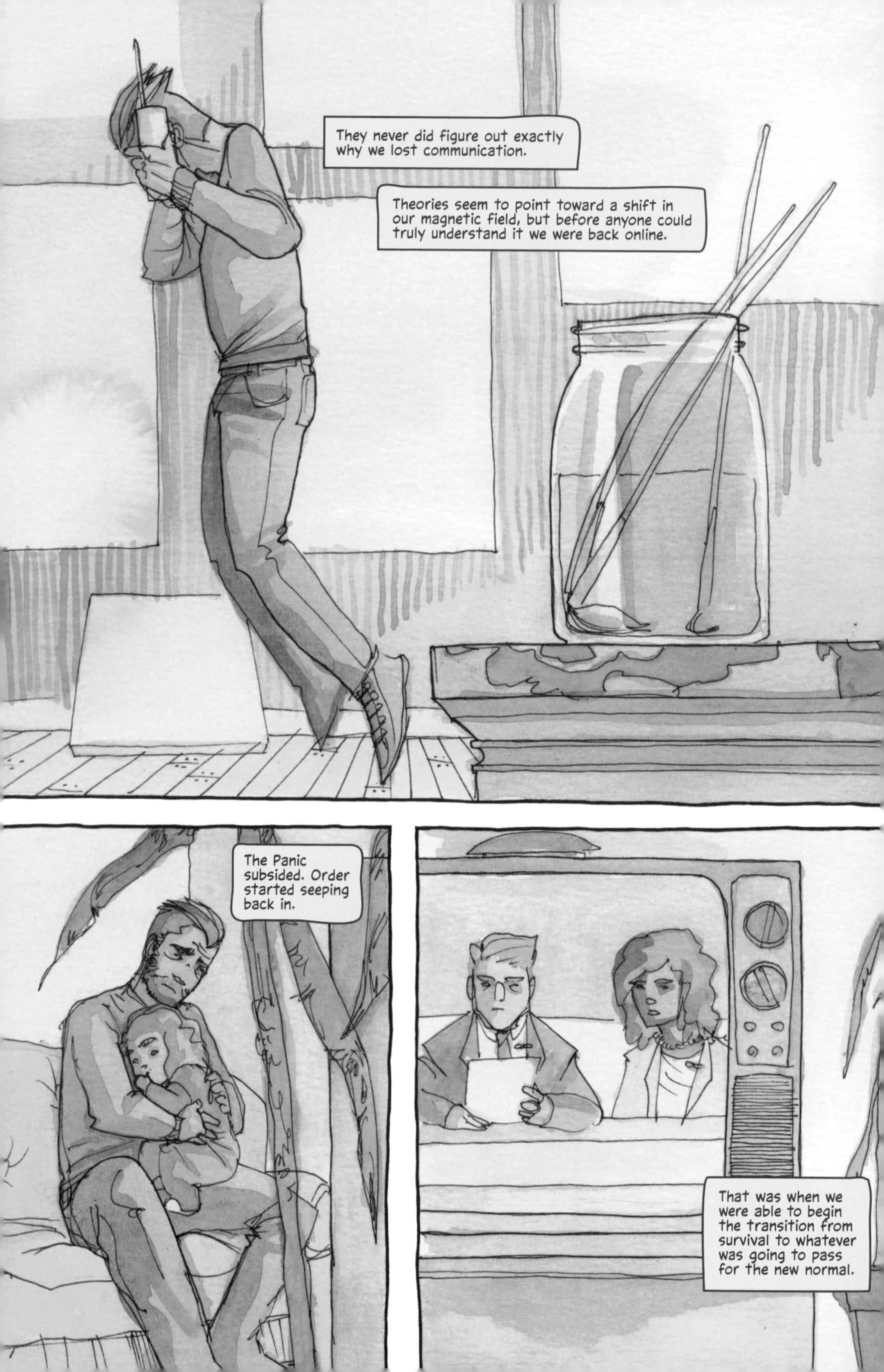
They never did figure out exactly why we lost communication.
Theories seem to point toward a shift in our magnetic field, but before anyone could truly understand it we were back online.
The Panic subsided. Order started seeping back in.
That was when we were able to begin the transition from survival to whatever was going to pass for the new normal.

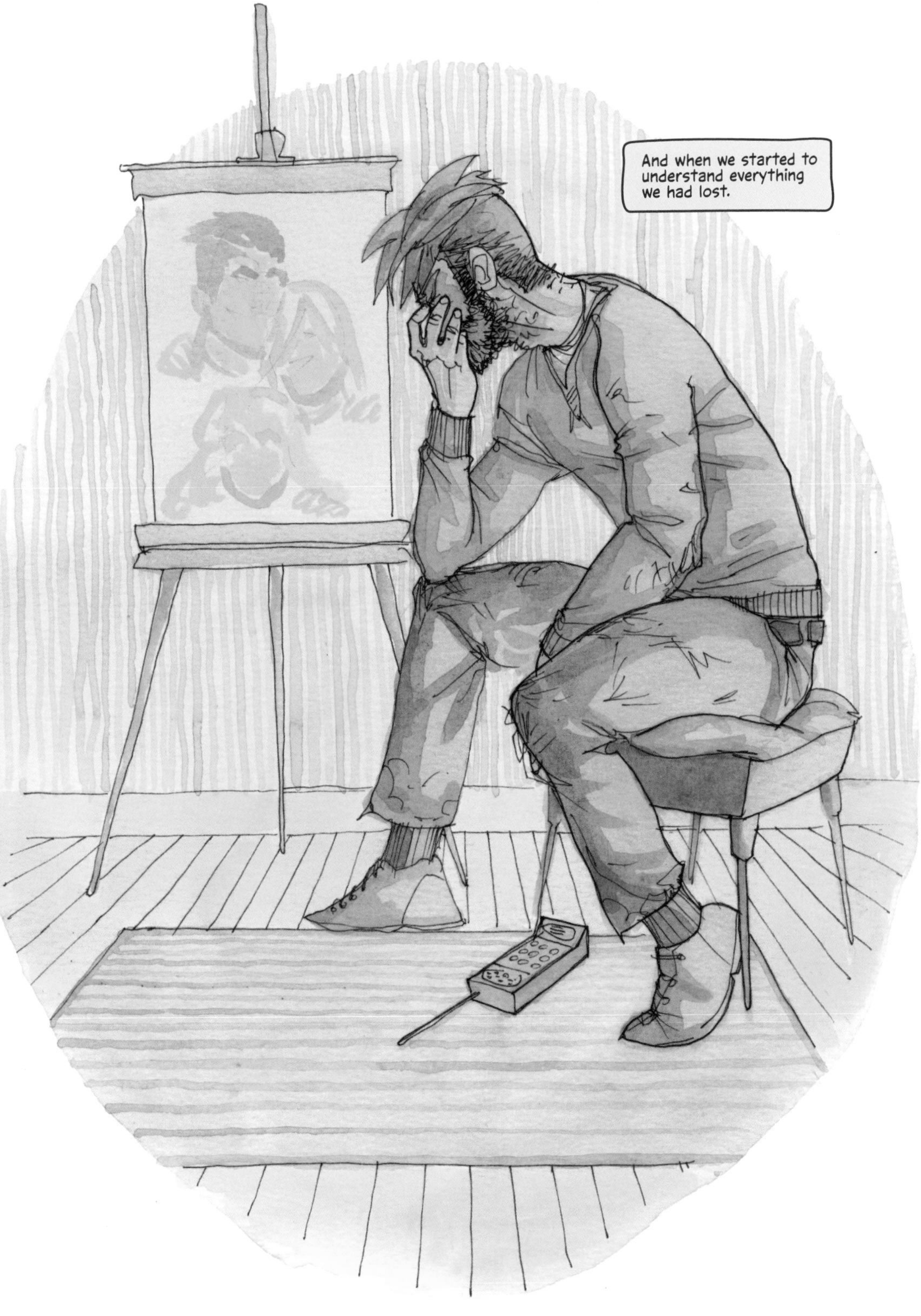
And when we started to understand everything we had lost.

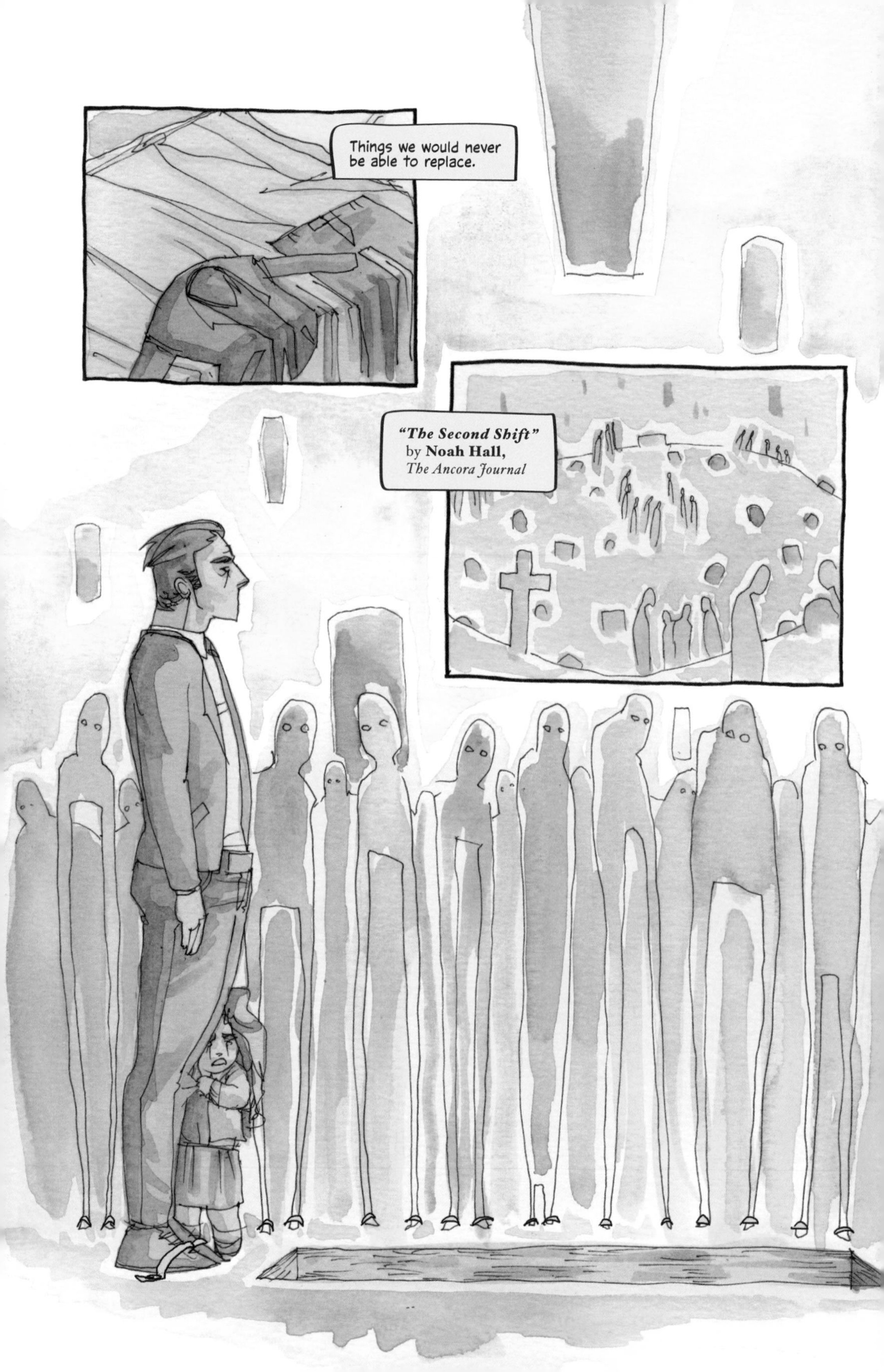
Things we would never be able to replace.
"The Second Shift" by Noah Hall, The Ancora Journal

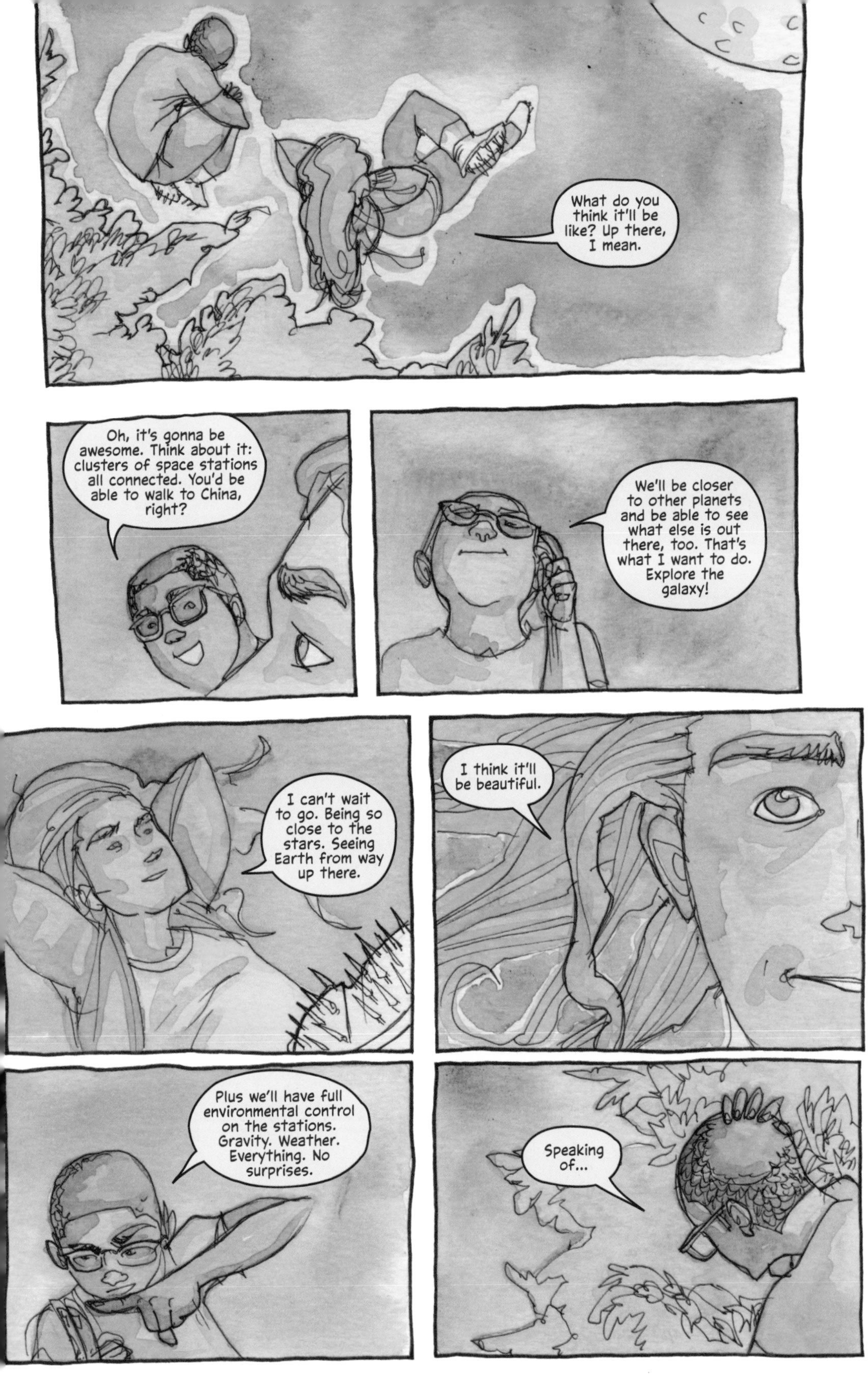
What do you think it'll be like? Up there, I mean.
Oh, it's gonna be awesome. Think about it: clusters of space stations all connected. You'd be able to walk to China, right?
We'll be closer to other planets and be able to see what else is out there, too. That's what I want to do. Explore the galaxy!
I can't wait to go. Being so close to the stars. Seeing Earth from way up there.
I think it'll be beautiful.
Plus we'll have full environmental control on the stations. Gravity. Weather. Everything. No surprises.
Speaking of...

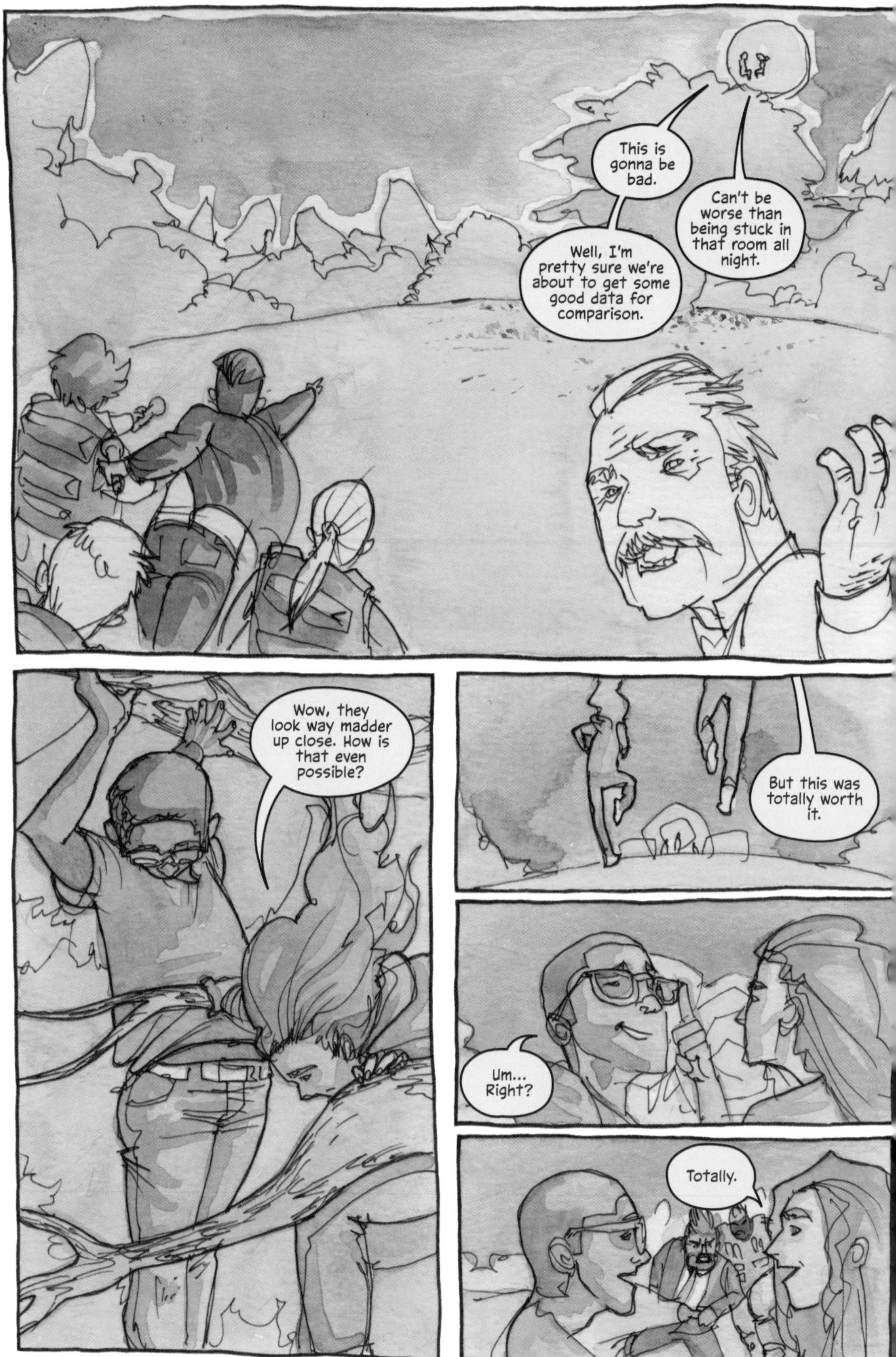
This is gonna be bad.
Can't be worse than being stuck in that room all night.
Well, I'm pretty sure we're about to get some good data for comparison.
Wow, they look way madder up close. How is that even possible?
But this was totally worth it.
Um... Right?
Totally.

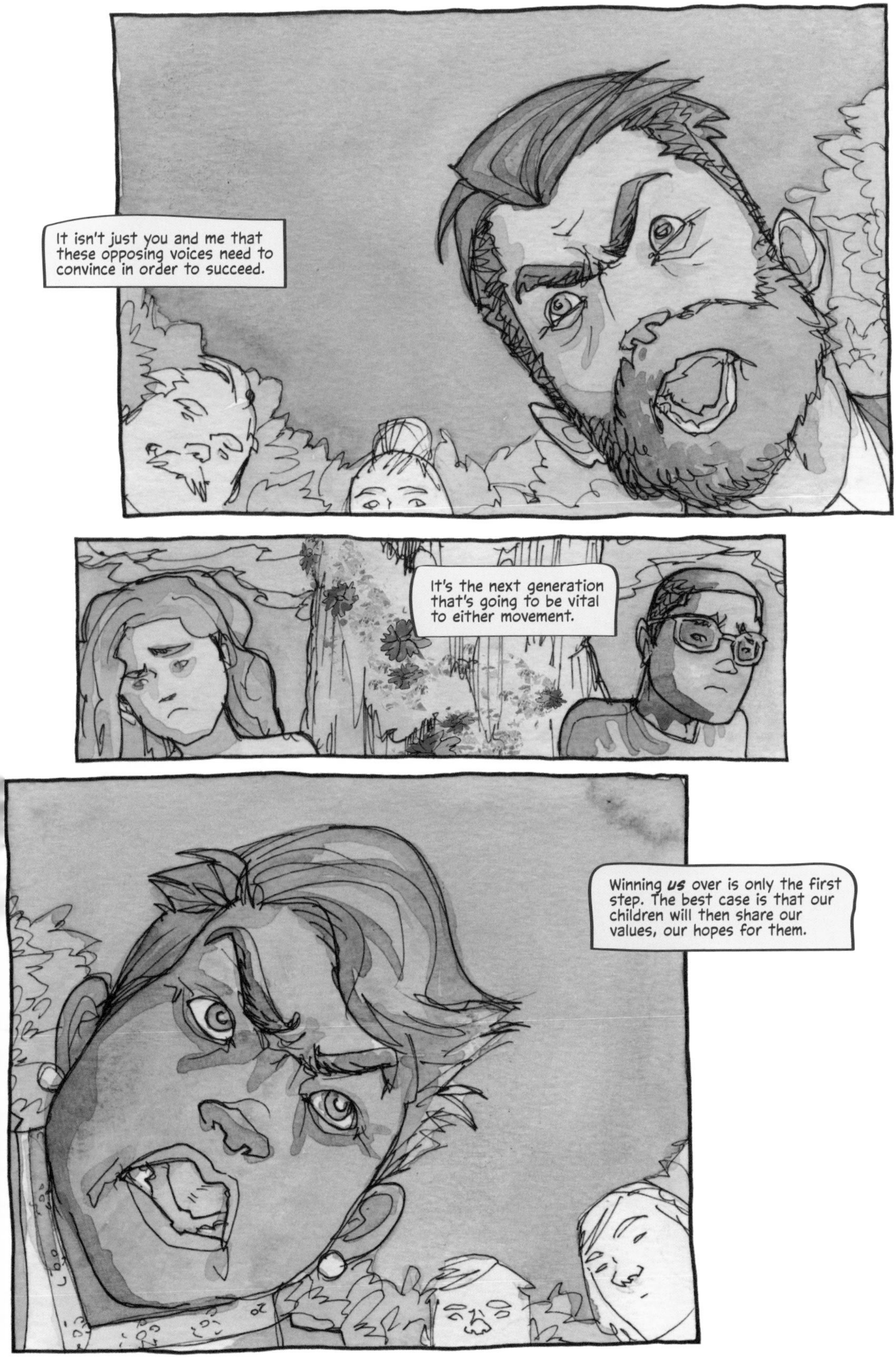

It isn't just you and me that these opposing voices need to convince in order to succeed.
It's the next generation that's going to be vital to either movement.
Winning *us* over is only the first step. The best case is that our children will then share our values, our hopes for them.

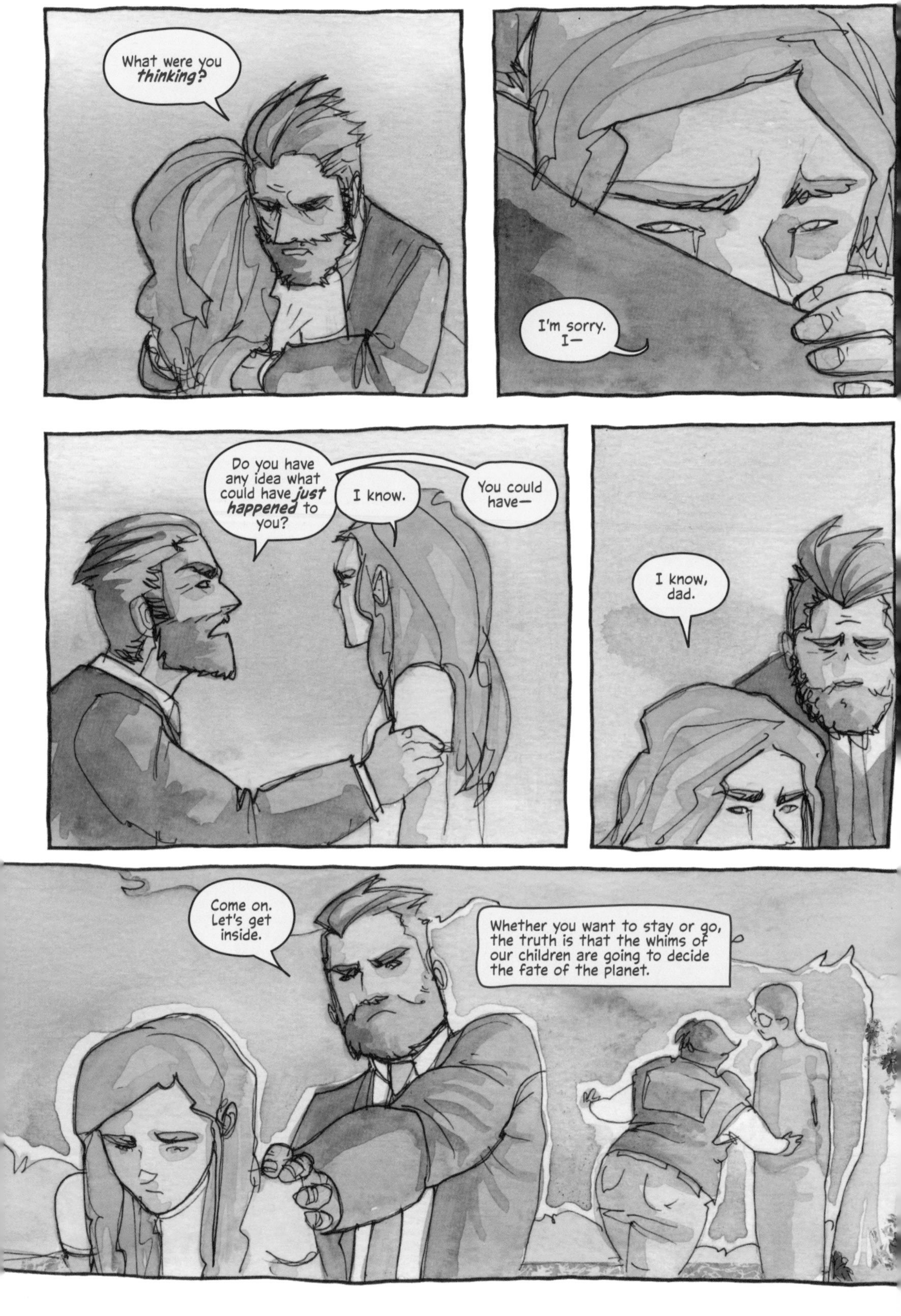

What were you *thinking?*
I'm sorry. I—
Do you have any idea what could have *just happened* to you?
I know.
You could have—
I know, dad.
Come on. Let's get inside.
Whether you want to stay or go, the truth is that the whims of our children are going to decide the fate of the planet.

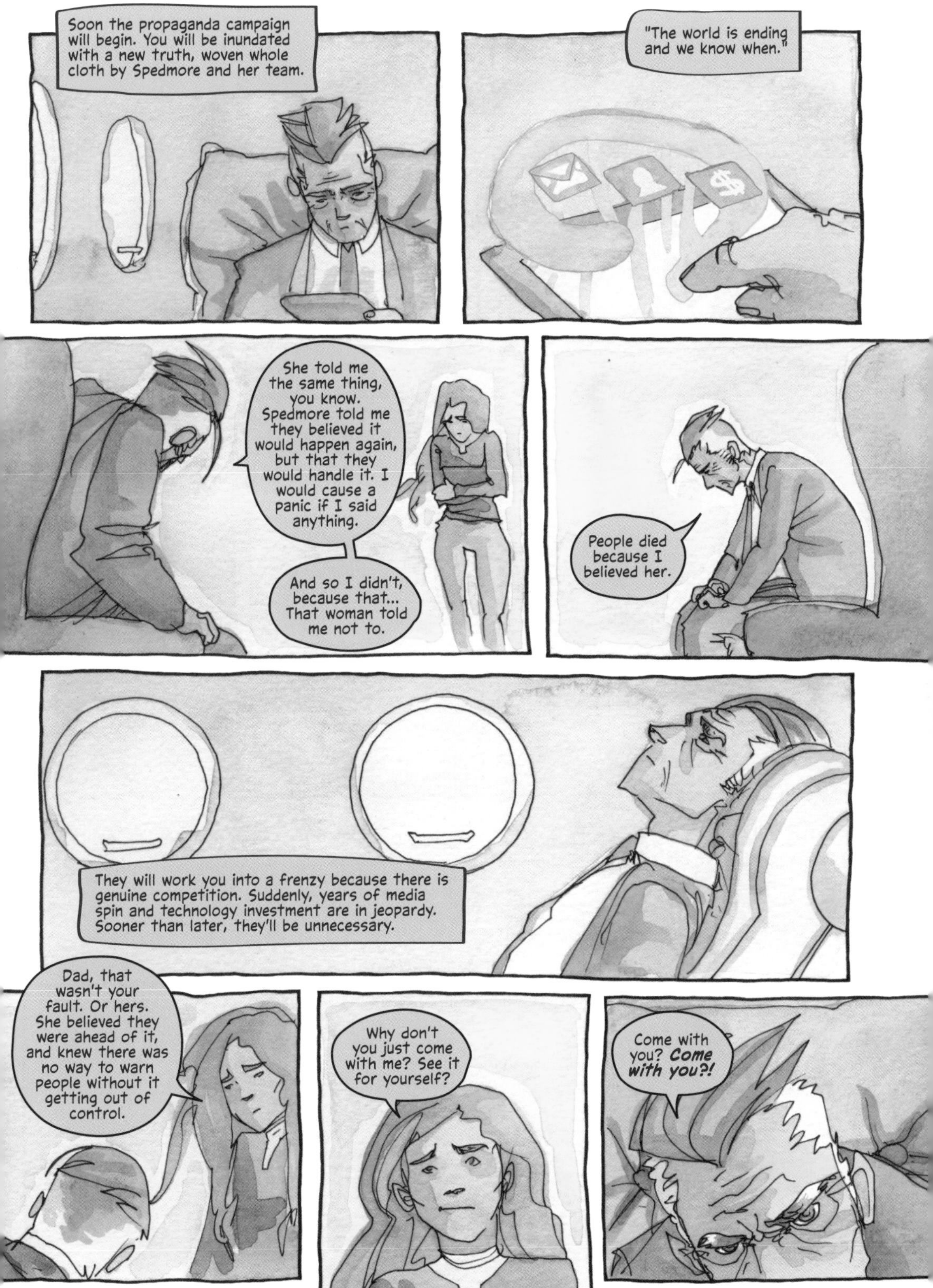
Soon the propaganda campaign will begin. You will be inundated with a new truth, woven whole cloth by Spedmore and her team.
"The world is ending and we know when."
She told me the same thing, you know. Spedmore told me they believed it would happen again, but that they would handle it. I would cause a panic if I said anything.
And so I didn't, because that... That woman told me not to.
People died because I believed her.
They will work you into a frenzy because there is genuine competition. Suddenly, years of media spin and technology investment are in jeopardy. Sooner than later, they'll be unnecessary.
Dad, that wasn't your fault. Or hers. She believed they were ahead of it, and knew there was no way to warn people without it getting out of control.
Why don't you just come with me? See it for yourself?
Come with you? **Come with you?!**

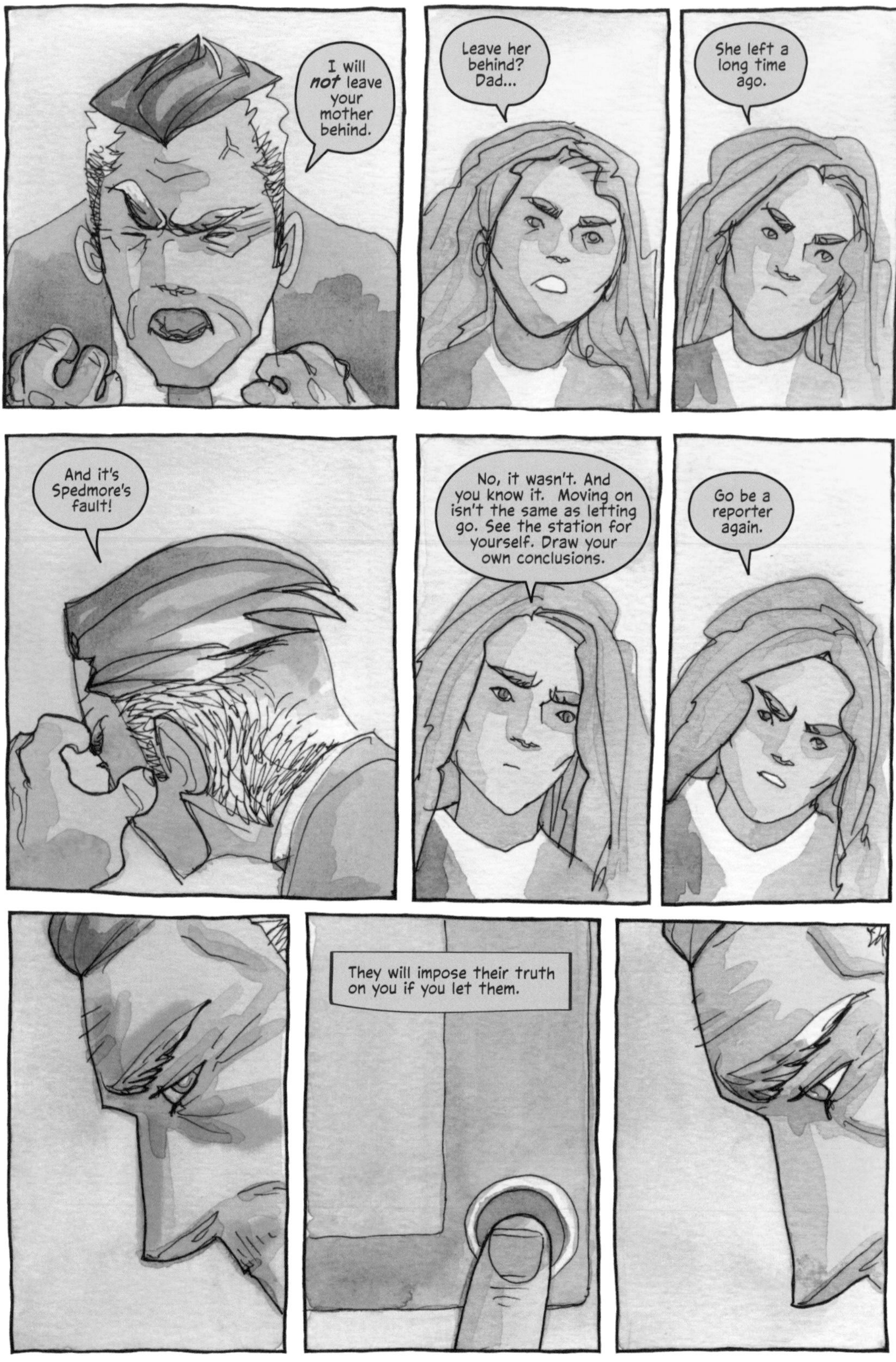
I will *not* leave your mother behind.
Leave her behind? Dad...
She left a long time ago.
And it's Spedmore's fault!
No, it wasn't. And you know it. Moving on isn't the same as letting go. See the station for yourself. Draw your own conclusions.
Go be a reporter again.
They will impose their truth on you if you let them.

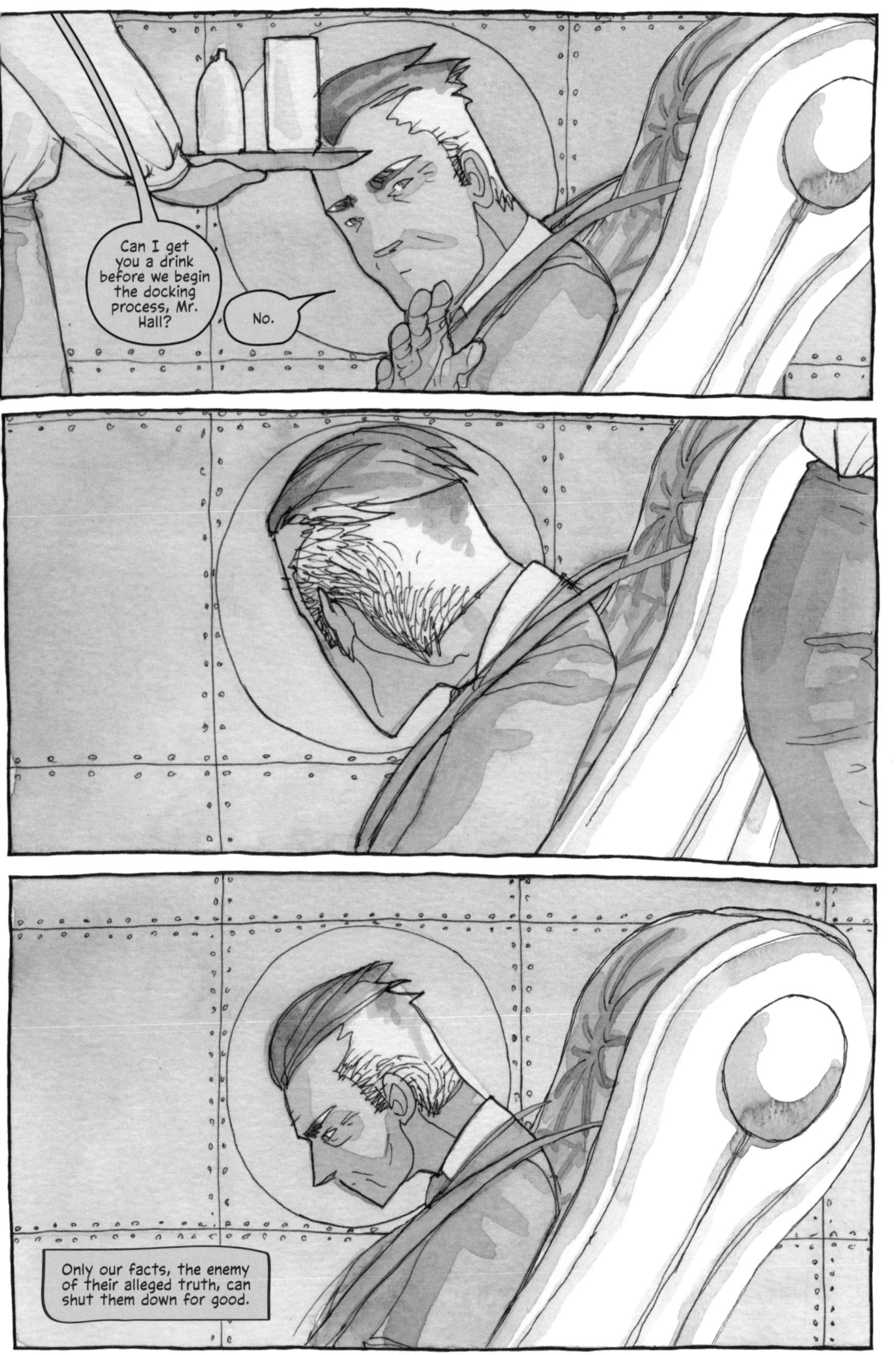
Can I get you a drink before we begin the docking process, Mr. Hall?
No.
Only our facts, the enemy of their alleged truth, can shut them down for good.

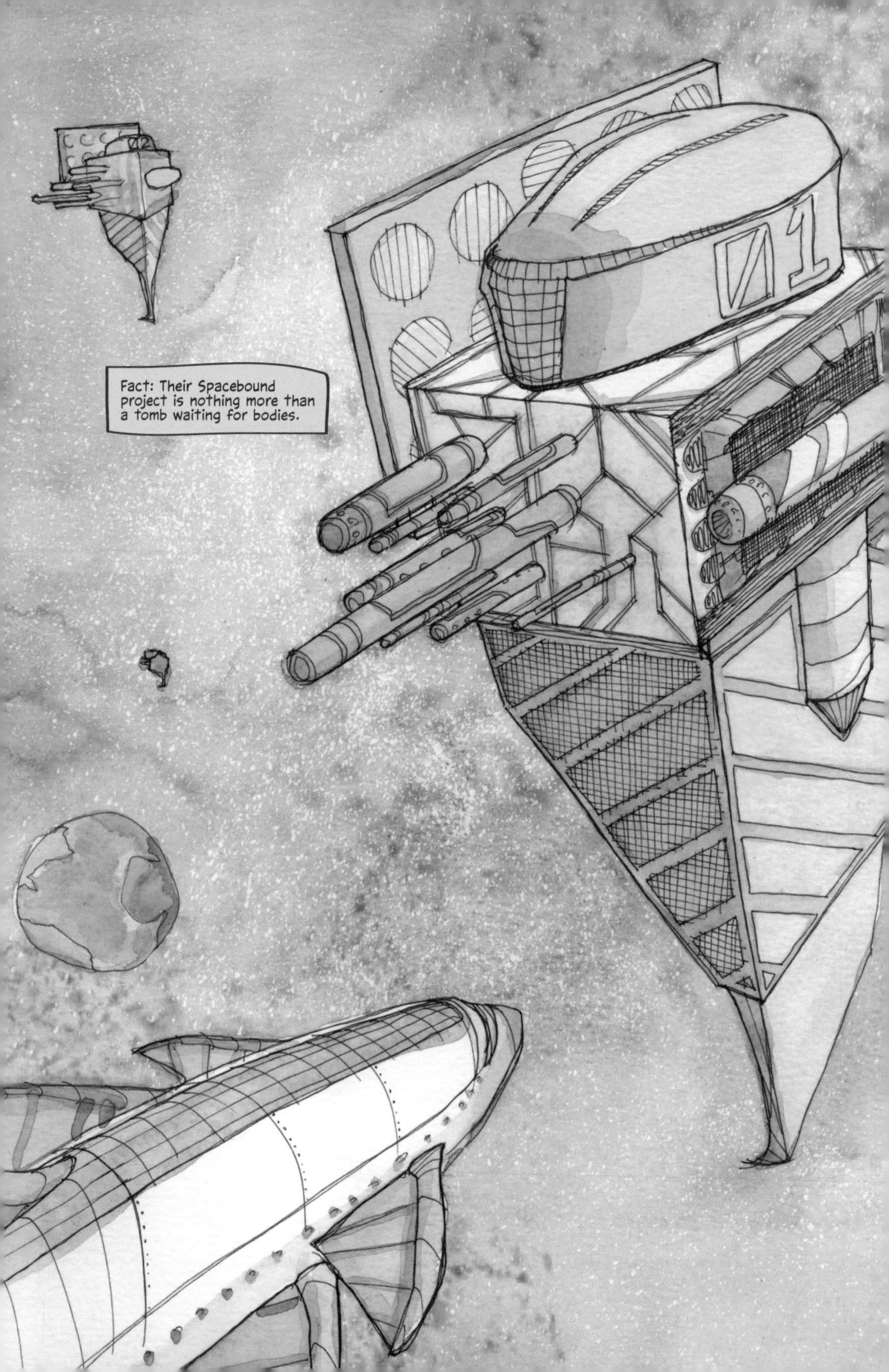
Fact: Their Spacebound project is nothing more than a tomb waiting for bodies.
Ø1

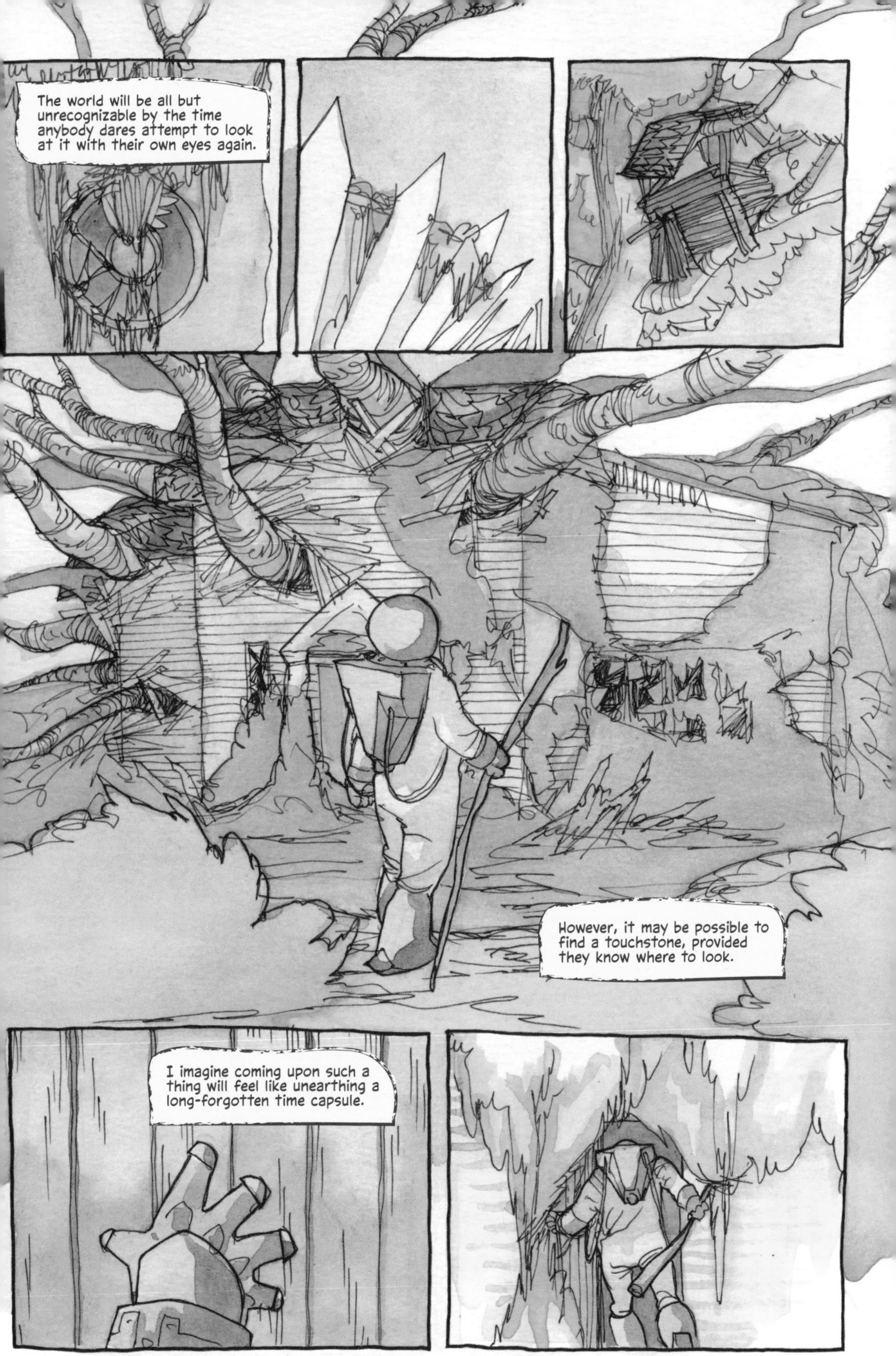

The world will be all but unrecognizable by the time anybody dares attempt to look at it with their own eyes again.
However, it may be possible to find a touchstone, provided they know where to look.
I imagine coming upon such a thing will feel like unearthing a long-forgotten time capsule.

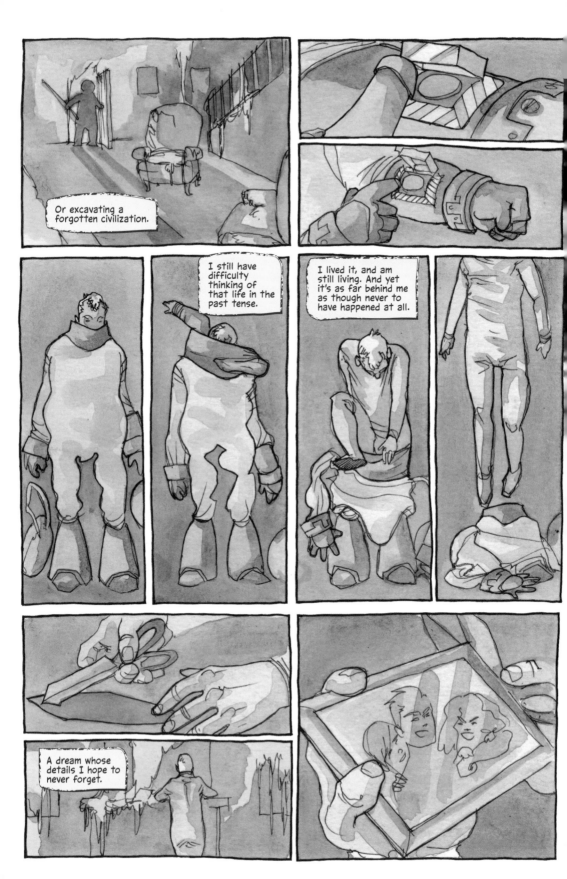

Or excavating a forgotten civilization.

I still have difficulty thinking of that life in the past tense.

I lived it, and am still living. And yet it's as far behind me as though never to have happened at all.

A dream whose details I hope to never forget.

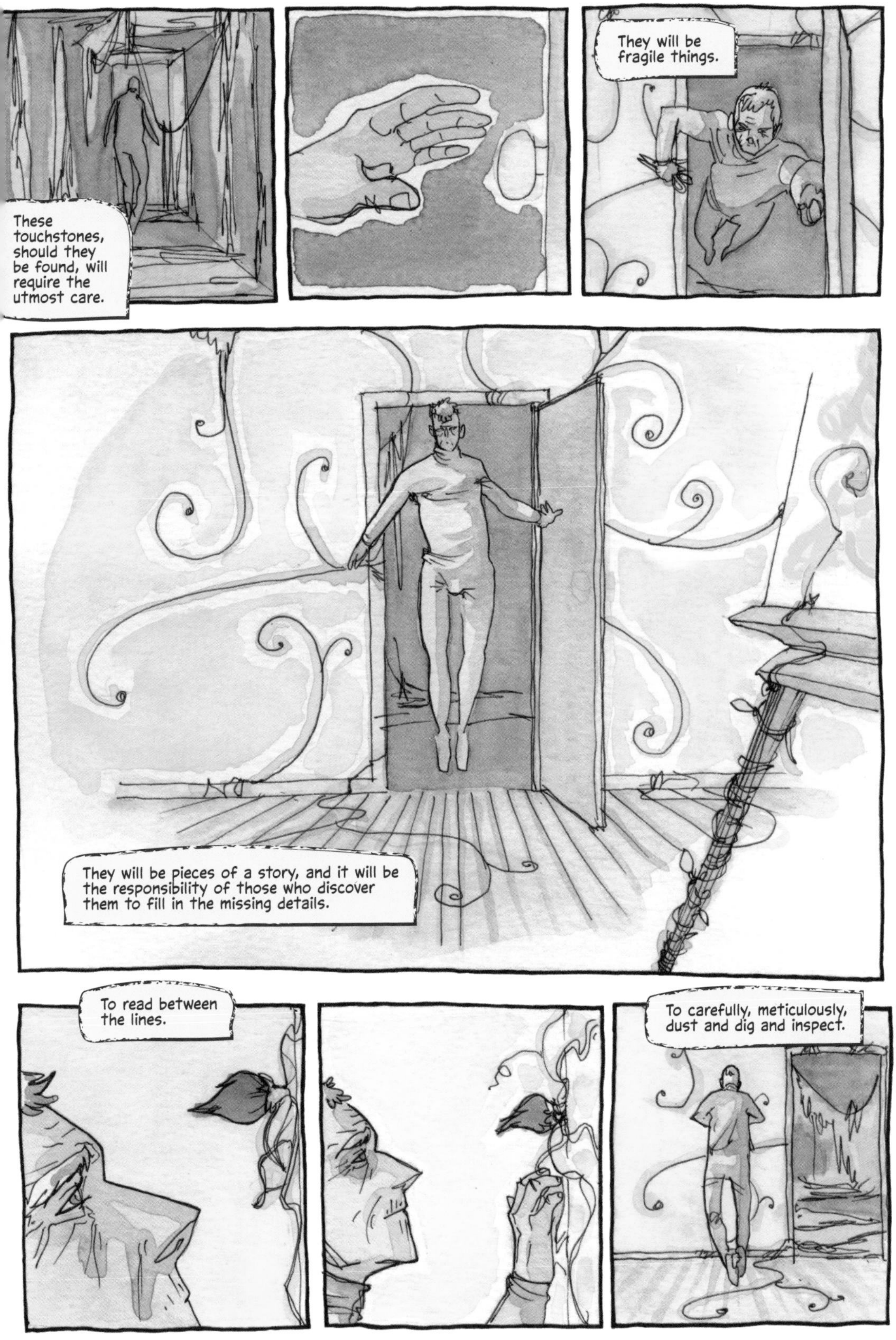
These touchstones, should they be found, will require the utmost care.
They will be fragile things.
They will be pieces of a story, and it will be the responsibility of those who discover them to fill in the missing details.
To read between the lines.
To carefully, meticulously, dust and dig and inspect.

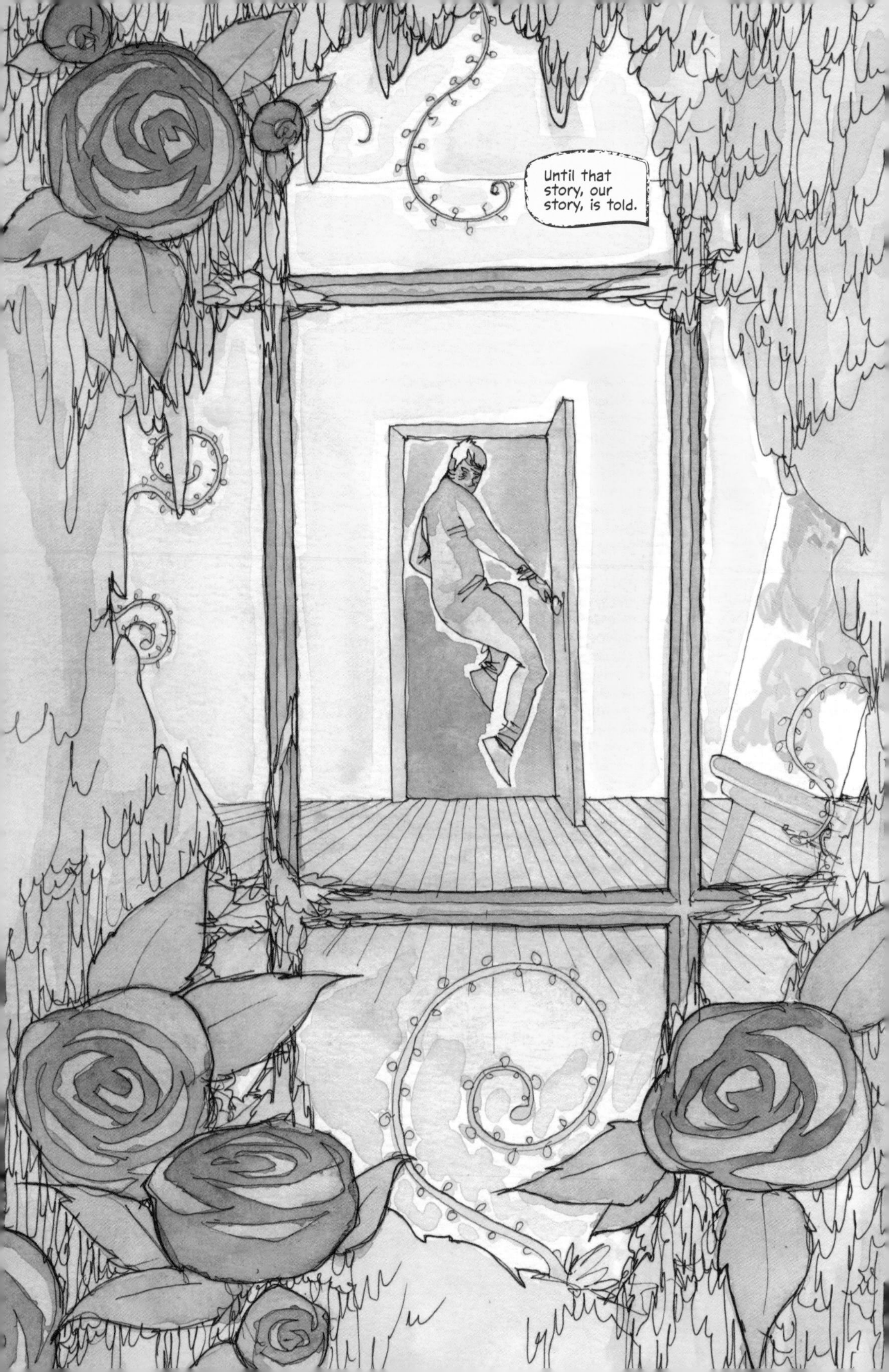
Until that story, our story, is told.

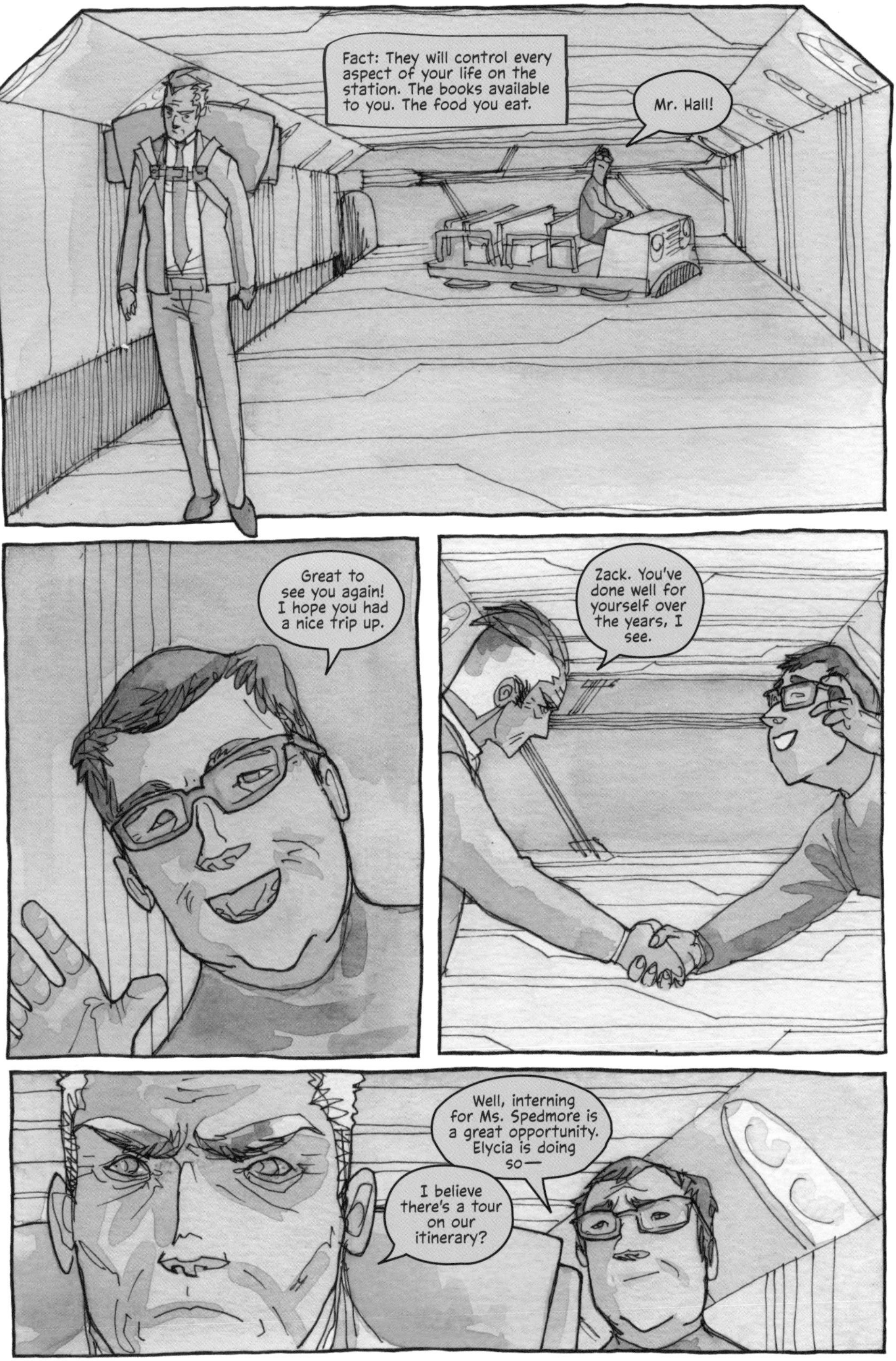
Fact: They will control every aspect of your life on the station. The books available to you. The food you eat.
Mr. Hall!
Great to see you again! I hope you had a nice trip up.
Zack. You've done well for yourself over the years, I see.
Well, interning for Ms. Spedmore is a great opportunity. Elycia is doing so—
I believe there's a tour on our itinerary?

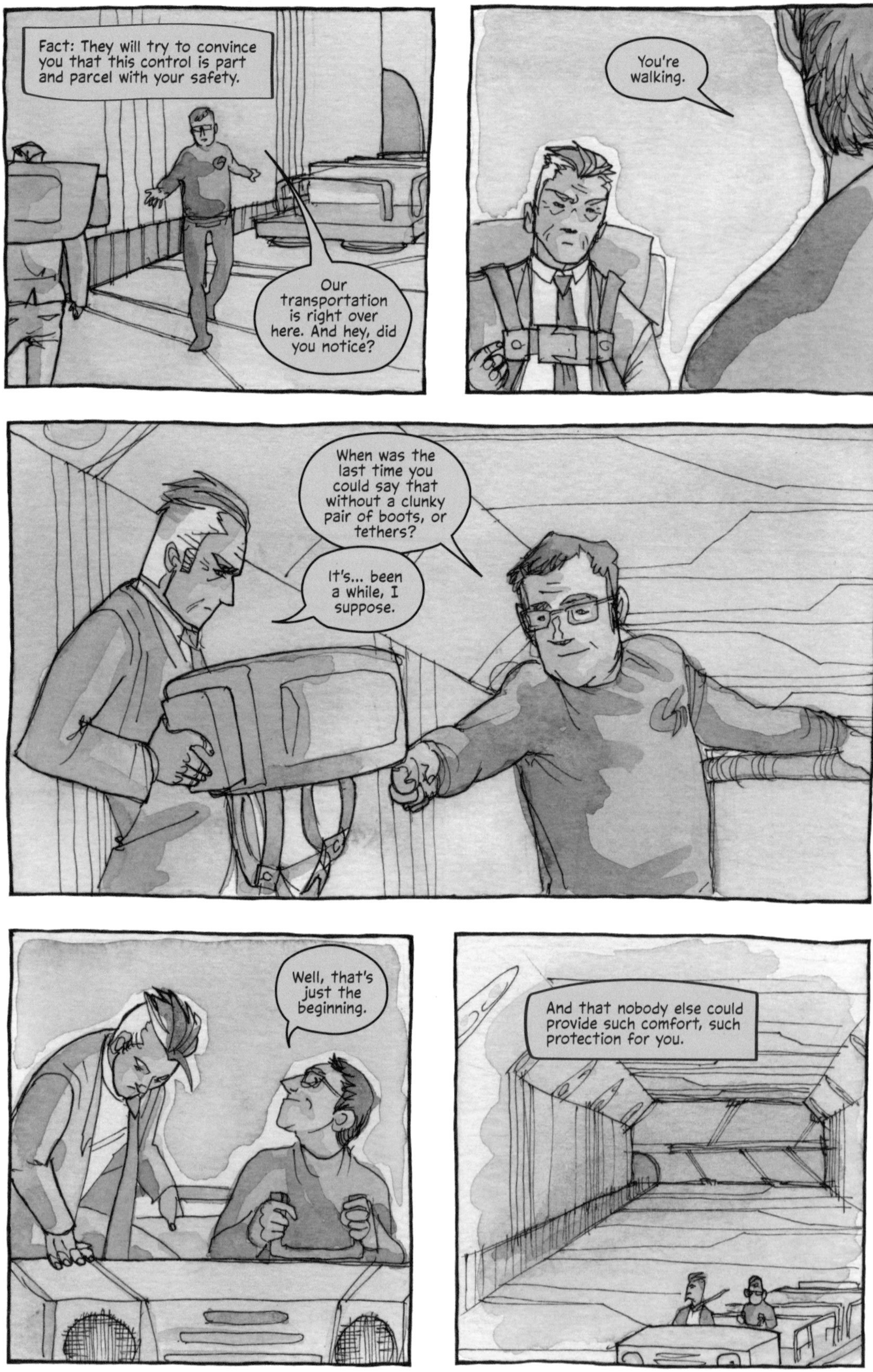

Fact: They will try to convince you that this control is part and parcel with your safety.
Our transportation is right over here. And hey, did you notice?
You're walking.
When was the last time you could say that without a clunky pair of boots, or tethers?
It's... been a while, I suppose.
Well, that's just the beginning.
And that nobody else could provide such comfort, such protection for you.

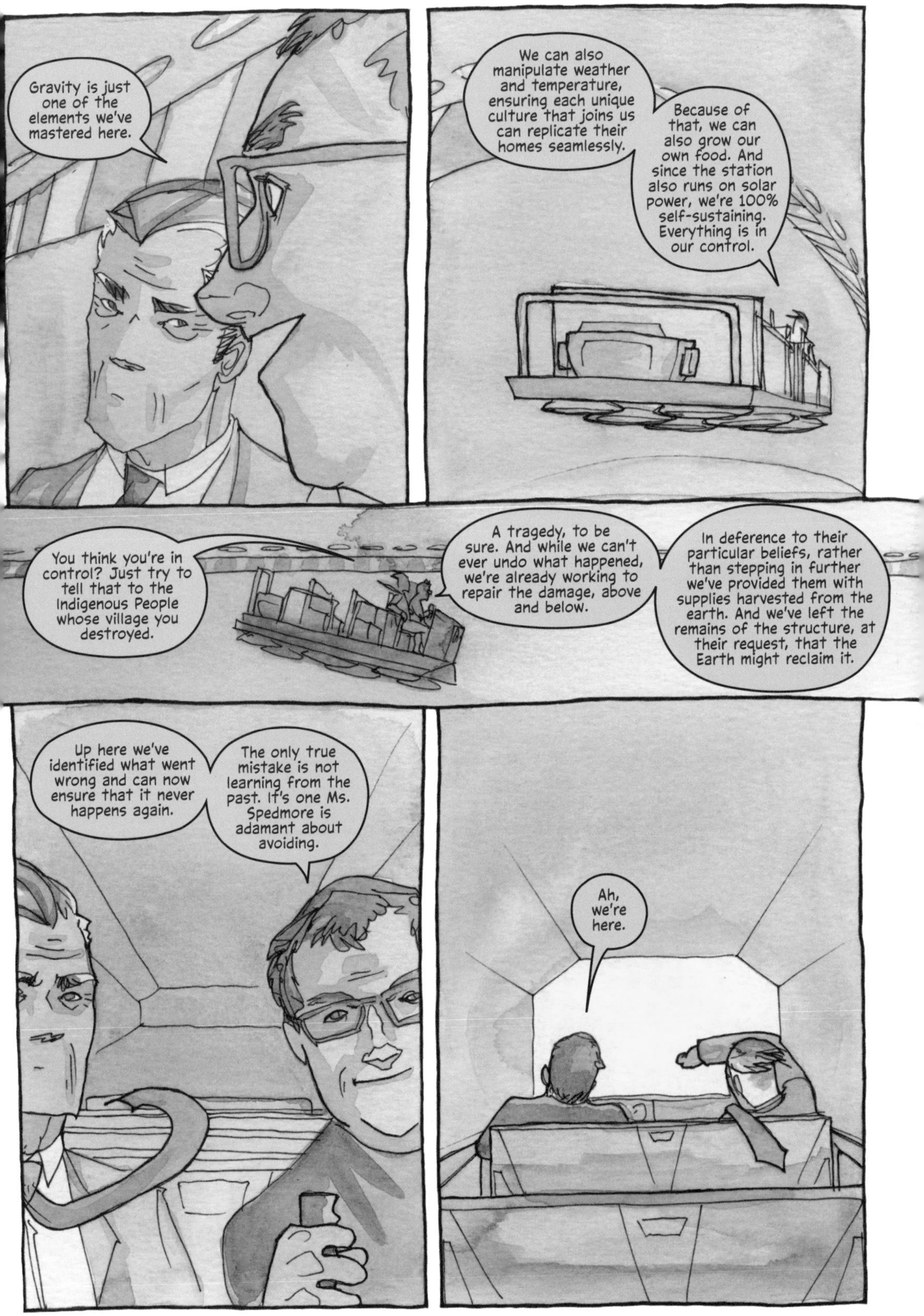
Gravity is just one of the elements we've mastered here.
We can also manipulate weather and temperature, ensuring each unique culture that joins us can replicate their homes seamlessly.
Because of that, we can also grow our own food. And since the station also runs on solar power, we're 100% self-sustaining. Everything is in our control.
You think you're in control? Just try to tell that to the Indigenous People whose village you destroyed.
A tragedy, to be sure. And while we can't ever undo what happened, we're already working to repair the damage, above and below.
In deference to their particular beliefs, rather than stepping in further we've provided them with supplies harvested from the earth. And we've left the remains of the structure, at their request, that the Earth might reclaim it.
Up here we've identified what went wrong and can now ensure that it never happens again.
The only true mistake is not learning from the past. It's one Ms. Spedmore is adamant about avoiding.
Ah, we're here.

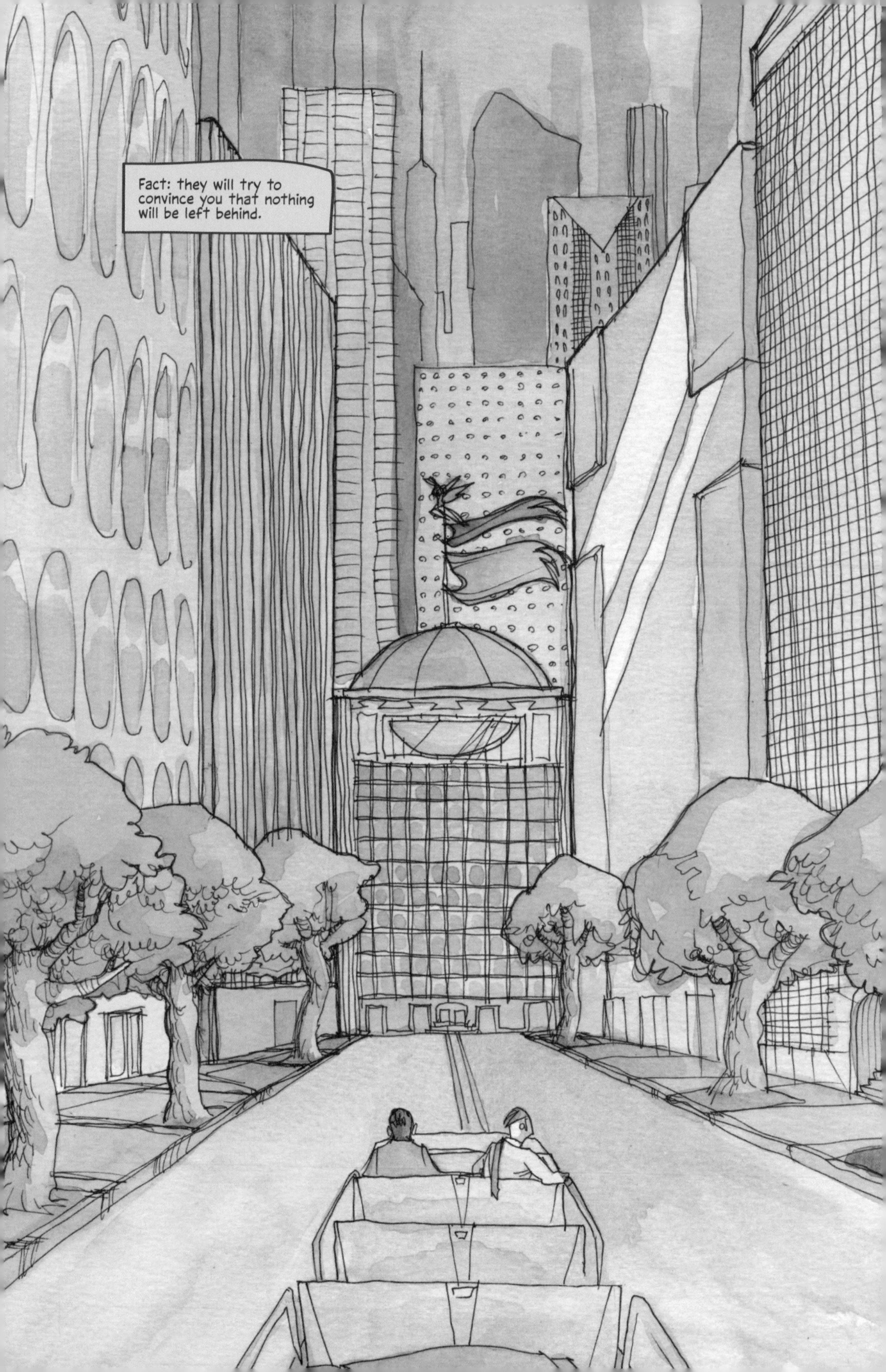
Fact: they will try to convince you that nothing will be left behind.

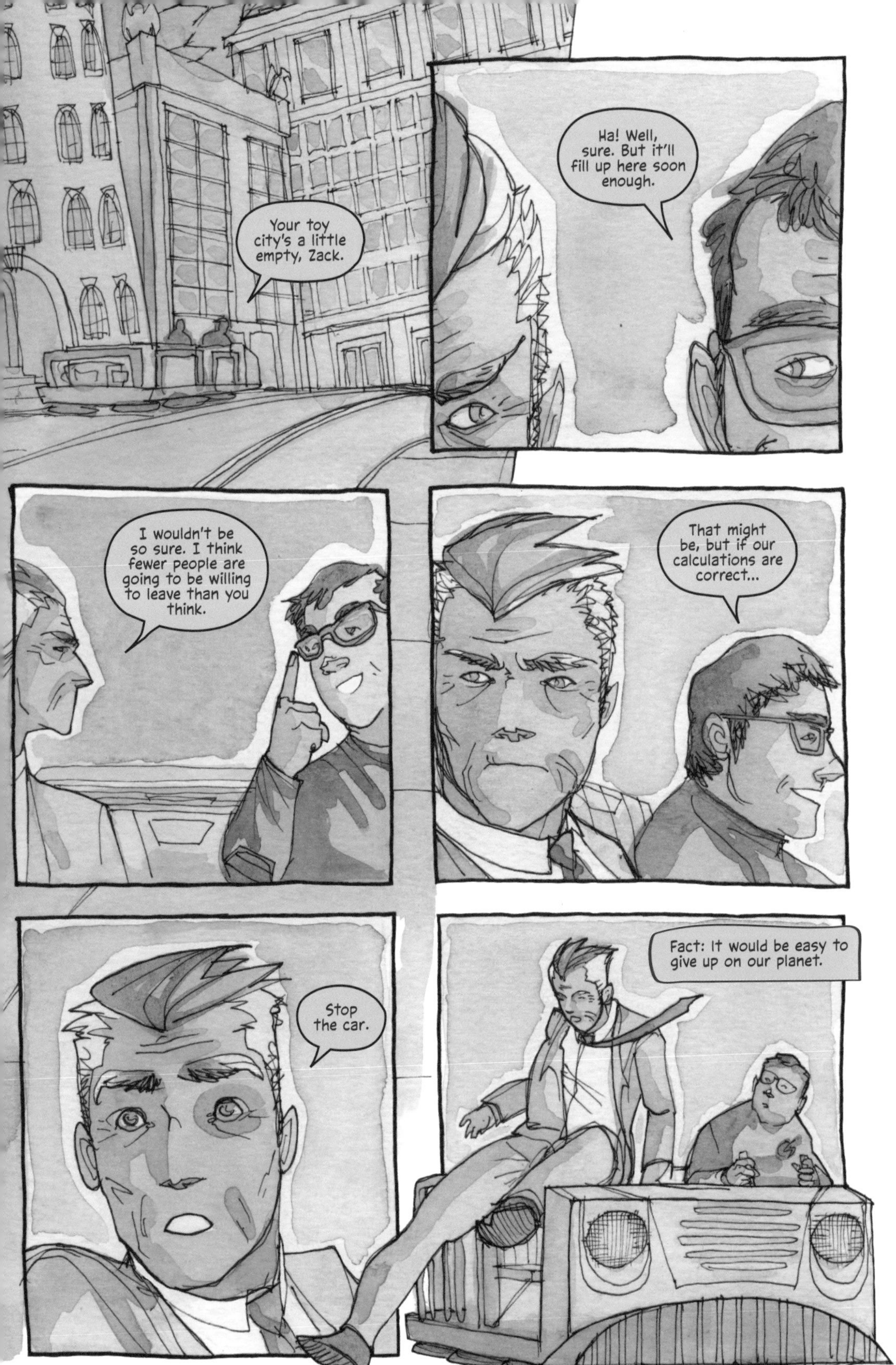
Your toy city's a little empty, Zack.
Ha! Well, sure. But it'll fill up here soon enough.
I wouldn't be so sure. I think fewer people are going to be willing to leave than you think.
That might be, but if our calculations are correct...
Stop the car.
Fact: It would be easy to give up on our planet.

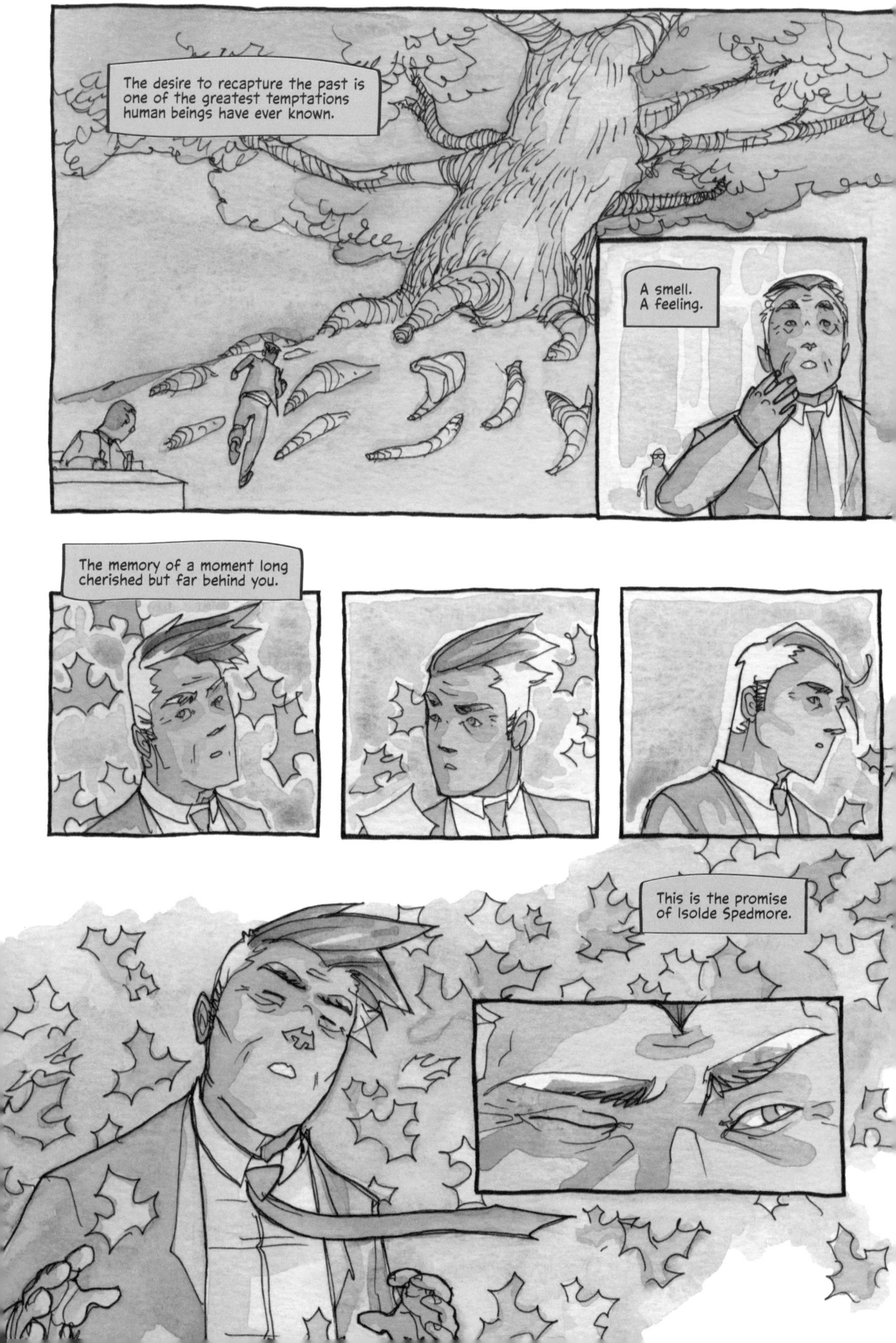
The desire to recapture the past is one of the greatest temptations human beings have ever known.
A smell. A feeling.
The memory of a moment long cherished but far behind you.
This is the promise of Isolde Spedmore.

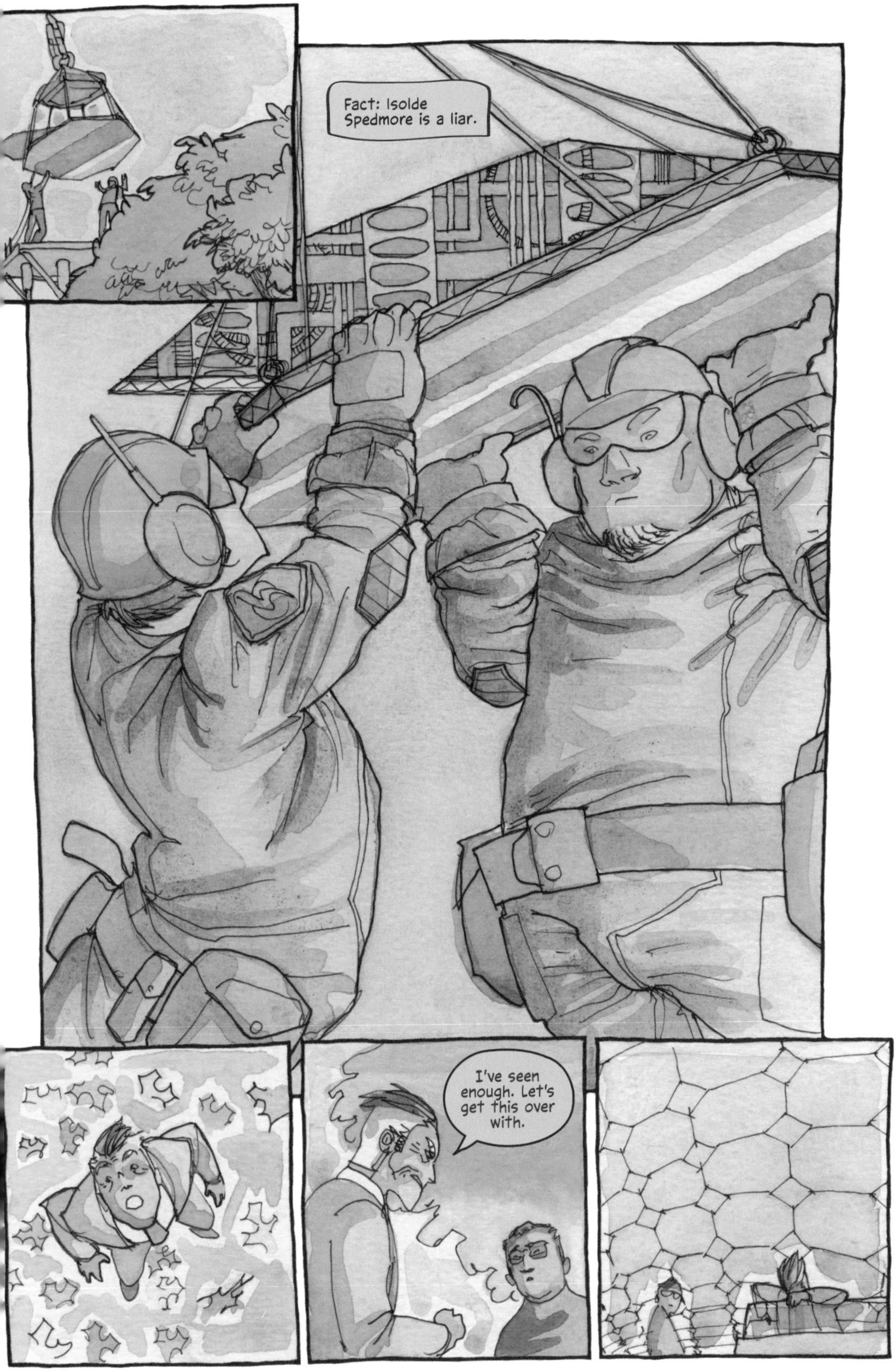
Fact: Isolde Spedmore is a liar.
I've seen enough. Let's get this over with.

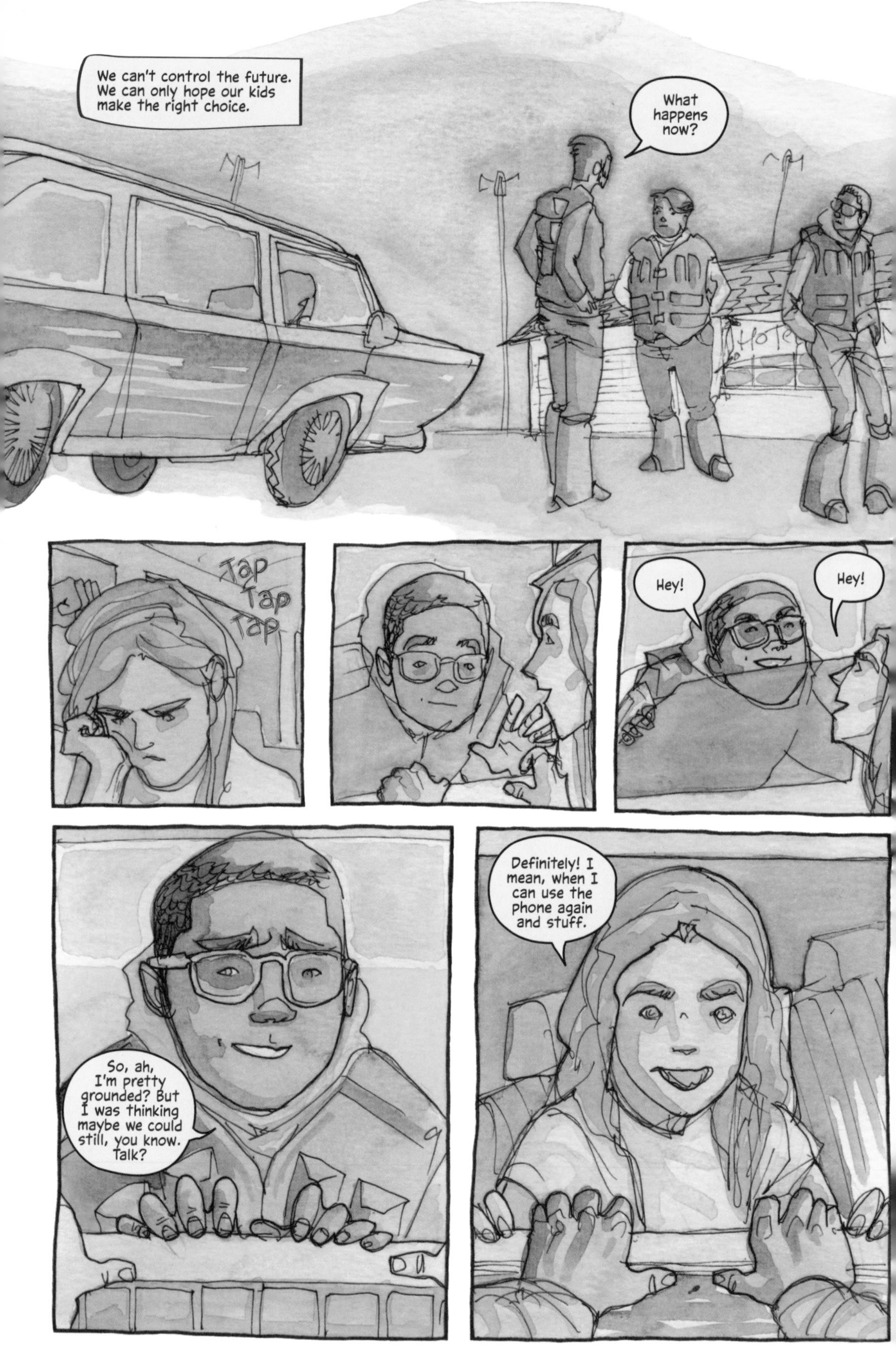
We can't control the future. We can only hope our kids make the right choice.
What happens now?
Tap Tap Tap
Hey!
Hey!
So, ah, I'm pretty grounded? But I was thinking maybe we could still, you know. Talk?
Definitely! I mean, when I can use the phone again and stuff.

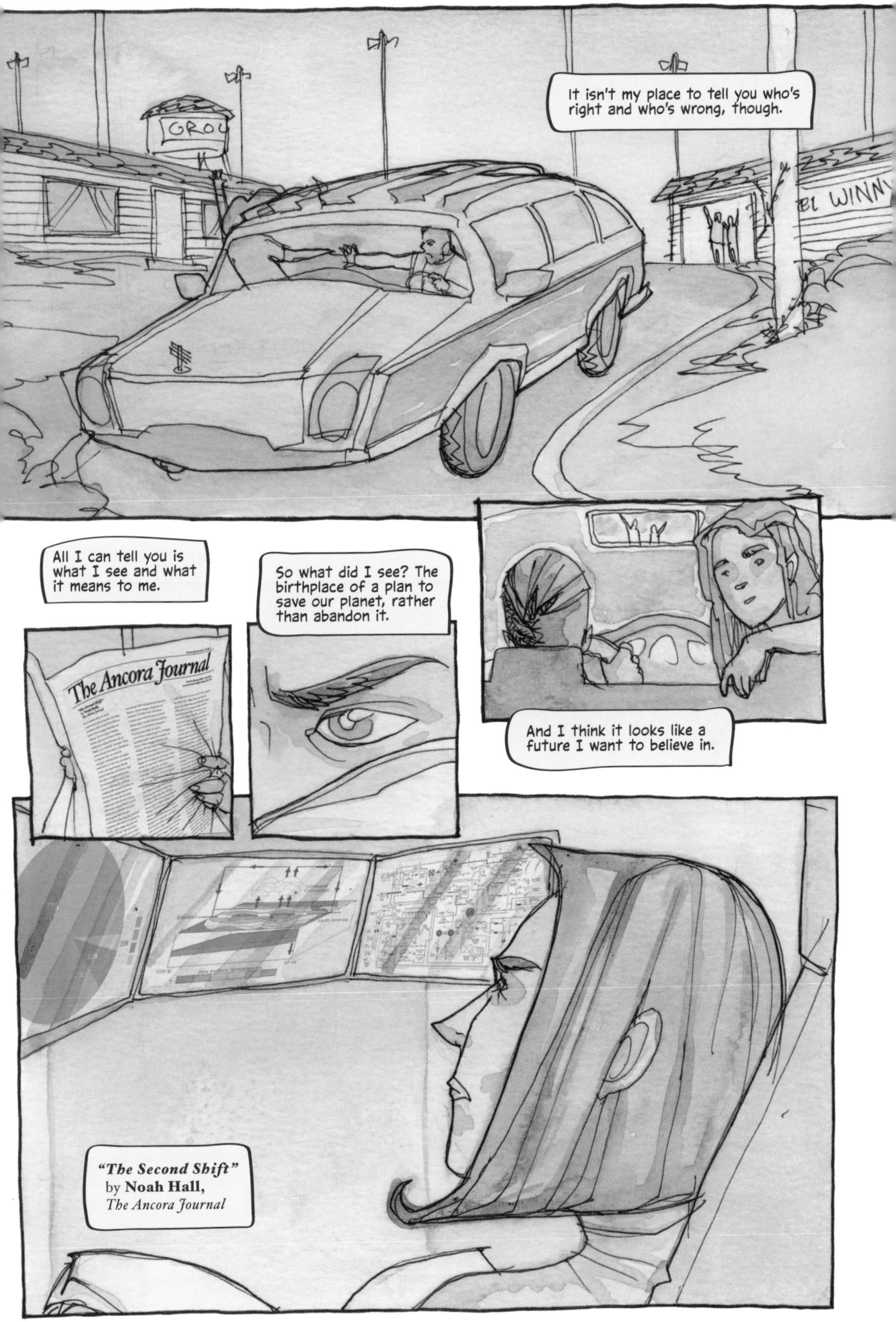
It isn't my place to tell you who's right and who's wrong, though.
All I can tell you is what I see and what it means to me.
So what did I see? The birthplace of a plan to save our planet, rather than abandon it.
The Ancora Journal
And I think it looks like a future I want to believe in.
"The Second Shift" by Noah Hall, The Ancora Journal

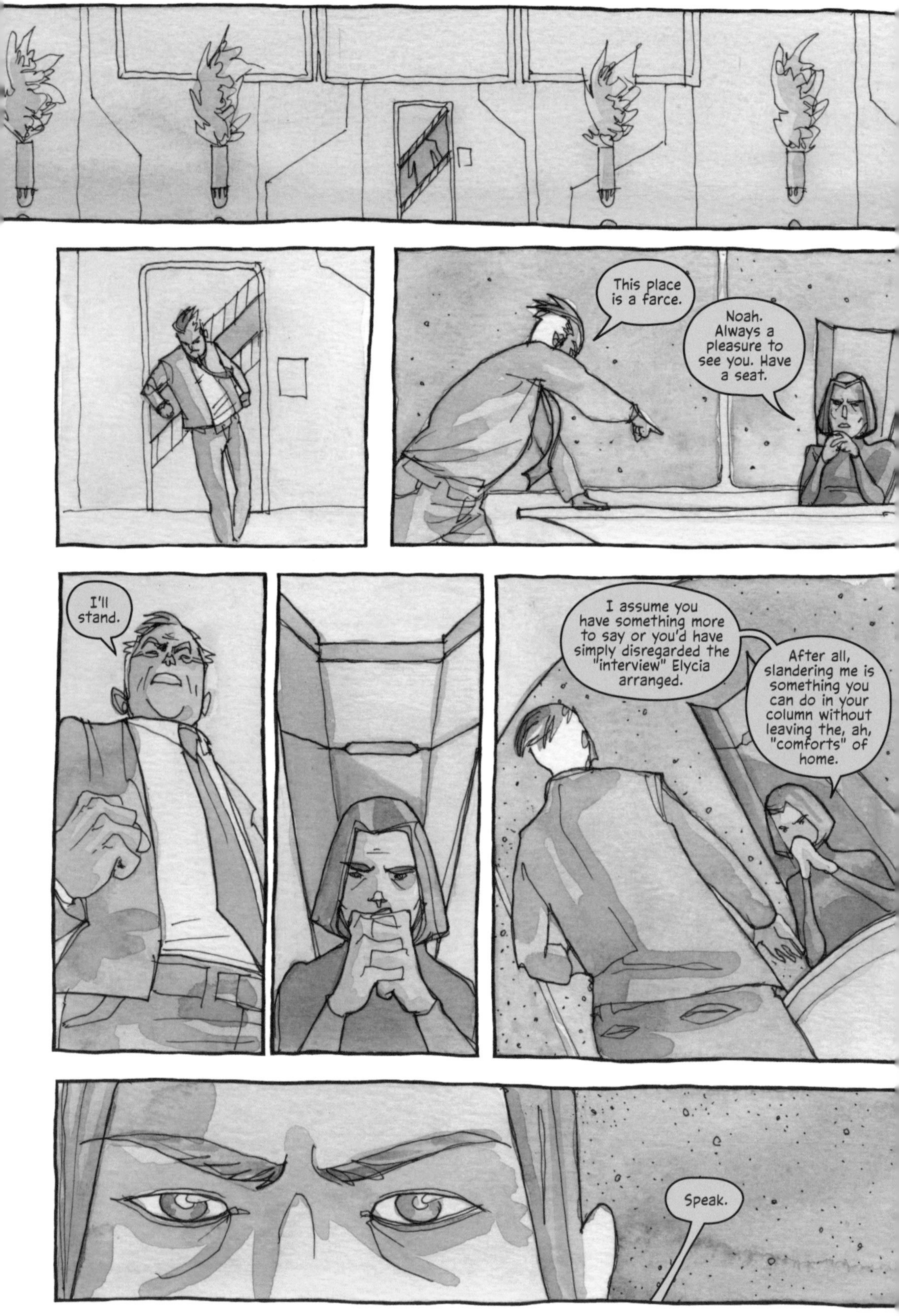
This place is a farce.
Noah. Always a pleasure to see you. Have a seat.
I'll stand.
I assume you have something more to say or you'd have simply disregarded the "interview" Elycia arranged.
After all, slandering me is something you can do in your column without leaving the, ah, "comforts" of home.
Speak.

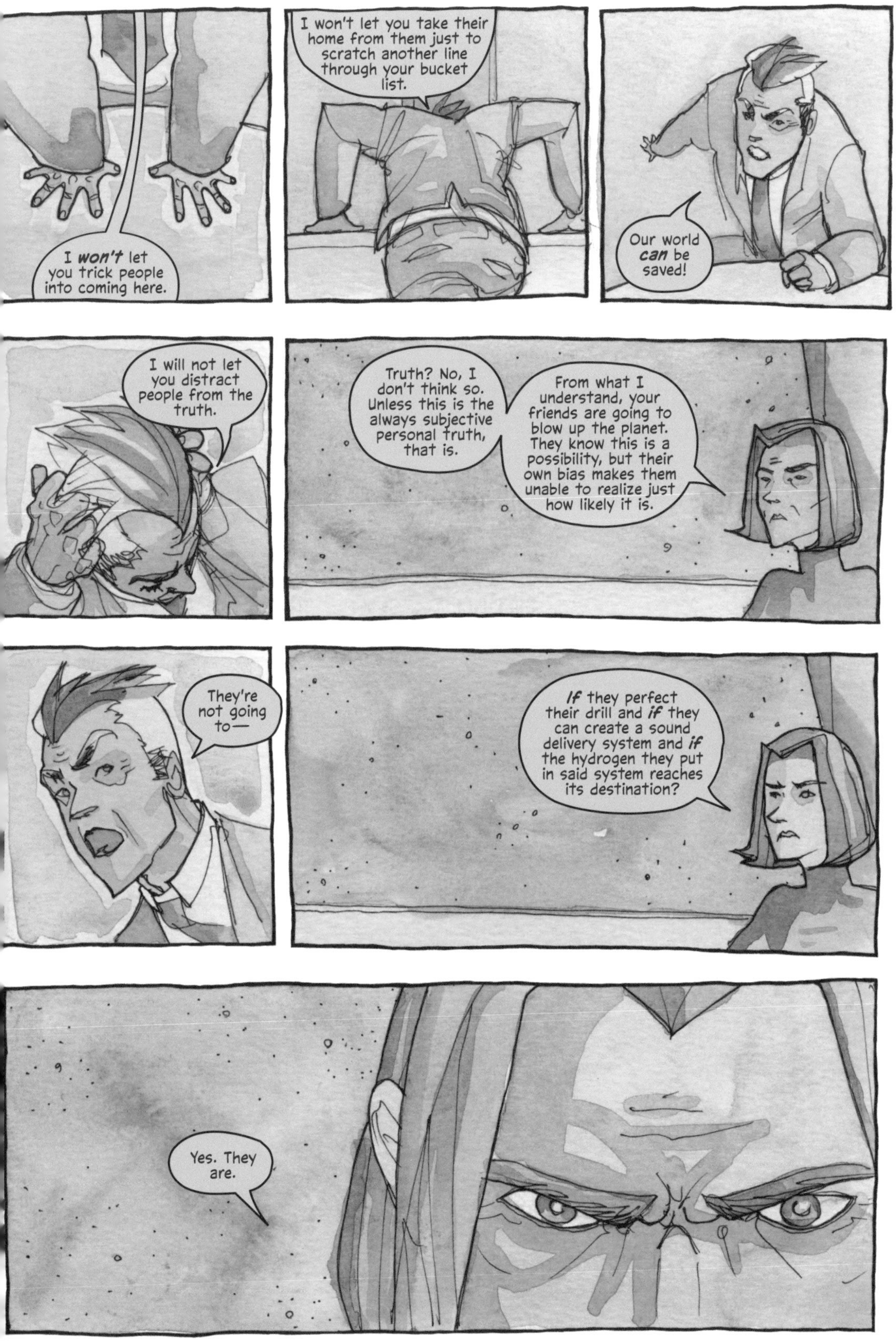
I *won't* let you trick people into coming here.
I won't let you take their home from them just to scratch another line through your bucket list.
Our world *can* be saved!
I will not let you distract people from the truth.
Truth? No, I don't think so. Unless this is the always subjective personal truth, that is.
From what I understand, your friends are going to blow up the planet. They know this is a possibility, but their own bias makes them unable to realize just how likely it is.
They're not going to—
If they perfect their drill and *if* they can create a sound delivery system and *if* the hydrogen they put in said system reaches its destination?
Yes. They are.

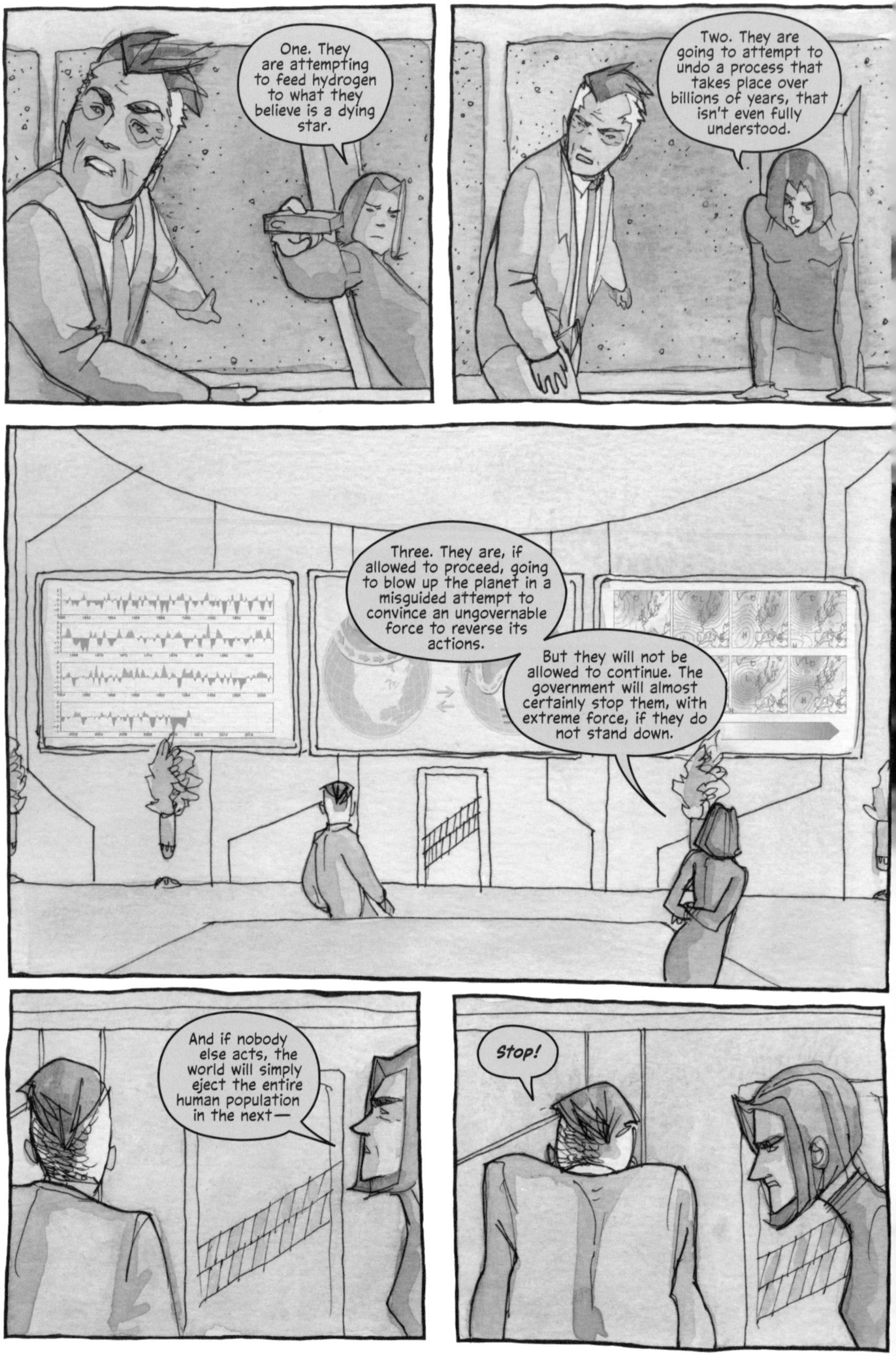
One. They are attempting to feed hydrogen to what they believe is a dying star.
Two. They are going to attempt to undo a process that takes place over billions of years, that isn't even fully understood.
Three. They are, if allowed to proceed, going to blow up the planet in a misguided attempt to convince an ungovernable force to reverse its actions.
But they will not be allowed to continue. The government will almost certainly stop them, with extreme force, if they do not stand down.
And if nobody else acts, the world will simply eject the entire human population in the next—
Stop!

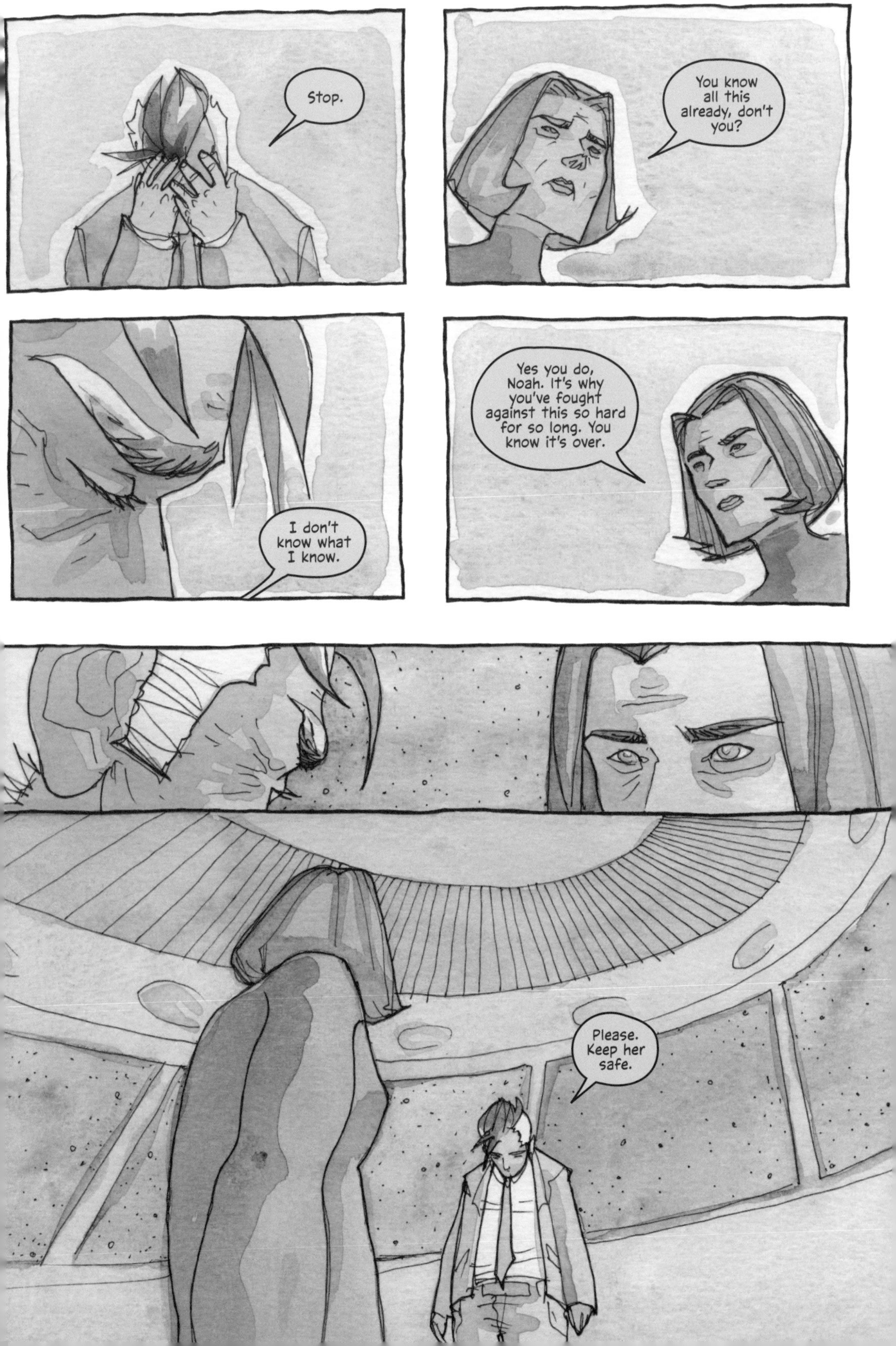
Stop.
You know all this already, don't you?
I don't know what I know.
Yes you do, Noah. It's why you've fought against this so hard for so long. You know it's over.
Please. Keep her safe.

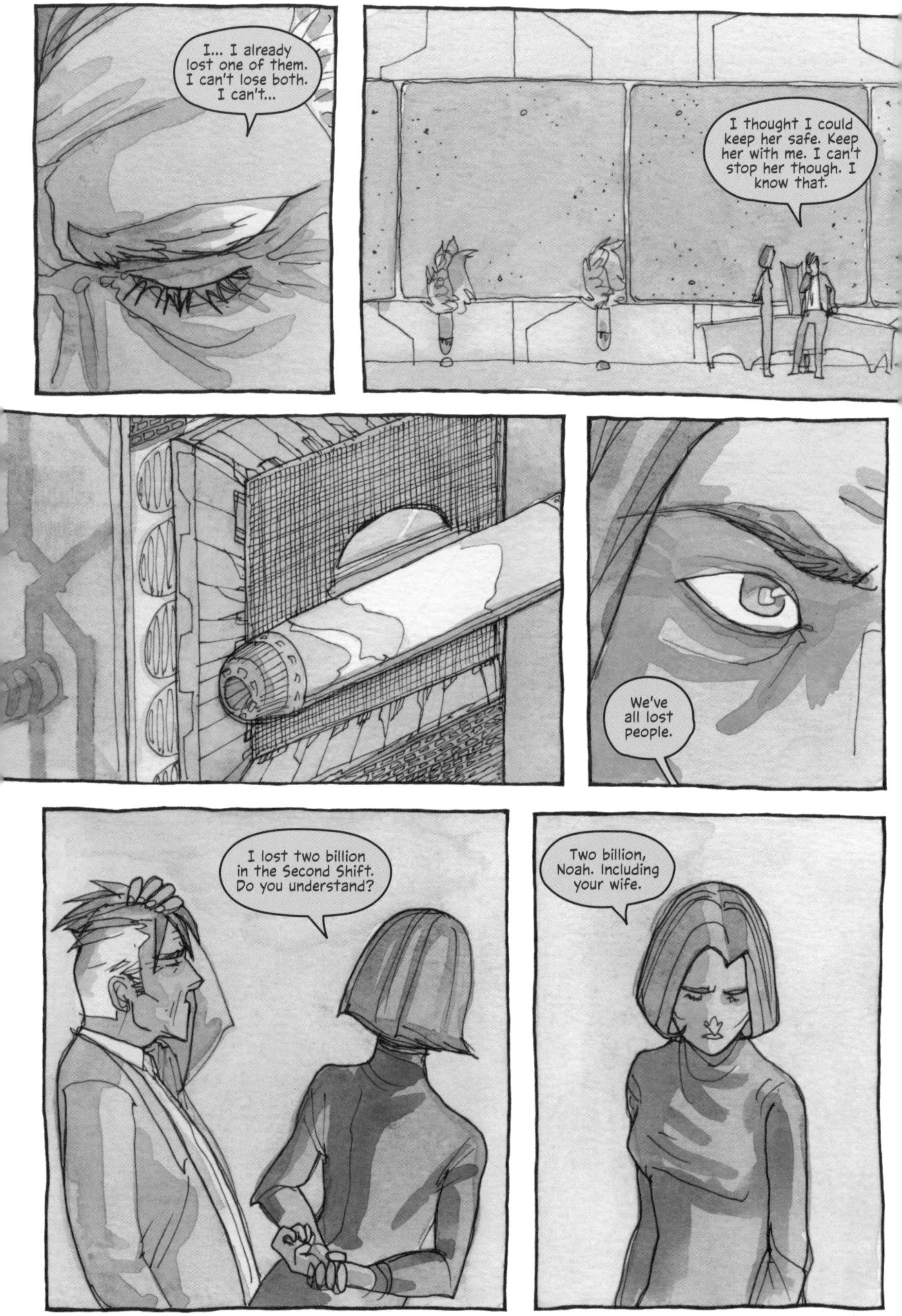
I... I already lost one of them. I can't lose both. I can't...
I thought I could keep her safe. Keep her with me. I can't stop her though. I know that.
We've all lost people.
I lost two billion in the Second Shift. Do you understand?
Two billion, Noah. Including your wife.

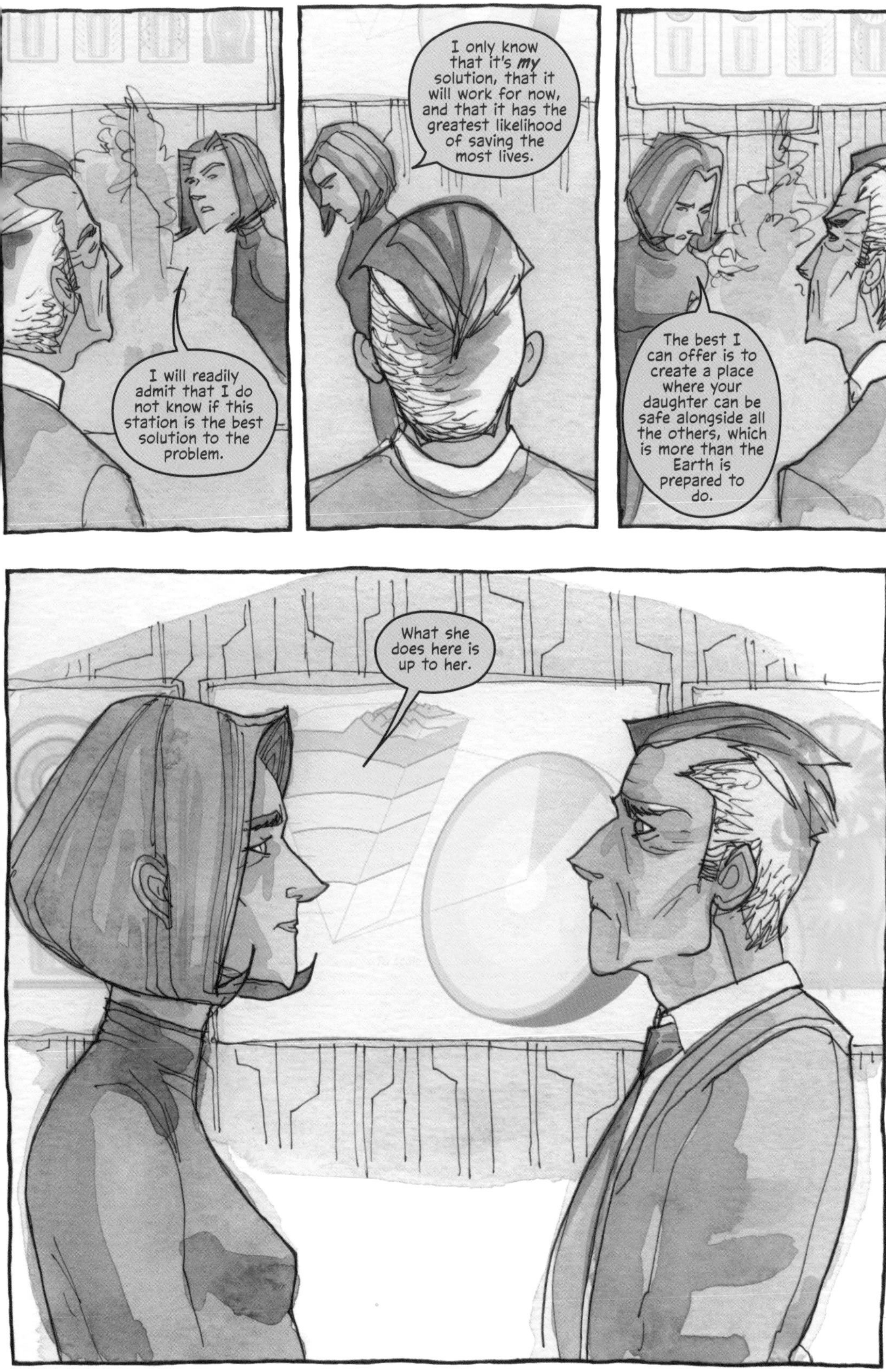
I will readily admit that I do not know if this station is the best solution to the problem.
I only know that it's *my* solution, that it will work for now, and that it has the greatest likelihood of saving the most lives.
The best I can offer is to create a place where your daughter can be safe alongside all the others, which is more than the Earth is prepared to do.
What she does here is up to her.

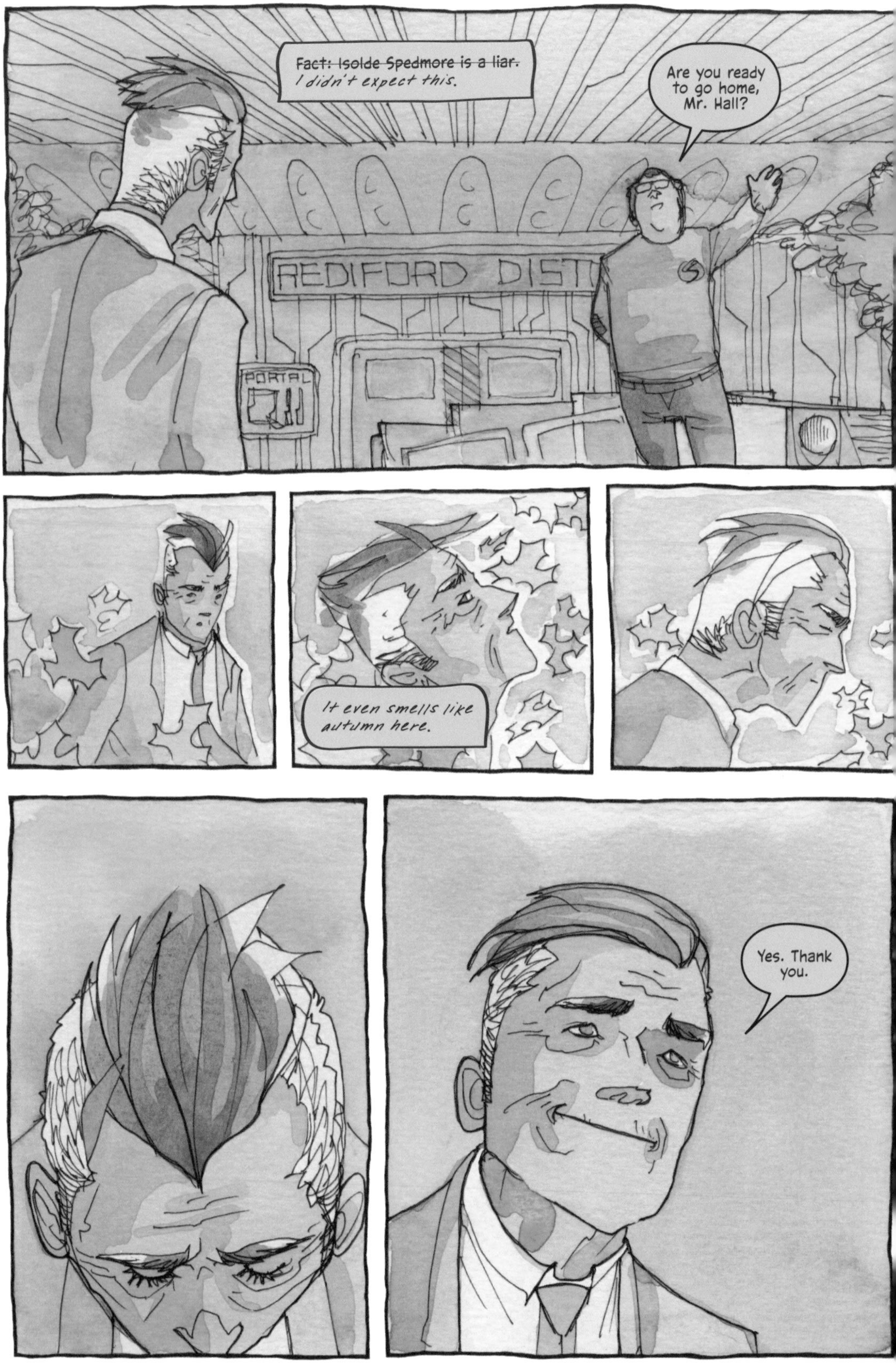
Fact: Isolde Spedmore is a liar.
I didn't expect this.
Are you ready to go home, Mr. Hall?
REDIFORD DIST
PORTAL
It even smells like autumn here.
Yes. Thank you.

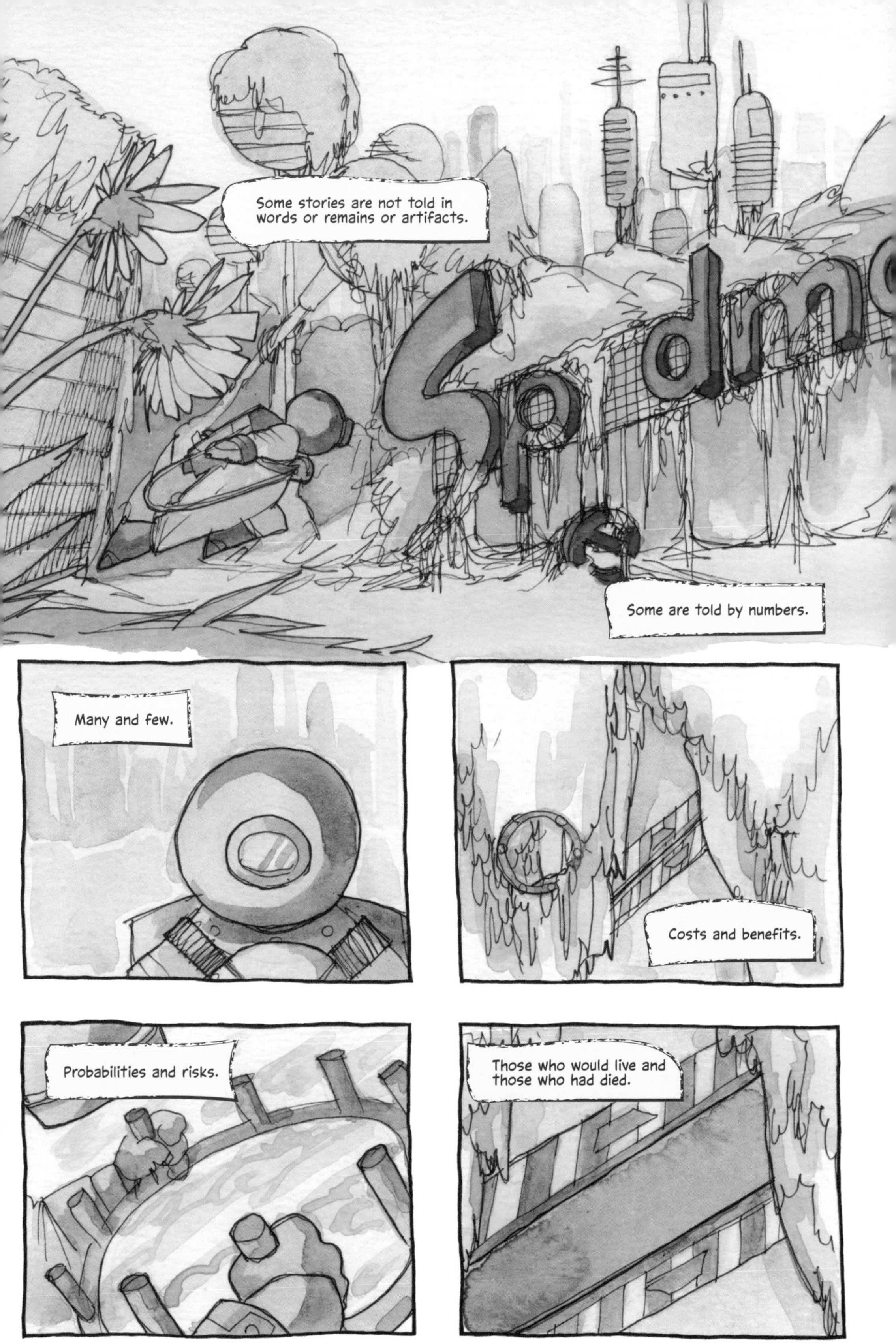
Some stories are not told in words or remains or artifacts.
Some are told by numbers.
Many and few.
Costs and benefits.
Probabilities and risks.
Those who would live and those who had died.

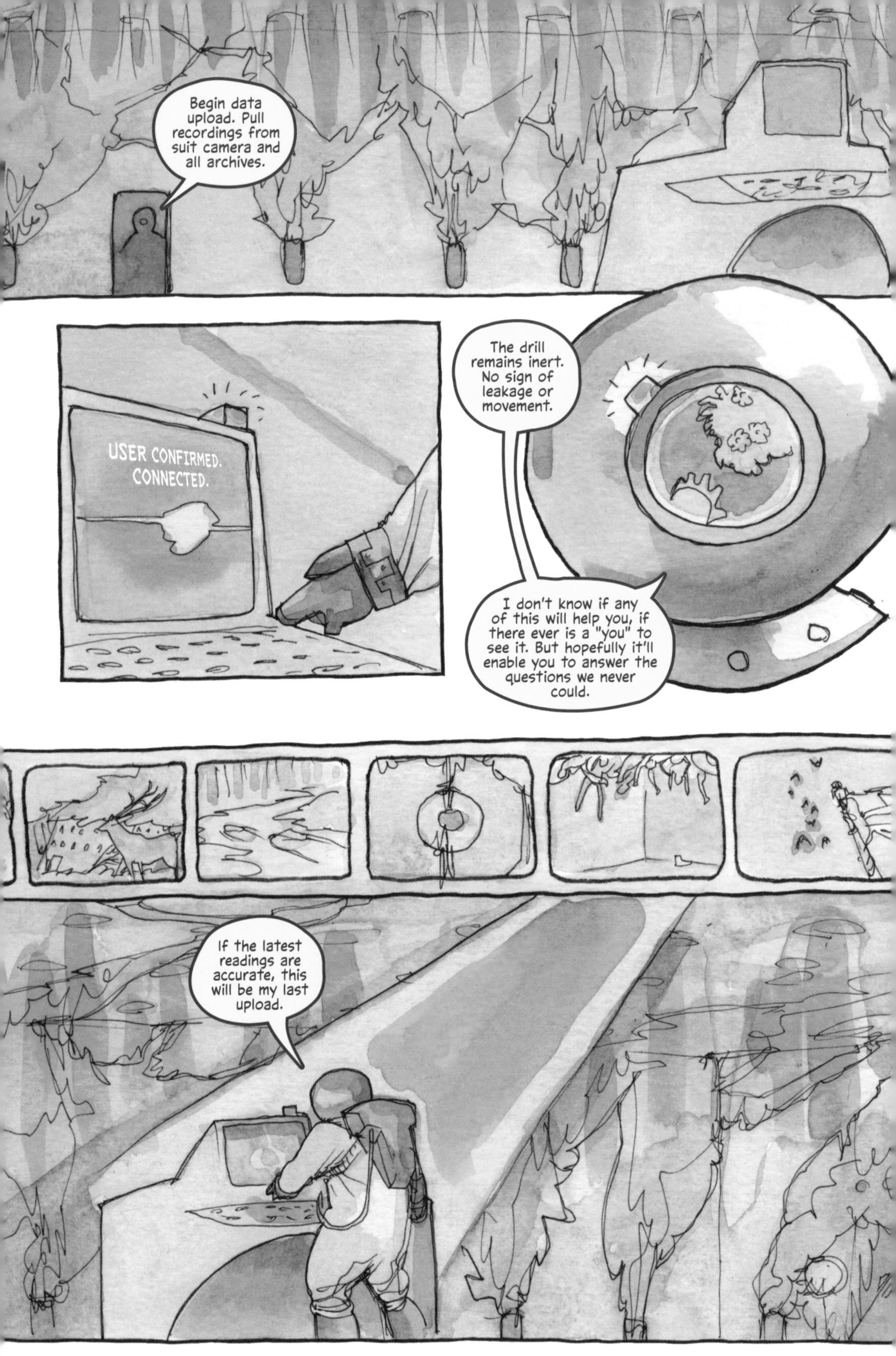
Begin data upload. Pull recordings from suit camera and all archives.
USER CONFIRMED. CONNECTED.
The drill remains inert. No sign of leakage or movement.
I don't know if any of this will help you, if there ever is a "you" to see it. But hopefully it'll enable you to answer the questions we never could.
If the latest readings are accurate, this will be my last upload.

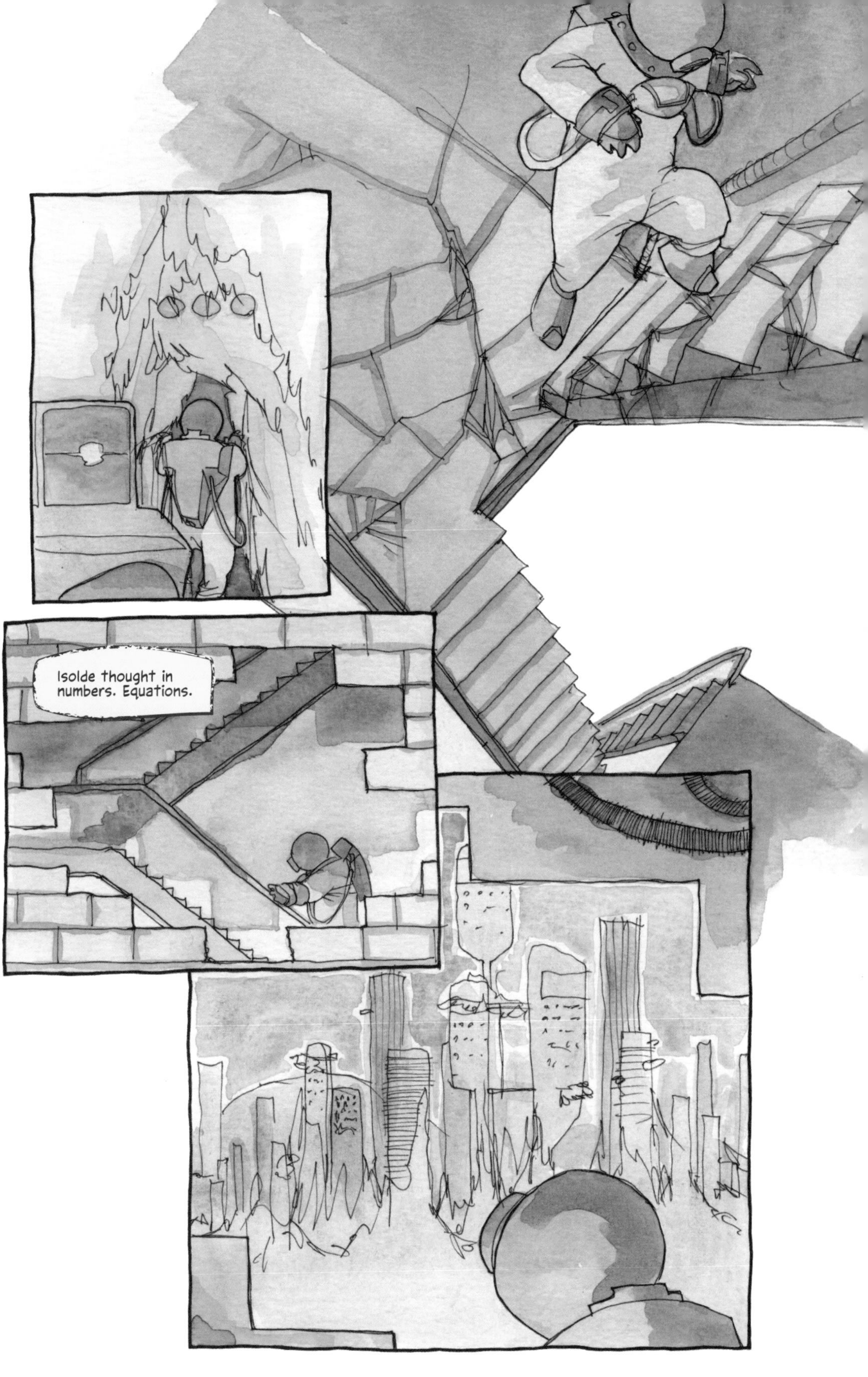
Isolde thought in numbers. Equations.

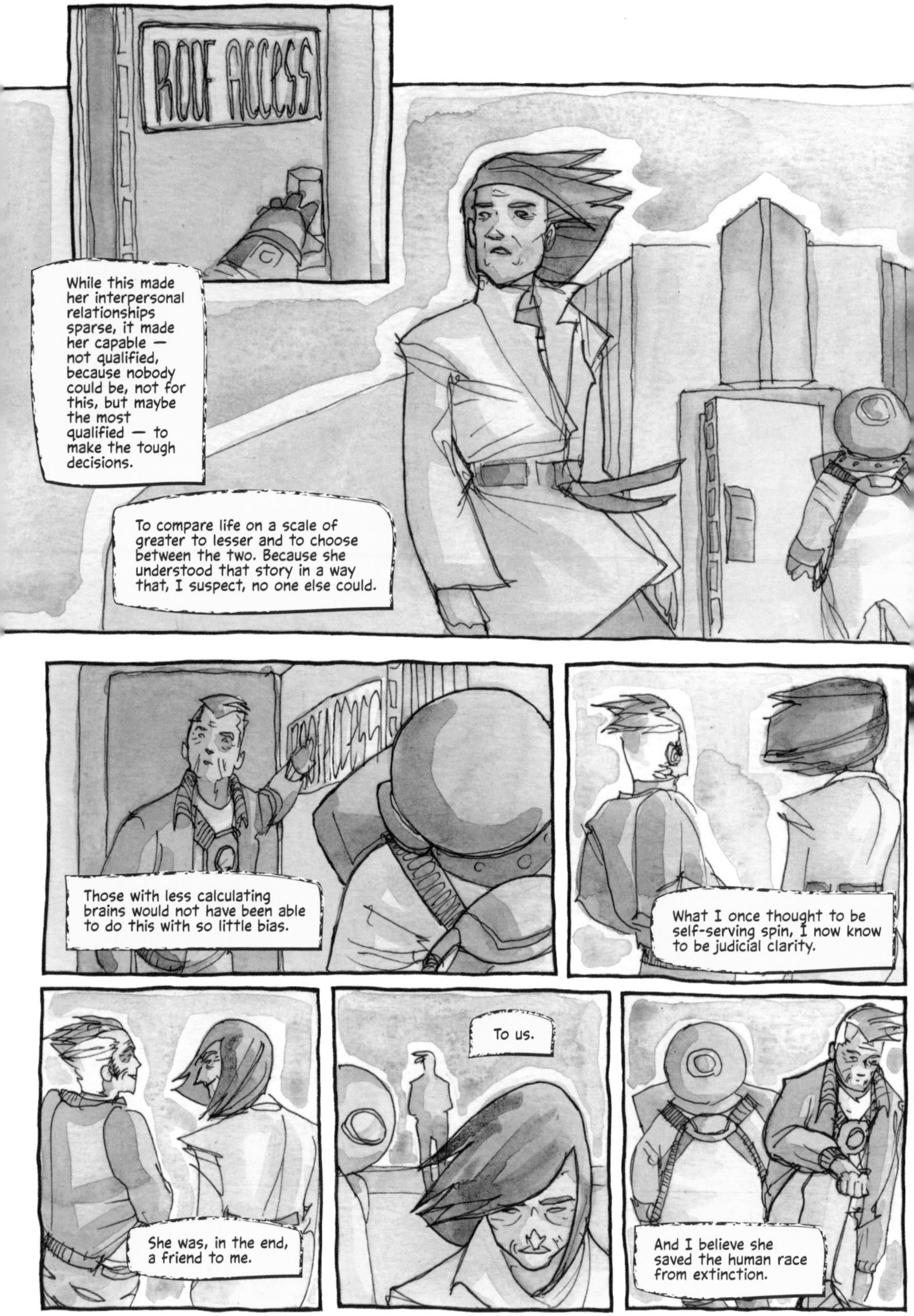
ROOF ACCESS
While this made her interpersonal relationships sparse, it made her capable — not qualified, because nobody could be, not for this, but maybe the most qualified — to make the tough decisions.
To compare life on a scale of greater to lesser and to choose between the two. Because she understood that story in a way that, I suspect, no one else could.
Those with less calculating brains would not have been able to do this with so little bias.
What I once thought to be self-serving spin, I now know to be judicial clarity.
She was, in the end, a friend to me.
To us.
And I believe she saved the human race from extinction.

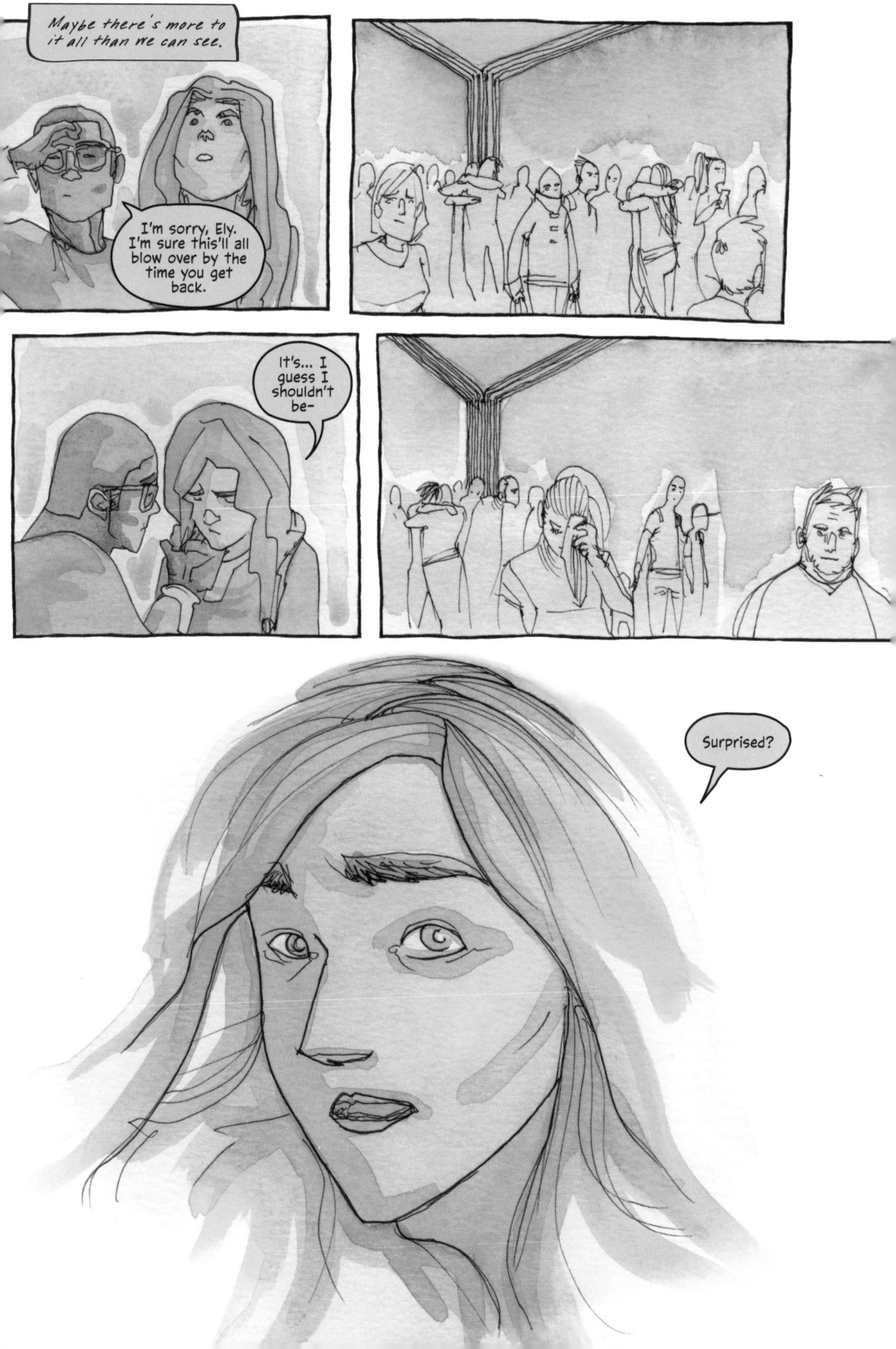

Maybe there's more to it all than we can see.
I'm sorry, Ely. I'm sure this'll all blow over by the time you get back.
It's... I guess I shouldn't be-
Surprised?

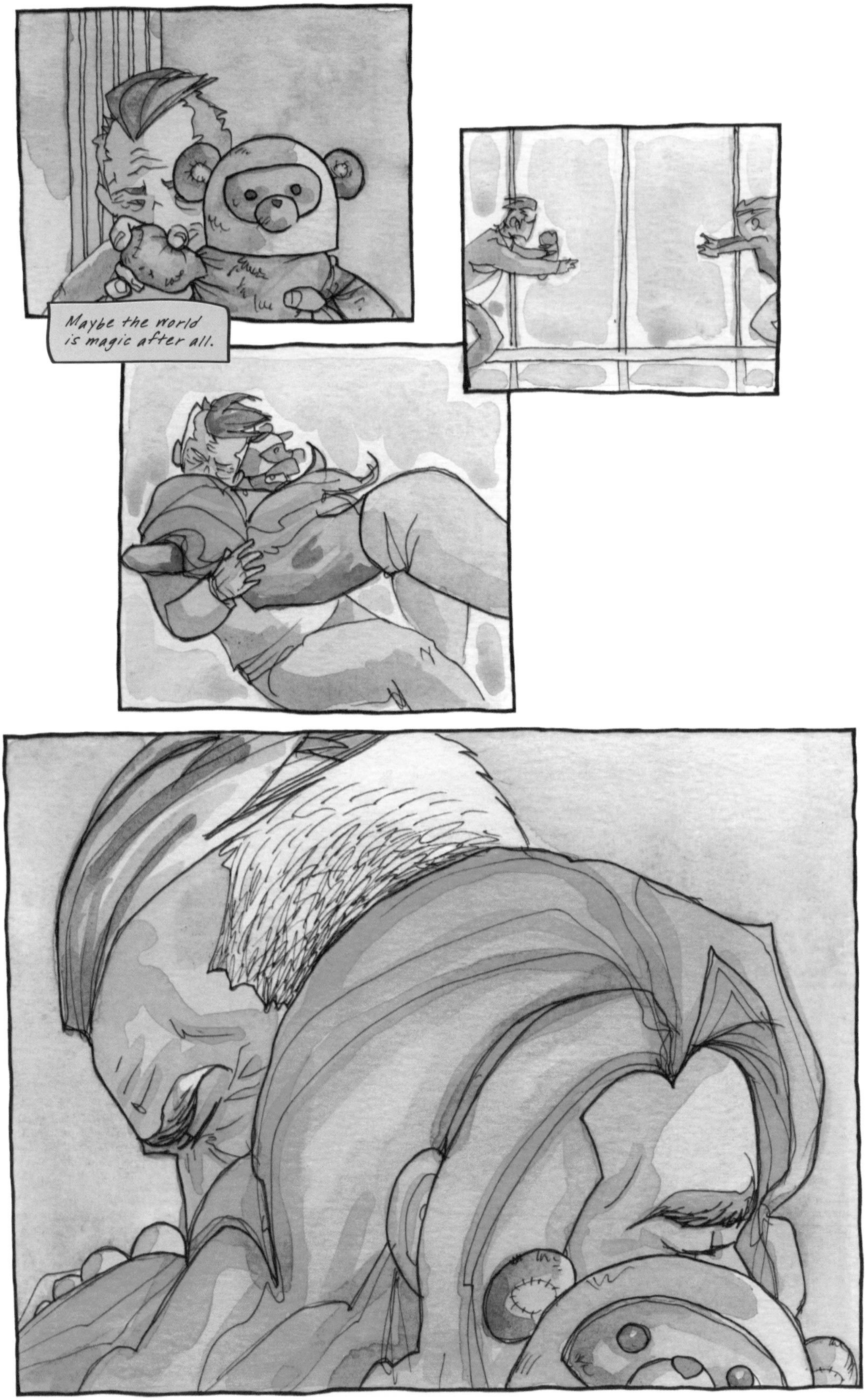
Maybe the world is magic after all.

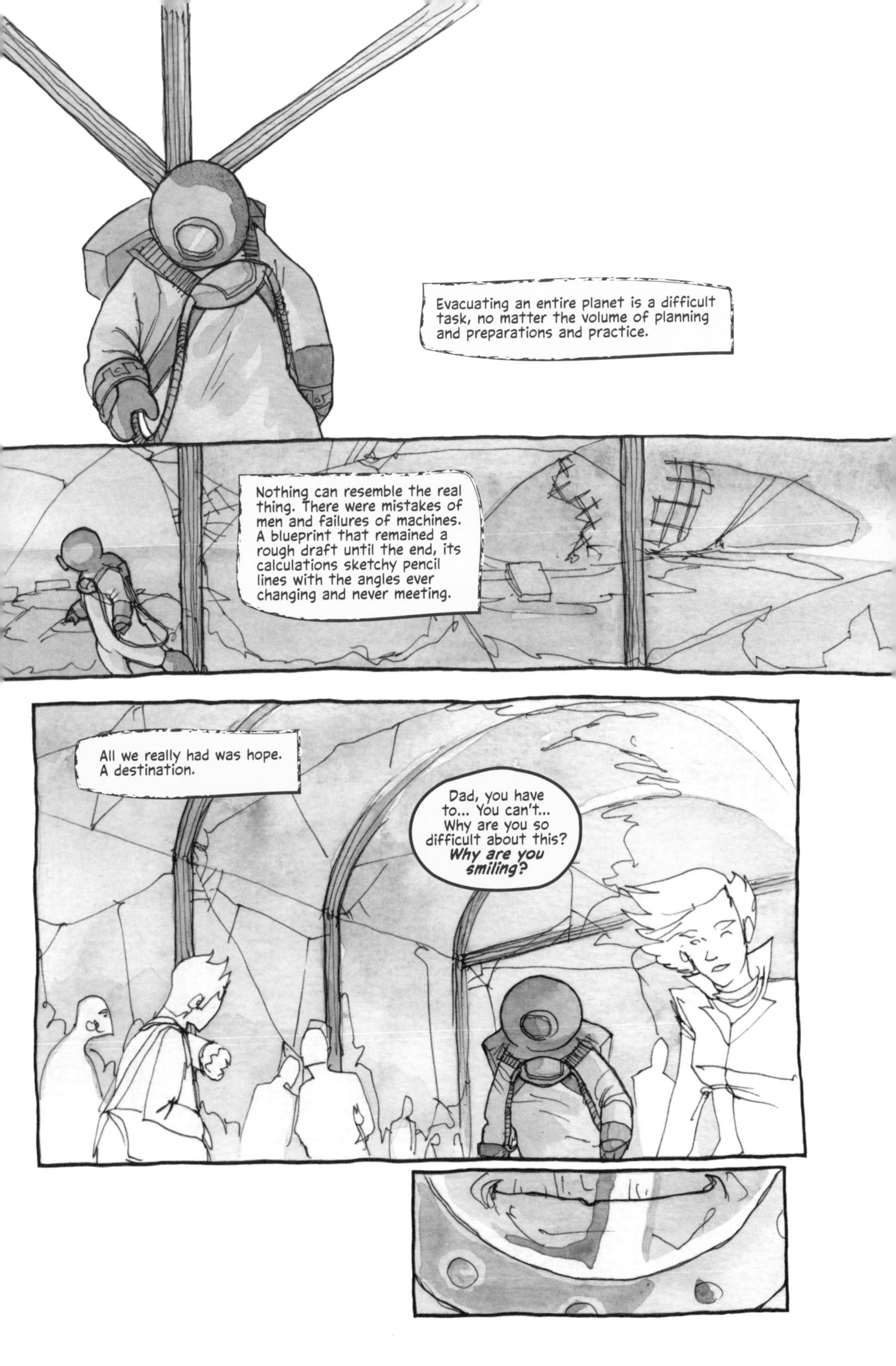
Evacuating an entire planet is a difficult task, no matter the volume of planning and preparations and practice.
Nothing can resemble the real thing. There were mistakes of men and failures of machines. A blueprint that remained a rough draft until the end, its calculations sketchy pencil lines with the angles ever changing and never meeting.
All we really had was hope. A destination.
Dad, you have to... You can't... Why are you so difficult about this? ***Why are you smiling?***

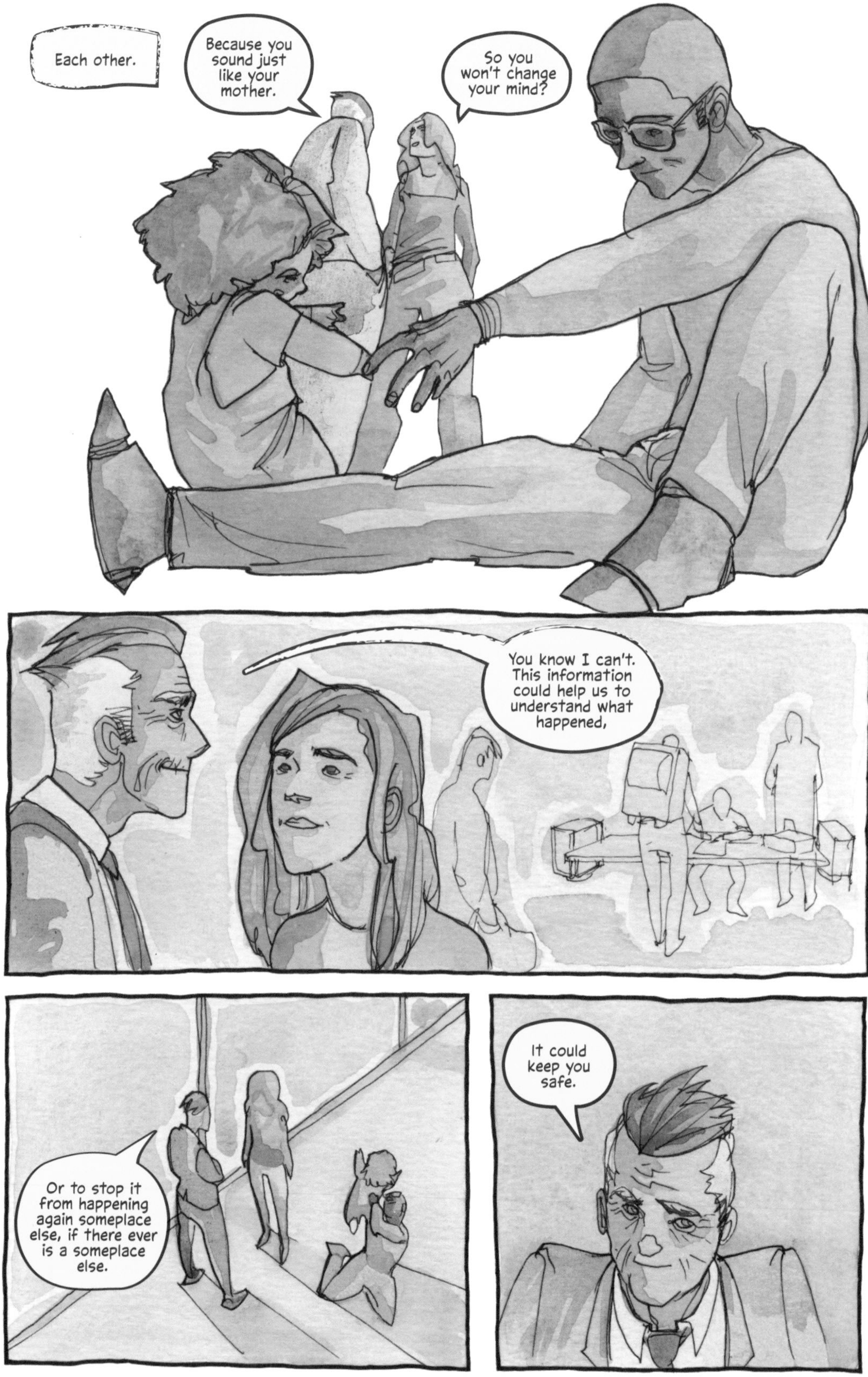
Each other.
Because you sound just like your mother.
So you won't change your mind?
You know I can't. This information could help us to understand what happened,
Or to stop it from happening again someplace else, if there ever is a someplace else.
It could keep you safe.

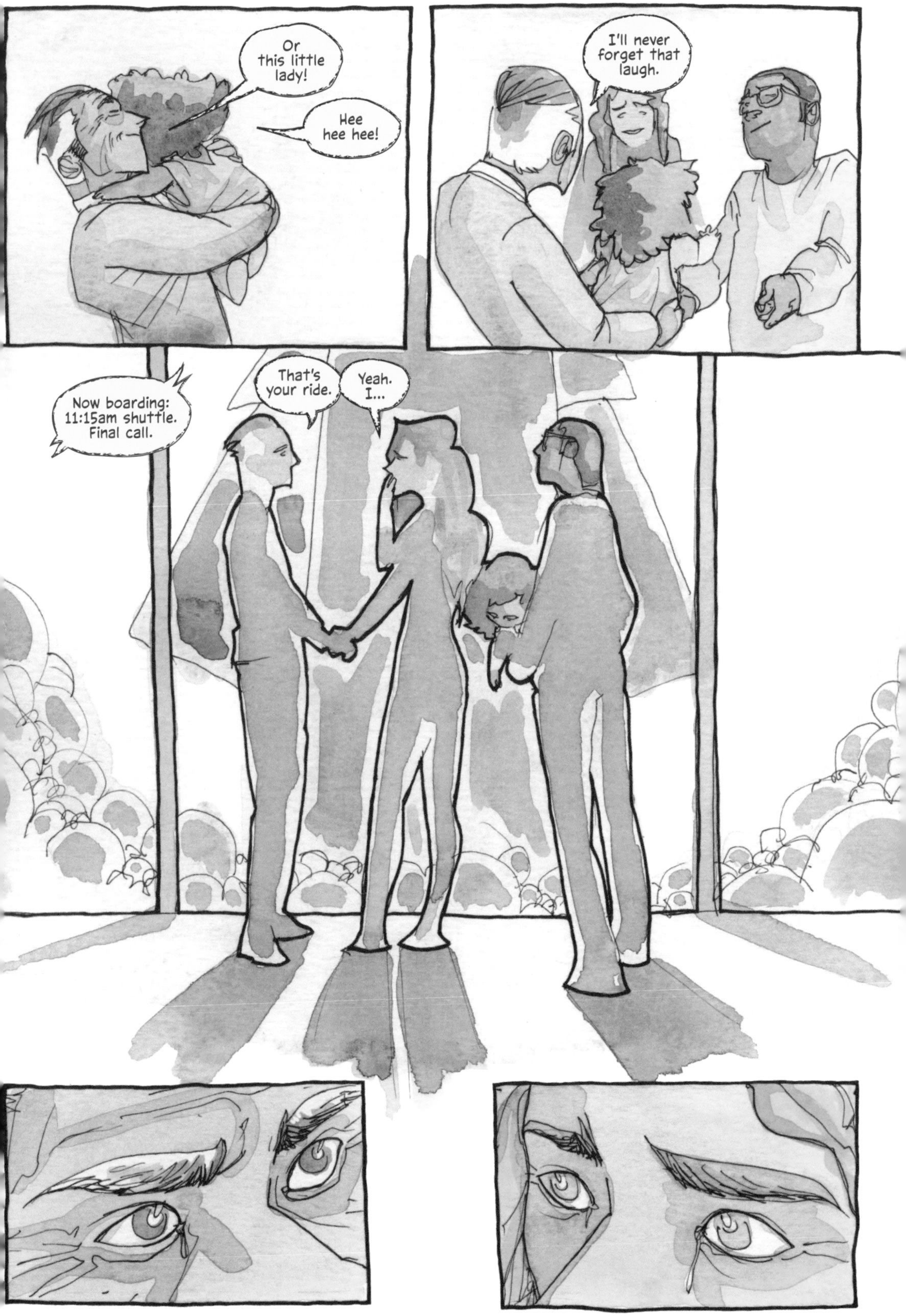

Or this little lady!
Hee hee hee!
I'll never forget that laugh.
Now boarding: 11:15am shuttle. Final call.
That's your ride.
Yeah. I...

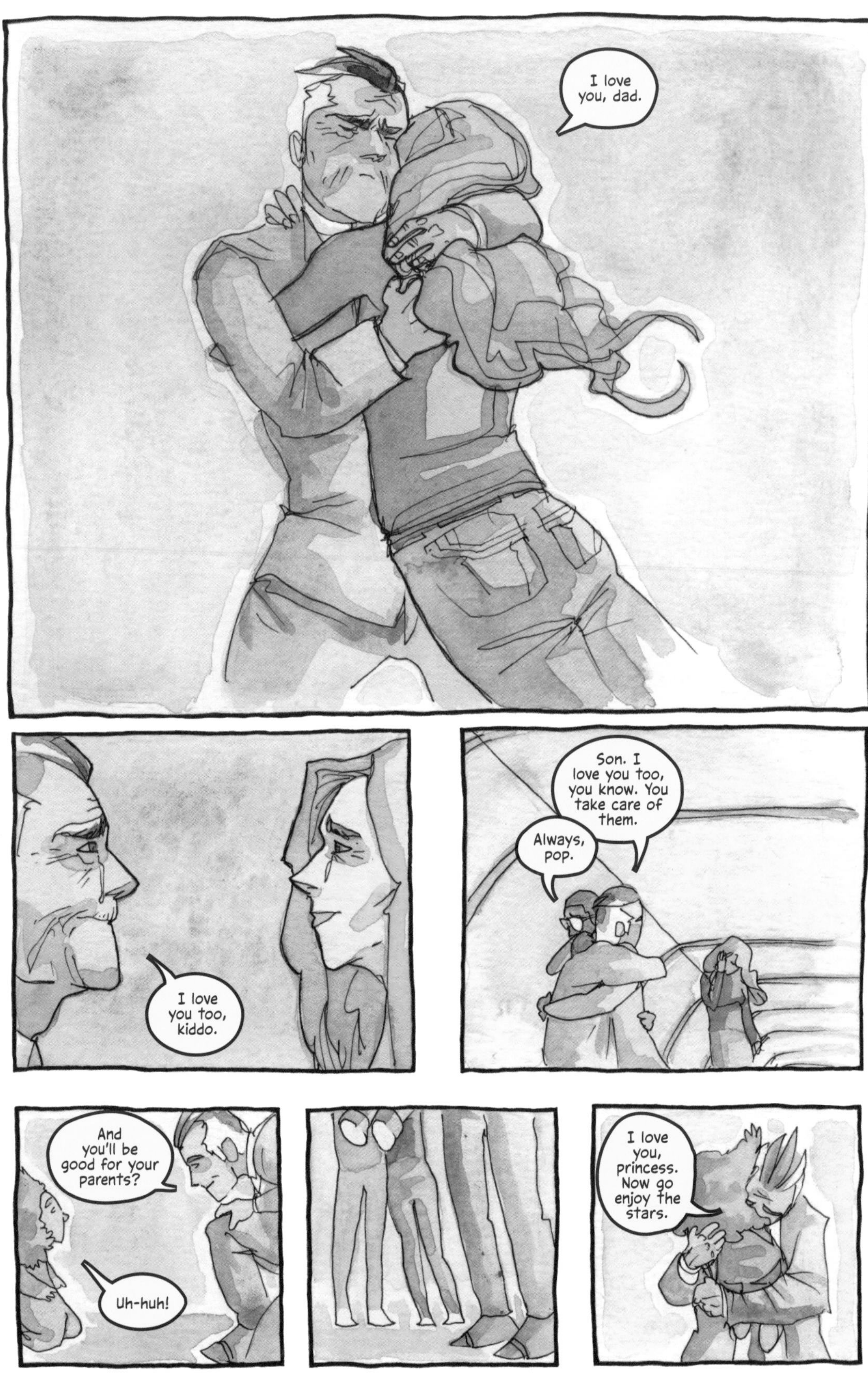
I love you, dad.
I love you too, kiddo.
Son. I love you too, you know. You take care of them.
Always, pop.
And you'll be good for your parents?
Uh-huh!
I love you, princess. Now go enjoy the stars.

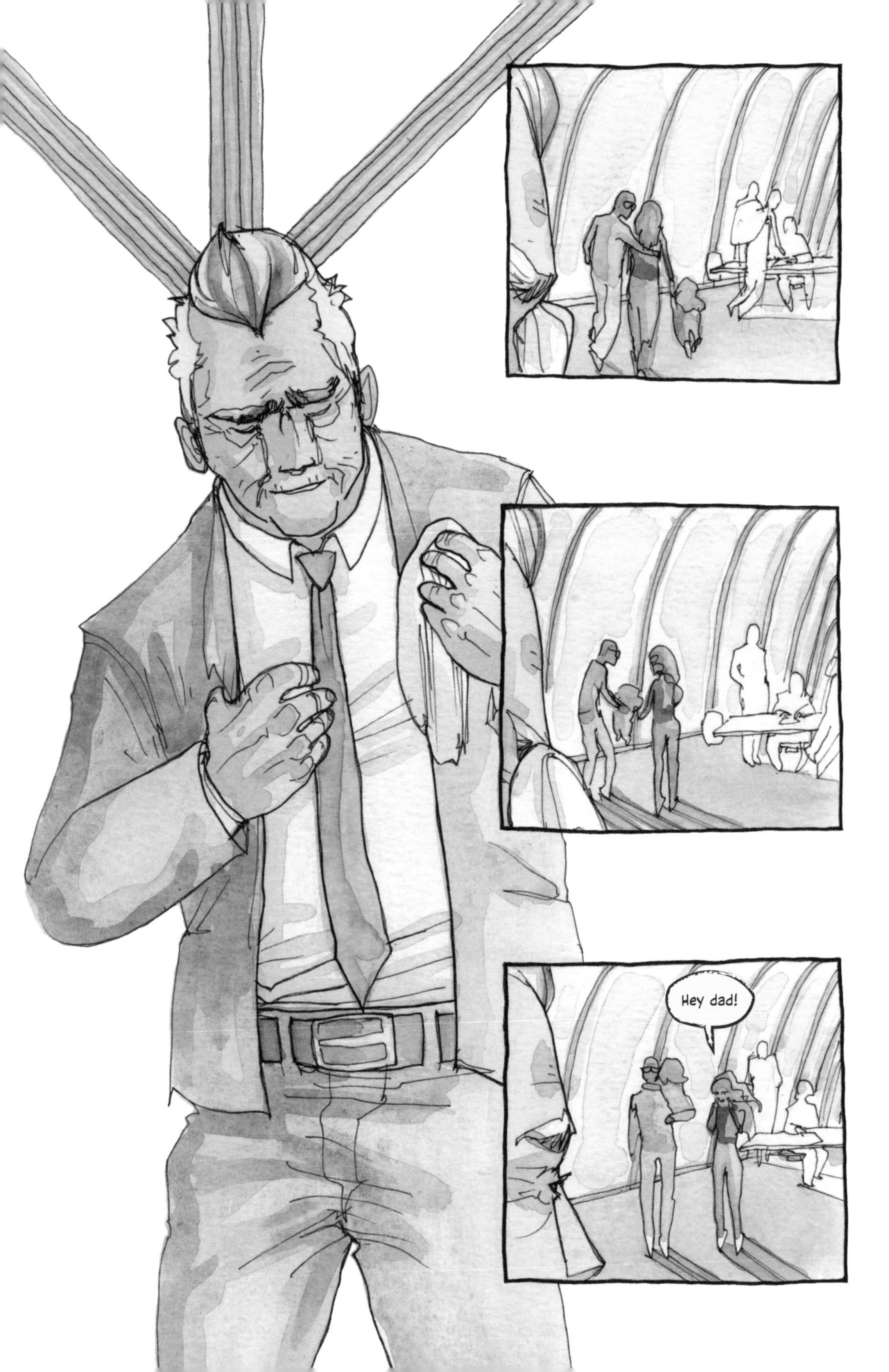
Hey dad!

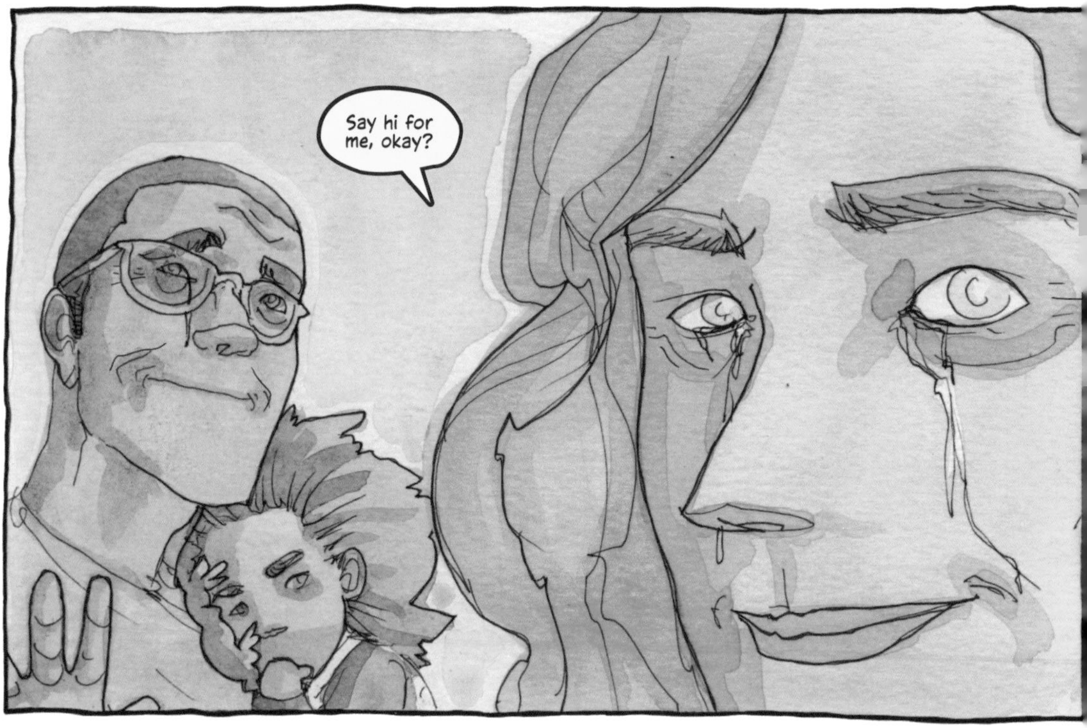
Say hi for
me, okay?

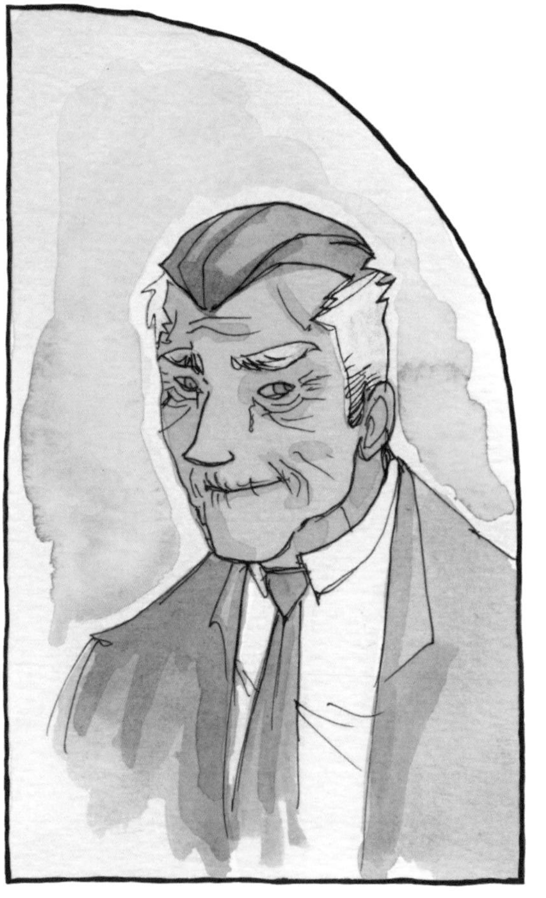

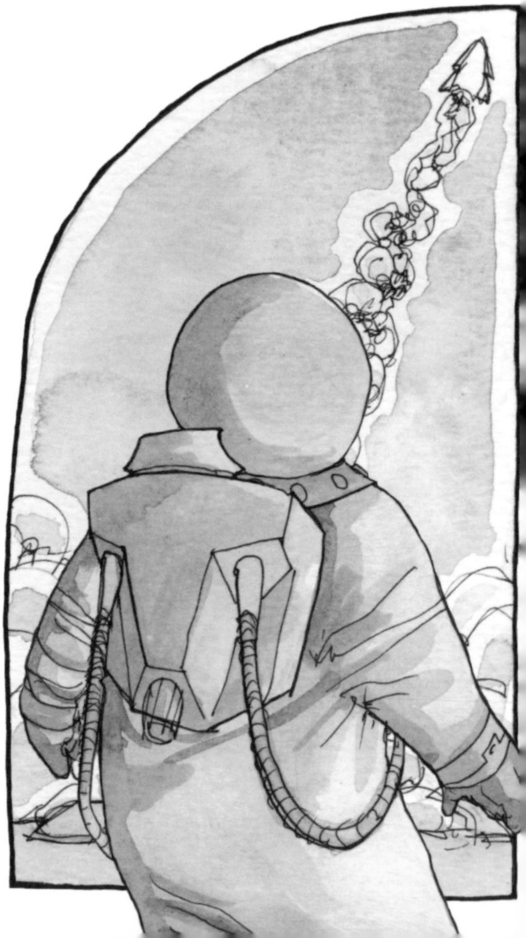

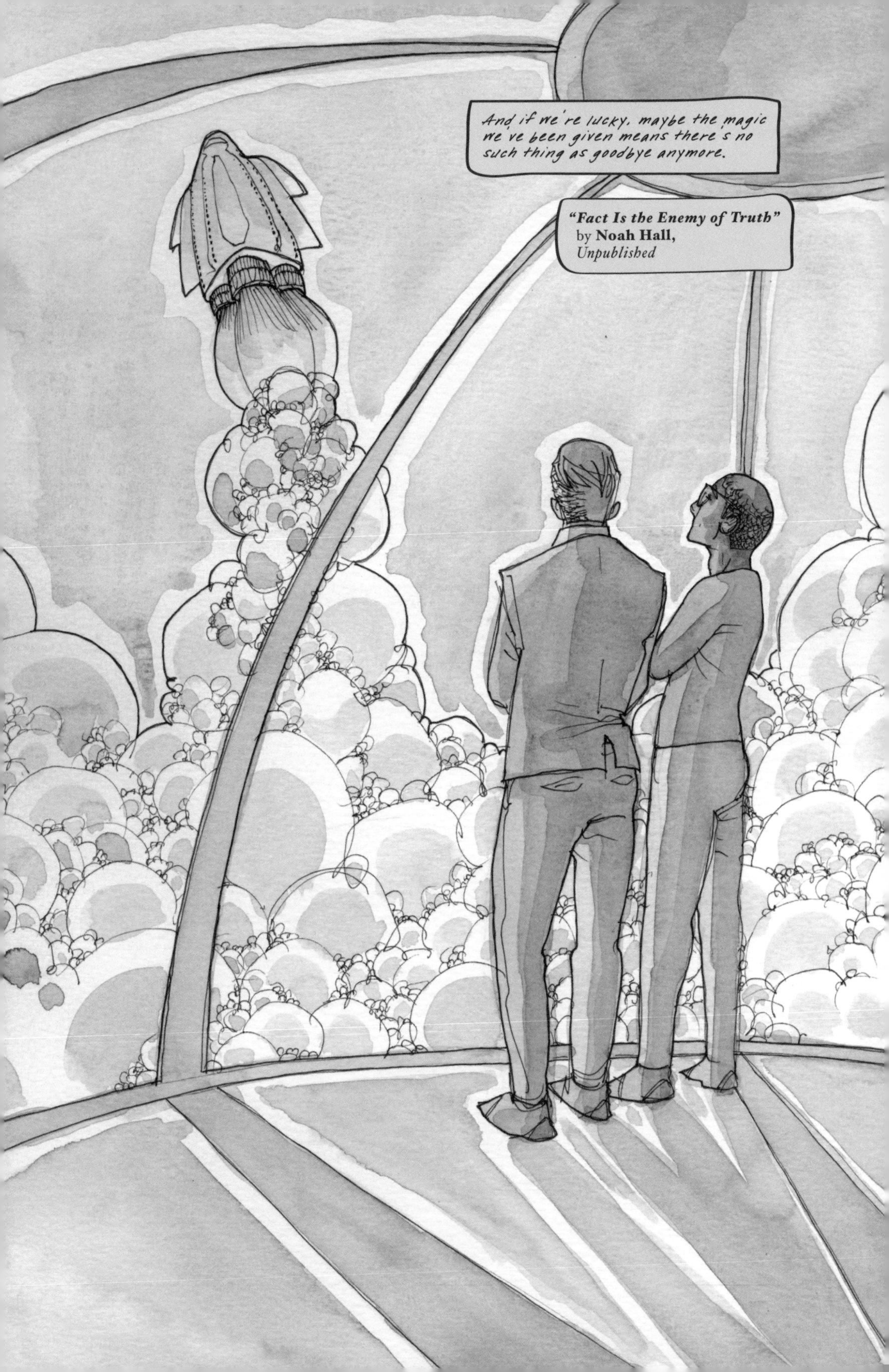
And if we're lucky, maybe the magic we've been given means there's no such thing as goodbye anymore.
"Fact Is the Enemy of Truth" by Noah Hall, Unpublished

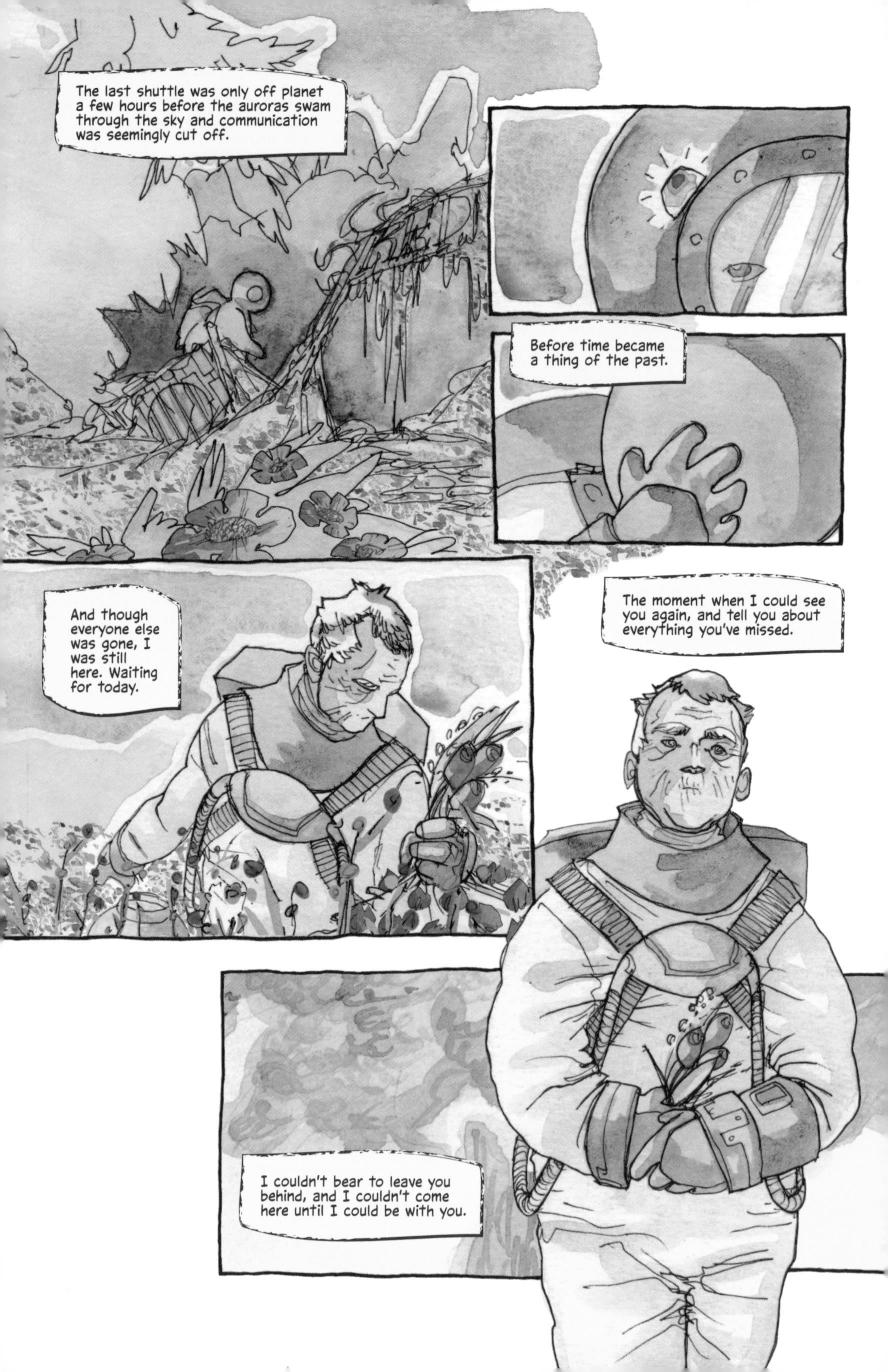
The last shuttle was only off planet a few hours before the auroras swam through the sky and communication was seemingly cut off.
Before time became a thing of the past.
And though everyone else was gone, I was still here. Waiting for today.
The moment when I could see you again, and tell you about everything you've missed.
I couldn't bear to leave you behind, and I couldn't come here until I could be with you.

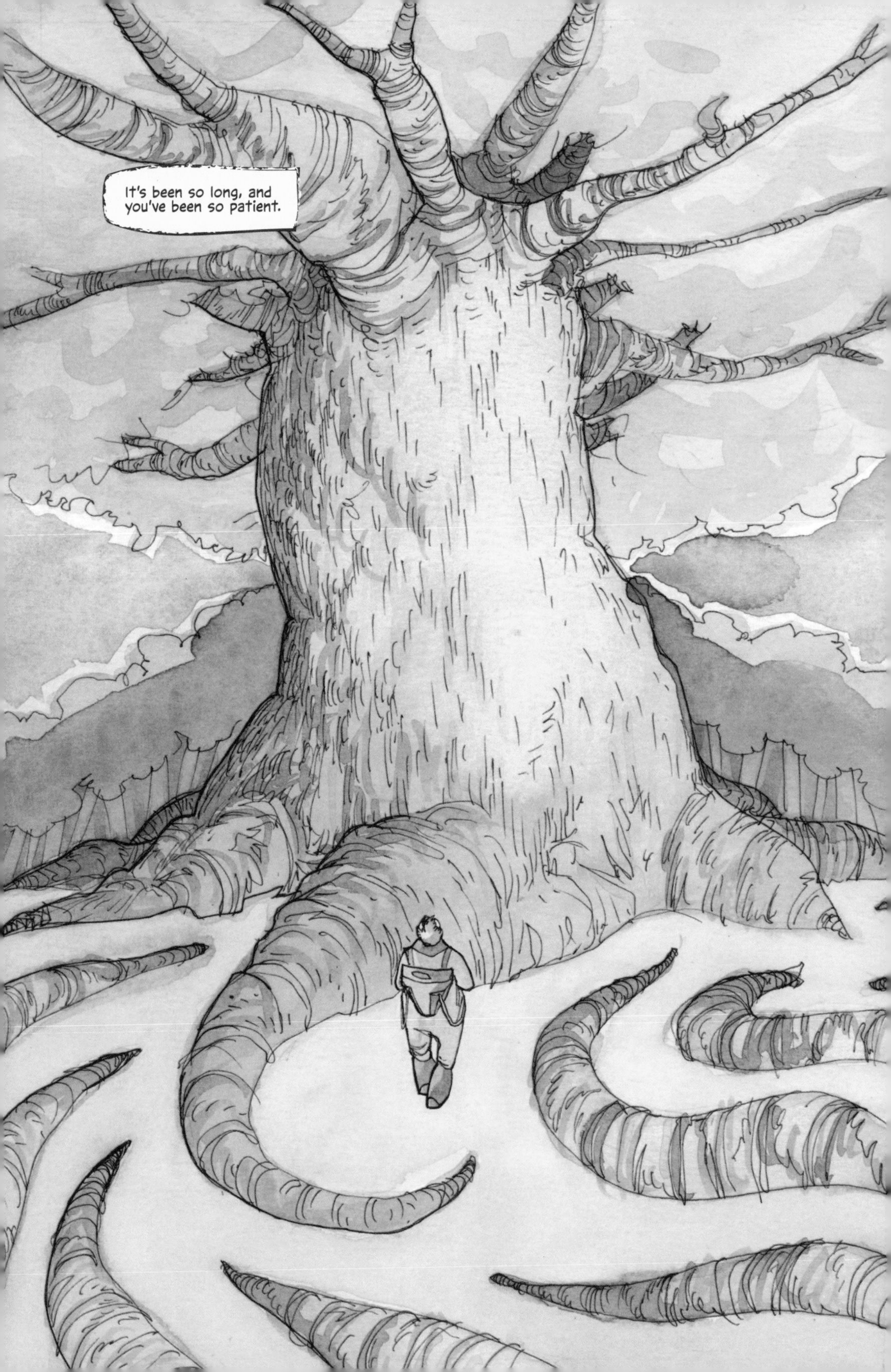
It's been so long, and you've been so patient.

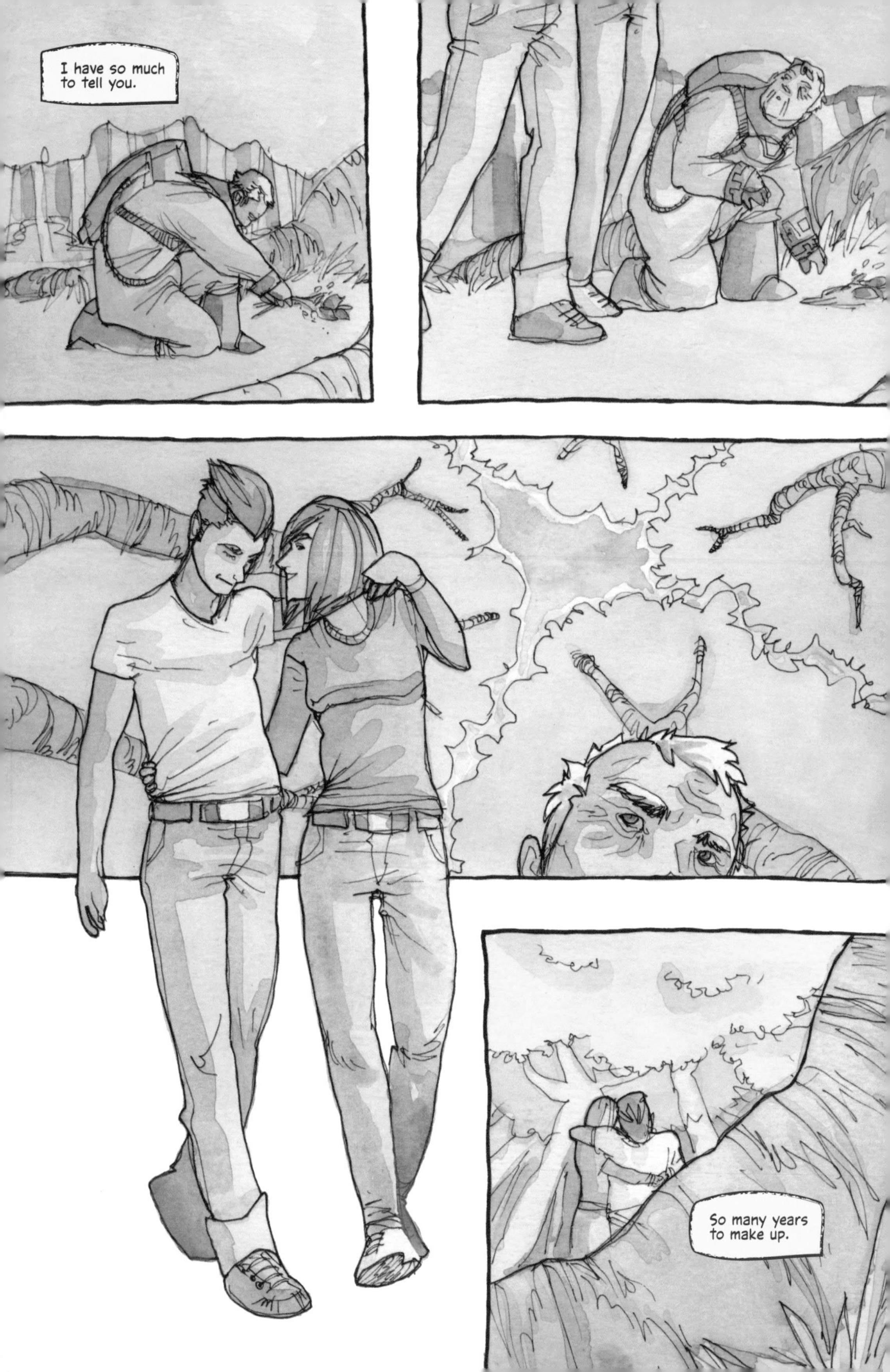
I have so much to tell you.
So many years to make up.

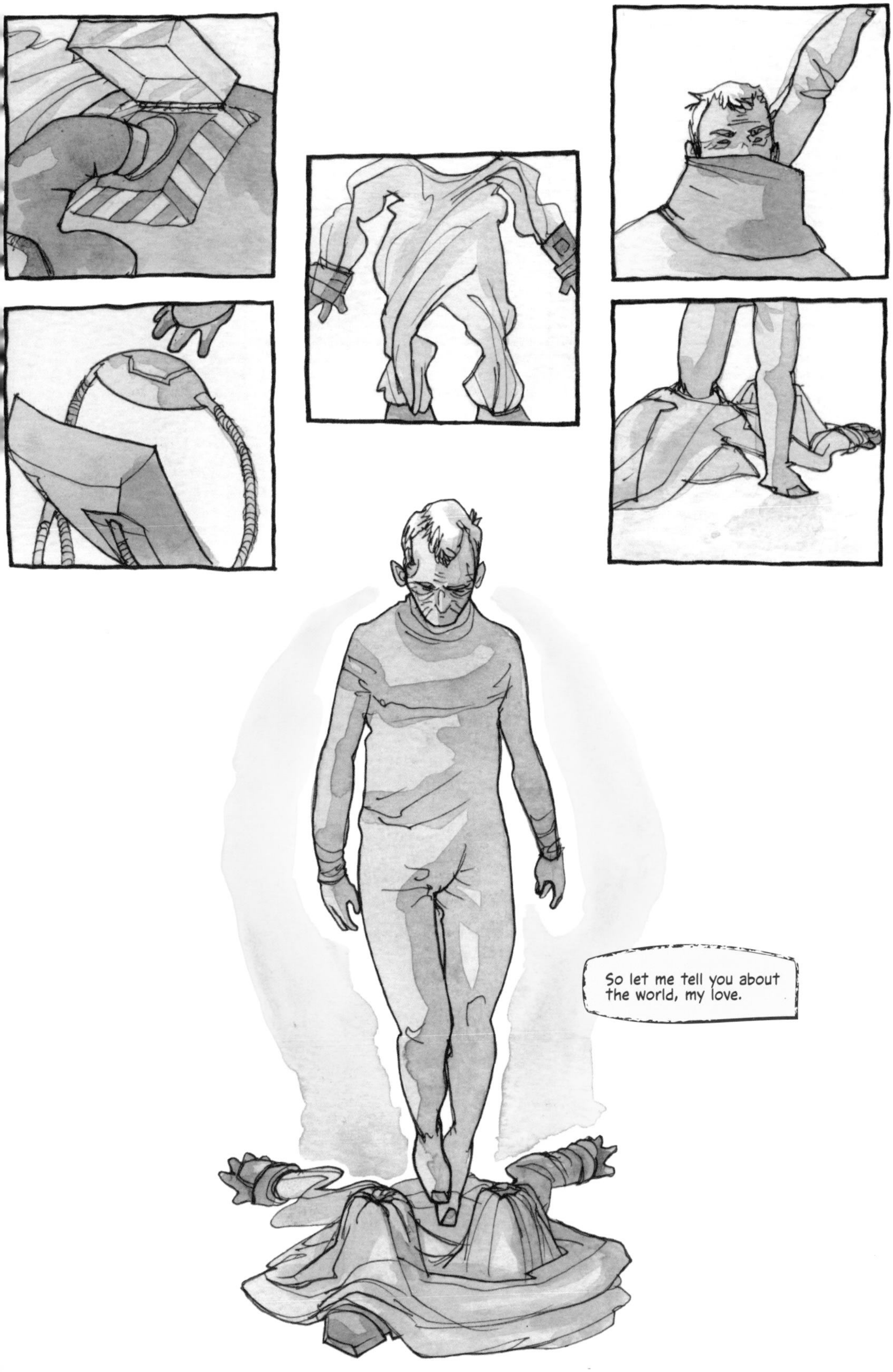
So let me tell you about the world, my love.

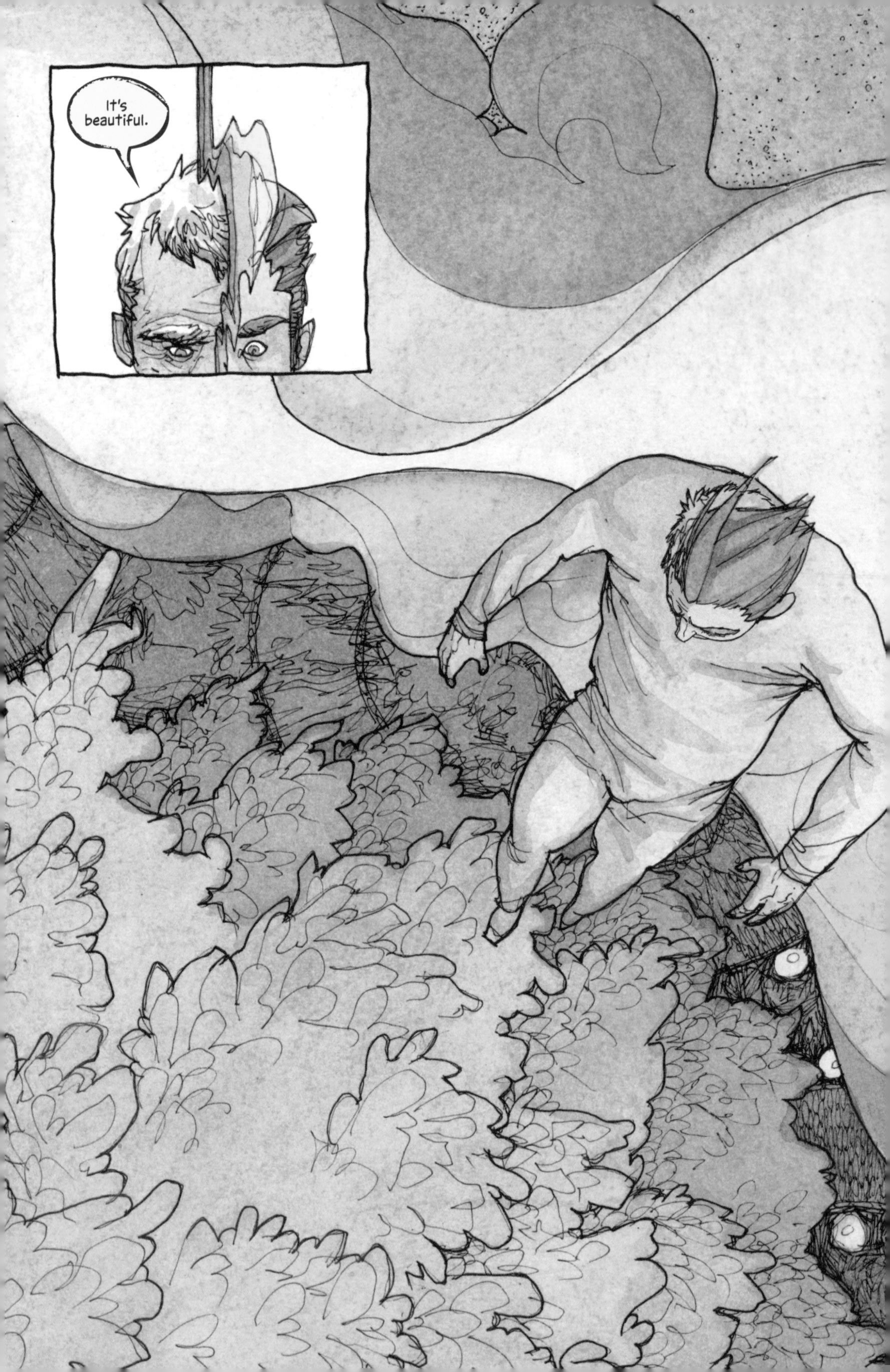
It's beautiful.

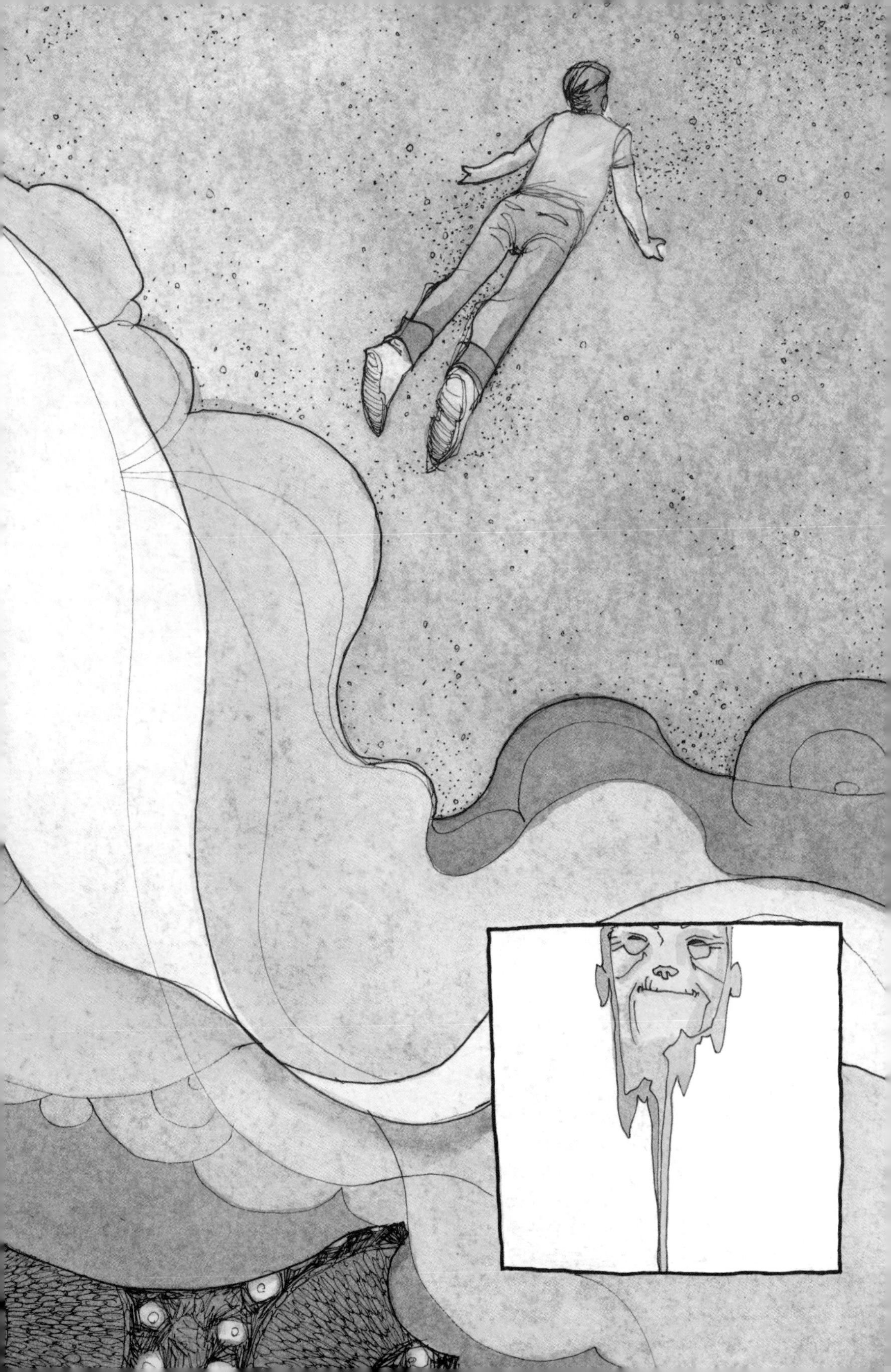

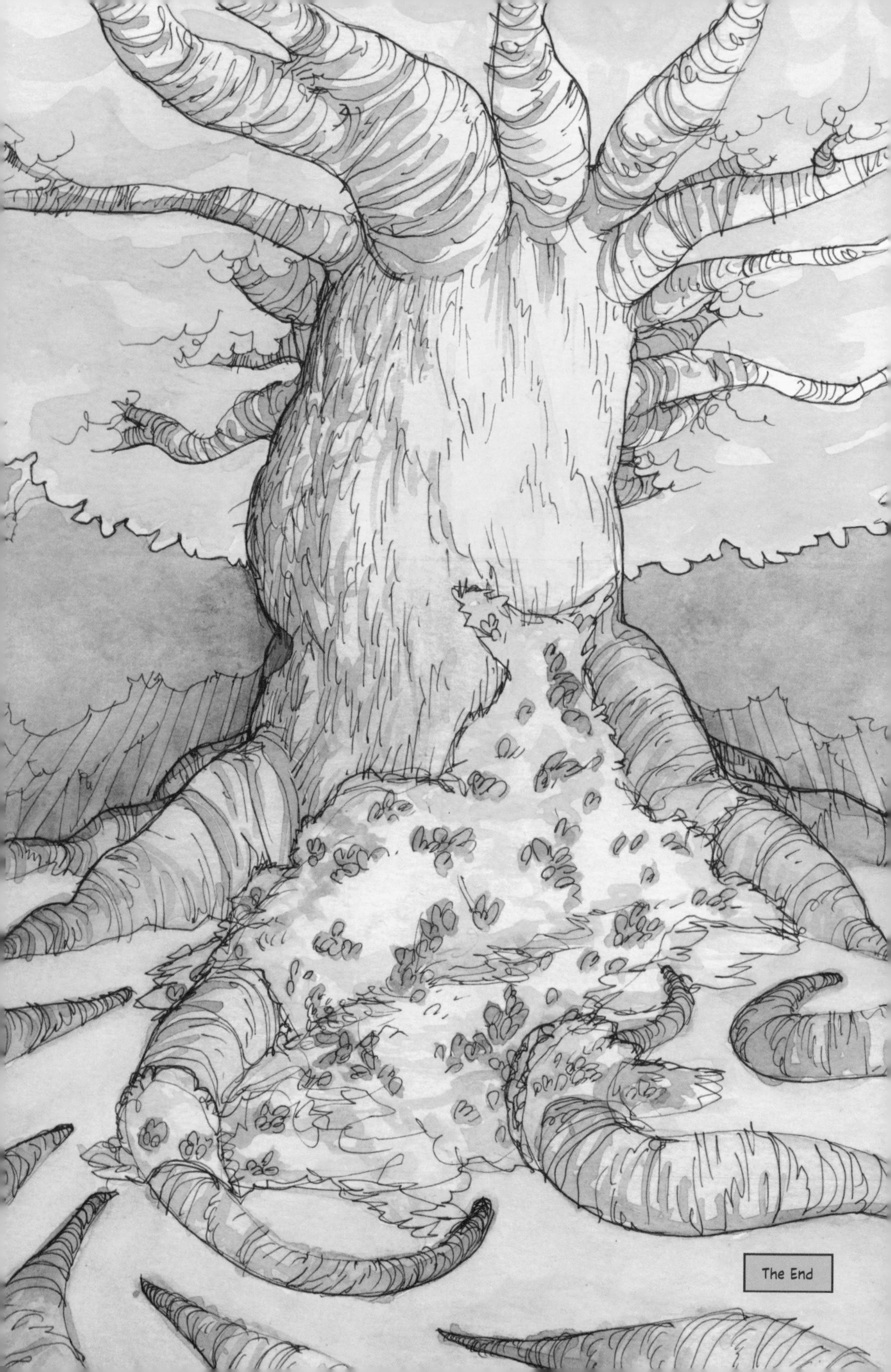
The End